The Secret of the League

The Story of a Social War

Ernest Bramah

The Secret of the League: The Story of a Social War

ISBN: 978-1-64799-961-2

CONTENTS

CONTENTS

CHAPTER I

IRENE

"I suppose I am old-fashioned"—there was a murmur of polite dissent from all the ladies present, except the one addressed—"Oh, I take it as a compliment nowadays, I assure you; but when I was a girl a young lady would have no more thought of flying than of"— she paused almost on a note of pained surprise at finding the familiar comparison of a lifetime cut off—"well, of standing on her head."

"No," replied the young lady in point, with the unfeeling candour that marked the youthful spirit of the age, "because it wasn't invented. But you went bicycling, and your mothers were very shocked at first."

"I hardly think that you can say that, Miss Lisle," remarked another of the matrons, "because I can remember that more than twenty years ago one used to see quite elderly ladies bicycling."

"After the others had lived all the ridicule down," retorted Miss Lisle scornfully. "Oh yes; I quite expect that in a few more years you will see quite elderly ladies flying."

The little party of matrons seated on the Hastings promenade regarded each other surreptitiously, and one or two smiled slightly, while one or two shuddered slightly. "Flying is very different, dear," said Mrs Lisle reprovingly. "I often think of what your dear grandfather used to say. He said"—impressively—"that if the Almighty had intended that we should fly, He would have sent us into the world with wings upon our backs."

There was a murmur of approval from all—all except Miss Lisle, that is.

"But do you ever think of what Geoffrey replied to dear grandpapa when he heard him say that once, mother?" said the unimpressed daughter. "He said: 'And don't you think, sir, that if the Almighty had intended us to use railways, He would have sent us into the world with wheels upon our feet?'"

"I do not see any connection at all between the two things," replied her mother distantly. "And such a remark seems to me to be simply irreverent. Birds are born with wings, and insects, and so on, but nothing, as far as I am aware, is born with wheels. Your grandfather used to travel by the South Eastern regularly every day, or how could he have reached his office? and he never saw anything wrong in using trains, I am sure. In fact, when you think of it you

1

will see that what Geoffrey said, instead of being any argument, was supremely silly."

"Perhaps he intended it to be," replied Miss Lisle with suspicious meekness. "You never know, mother."

Such a remark merited no serious attention. Why should any one, least of all a really clever young man like Geoffrey, deliberately intend to be silly? There was too often, her mother had observed, an utter lack of relevance in Irene's remarks.

"I think that it is a great mistake to have white flying costumes as so many do," observed another lady. "They look—but perhaps they wish to."

"Certainly when they use lace as well it really seems as though they do. Oh!"

There was a passing shadow across the group and a slight rustle in the air. Scarcely a dozen yards above the promenade a young lady was flying strongly down the wind with the languid motion of the "swan stroke." She wore white—and lace trimming. Mrs Lisle gazed fixedly out to sea. Even Irene felt that the vision was inopportune.

"There are always some who overdo a thing," she remarked. "There always have been. That was only Velma St Saint of the New Gaiety; she flies about the front every day for the advertisement of the thing: I wonder that she doesn't drop handbills as she goes. There's plenty of room up on the Castle Hill—in fact, you aren't supposed to fly west of the Breakwater—but there will always be some——" A vague resentment closed the period.

"Are you staying at the Palatial this time?" asked the lady who had mentioned lace, feeling it tactful to change the subject. "I think that you used to."

"Oh, haven't you seen?" was the reply. "The Palatial has been closed for the last six months."

"Yes, it's a great pity," remarked another. "It looks so depressing too, right on the front. But they simply could not go on. I suppose that the rates here are something frightful now."

"Oh, enormous, my dear; but it was not that alone. The Palatial has always aimed at being a 'popular' hotel, and so few of the upper middle class can afford hotels now. Then the new tax on every servant above one—calculated as fifty per cent. of their wages, I think, but there are so many new taxes to remember—proved the last straw."

"Yes, it is fifty per cent. I remember because I had to give up my between-maid to pay the cook's tax. But I thought that hotels were to be exempt?"

"Not in the end. It was argued that hotels existed for the

2

convenience of the monied classes, and that they ought to pay for it. So a large number of hotels are closed altogether; others work with a reduced staff, and a great many servants have been thrown out of employment."

Miss Lisle laughed unpleasantly. "A good thing, too," she remarked. "I hate hotel servants. So does everybody. It is the only good thing I have heard of the Labour Government doing."

"I am sure I don't hate them," said Mrs Lisle, looking round with pathetic resignation, "although they certainly had become rather grasping and over-bearing of late. But it was quite an unforeseen development of the scheme that so many should lose their places. Indeed the special object of the tax was to create a fund—'earmarked' I think they call it—out of which to meet the growing pension claim, now that so few of the servant class think it worth while to save."

Miss Lisle laughed again, this time with a note of genuine amusement.

("A most unpleasant girl, I fear," murmured the lady who had raised the white costume question, to her neighbour in a whisper: "so odd.")

"It made a great difference at the registry offices. There are a dozen maids to be had any day where there were really none before. Only one cannot afford to keep them now."

There was a word, a sigh, and an "Ah!" to mark this point of agreement among the four ladies.

"I am afraid that the Government confiscation of all dividends above five per cent. bears very heavily on some," remarked one after a pause. "I know a poor soul of over sixty-five, nearly blind too, whose husband had invested all his savings in the company he had worked for because he knew that it was safe, and, having a good reserve, intended to pay ten per cent. for a long time. When he died it brought her in fifty pounds a year. Now——"

There were little signs of sympathy and commiseration from the group. The sex was beginning to take an unwonted interest in terms financial—per centage, surrender value, trustee stock, unearned increment, and so on. They had reason to do so, for revolutionary finance was very much in the air, or, rather, had come tangibly down to earth at length: not the placid city echoes that were wont to ripple gently across the breakfast-table a few years earlier without leaving any one much better or much worse off, but the galvanic adjustment that by a stroke made the rich well-to-do, the well-to-do just so-so, the struggling poor, and left the poor where they were before. The frenzied effort that in a session strove to tear up the trees of the forest and leave the plants beneath untouched; to

3

pull to pieces the intertwined fabric of a thousand years' growth and to create from it a bundle of straight and equal twigs; in a word, to administer justice on the principle of knocking out one eye in all the sound because a number of people were unfortunately born or fallen blind.

"Five and twenty," mused Mrs Lisle. "I suppose it is just possible."

"It is really less than that," explained the other. "You may have noticed that as it is now no good making more than five per cent., most companies pay even less. There is no incentive to do well."

"One hears of even worse cases on every hand," said another of the ladies. "I am trying to interest people in a poor deformed creature whose father left her an annuity derived from ground rents in the City.... As it has been worked out I think that she owes the Incomes Adjustment Department lawyers something a year now. But private charity seems almost to have ceased altogether. Have you heard that 'Jim's' is closed?"

It was true. St James's Hospital, whose unvarnished record was, "Three hundred of the very poor treated freely each day," was a thing of the past, and across its portal, where ten years before a couple of stalwart gentlemen wearing red ties had rested for a moment, while they lit their pipes, a banner with the strange device, "Curse your Charity!" now ran the legend, "Closed for want of Funds."

"I wonder sometimes," mused the last speaker, "why some one doesn't do something."

"But," objected another, "what is there to do? What is there?"

They all agreed that there was nothing—absolutely nothing. Every one else was tacitly making the same admission; that was the fatal symptom.

Miss Lisle jumped up and began to move away unceremoniously.

"Where are you going, dear?" asked her mother in mild reproof.

"Oh, anywhere," replied Irene restlessly.

"But what for?" persisted Mrs Lisle.

"Oh, anything."

"That is 'nothing,' Miss Lisle," smiled the tactful lady of the party, anxious to smooth over the awkwardness of the moment.

"No, it is at least something," flung back the girl brusquely; and with swinging strides she set off at a furious pace towards the open country.

"Irene is a little impulsive at times," apologized her mother, sitting back with placidly folded hands.

4

CHAPTER II

THE PERIOD, AND THE COMING OF WINGS

An intelligent South Sea Islander, who had been imported into this country to stimulate missionary enterprise, on his return had said that the most marked characteristic of the English of the period was what they called "snap."

The nearest equivalent in his own language signifying literally "quick hot words," he had some difficulty in conveying the impression he desired, and his circle had to rest content that "snap" permeated the journalism, commerce, politics, drama, and social life of the English, had assailed their literature, and was beginning to influence religion, art, and science. It may be admitted that the foreign gentleman's visit had coincided with a period of national stress, for the week in question had embraced the more entertaining half of a general election, seen the advent of two new farthing daily papers, and been marked by the Rev. Sebastian Tauthaul's striking series of addresses from the pulpit of the City Sanctum, entitled "If Christ put up for Battersea." It had also included the launching of a new cocoa, a new soap, and a new concentrated food.

The new food was called "Chip-Chunks." "A name which I venture to think spells success of itself," complacently remarked its inventor. "A very good name indeed," admitted his advertising manager. "It has the great desideratum that it might be anything, and, on the other hand, it might equally well be nothing." "Just so," said the inventor with weighty approval; "just so." A "snap-line" was required that would ineradicably fix Chip-Chunks in the public mind, and "Bow-wow! Feel chippy? Then champ Chip-Chunks" was found in an inspired moment. It was, of course, fully cooked and already quite digested. It was described as the delight of the unweaned infant, the mainstay of the toothless nonagenarian, and so simple and wholesome that it could be safely taken and at once assimilated by the invalid who had undergone the operation of having his principal organ of digestion removed. So little, indeed, remained for nature and the human parts to do in the matter of Chip-Chunks as to raise the doubt whether it might not be simpler and scarcely less nutritive to open the tin and pour the contents down the drain forthwith.

As Chip-Chunks was designed for those who were disinclined to exercise the functions of digestion, so Isabella soap made an appeal to those who disliked work and had something of an

5

antipathy to soap at all. One did not wash with Isabella, it was assured: one sat down and watched it. It had its "snap-lines," too:

"You write it 'wash,' but you call it 'wosh.'

"What is the difference?

"There is 'a' difference.

"There is also 'a' difference between Isabella soap and all other soaps:

"All the difference.

"That's our point. Put it in your washtub and watch it."

Cocoa was approached in a more sober spirit. Soap may blow bubbles of light and airy fancy, pills ricochet from one gay conceit to another, meat extracts gambol with the irresponsible exuberance of bulls in china cups, but cocoa relied upon sincerity and statistics. Kingcup cocoa was the last word of the expert. It won its way into the great heart of the people by driving home the significant fact that it contained .00001 per cent. more phosphorus, and .000002 per cent. less of something fatty, than any other cocoa in existence. When the newspaper reader of the period had been confronted by this assertion, in various guises, seventeen thousand times, he had reached a state of mind in which .00001 per cent. more phosphorus and .000002 per cent. less fat represented the difference between vigorous manhood and drivelling imbecility.

The Rev. Sebastian was all "snap." His topical midday addresses—described by himself as "Seven minutes sandwich-sermonettes"—have already been referred to. Young men who were pressed for time were bidden to bring their bath buns or buttered scones and eat openly and unashamed. Workmen with bread and cheese and pots of beer were welcomed with effusion. This particular series extended over the working days of a week, and was subdivided thus:

Monday.—The Issues before the Constituency.
Tuesday.—His Address to the Electors.
Wednesday.—The Day of the Contest.
Thursday.—Which Way are you Voting?
Friday.—Spoiled Papers.
Saturday.—At the Top of the Poll and the Leader of our Party.

Of the new papers, of their sprightliness, their enterprise, their general all-roundness, their almost wicked experience of the ways of the world, from a quite up-to-date fund of junior office witticism to a knowledge of the existence of actresses who do not act, outwardly respectable circles of society who play cards for money on Sunday, and (exclusively for the benefit of their readers)

6

places where quite high-class provisions (only nominally damaged) could be bought cheap on Saturday nights, it is unnecessary to say much. Of their irresponsible cock-sureness, their bristling combativeness, their amazing powers of prophetic penetration, and, it must be confessed, their ineradicable air of somewhat second-rate infant phenomenonship, their crumbling yellow files still bear witness. As a halfpenny is half a penny, so a farthing is half a halfpenny, and the mind that is not too appalled by the possibilities of the development can people for itself this journalistic Eden.

The Whip described its programme as "Vervy and nervy; brainy and champagny." The Broom relied more on solider attractions of the "News of the World in Pin Point Pars" and "Knowledge in Nodules" order. Both claimed to be written exclusively by "brainy" people, and both might have added, with equal truth, read exclusively by brainless. Avowedly appealing "to the great intellect of the nation," neither fell into the easy mistake of aiming too high, and the humblest son of toil might take them up with the fullest confidence of finding nothing from beginning to end that was beyond his simple comprehension.

But the most cursory review of national "snappishness" would be incomplete if it omitted the field of politics, especially when the period in question contained so concentrated an accumulation of "snap" as a general election. Contests had long ceased to be decided on the merits of individuals or of parties, still less to be the occasions for deliberate consideration of policy. Each group had its label and its "snap-cries." The outcome as a whole—the decision of each division with few exceptions—lay in the hands of a class which, while educated to the extent of a little reading and a little writing, was practically illiterate in thought, in experience, and in discrimination. To them a "snap-cry" was eminently suited, as representing a concrete idea and being in fact the next best argument to a decayed egg. That national disaster had never so far been evolved out of this rough-and-ready method could be traced to a variety of saving clauses. At such a time the strict veracity of the cries raised was not to be too closely examined; indeed, there was not the time for contradiction, and therein lay the essence of some of the most successful "snaps."

Misrepresentation, if on a sufficiently large scale, was permissible, but it was advisable to make it wholesale, lurid, and applied not to an individual but to a party—emphasising, of course, the fact that your opponent was irretrievably pledged to that party through thick and thin.

In other words, it was quite legitimate for A to declare that the policy of the party to which his opponent B belonged was a policy of

7

murder, rapine, piracy, black-mail, highway robbery, extermination, and indiscriminate bloodshed; that they had swum to office on a sea of tears racked from the broken hearts of an outraged peasantry, risen to power on the apex of a smoking hecatomb of women and children, and kept their position by methods of ruthless barbarism; that assassination, polygamy, thuggeeism, simony, bureaucracy, and perhaps even an additional penny on the poor man's tea, would very likely be found included in their official programme; that they were definitely pledged to introduce Kalmucks and Ostyaks into the Government Dock-yards, who would work in chained gangs, be content with three farthings for a fourteen hours' day, and live exclusively on engine waste and barley-water.

This and much more was held to be fair political warfare which should not offend the keenest patriot. But if A so far descended to vulgar personalities as to accuse B himself of employing an urchin to scare crows at eightpence a day when the trade union rate for crow-scaring was ninepence, he stood a fair chance of having an action for libel or defamation of character on his hands in addition to an election.

Under such a system the least snappy went to the wall. Happy was the man who was armed not necessarily with a just cause, but with a name that lent itself to topical alliteration. Who could resist the appeal to

Vote for	Frank	Blarney.
	Fresh	Brooms in Parliament.
	Fewer	Bungles during the next five years.
	Financial	Betterment at home.
	Free	Breakfast tables for the People.
	Flourishing	Businesses all round.

—especially when it was coupled with the reminder that

Every vote given to A. J. Wallflower is a slice of bread filched from your innocent children's hard-earned loaf.

Of course the schools could not escape the atmosphere. The State-taught children were wonderfully snappy—for the time being. Afterwards, it might be noticed, that when the props were pulled away they were generally either annoyingly dull or objectionably pert, or, perhaps, offensively dully-pert, according to whether their nature was backward or forward, or a mixture of both. The squad-drilled units could remember wonderfully well—for the time; they could apply the rules they learned in just the way they were taught to apply them—for the time. But they could not remember what they had not been drilled to remember; they could not apply the

8

rules in any other way; they could not apply the principles at all; and they could not think.

High and low, children were not allowed to think; with ninety-nine mothers out of a hundred its proper name was "idleness." "I do not like to see you sitting down doing nothing, dear," said every mother to every daughter plaintively. "Is there no sewing you might do?" So the would-be thoughtful child was harried into working, or playing, or eating, or sleeping, as though a mind contentedly occupied with itself was an unworthy or a morbid thing.

Yet it was a too close adherence to the national character that proved to be the undoing of Wynchley Slocombe, who is now generally admitted to have been the father of the form of aerial propulsion so widely enjoyed to-day. Like everybody else, he had read the offer of the Traffic and Locomotion Department of a substantial reward for a satisfactory flying-machine, embracing "any contrivance ... that would by demonstration enable one or more persons, freed from all earth-support or connection (a) to remain stationary at will, at any height between 50 and 1500 feet; (b) at that height to travel between two points one mile apart within a time limit of seven minutes and without deviating more than fifty yards from a straight line connecting the two points; (c) to travel in a circle of not less than three miles in circumference within a time limit of fifteen minutes." Wynchley took an ordinary intelligent interest in the subject, but he had no thought of competing.

It was not until the last day of the period allowed for submitting plans that Wynchley's great idea occurred to him. There was then no time for elaborating the germ or for preparing the requisite specifications, even if he had any ability to do so, which he had not, being, in fact, quite ignorant of the subject. But he remembered hearing in his youth that when a former Government of its day had offered a premium for a convenient method of dividing postage stamps (until that time sold in unperforated sheets and cut up as required by the users), the successful competitor had simply tendered the advice, "Punch rows of little holes between them." In the same spirit Wynchley Slocombe took half a sheet of silurian notepaper (now become famous, and preserved in the South Kensington Museum) and wrote on it, "Fasten on a pair of wings, and practise! practise!! practise!!!" It was to be the aerial counterpart of "Gunnery! Gunnery!! Gunnery!!!"

Unfortunately, the departmental offices were the only places in England where "snap" was not recognised. Wynchley was regarded as a suicidal lunatic—a familiar enough figure in flying-machine circles—and his suggestion was duly pigeon-holed without consideration.

9

The subsequent career of the unhappy man may be briefly stated. Disappointed in his hopes of an early recognition, and not having sufficient money at his disposal to demonstrate the practicability of his idea, he took to writing letters to the President of the Board, and subsequently to waylaying high officials and demanding interviews with them. Dismissed from his situation for systematic neglect of duty, he became a "poor litigant with a grievance" at the Law Courts, and periodically applied for summonses against the Prime Minister, the Lord Mayor of London, and the Archbishop of Canterbury. Still later his name became a by-word as that of a confirmed window-breaker at the Government offices. A few years afterwards, a brief paragraph in one or two papers announced that Wynchley Slocombe, "who, some time ago, gained an unenviable notoriety on account of his hallucinations," had committed suicide in a Deptford model lodging-house.

In the meanwhile two plans for flying-machines had been selected as displaying the most merit, and their inventors were encouraged to press on with the construction under a monetary grant. Both were finished during the same week, and for the sake of comparison they were submitted to trial on the same day upon Shorncliffe plain. Vimbonne VI., which resembled a much-distended spider with outspread legs, made the first ascent. According to instructions, it was to demonstrate its ability to go in a straight line by descending in a field near the Military Canal, beyond Seabrook, but from the moment of its release it continued to describe short circles with a velocity hitherto unattained in any air-ship, until its frantic constructor was too dizzy to struggle with its mechanism any longer. The Moloch was then unmoored, and took up its position stationary at a height of 1000 feet with absolute precision. It was built on the lines of a gigantic centipede, with two rows of clubby oars beneath, and ranked as the popular favourite. Being instructed, for the sake of variety, to begin with the three mile circle, the Moloch started out to sea on the flash of the gun, the sinuous motion that rippled down its long vertebrate body producing an effect, accidental but so very life-like, that many of the vast concourse assembled on the ground turned pale and could not follow it unmoved....

There have been many plausible theories put forward by experts to account for the subsequent disaster, but for obvious reasons the real explanation can never progress beyond the realms of conjecture, for the Moloch, instead of bending to the east, encircling Folkestone and its suburbs, and descending again in the middle of Shorncliffe Camp, continued its unswerving line towards the coast of France, and never held communication with civilised man again.

So exact was its course, however, that it was easy to trace its passage across Europe. It reached Boulogne about four o'clock in the afternoon, and was cheered vociferously under the pathetic impression that everything was going well. Amiens saw it a little to the east in the fading light of evening, and a few early citizens of Dijon marked it soon after dawn. Its passage over the Alps was accurately timed and noted at several points, and the Italian frontier had a glimpse of it, very high up, it was recorded, at nightfall. A gentleman of Ajaccio, travelling in the interior of the island, thought that he had seen it some time during the next day; and several Tripoli Greeks swore that it had passed a few yards above their heads a week later; but the testimony of the Corsican was deemed the more reliable of the two. A relief expedition was subsequently sent out and traversed a great part of Africa, but although the natives in the district around the Albert Nyanza repeatedly prostrated themselves and smacked their thighs vigorously—the tribal signs of fear and recognition—when shown a small working model of the Moloch, no further trace was ever obtained of it.

The accident had a curious sequel in the House of Commons, which significantly illustrates how unexpected may be the ultimate developments of a chain of circumstance. It so happened that in addition to its complement of hands, the Moloch carried an assistant under-secretary to the Board of Agriculture. This gentleman, who had made entomology a lifelong study, was invaluable to his office, and the lamentable consequence of his absence was that when the President of the Board rose the following night to answer a question respecting the importation of lady-birds to arrest an aphis plague then devastating the orchards of the country, he ingenuously displayed so striking an unfamiliarity with the subject that his resignation was demanded, the Government discredited, and a dissolution forced. In particular, the hon. gentleman convulsed the House by referring throughout to lady-birds as "the female members of the various feathered tribes," and warmly defending their importation as the only satisfactory expedient in the circumstances.

Wynchley's suggestion remained on file for the next few years, and would doubtless have crumbled to dust unfruitfully had it not been for a trivial incident. A junior staff clerk, finding himself to be without matches one morning, and hesitating to mutilate the copy of—let us say, the official Pink Paper which he was reading at the moment, absent-mindedly tore a sheet haphazard from a bundle close at hand. As he lit his cigarette, the name of Wynchley

11

Slocombe caught his eye and stirred a half-forgotten memory, for the unfortunate Wynchley had been a stock jest in the past.

Herbert Baedeker Phipps now becomes a force in the history of aerial conquest. He smoothed out the paper from which he had only torn off a fragment, read the stirring "Practise! Practise!! Practise!!!" (at least it has since been recognised to be stirring— stirring, inspired, and pulsating with the impassioned ardour of neglected genius), and pondered deeply to the accompaniment of three more cigarettes. Was there anything in it? Why could not people fly by means of artificial wings? There had been attempts; how did the enthusiasts begin? Usually by precipitating themselves out of an upper window in the first flush of their self-confidence. They were killed, and wings fell into disfavour; but the same result would attend the unsophisticated novice who made his first essay in swimming by diving off a cliff into ten fathoms deep of water. Here, even in a denser medium, was the admitted necessity for laborious practice before security was assured.

Phipps looked a step further. By nature man is ill-equipped for flying, whereas he possesses in himself all the requisites for successful propulsion through the water. Yet he needs practice in water; more practice therefore in air. For thousands of years mankind has been swimming and thereby lightening the task for his descendants, to such an extent that in certain islands the children swim almost naturally, even before they walk; whereas, with the solitary exception of a certain fabled gentleman who made the attempt so successfully and attained such a height that the sun melted the wax with which he had affixed his wings (Styckiton in convenient tubes not being then procurable), no man has ever flown. More, more practice. The very birds themselves, Phipps remembered, first require parental coaching in the art, while aquatic creatures and even the amphibia take to that element with developed faculties from their birth. Still more need of practice for ungainly man. Here, he was convinced, lay the whole secret of failure and possible success. "Practise! Practise!! Practise!!!" The last word was with Wynchley Slocombe.

12

CHAPTER III

THE MILLION TO ONE CHANCE

So wings came—to stay, every one admitted, although most people complained that after all flying was not so wonderful when one could do it as they thought it would have been. For at the first glance the popular fancy had inclined towards pinning on a pair of gauzy appendages and soaring at once into empyrean heights with the spontaneity of a lark, or of lightly fluttering from point to point with the ease and grace of a butterfly. They found that a pair of wings cost rather more than a high-grade bicycle, and that the novice who could struggle from the stage into a net placed twenty yards away, after a month's course of daily practices, was held to be very promising. There was no more talk of England lying at the mercy of any and every invader; for one man, and one only, had so far succeeded in crossing even the Channel, and that at its narrowest limit. For at least three years after the conversion of Phipps the generality of people gleaned their knowledge of the progress of flying from the pages of the comic papers. To the comic papers wings had been sent as an undiluted blessing.

But if alatics, in their infancy, did not come up to the wider expectation, there were many who found in it a novel and exhilarating sport. There were also those who, discovering something congenial in the new force, set quietly and resolutely to work to develop its possibilities and to raise it above the level of a mere fashionable novelty. There have always been some, a few, not infrequently Englishmen, who have unostentatiously become preeminent in every development of science with a fixity of purpose. Their names rarely appear in the pages of history, but they largely write it.

Hastings permitted mixed flying. It was a question that had embittered many a town council. To one section it seemed intolerable that a father, a husband, or a brother should be torn for twenty minutes from the side of his female relatives; to the opposing section it seemed horrible that coatless men should be allowed to spread their wings within a hundred and fifty yards of shoeless women.

"I have no particular convictions," one prominent citizen remarked, "but in view of the existing railway facilities it is worth while considering whether we shall have any visitors at all this season if we stand in the way of families flying down together." The humour of the age was flowing mordaciously, even as the wit of France had done little more than a century before. The readiest jests carried a tang, whether turning upon personal poverty, municipal extravagance, or national incapacity. Opinion being evenly divided, the local rate of seventeen shillings in the pound influenced the casting vote in favour of mixed flying. There were necessary preparations, including a captive balloon in which an ancient mariner, decked out with a pair of wings like a superannuated Cupid, was posted to render assistance to the faltering. The rates at once rose to seventeen shillings and sixpence, but the principle of the enterprise was admitted to be sound.

So on this pleasant summer afternoon—an ideal day for a fly, said every one—the heights above the old town were echoing to the ceaseless gaiety of the watching crowd, for alatics had not yet ceased to be a novelty, while the air above was cleft by a hundred pairs of beating wings.

"A remarkable sight," said an old man who had opened conversation with the sociable craving of the aged; "ten years ago we little expected this."

"Why, no," replied his chance acquaintance on the seat; "if I remember rightly, the tendency was all towards a combination either of a balloon and a motor-car or of a submarine and a band-box."

"You don't fly yourself?"

The young man—and he was a stalwart enough youth—looked at himself critically as if mentally picturing the effect of a pair of wings upon his person. "Well, no," he replied; "one doesn't get the time for practice. Then consider the price of the things. And the annual licence—oh, they won't let you forget that, I assure you. Well, is it worth it?"

The old man shook his head in harmonious agreement; decidedly for him it was not worth it. "Perhaps you are in Somerset House?" he remarked tentatively. It is not the young who are curious; they have the fascinating study of themselves.

"Not exactly," replied the other, veiling by this diplomatic ambiguity an eminent firm of West End drapers; "but I happen to have rather exceptional chances of knowing what is going on behind the scenes in London. I can assure you, sir, that in spite of the last sixpence on the income-tax and the hen-roost tax, the Chancellor of the Exchequer has sent out stringent orders to whip up every penny in the hope of lessening a serious deficit."

"There may possibly be a deficit," admitted the old man with bland assurance; "but what do a few millions, either one way or the other, matter to a country with our inexhaustible resources? We are

14

certainly passing through a period of financial depression, but the unfailing lesson of the past has been that a cycle of bad years is inevitably followed by a cycle of good years, and in the competition with foreign countries our advantage of free trade ensures our pre-eminence." For it is a mistake now to ascribe optimism to youth. Those youths have by this time grown up into old men. Age is the optimist because it has seen so many things "come right," so many difficulties "muddled through." Also because they who would have been pessimistic old men have worried themselves into early graves. Your unquenchable optimist needs no pill to aid digestion. "Then," he concluded, "why trouble yourself unnecessarily on a beautiful day like this!"

"Oh, it doesn't trouble me," laughed the other man; "at least the deficit doesn't; nor the income-tax, I regret to say. But I rather kick at ten per cent. on my season ticket and a few other trifles when I consider that there used to be better national value without them. And I rather think that most others have had about enough of it."

"Patience, patience; you are a young man yet. Look round. I don't think I ever saw the grass greener for the time of the year, and in my front garden I noticed only to-day that the syringa is out a full week earlier than I can remember.... Eh! What is it? Which way? Where?"

The clerk was on his feet suddenly, and standing on the seat. Every one was standing up, and all in a common impulse were pointing to the sky. Some—women—screamed as they stood and watched, but after a gasp of horrified surprise, like a cry of warning cut short because too late, the mingling noises of the crowd seemed to shrink away in a breath. Every one had read of the sickening tragedies of broken cross-rods or of sudden loss of wing-power—ærolanguisis it was called—and one was taking place before their eyes. High up, very high at first, and a little to the east, a female figure was cleaving headlong through the air, and beyond all human power to save.

So one would have said; so every one indeed assumed; and when a second later another figure crossed their range it only heralded a double tragedy. It drew a gasp ... a gasp that lingered, spun out long and turned to one loud, tumultuous shout. The next minute men were shouting incoherently, dancing wildly, shaking hands with all and any, and expressing frantic relief in a hundred frantic ways.

Thus makes his timely entry into this chronicle Gatacre Stobalt, and reviewing the progress of flying as it then immaturely stood, it is not too much to say that no other man could have turned that tragedy. With an instinctive judgment of time, distance, angle,

15

and his own powers, Stobalt, from a hundred feet above, had leapt as a diver often leaps as he leaves the plank, and with rigid outstretched wings was dropping earthward on all but a plummet line. It was the famous "razor-edge" stroke at its narrowest angle, the delight of strong and daring fliers, the terror of those who watched beneath. It may be realised by ascending to the highest point of St Paul's and contemplating a dive into the flooded churchyard.

The moment was a classic one in the history of the wing. The air had claimed its victims as the waters have; and there was a legitimate pride, since the enterprise was no longer foolhardy, that they had never been withheld. But never before had a rescue been effected beyond the limits of the nets; it was not then deemed practicable and the axiom of the sport "A broken wing is a broken neck," so far held good. Yet here was a man, no novice in the art, deliberately pointing sheer to earth on a line that must bring him, if unswervingly maintained, into contact with the falling girl beneath. Up to that point the attempt would have been easy if daring, beyond it nothing but the readiest self-possession and the most consummate skill could avert an irretrievable disaster to himself.

"You have not even had the curiosity to ask if I am hurt yet." Her voice certainly was.

"$X = - 4 \{C^2\} \{x^3\}$," murmured Stobalt abstractedly. "I assure you," he explained, leaving the higher mathematics at her reproach, "that I had quite satisfied myself that you were not.... It all turns on the extra tension thrown on the crank by the additional three feathers. I am convinced that English makers have gone as far as they safely can in that direction." He glanced at her wings as he mused. They were of the familiar detached feather—or "venetian blind," as it was commonly called—pattern, and wonderfully graceful in their long sweep and elegant poise. Made of the purest white celluloid, just tinted with a delicate and deepening pink at the base, they harmonised with her sea-green costume as faultlessly as the lily with the leaves it springs from. Stobalt himself used the more difficult but much more powerful "bat" shape, built up of gold-beaters' skin; he had already folded them in rest, but in those early days the prudish conventions of the air debarred the girl from seeking a like repose.

"I should certainly discard the three outside feathers," he summed up.

"I shall certainly discard the whole thing," she replied. "I do not know which felt the worse—being killed or being saved."

He made a gesture that would seem to say that the personal

16

details of the adventure were better dismissed. He was plainly a man of few words, but the mechanical defect still held his interest.

"One understands that a brave man always dislikes being thanked," she continued a little nervously; "and, indeed, what can I say to thank you? You have saved my life, and I know that it must have been at a tremendous risk to yourself."

"I think," he said, "that the sooner you forget the incident.... That and the removal of those three feathers." His gestures were deliberate and the reverse of vivacious, but when he glanced up and moved a hand, it at once conveyed to the girl that in his opinion nothing else need stand in the way of her recovered powers and confidence.

"And there is," she said timidly, "nothing?" Precisely what there might be had not occurred to her satisfactorily.

"Nothing," he said, without the air of being heroic in his generosity. "Unless," he added, "you care to promise that you will not let——" He stopped with easy self-possession and turned enquiringly to a man in some official dress who had suddenly appeared in the glade.

"Have you a licence?" demanded the official, ignoring Stobalt and addressing himself in a style that at one time would have been deemed objectionably abrupt, to the lady. He was in point of fact a policeman, and from a thong on his wrist swung a truncheon, while the butt of a revolver showed at his belt. He wore no number or identifying mark, for it had long since been agreed that it must be objectionable to their finer feelings to treat policemen as though they were—one cannot say convicts, for a sympathetic Home Secretary had already discontinued the numbering of convicts on the ground that it created a state of things "undistinguishable from slavery," though not really slavery—but as though they were railway bridges or district council lamp-posts. "Treat a man as a dog, and he becomes a dog," had been the invincible argument of the band of humanitarians who had introduced what was known as the "Get-up-when-you-like-and-have-what-you-want" system of prison discipline, and "Treat a man as a lamp-post, and he becomes a lamp-post," had been the logical standpoint of the Amalgamated Union of Policemen and Plain Clothes Detectives.

"Yes," replied the girl, and her voice had not quite that agreeable intonation that members of the force usually hear from the lips of fair young ladies nowadays. "Do you wish to see it?"

"What else should I ask you if you had one for?" he demanded with the innate boorishness of the heavy-witted man. "Of course I want to see it."

She opened the little bag that hung from her girdle and handed him a paper without a word.

"Muriel Ursula Percy Sleigh Hampden?" It would be idle to pretend that the names pleased him, or that he tried to veil his contempt.

"Yes," she replied.

He indicated his private disbelief—or possibly merely took a ready means of exercising his authority in a way that he knew to be offensive—by producing a small tin box from one of his pockets and passing it to her without any explanation. The requirement was so universal in practice, however, that no explanation was necessary, for the signature, as the chief mark of identification, had long been superseded by the simpler and more effective thumb-sign. Miss Hampden made a slight grimace when she saw the condition of the soft wax which the box contained, but she obediently pressed it with her thumb and passed it back again. As her licence bore another thumb-sign, stamped in pigment, it was only necessary for the constable to compare the two (a process simplified by the superimposing glass, a contrivance not unlike a small opera-glass with converging tubes) in order to satisfy himself at once whether the marks were the impress of the same thumb. Apparently they were, for with a careless "Right-O," he proceeded on his way, swinging his truncheon with an easy grace, and occasionally striking off the end of an overhanging branch.

"I wonder," said Stobalt, when at length the zealous officer had quite disappeared in search of other fields for tactful activity, "I wonder if you are a daughter of Sir John Hampden?"

"Yes," she replied, looking at him with renewed interest. "His only daughter. Do you know my father?"

He shook his head. "I have been away, but we see the papers sometimes," he said. "The Sir John I mean," he explained, as though the point were a matter of some moment, "was a few years ago regarded as the one man who might unite our parties and save the position."

"There is only one Sir John Hampden," she replied. "But it was too late."

"Oh yes," he admitted vaguely, dismissing the subject.

Both were silent for a few minutes; it might be noticed that people often became thoughtful when they spoke of the past in those years. Indeed, an optimist might almost have had some ground for believing that a thinking era had begun.

When he spoke again it was with something of an air of constraint. "You asked me just now if there was—anything. Well, I have since thought——"

18

"Yes?" she said encouragingly.

"I have thought that I should like to meet your father. I hear everywhere that he is the most inaccessible man in London; but perhaps if you could favour me with a line of introduction——"

"Oh yes," she exclaimed gladly. "I am sure that he would wish to thank you. I will write to-morrow."

"I have paper and a pencil here," he suggested. "I have been a sailor," he added, as though that simple statement explained an omnipercipient resourcefulness; as perhaps it did.

"If you prefer it," she said, accepting the proffered stationery. It did not make the least difference, she told herself, but this business-like expedition chilled her generous instincts.

"I leave for town to-night," was all he vouchsafed.

For a few minutes she wrote in silence, while he looked fixedly out to sea. "What name am I to write, please?" she asked presently.

"Oh, Salt—George Salt," he replied in a matter-of-fact voice, and without turning his head.

"Is it 'Mr Salt,' or 'Captain,' or——?"

"Just 'Mr,' please. And"—his voice fell a little flat in spite of himself, but he did not meet her eyes—"and would it be too much if I asked you to mention the circumstances under which we met?"

She bent a little lower over the paper in a shame she could not then define. "I will not fail to let my father know how heroic you have been, and to what an extent we are indebted to you," she replied dispassionately.

"Thank you." Suddenly he turned with an arresting gesture, and impulsive speech trembled on his tongue. But the sophistries of explanation, apology, self-extenuation, were foreign to the nature of this strong keen-featured man, whose grey and not unkindly eyes had gained their tranquil depth from long intercourse with sea and sky—those two masters who teach the larger things of life. The words were never spoken, his arm fell down again, and the moment passed.

"I have never," he was known to say with quiet emphasis in later years, "regretted silence. I have never given way to an impulse and spoken hastily without regretting speech."

The London evening papers were being cried in the streets of the old Cinque Port as "George Salt" walked to the station a few hours later. A general election was drawing to its desultory close, but the results seemed to excite curiously little interest among the well-dressed, leisured class that filled the promenades. It was a longer sweep of the pendulum than had ever been anticipated in the days when politics were more or less the pastime of the rich, and the working classes neither understood nor cared to understand them—

only understood that whatever else happened nothing ever came their way.

The man who had been a sailor bought two papers of very different views, the Pall Mall Gazette and the orthodox labour organ called The Masses. Neither rejoiced, but to despair The Masses added a note of ingenuous surprise as it summarised the contest as a whole. This was how the matter stood:

Position of Parties at the Dissolution

Labour Members	300
Socialists	140
Liberals	112
Unionists	40

Party Gains

Socialist Gains	204
Moderate Labour Gains	5
Imperial Party Gains	0

Position of Parties in the New Parliament

Socialists	344
Moderate Labour Party (all groups)	179
Combined Imperial Party (Liberals Unionists)	68

(The above returns do not include the Orkney and Shetland Islands.)

Socialist majority over all possible combinations 97

There is no need to trace the development of political events leading up to this position. It lends itself to summary. The Labour party had come into power by pointing out to voters of the working classes that its members were their brothers, and promising them a great deal of property belonging to other people and a good many privileges which they vehemently denounced in every other class.

20

When in power they had thrown open the doors of election to one and all. The Socialist party had come into power by pointing out to voters of the working classes that its members were even more their brothers, and promising them a still larger share of other people's property (some, indeed, belonging to the more prosperous of the Labour representatives then in office) and still greater privileges. Yet the editor of The Masses was both pained and surprised at the result.

CHAPTER IV

THE COMPACT

A strong man and a prominent politician, Sir John Hampden had occupied the unfamiliar position in Parliament of belonging to no party. To no party, that is, as the term had then been current in English politics; for, more discerning than most of his contemporaries, he had foreseen the obliteration of the existing boundaries and the phenomenal growth of purely class politics even in the old century. It was, he recognised, to be that development of the franchise with which the world was later to become tolerably familiar: civil war on constitutional lines. His warnings fell on very stony ground. The powers that had never yet prepared for war abroad until the enemy had comfortably occupied all the strategic points, lest they should wound some wily protesting old gentleman's susceptibilities, were scarcely likely to take time by the forelock—or even by a hind fetlock, to enlarge the comparison—at home. While the Labour party was bringing pressure upon the Government of the day to grant an extension of suffrage that made Labour the master of eight out of every ten constituencies, the two great classical parties were quarrelling vehemently whether £5000 should be spent upon a sanatorium at Hai Yang and £5,000,000 upon a dockyard at Pittiescottie, or £5,000,000 upon a dockyard at Hai Yang and £5000 upon a sanatorium at Pittiescottie. When it is added that the Labour party was definitely pledged to the inauguration of universal peace by declining to go to war on any provocation, and looked towards wholesale disarmament as the first

21

means of economy on attaining office, the cataclysmal humour of the situation becomes apparent.

They attained office, as it has been seen, thanks largely to the great Liberal party whom they succeeded. The great Liberal party, like the editor of The Masses some years later, was pained and surprised at this ingratitude. The great Liberal party had never contemplated such a development, and through thick and thin had insisted upon regarding the Labour party as its ally, notwithstanding the fact that the "ally" had always laughed uproariously at the "alliance," and had pleasantly announced its intention of strewing Westminster with the wreckage of all existing capitalistic parties when once it was strong enough to do so.

Little wonder that that great Liberal Administration was destined to pass down to future ages as the "House of Pathetic Fools." Posterity adjudicated that no greater example of servile fatuousness could be produced. This was unjust, for on 20th June 1792, Louis XVI., certainly, let it be admitted, harder pressed, had accepted a red "cap of liberty," and putting it on in obedience to the command of the "extreme party" of his time, had bowed right and left with ingratiating friendliness, while a Labour gentleman, bearing upon a pike a raw cow's heart labelled "The heart of an aristocrat," roared out, with his twenty thousand friends, an amused approval.

It was out of the material of the two great traditional parties that Sir John Hampden tried to create his "class" coalition to meet the new conditions. The spectacle of working men suddenly dropping party differences and merging into a solid phalanx of labour was before their eyes, but the Tories were disintegrated and inert, the Whigs self-satisfied and cock-sure. The years of grace— just so many years as Sir John was before his contemporaries— passed. Then came a brief period, desperate indeed, but not hopeless, while something might yet be done; but the leaders of the historical parties were waiting for some happy chance by which they might retract and yet preserve their dignity. It was during this crisis that the party whose idea of dignity was symbolised by the escort of a brass band on a green-grocer's cart, abolished the House of Lords, suspended the naval programme, and confiscated all ecclesiastical landed property. Panic reigned, but there could be no appeal, for the party in power had never concealed their aims and aspirations, and now that they had been returned, they were only carrying out their promises.

That is putting their position so mildly as to be almost unjust. They were, indeed, among political parties the only one immaculate and beyond reproach. All others had trimmed and whittled, promised and recalled, sworn and forsworn, till political assurances were emptier than libertines' vows. The Socialists had nailed their manifesto to the mast, and no man could charge them with duplicity. On every platform from Caithness to Cornwall they had stood openly and declared: We are the enemies to Capital; we are at war with Society as it is at present constituted; we are for the forcible distribution of wealth, however come by, the abolition of class distinctions, and the levelling of humanity, with the unskilled labourer as the ideal standard.

"Good fellows all," had, in effect, declared their Liberal "allies," "and they do not really mean that—not phraseologically accurately, that is. We go in for a little, say, serpent-charming ourselves at election times, and when these excellent men are in Parliament the refining influence of the surroundings will tone them down wonderfully, and they will turn out thoroughly moderate and conciliatory members."

"Don't you make any error about that, comrades," the Socialistic-Labour candidates had replied; and with a candour unparalleled in the history of electioneering they had not merely hinted this or said it among themselves, but had freely and honourably proclaimed it to the four winds. "If you like to help us just now that's your affair, and we are quite willing to profit by it. But if you knew what you were doing, you would go home and all have the nightmare."

"So naïve!" smiled the great Liberal party. "Suppose they have to talk like that at present to please the unemployed."

Then came the deluge. Sir John Hampden could have every section of the middle and upper class political parties to lead if he so deigned, but wherever else he might lead them there was no possible hope of it being to St. Stephen's. It was, as his daughter had said, then too late. Labour members of one complexion or another had captured three-quarters of the constituencies, and there was not the slightest chance of ousting them.

So it came about that in less than a decade from the first alarm, the extremity of the patriot's hope was that in perhaps twenty years' time, when the country was reduced to bankruptcy and the position of a third class power, and when there was no more property to confiscate in the interest of the working class voter, a popular rising or a foreign invasion might again place a responsible administration in power. But in the meantime the organisations of the old parties fell to pieces, the parties themselves ceased to be powers, their leaders were half forgotten. Sir John Hampden might still be a rallying point if he raised a standard in a time of renewed hope, but there was no hope, and Sir John was reported to have broken his staff, drowned his books, and cut himself off from politics in the bitterness of his indignation and impotent despair.

It was in something very like this mood that George Salt found him, and it was an issue of the mood that would have made him inaccessible to a less resourceful man. Day after day he had denied himself to his old associates, and little disappointed hucksters who were anxious to betray their party for their conscience' sake—provided there was a definite offer of a more lucrative position in a new party—vainly shadowed his doorway with ready-made cabals in their pocket-books. But the man who had been a sailor and spoke few words had an air that carried where fluency and self-assurance failed. Even then, almost at his first words, Sir John would have closed the subject, definitely and without discussion.

"Politics do not concern me, Mr Salt," he said, rising, with an angry flash in the eyes whose fighting light gave the lie to the story of abandoned hope. "If that is your business you have reached me by a subterfuge."

"Having reached you," replied Salt, unmoved, "will you allow me to put my suggestions before you?"

"I have no doubt that they are interesting," replied the baronet, falling into smooth indifference, "but, as you may see, I am exclusively devoted to Euplexoptera now." It might be true, for the table before him was covered with specimens, scientific instruments and entomological works, while not even a single newspaper betrayed an interest in the day; but a world of bitterness smouldered beneath his half-scornful admission. "If," he continued in the same vein, "you have an idea for an effective series of magic lantern slides, you will find the offices of the Union of Imperial Agencies in Whitehall."

The first act to which the new Government was pledged was the evacuation of Egypt, and the mighty counterblast from the headquarters of the remnant of the great opposing organisation was, it should be explained, a travelling magic lantern van, designed to satisfy rural voters as to the present happy condition of the fellahin!

"Possibly you would hardly complain that I am not prepared to go far enough," replied the visitor. "But in order to discuss that, I must have your serious attention."

"I have already expressed myself," replied Sir John formally. "I am not interested."

"If you will hear me out and then repeat that, I will go," urged Salt with desperate calmness. "Yet I have thrown up the profession of my life because I hold that there is a certain remedy. And I have come a hundred miles to-night to offer it to you: for you are the man. Realise that I am vitally concerned."

"I am very sorry," replied Sir John courteously, but without the faintest encouragement, "but the matter is beyond me. Leave me, and try some younger, less disillusionised man."

"There is no other man who will serve my purpose." Sir John stared hard, as well he might: others had not been in the habit of appealing to him to serve their purposes. "You are the natural leader of our classes. You alone can inspire them; you alone have the authority to call them to any effort."

"I have been invited to lead a hundred forlorn hopes," replied Sir John. "A dozen years—nine years—aye, perhaps even six years ago any one of them might have been sufficient. Now—I have my earwigs. Good night, Mr Salt."

The dismissal was so unmistakably final that the most stubborn persistence could scarcely ignore it. Mr Salt rose, but only to approach the table by which Sir John was standing.

"I wished to have you with me on the bare merits of my plan," he said in a low voice, "but you would not. But you shall save England in spite of your dead heart. Read this letter."

For a moment it seemed doubtful how Hampden would take so brusque a demand. Another second and he might have imperiously ordered Salt to leave the house, when his eyes fell with a start upon the writing thrust before him, and taking the letter in his hand he read it through, read it twice.

"Little fool!" he said, so low that it sounded tenderly; "poor little fool!" Then aloud: "Am I to understand that you have saved my daughter's life?"

"Yes," replied George Salt, and even the tropical sunburn could not cover his hot shame.

"At great personal risk to yourself?"

Again the reply was, "Yes," without an added word.

"Why did you not let me know of this before?"

"Does that matter now?" It had been his master card, but a very humiliating one to play throughout: to trade upon that moment's instinctive heroism, to assert his bravery, to apprise it at its worth, and to claim a fit return.

"No," admitted Sir John with intuition, "I don't suppose it does. The position then is, that instead of exchanging the usual compliments applicable to the occasion, I express my gratitude by listening to your views on the political situation? And further," he continued, with the same gentle air of irony, accepting Salt's silent acquiescence, "that I proceed to liquidate my obligation fully by

25

identifying myself with a scheme which you have in your pocket for averting national disaster?"

"No," replied Salt sharply. "That is for you to accept or reject unconditionally on your own judgment."

"Very well. I am entirely at your service now."

"In the first place, then, I ask you to admit that a state of civil war morally exists, and that the only possible hope for our existence lies in adopting the methods of covert civil war to secure our ends."

"Admit! Good God! I have been shrieking it into deaf ears for half my life, it seems," cried Sir John, suddenly stirred despite himself. "They called me the Phantom Storm-petrel—'Wolf-cry' Hampden, Heaven knows what not—through an entire decade. Admit! Go on, Mr Salt. I accept your first clause more easily than Lord Stirling swallowed Socialistic amendments to his own Bills, and that is saying a great deal."

"Then," continued Salt, taking a bundle of papers from an inner pocket and selecting a docket of half a dozen typewritten sheets from it, "I propose for your acceptance the following plan of campaign."

He looked round the littered desk for a vacant space on which to lay the document. With an impetuous movement of his arm Sir John swept books, trays, and insects into one chaotic heap, and spreading the summary before him plunged into it forthwith.

CHAPTER V

THE DOWNTRODDEN

"Kumreds," announced Mr Tubes with winning familiarity, "I may say now and once and for all that you've thoroughly convinced me of the justice of your claims. But that isn't saying that the thing's as good as done, so don't go slinging it broadcast in the next pub you come to. There's our good kumred the Chancellor of the Exchequer to be taken into account, and while I'm about it let me tell you straight that these Cabinet jobs, whether at twenty, fifty, or a hundred quid a week, aren't the softest things going, as some of you chaps seem to imagine."

"Swap you, mate, then," called out a facetious L. & N. W.

fireman. "Yus, and throw the missis and kids into the bargain. Call it a deal?"

In his modest little house the Right Hon. James Tubes, M.P., Secretary of State for the Home Department, was receiving a deputation. Success, said his friends, had not spoiled him; others admitted that success had not changed him. From the time of his first appearance in Parliament he had been dubbed "Honest Jim" (perhaps a somewhat empty compliment in view of the fact that every Labour constituency had barbed unconscious satire at its own expense by distinguishing its representative as "Honest" Tom, Dick, or Harry), and after his elevation to Cabinet rank he still remained honest. More to the point, because more apparent, he remained unpretentious. It is true that he ceased to wear, as a personal concession to the Prime Minister, by whose side he sat, the grimy coal miner's suit in which he had first appeared in the House to the captivating of all hearts; but, more fortunate than Caractacus, he escaped envy by continuing to occupy his humble villa in Kilburn. The expenses of a Cabinet Minister, even in a Socialist Government, must inevitably be heavier than those of a private member, but this admirable man illustrated the uselessness of riches by continuing to live frugally but comfortably upon a tenth of his official income. According to intimate rumour he prudently invested the superfluous nine-tenths against a rainy day in the gilt-edged securities of countries where Socialism was least rampant.

Mr Tubes never refused to see a deputation, and when their views had been laid before him it was rare indeed that he was not able to declare a warm personal interest in their objects. True, he could not always undertake to carry their recommendations into effect; as a Minister he could not always express official approval of them, but they were rarely sent away without the moral support of that wink which is proverbially as significant as a more compromising form of agreement. Whether the particular expression of the great voice of the people was in the direction of the State adoption of Zulu orphans, or the compulsory removal of park palings from around private estates, the deputation could always go away with the inward satisfaction that however his words might read to outsiders on the morrow, they knew that as a man and a comrade, he, Jim Tubes, was with them heart and soul. "It costs nothing," he was wont to remark broad-mindedly to his home circle—referring, of course, to his own sympathetic attitude; for some of the ingenuous proposals which he countenanced were found in practice to prove very costly indeed—"and who knows what may happen next?"

But on this occasion, as far as compliance lay within his

27

power, there had been no need for mental reservation. The railway-men had been patient under capitalistic oppression in the past; they were convincing now in argument; and they were moderate in their demands for the future. It was no "Væ victis!" that these sturdy wearers of green corduroy trousers held out to their employers, but a cheery "Come now, mates. Fair does and we'll mess along somehow till the next strike."

Mr Drugget, M.P., introduced the deputation. It consisted of railway workers of all the lower grades with the exception of clerks. After many ineffectual attempts to get clerks to enter the existing Labour ring, it had been seriously proposed by the Labour wirepullers (who loved them in spite of their waywardness, and would have saved them, and their votes and their weekly contribution, from themselves) that they should form a Union of their own in conjunction with shop assistants and domestic servants. When the clerks (of whom the majority employed domestic servants directly or indirectly in their homes or in their lodgings) laughed slightly at the proposal; when the shop assistants smiled self-consciously, and when the domestic servants giggled openly, the promoters of this amusing triple alliance cruelly left them to their fate thenceforward, pettishly declaring that all three were a set of snobs—a designation which they impartially applied to every class of society except their own, and among themselves to every minute subdivision of Labour except the one which they adorned.

It devolved upon a rising young "greaser" in the service of the Great Northern to explain, as spokesman, the object of the visit. Under the existing unfair conditions the directors of the various companies were elected at large salaries by that unnecessary and parasitic group, the shareholders, while the workmen—the true creators of every penny of income—had no direct hand in the management of affairs. When they wished to approach the chief authorities it was necessary for them to send delegates from their Union, who were frequently kept waiting ten minutes in an ante-room; and although of late years their demands were practically always conceded without demur, the position was anomalous and humiliating. What seemed only reasonable to them, then, was that they should have the right to elect an equal number of directors from among themselves, who should sit on the Board with the other directors, have equal powers, and receive similar salaries.

"To be, in fact, your permanent deputation to the Board," suggested the Home Secretary.

"That's it—with powers," replied the G. N. man.

"There'll be some soft jobs going—then," murmured a shunter, who was getting on in years, reflectively.

"No need for the missis to take in young men lodgers if you get one, eh, Bill?" said his neighbour jocosely.

Whether it was the extreme unlikelihood of his ever being made a director, or some other deeper cause, the secret history of the period does not say, but Bill turned upon his innocent friend in a very aggressive mood.

"What d'yer mean—young men lodgers?" he demanded warmly. "What call have you to bring that up? Come now!"

"Why, mate," expostulated the offending one mildly, "no one said anything to give any offence. What's the 'arm? Your missis does take in lodgers, same as plenty more, don't she? Well, then!"

"I can take a 'int along the lines as well as any other," replied Bill darkly. "It's gone far enough between pals. See? I never said anything about your sister leaving that there laundry, did I? Never, I didn't."

"And what about it if you did?" demanded the neighbour, growing hot in his turn. "I should think you'd have enough——"

"Gentlemen, gentlemen," expostulated the glib young spokesman, as the voices rose above the conversational whisper, "let us have absolute unanimity, if you please—expressed in the usual way, by all saying nothing together."

"Wha's matter with Bill?" murmured the next delegate with polite curiosity.

"Seems to me the little man is troubled with his teef," replied the unfortunate cause of the ill-feeling, with smouldering passion. "Strike me if he isn't. Ah!" And seeing the impropriety of relieving his feelings in the usual way in a Cabinet Minister's private study, he relapsed into bitter silence.

Mr Tubes having expressed his absolute approval of this detail of the programme, the second point was explained. Why, it was demanded, should the provisions of the Employers' Liability Act apply only to the hours during which a man was at work? Furthermore, why should they apply only to accidents? Supposing, said Mr William Mulch, the spokesman in question, that a bloke went out in a social way among his friends, as any bloke might, caught the small-pox, and got laid up for life with after-effects, or died? Or suppose the bloke, after sweating through a day's work, went home dog-tired to his miserable hovel, and broke his leg falling over the carpet, or poisoned his hand opening a tin of sardines? They looked to the present Government to extend the working of the Act so as to cover the disablement or death of employés from every cause whatever, natural death included, and

29

wherever they might be at the time. Under the present unfair and artificial conditions of labour, the work-people were nothing but the slaves and chattels of capitalists, and it was manifestly unfair that the latter should escape their responsibilities after exploiting a man's labour for their own greedy ends, simply because he happened to die of hydrophobia or senile decay, or because the injury that disabled him was received outside the fœtid, insanitary den where in exchange for a bare sordid pittance his flesh was ground from his bones for eight hours daily.

The Right Hon. gentleman expressed his entire concurrence with this provision also, and roused considerable enthusiasm by mentioning that some time ago he had independently arrived at the conclusion that such a clause was urgently required.

Before the next point was considered, Comrade Tintwistle asked permission to say a few words. He explained that he had no intention of introducing a discordant note. On the contrary, he heartily supported the proposal as far as it went, but—and here he wished to say that though he only voiced the demands of a minority, it was a large, a growing, and a noisy minority—it did not go far enough. The contention of those he represented was that the responsibility of employers ought to extend to the wives and families of their work-people. Many a poor comrade was sadly harassed by having to keep a crippled child who would never be a bread-winner, or an ailing wife who was incapable of looking after his home comfort properly. They were fighting over again the battle that they had won in the matter of free meals for school children. It had taken years to convince people that it was equally necessary that children who did not happen to be attending school should have meals provided for them, and even more necessary to see that their mothers should be well nourished; it had taken even longer to arrive at the logical conclusion that if free meals were requisite, free clothes were not a whit less necessary. No one nowadays doubted the soundness of that policy, yet here they were again timorously contemplating half-measures, while the insatiable birds of prey who sucked their blood laughed in their sleeve at the spectacle of the British working men hiding their heads ostrich-like in the shifting quicksand of a fool's paradise.

The signs of approval that greeted this proposal showed clearly enough that other members of the deputation had sympathetic leanings towards the larger policy of the minority. Mr Tubes himself more than hinted at the possibility of a personal conversion in the near future. "In the meantime," he remarked, "everything is on your side. Your position is logical, moderate, and just. All can admit that, although we may not all exactly agree as to

30

whether the time is ripe for the measure. With every temptation to wipe off some of the arrears of injustice of the past, we must not go so far as to kill the goose that lays the golden egg."

"How do you make that out?" demanded an unsophisticated young signalman. "It's the work of the people that produces every penny that circulates."

"Oh, just so," replied Tubes readily. "That is the real point of the story. It was the grains of corn that made the eggs, and the goose did nothing but sit and lay them. We must always have our geese." He turned to the subject in hand again with a laugh, and approved a few more modest suggestions for abolishing "privileges."

"The last point," continued the spokesman, "is one that closely concerns the principles that we all profess. I refer to the obsolete and humiliating anachronism that with a Government pledged to the maintenance of social equality in office, at any hour of the day, at practically every railway station throughout the land you will still see trains subdivided as regards designation and accommodation into first, second, and third classes. It is a distinction which to us, as the representatives of the so-called third class, is nothing more or less than insulting. Why should me and my missis when we travel be compelled to sit where the accidents generally happen and have to put up with eighteen in a compartment, when smug clerks and saucy ladies' maids, who are no better than us, enjoy the comparative luxury of only fifteen in a compartment away from the collisions, and snide financiers and questionable duchesses, who are certainly a good deal worse, sit in padded rooms, well protected front and rear, and never know what it is to be packed more than six a-side? If that isn't class distinction I should like to know what is. It isn't—Gawd help us!—that we wish to mix with these people, or that we envy their position or covet their wealth. Such motives have never entered into the calculations of those who have been foremost in Socialistic propaganda. But as thoughtful and self-respecting units of an integral community we object to being segregated by the imposition of obsolete and arbitrary barriers, we do resent the artificial creation of social grades, and we regard with antagonism and distrust the unjust accumulation of labour-created wealth in the hands of the idle and incapable few.

"But if this is the standpoint of the great mass of the democracy, to us of the Amalgamated Unions of Railway Workers and Permanent Way Staffs the invidious distinction has a closer significance. As ordinary citizens our sense of equality is outraged by the demarcations I have referred to; but as our work often places us in a temporary subordination to the occupants of these so-called first and second classes, whom we despise intellectually and resent

31

economically, we incur the additional stigma of having to render them an external deference which we recognise to be obsolete and servile. The Arden and Avon Valley case, which earned the martyrdom of dismissal for William Jukson and ultimately involved forty thousand of us in a now historic strike, simply because that heroic man categorically refused to the doddering Duke of Pentarlington any other title than the honourable appellation of 'Comrade,' is doubtless still fresh within your minds. We lost on that occasion through insufficiency of funds, but the ducal portmanteau over which William Jukson took his memorable stand, will yet serve as a rallying point to a more successful issue."

Mr Mulch paused for approbation, which was not stinted, but before he could resume, a passionate little man who had been rising to a more exalted state of fervour with every demand, suddenly hurled himself like a human wedge into the forefront of the proceedings.

"Kumrids!" he exclaimed, breathless from the first, "with your kind permission I would say a few words embodying a suggestion which, though not actually included in the agenda, is quite in 'armony with the subject before us."

"Won't it keep?" suggested a tired delegate hopefully.

"The suggestion is briefly this," continued the little man, far too enthusiastic to notice any interruption, "that as a tribute to William Jukson's sterling determination and as a perpetual reminder of the issues raised, we forthwith add to the banners of the Amalgamated Unions one bearing an allegorical design consisting of two emblematic figures struggling for the possession of a leather portmanteau with the words 'No Surrender!' beneath. The whole might be made obvious to a person of the meanest intelligence by the inscription 'A. and A. V. Ry. Test Case. W. J. upholds the Principles of Social Democracy and Vindicates the People's Rights,' running round."

"Why should he be running round?" asked a slow-witted member of the deputation.

"Who running round?" demanded the last speaker, amenable to outside influence now that he had said his say.

"William Jukson. Didn't you say he was to be on this banner vindicating the people's rights running round? He stood there on the platform, man to man, so I've always heard."

The redoubtable Jukson's champion cast a look of ineffable contempt upon his simple brother and made a gesture expressive of despair. "That's all," he said, and sat down.

Mr Mulch resumed his interrupted innings. "The suggestion will doubtless receive attention if submitted through the proper channels," he remarked a little coldly. It was one thing to take the indomitable Jukson under his own ægis; quite another to countenance his canonisation at a period when strenuous candidates were more numerous than remunerative niches. "But to revert to the subject in hand from which we have strayed somewhat. It only remains for me to say that all artificial distinctions between class and class are distasteful to the people at large, detestable to the powerful Unions on whose behalf we are here to-day, and antagonistic to the interests of the community. We confidently look, therefore, to the present Government to put an end to a state of things that is inconsistent with the maintenance of practical Socialism."

Towards this proposal, also, Mr Tubes turned a friendly ear, but he admitted that in practice his sympathies must be purely platonic, for the time at least. In truth, the revenue yielded by the taxation of first and second class tickets was so considerable that it could not be ignored. Many people adopted the third class rather than suffer the exaction, and the receipts of all the railway companies in the kingdom fell considerably—to the great delight of that large section of the Socialistic party that had not yet begun to think. But the majority of the wealthy still paid the price, and not a few among the weak, aged, and timorous, among children, old men, and ladies, were driven to the superior classes which they could ill afford by the increased difficulty of finding a seat elsewhere, and by the growing truculence of the workmen who were thrust upon them in the thirds. For more than a decade it had been observed that when a seat in tram or train was at stake the age of courtesy was past, but a new Burke, listening to the conversation of those around, might too frequently have cause to think that the age of decency had faded also. Another development, contributing to the maintenance of the higher classes, was the fact that one was as heavily mulcted if he turned to any of the other forms of more exclusive travelling. Private carriages of all kinds were the butt of each succeeding Budget, even bicycles (unless owned by workmen) were not exempt; and so heavily was the Chancellor's hand laid upon motor cars (except such as were the property of Members of Parliament) that even the Marquis of Kingsbery was satisfied, and withdrew his threat to haunt the Portsmouth Road with an elephant gun.

And yet, despite the persistence of a Stuart in imposing taxation and the instincts of a Vespasian in making it peculiarly offensive, the Treasury was always in desperate straits. The reason was not far to seek. In the old days Liberal governments had at times proved extravagant; Tory governments had perhaps oftener proved even more extravagant; but in each case it was the tempered profusion of those who through position and education were too careless to count their pence and too unconcerned to be dazzled by their pounds. The Labour and the Socialist administrations proved superlatively extravagant: and there is nothing more irredeemable than the spendthrift recklessness of your navvy who has unexpectedly "come into money." The beggar was truly on horseback, or, to travel with the times, he had set off in his motor car, and he was now bowling along the great high-road towards the cliff-bound sea of national perdition, a very absent-minded beggar indeed, with a merry hand upon the high speed gear.

"I am with you heart and soul," therefore declared Mr Tubes as a man, and as a member of the Cabinet added—"in principle. But the contemplated Act for providing State maintenance of strikers, in strikes approved of by the Board of Trade, makes it extremely undesirable to abolish any of the existing sources of revenue, at least until we see what the measure will involve."

"Save on the Navy, then," growled a malcontent in the rear rank.

"We have already reduced the Navy to the fullest extent that we consider it desirable to go at present; that is to say, to the common-sense limit—equality with any one of the other leading powers."

"The Army, then."

"We have already reduced the Army very considerably, but with a navy on the lines which I have indicated and an army traditionally weaker at the best than those of the great military powers, which are also naval powers, is it prudent?" The gesture that closed the sentence clearly expressed Mr Tubes's own misgivings on the subject. He had always been regarded as a moderate though a vacillating man among his party, and the "reduce everything and chance it" policy of a powerful section of the Cabinet disturbed his rest at times.

"Why halt ye between two opinions?" exclaimed a clear and singularly sweet voice from the doorway. "Temporise not with the powers of darkness when the day of opportunity is now at hand. Sweep away arms and armies, engines of war and navies, in one vast and irresistible wave of Universal Brotherhood. Beat the swords into ploughshares, cast your guns into instruments of music, let all strife cease. Extend the hand of friendship and equality not only man to man and class to class, but nation to nation and race to race. Make a great feast, and in love and fellowship compel them to come in: so shall you inaugurate the reign of Christ anew on earth."

Every one looked at the speaker and then glanced at his neighbour with amusement, contempt, enquiry, here and there

34

something of approval, in his eye. "The Mad Parson," "Brother Ambrose," "The Ragged Priest," "St Ambrose of Shadwell," ran from lip to lip as a few recognised the tonsured barefoot figure standing in his shabby cassock by the door. Mr Tubes alone, seated out of the range of whispers and a victim to the defective sight that is the coal-pit heritage throughout the world, received no inkling of his identity, and, assuming that he was a late arrival of the deputation, sought to extend a gentle conciliation.

"The goal of complete disarmament is one that we never fail to strive for," he accordingly replied, "but our impulsive comrade must admit that the present is hardly the moment for us to make the experiment entirely on our own. Prudence——"

"Prudence!" exclaimed the ragged priest with flashing vehemence. "There is no more cowardly word in the history of that Black Art which you call Statecraft. All your wars, all your laws, all tyranny, injustice, inhumanity, all have their origin in a fancied prudence. It marks the downward path in whitened milestones more surely than good intentions pave that same decline. Dare! dare! dare! man. Dare to love your brother. Herod was prudent when he sought to destroy all the children of Bethlehem; it was prudence that led Pilate to deliver up our Master to the Jews. The deadly ignis fatuus of prudence marched and counter-marched destroying armies from the East and from the West through every age, formed vast coalitions and dissolved them treacherously, made dynasties and flung them from the throne. It led pagan Rome, it illumined the birth of a faith now choked in official bonds, it danced before stricken Europe, lit the martyrs' fires, lured the cold greed of commerce, and now hangs a sickly beacon over Westminster. But prudence never raised the fallen Magdalene nor forgave the dying thief. Christ was not prudent."

"Christ, who's 'e?" said a man who had a reputation for facetiousness to maintain. "Oh! I remember. He's been dead a long time."

Ambrose turned on him the face that led men and the eye that quelled. "My brother," he almost whispered across the room, "if you die with that in your heart it were better for you that He had never lived."

There was something in the voice, the look, the presence, that checked the ready methods by which a hostile intruder was wont to be expelled. All recognised a blind inspired devotion beside which their own party enthusiasm was at the best pale and thin. Even to men who were wholly indifferent to the forms of religion, Ambrose's self-denying life, his ascetic discipline, his fanatical whole-heartedness, his noble—almost royal—family, and the magnetic

35

influence which he exercised over masses of the most wretched of the poor and degraded gave pause for thought, and often extorted a grudging regard. Not a few among those who had dispassionately watched the rise and fall of parties held the opinion that the man might yet play a wildly prominent part in the nation's destinies and involve a tragedy that could only yet be dimly guessed: for most men deemed him mad.

"Whatever you may wish to say this is neither the time nor the place," said Mr Drugget mildly. "We are not taking part in a public meeting which invites discussion, but are here in a semi-private capacity to confer with the Home Secretary."

"There is no time or place unseasonable to me, who come with Supreme authority," replied Ambrose. "Nor, if the man is worthy of his office, can the Home Secretary close his ears to the representative of the people."

"The people!" exclaimed a startled member of the Amalgamated Unions. "What d'yer mean by the 'representative of the people'? We are the representatives of the people. We are the people!"

"You?" replied Ambrose scornfully, sweeping the assembly with his eye and returning finally with a disconcerting gaze to the man who spoke, "you smug, easy, well-fed, well-clad, well-to-do in your little way, self-satisfied band of Pharisees, you the people of the earth! Are you the poor, are you the meek, the hungry, the persecuted? You are the comfortable, complacent bourgeoisie of labourdom. You can never inherit the Kingdom of Christ on earth. Outside your gates, despised of all, stand His chosen people."

There was a low, rolling murmur of approval, growing in volume before it died away, but it rose not within the chamber but from the road outside.

"Mr Tubes," whispered the introducer of the deputation uneasily, "give the word, sir. Shall we have this man put out?"

"No, no," muttered Tubes, with his eyes fixed on the window and turning slightly pale; "wait a minute. Who are those outside?"

The Member of Parliament looked out; others were looking too, and for a moment not only their own business was forgotten, but the indomitable priest's outspoken challenge passed unheeded in a curious contemplation of his following. At that period the sight was a new one in the streets of London, though afterwards it became familiar enough, not only in the Capital, but to the inhabitants of every large town and city throughout the land.

Ambrose had been called "The Ragged Priest," and it was a very ragged regiment that formed his bodyguard; he was "The Mad Parson," and an ethereal mania shone in the faces of many of his followers, though as many sufficiently betrayed the slum-bred cunning, the inborn brutishness of the unchanged criminal and the hooligan, thinly cloaked beneath a shifty mask of assumed humility. As became "St Ambrose," the banners which here and there stood out above the ranks—mere sackcloth standards lashed to the roughest poles—nearly all bore religious references in their crude emblems and sprawling inscriptions. The gibes at charity, the demands for work of an earlier decade had given place to another phase. "Christ is mocked," was one; "Having all things in common," ran another; while "As it was in the beginning," "Equality, in Christ," "Thy Kingdom come," might frequently be seen. But a more significant note was struck by an occasional threat veiled beneath a text, as "The sun shall be turned into darkness, the moon into blood," though their leader himself never hinted violence in his most impassioned flights. Among the upturned faces a leisurely observer might have detected a few that were still conspicuous in refinement despite their sordid settings—women chiefly, and for the most part fanatical converts who had been swept off their feet by Ambrose's eloquence in the more orthodox days when he had thrilled fashionable congregations from the pulpit of a Mayfair church. Other women there were in plenty; men, old and young; even a few children; dirty, diseased, criminal, brutalised, vicious, crippled, the unemployed, the unemployable. Beggars from the streets, begging on a better lay; thieves hopeful of a larger booty; malcontents of every phase; enemies of society reckoning on a day of reckoning; the unfortunate and the unfortunates swayed by vague yearnings after righteousness; schemers striving for their private ends; with a salting of the simple-hearted; all held together so far by the vehement personality of one fanatic, and glancing down the ranks one could prophesy what manner of monster out of the depths this might prove when it had reached rampant maturity. Poverty, abject poverty, was the dominant note; for all who marched beneath the ragged banner must go in rags.

Mr Drugget was the first to recover himself. "Look here," he said, turning to Ambrose aggressively, "I don't quite catch on to your game, but that's neither here nor there. If you want to know what I call it, I call it a bit of blasted impertinence to bring a mob like that to a man's private house, no matter who he may be. What's more, this is an unlawful gathering according to Act of Parliament."

"That which breaks no divine commandment cannot be unlawful," replied Ambrose, unmoved. "I recognise no other law. And you, who call yourselves Socialists and claim equality, what are your laws but the old privileges which you denounced in others

37

extended to include yourselves, what your equality but the spoliation of those above you?"

"We are practical Socialists," exclaimed one or two members with dignity. "As reasonable men we recognise that there must be a limit somewhere."

"Practical is the last thing you can claim to be. You are impractical visionaries; for it would be as easy for a diver to pause in mid-air as for mankind to remain at a half-way house to Equality. All! All! Every man-made distinction must be swept away. Neither proprietor nor property, paid leader nor gain, task-work nor pride of place; nothing between God and man's heart. That is the only practical Socialism, and it is at hand."

"Not while we're in office," said the Home Secretary shortly.

"Mene, Mene, Tekel, Upharsin," cast back Ambrose. "Where is now the great Unionist party? In a single season the sturdy Liberal stronghold crumbled into dust. You deposed a Labour government that was deemed invulnerable in its time. Beware, the hand is already on the wall. Those forces which you so blindly ignore will yet combine and crush you."

It was not unlikely. In former times it would have required barricades and some personal bravery. But with universal suffrage the power of the pauper criminal was no less than that of the ducal millionaire, and the alcohol lunatic, presenting himself at the poll between the spasms of delirium tremens, was as potent a force as the philosopher. A party composed of paupers, aliens, chronic unemployed, criminals, lunatics, unfortunates, the hysterical and degenerate of every kind, together with so many of the working classes as might be attracted by the glamour of a final and universal spoliation, led by a sincere and impassioned firebrand, might yet have to be reckoned with.

"And you, comrade?" said a railway-man with pardonable curiosity. "When you've had your little fling, who's going to turn you out and come in?"

"We!" exclaimed Ambrose with a touch of genuine surprise; "how can you be so blind! We represent the ultimate destiny of mankind."

In another age and another place a form of government called the States General, and largely composed of amiable clerics, had been called up to redress existing grievances. Being found too slow, it gave place to the National Assembly, and, to go yet a little faster, became the Legislative Assembly. This in turn was left behind by the more expeditious Girondins, but as even they lagged according to the bustling times, the Jacobins came into favour. The ultimate development of quick-change Equality was reached in the

38

Hébertists. From one to another had been but a step, and they were all "The People"; but while the States General had looked for the millennium by the abolition of a grievance here and there, and the lightening of a chafing collar in the mass, the followers of Hébert found so little left for them to abolish that they abolished God. The experiment convinced the sagest of the leaders that human equality is only to be found in death, and, true to their principles, they "equalised" a million of their fellow-countrymen through the instrumentality of the guillotine, and other forms of moral suasion. Grown more tender-hearted, "The People" no longer thirsted for another section of "The People's" blood—only for their money; and in place of Fouquier-Tinville and the Gentleman with the Wooden Frame, their instruments of justice were represented by a Chancellor of the Exchequer, and an individual delivering blue papers.

"We represent the ultimate destiny of mankind: absolute equality," announced Ambrose. "Any other condition is inconsistent with the professions to which your party has repeatedly pledged itself. Will you, my brother," he continued, addressing himself to the Home Secretary, "receive a deputation?"

The deputation was already waiting at the outer door, three men and three women. It included a countess, a converted housebreaker, and an anarchist who had become embittered with life since the premature explosion of one of his bombs had blown off both his arms and driven him to subsist on the charitable. The other three were uninteresting nonentities, but all were equal in their passion for equality.

"We are all pledged to the principle of social equality, and every step in that direction that comes within the range of practical politics must have our sympathy," replied Mr Tubes. "Further than that I am not prepared to commit myself at present. That being the case, there would be no object in receiving a deputation." To this had Mr Tubes come at last.

"The unending formula," said Brother Ambrose with weary bitterness. "... Bread, and you give them stones ... Man," he cried with sudden energy, "almost within your grasp lies the foundation of New Jerusalem, tranquil, smiling, sinless. What stands in your way? Nothing, nothing! truly nothing but the heavy shadow of the old and cruel past. Throw it off; is it not worth doing? No more spiritual death, no more sorrow of the things of this world, nor crying, 'Neither shall there be any more pain: for the former things are passed away.'"

"I have nothing more to say," responded the Home Secretary coldly, bending over his desk to write.

"Then I have much more to do," retorted Ambrose impetuously, "and that shall be with the sword of my mouth." He strode from the room with an air that no amount of legislative equality could ever confer upon any of those he left behind, and a moment later his ragged escort was in motion homeward—slumward.

"Kumreds," said Mr Tubes, looking up, "the harmony of the occasion has been somewhat impaired by an untoward incident, but on the whole I think that you may rest well satisfied with the result of your representations. Having another appointment I must now leave you, but I have given instructions for some beer and sandwidges to be brought in, and I trust that in my enforced absence you will all make yourselves quite at home." He shook hands with each man present and withdrew.

"Beer and sandwidges!" muttered Comrade Tintwistle, with no affectation of delight, to a chosen spirit. "And this is the man we pay fifty quid a week to!"

"Ah!" assented the friend, following Mr Tubes's hospitable directions by strolling round the room and fingering the ornaments. "Well, when it comes to a general share-out I don't know but what I should mind having this here little round barometer for my parlour."

"Neat little thing," assented Tintwistle with friendly interest. "What does it say?"

"Seems to be dropping from 'Change' to 'Stormy,'" read the friend.

CHAPTER VI

MISS LISLE TELLS A LONG POINTLESS STORY

Sir John Hampden lived within a stone-throw of the Marble Arch; George Salt had established himself in Westminster; and about midway between the two, in the neighbourhood of Pall Mall, a convenient but quite unostentatious suite of offices had been taken and registered as the headquarters of the Unity League.

The Unity League was a modern organisation that had come

into existence suddenly, and with no great parade, within a week of that day when George Salt had forced Hampden to hear what he wished to say, a day now nearly two years ago. The name was simple and commonplace, and therefore it aroused neither curiosity nor suspicion; it was explained by the fact that it had only one object: "By constitutional means to obtain an adequate representation of the middle and upper classes in Parliament," a phrase rendered by the lighter-hearted members colloquially as "To kick out the Socialists." The Government, quite content to govern constitutionally (in the wider sense) and to be attacked constitutionally (in the narrower sense), treated the existence of the Unity League as a playful ebullition on the part of the milch sections of society, and raised the minimum income-tax to four and threepence as a sedative.

At first the existence of the League met with very little response and no enthusiasm among those for whom it was intended. It had become an article of faith with the oppressed classes that no propagandism could ever restore an equitable balance of taxation. Every change must inevitably tend to be worse than the state before. To ask the working classes (the phrase lingered; by the demarcation of taxation it meant just what it conventionally means to-day, and, similarly, it excluded clerical workers of all grades)—to ask this privileged class which dominated practically every constituency to throw out their own people and put in a party whose avowed policy would be to repeal the Employers' Liability Act (Extended), the Strikes Act, the Unemployed Act, the Amended Companies Act, the Ecclesiastical Property Act, the infamous Necessity Act, and a score of other preposterous Acts of Injustice before they even gave their attention to anything else, had long been recognised to be grotesque. A League, therefore, which spoke of working towards freedom on constitutional lines fell flat. The newspapers noticed it in their various individual fashions, and all but the Government organs extended to it a welcome of cold despair. The general reader gathered the impression that he might look for its early demise.

The first revulsion of opinion came when it was understood that Sir John Hampden had returned to public life as the President of the League. What his name meant to his contemporaries, how much the League gained from his association, may be scarcely realised in an age existing under different and more conflicting conditions. Briefly, his personality lifted the effort into the plane—not of a national movement, for with the nation so sharply riven by two irreconcilable interests that was impossible, but certainly beyond all cavil as to motives and methods. When it was further

41

known that he was not lending his name half-heartedly as to a forlorn hope, or returning reluctantly as from a tardy sense of duty, men began to wonder what might lie behind.

The first public meeting of the newly formed League deepened the impression. Men and women of the middle and upper classes were invited to become members. The annual subscription being a guinea, none but adults were expected. Those of the working class were not invited. If the subscription seemed large, the audience was asked to remember what lay at stake, and to compare with it the case of the artisan cheerfully contributing his sixpence a week to the strike fund of his class. "As a result there is a Strikes Act now in force," the President reminded them, "and the artisan no longer pays the cost——"

"No, we do," interjected a listener.

"I ask you to pay it for three years longer; no more, perhaps less," replied Hampden with a reassuring smile, and his audience stared.

If the subscription seemed large for an organisation of the kind the audience was assured that it was by no means all, or even the most, that would be expected of them. They must be prepared to make some sacrifice when called upon; the nature he could not indicate at that early stage. No balance sheet would be published; no detailed reports would be issued. There would be no dances, no garden-parties, no club houses, no pretty badges. The President warned them that membership offered no facilities for gaining a precarious footing in desirable society, through the medium of tea on the Vicarage lawn, or croquet in the Home Park. "We are not playing at tin politics nowadays," he caustically remarked.

That closed the exordium. In a different vein Hampden turned to review the past, and with the chartered freedom of the man who had prophesied it all, he traced in broad lines and with masterly force the course of Conservative ineptitude, Radical pusillanimity, Labour selfishness, and Socialistic tyranny. What would be the crowning phase of grab government? History foreshadowed it; common-sense certified it. Before the dark curtain of that last stupendous act the wealth and wisdom, the dignity and responsibility of the nation, stood in paralysed expectancy.

There was a telling pause; a dramatic poignant silence hung over the massed crowd that listened to the one man who could still inspire a kindling spark of hope. Then, just at the opportune moment, a friendly challenge gave the effective lead:

"And what does Sir John Hampden offer now?"

"Absolute victory," replied the speaker, with the thrilling energy of quiet but assured conviction, "and with it the ending of

42

this nightmare dream of life in which we are living now, when every man in his half-guilty helplessness shuns his own thoughts, and all are filled with a new unnatural pain: the shame of being Englishmen. Blink the fact or not, it is civil war upon which we are now engaged. Votes are the weapons, and England and her destiny, nothing more or less, are the stakes. It has frequently been one of the curious features even of the most desperate civil struggles of the past, that while battles were raging all around, towns besieged, and thrones falling, commerce was at the same time being carried on as usual, wordy controversies on trivial alien subjects were being hotly discussed by opposing sections, as though their pedantic differences were the most serious matters in the world, and the ordinary details of everyday life were proceeding as before. So it is to-day, but civil, social, war is in our midst, and—again blink it or not—we are losing, and wage it as it is being waged we shall continue to lose. I am not here to-day to urge the justice of our cause, to palliate unwise things done, to indulge in regrets for wise things left undone. One does not discuss diplomacy in the middle of a battle. I am here to hold out a new hope for the triumph of our cause, for the revival of an era of justice, for the recovered respect of nations. I have never been accused of undue optimism, yet fully weighing my words, I stand on this platform to-night to share with you my conviction that it is within our power, in three years' time, to send an overwhelming majority of our reconstructed party into power, to reduce the income-tax to a sane and normal level, and to recommence the building up of a treasonably neglected navy."

Another man—perhaps any other man—would have been met by ridicule, but Hampden's reputation was unique. The one point of emphasis that could not fail to impress itself upon every listener was that there was something behind all this. It was a point that did not convey itself half so forcefully in the newspaper reports, so that, as Socialists and their friends did not attend the meetings (even as members of the wealthier classes had ignored Socialistic "vapourings" in days gone by), any menace to the Government that the League might contain was lost on them for the present. It was the moral of an old fable: the Dog in Luxury grown slothful and unready.

The subscription deterred few. It was an epoch when everything was, apparently, being given away for nothing; though never had the grandfatherly maxim that in business nothing ever is offered without its price, been so keenly observed. But superficially, to ride in a penny 'bus entitled one to a probable pension for life; to buy a pound of tea was only the preliminary to being presented with a motor-car or a grand piano. Fortunes lurked in cigarette boxes,

43

whole libraries sprang gratuitously from the columns of the daily papers; not only oxen, but silver spoons inexhaustible were compressed within the covers of each jar of meat extract, and buried treasure, "Mysterious Millionaires," and "Have-you-that-ten-pound-note?" men littered the countryside. To be asked to subscribe a guinea for nothing definite in return, was therefore a pleasing novelty which took amazingly. So, too, the idea of participating in some sort of legal revolution which would entail sacrifices and result in unexpected developments, was found to be delightfully invigorating. How the movement spread is a matter of history. Incomes had been reduced wholesale, yet, so great was the confidence in Hampden's name, that many members sent their subscription ten times told. When he asked, as he frequently did at the close of a meeting, for recruits who were willing to devote their whole time unpaid to the work in various departments, more than could be accepted were invariably forthcoming. All members proselytised on their own initiative, but within these there were thousands of quiet and devoted workers who were in close touch with the office of the League. They acted on detailed instructions in their methods, and submitted regular reports of progress and of the state of public feeling in every part of the kingdom and among every class of the community. To what length the roll of membership had now extended only two men knew, even approximately. All that could be used as a guide was the fact that it was the exception rather than the rule anywhere to find a family among the classes aimed at, that did not contain at least one member; while London, within the same indicated limits, had practically gone solid for membership.

And George Salt? The public knew nothing of him; his name did not appear in connection with the League, nor did he ever take a place among the notables upon the platform at its meetings. But the thousands of the inner ring knew him very well, and few whose business led them to the offices missed encountering him. He was officially supposed to be a League secretary to Sir John Hampden, endowed with large discretionary powers.

At the moment when this chapter opens he was receiving in his office a representative of the leading Government organ: a daily paper which purveyed a mixture of fervent demagogism and child-like inconsistency, for the modest sum of one halfpenny. The Tocsin, as it was called, was widely read by a public who believed every word it contained, with that simple credulity in what is printed which is one of the most pathetic features of the semi-illiterate.

Mr Hammet, the representative of The Tocsin, had come to find out what was really behind the remarkable spread of the Unity

League. Possibly members of the Government were beginning to fidget. Salt had seen him for the purpose of telling him everything else that he cared to know. To enquirers, the officials of the League were always candid and open, and laughingly disclaimed any idea of a mysterious secret society. So Salt admitted that they really hoped for a change of public opinion shortly; that they based their calculation on the inevitable swing of the pendulum, and so forth. He allowed it to be drawn easily from him that they had great faith in party organisation, and that perhaps—between themselves and not for publication—the Government would be surprised by a substantial lowering of their majority at the next election, as a result of quiet, unostentatious "spade work." "As a party we are not satisfied with the state of things," he said. "We cannot be expected to be satisfied with it, and we are certainly relying on a stronger representation in opposition to make our views felt."

"Quite right," said Mr Hammet sympathetically. He closed the note-book in which he had made a few entries and put it away, to indicate that his visit was officially at an end, and whatever passed between them now was simply one private gentleman talking to another, and might be regarded as sacredly confidential. Salt also relaxed the secretarial manner which he had taken the pains to acquire, and seemed as though he would be glad of a little human conversation with a man who knew life and Fleet Street: which meant, of course, that both were prepared to be particularly alert.

"I was at one of your meetings the other night—the Albert Hall one," remarked the newspaper man casually. "Your Chief fairly took the crowd with him. No being satisfied with a strong opposition for him! Why, he went bald-headed for sweeping the country and going in with a couple of hundred majority or so."

Salt laughed appreciatively. "No good being down-hearted," he replied. "That was the end of all the old organisations. 'We see no hope for the future, so you all may as well mark time,' was their attitude, and they dropped out. 'When anything turns up we intend being ready for it, so come in now,' we say."

"Seems to take all right too," admitted Mr Hammet. "I was offered a level dollar by a friend of mine the other day that you had over half a million members. I took it in a sporting spirit, because I know that half a million needs a lot of raking in, and I put it at rather less myself—but, of course, as you are close about it we can never settle up." Half a million, it may be observed, was everybody's property, as an estimate on "excellent authority."

"We don't publish figures, as a matter of fact," admitted Salt half-reluctantly, "but I don't know why there should be any very particular secret about it——"

45

"Oh, every office has its cupboards and its skeletons," said Mr Hammet generously. "But if one could see inside," he added with a knowing look, "I think that I should win."

"No," exclaimed Salt suddenly. "I don't mind telling you in confidence. We have passed the half million: passed it last—well, some time ago."

"Lucky for me that it is in confidence," remarked the pressman with a grimace, "or I should have to pay up. What is the exact figure, then?" he ventured carelessly.

"No one could quite tell you that," replied Salt, equally off-hand.

"Six hundred thousand?" suggested Mr Hammet.

"Oh, that is a considerable advance,—a hundred thousand," admitted Salt with transparent disappointment. It is not pleasant when you have impressed your man to have him expecting too much the next minute.

"I was thinking of the old Buttercup League," said Mr Hammet. "You took the remains over, lock, stock, and barrel, I believe?"

"Yes, all that would come. Half belonged to your party really, and half of the remainder were children. What an organisation that was in its time! A million and a half!" The smart young newspaper man noted Mr Salt's open admiration for these figures. It convinced him that the newer League was not yet within measurable distance of half that total.

"And in the end it did—what?" he remarked.

Salt was bound to apologise. "What is there to do, after all?" he admitted. "What can you do but keep your people together, show them where their interest lies, and wait?"

"And rake in the shekels?" suggested Mr Hammet airily.

"Oh, that!" agreed Salt a little uneasily. "Of course one has to look after the finances."

"Ra-ther," agreed Mr Hammet. "Wish I had the job. Do you smoke here as a general thing?"

"Oh yes," replied Salt, who never did. "Try one of these."

"Fairish cigars. Better than you'd find in the old man's private box up at our show," was the verdict. "But then we haven't a revenue of half a million."

"Of course I rely on you not to say anything about our numbers," said the secretary anxiously.

The visitor made a reassuring gesture, expressive of inviolable secrecy. "Though I suppose you have to make a return for income-tax purposes," he mused. "My aunt! what an item you must have!"

"No," replied Salt. "We do not pay anything."

46

Mr Hammet stared in incredulous surprise. "How do you manage to work it?" he demanded familiarly. "You don't mean that they have forgotten you?"

"No; it's quite simple," explained Salt. "Your friends made the funds and incomes of Trades Unions sacred against claims and taxes of every kind a few years ago, and we rank as a Trade Union."

"Don't call them my friends, please God," exclaimed Mr Hammet with ingratiating disloyalty. "I work as in a house of bondage. You don't publish any balance-sheet, by the way, do you?"

"No, we don't see why we should let every one know how the money is being spent. No matter how economically things are carried on there are always some who want to interfere."

"Especially if they sampled your weeds," suggested the visitor pleasantly. "Pretty snug cribs you must have, but that's not my business. Between ourselves, what does Sir John draw a year?"

"Nothing," protested Salt eagerly, too eagerly. "As President of the League he does not receive a penny."

Sharp Mr Hammet, who prided himself upon being a terror for exposures and on having a record of seven flagrant cases of contempt of court, read the secretary's eagerness like an open book. "But then there are Committees, Sub-committees, Executives, Emergency Funds, and what not," he pointed out, "and our unpaid League President may be Chairman of one, and Secretary of another, and Grand Master of a third with a royal salary from each, eh? Can you assure me——"

"Oh, well; of course," admitted Salt, cornered beyond prevarication, "that is a private matter that has to do with the officials of the League alone. But you may take it from me that every one in these offices earns his salary whatever it may be."

Mr Hammet smiled his polite acquiescence broadly.

"Same here, changing the scene of action to Stonecutter Street," he commented. "Do you happen to know how Sir John came to start this affair? Well, Tagg M.P. met Miss Hampden once and wanted to marry her. He called on Sir John, who received him about as warmly as a shoulder of Canterbury lamb even before he knew what his business was. When he did know, he gave such an exhibition of sheet lightning that Tagg, who is really a very level-headed young fellow in general, completely lost his nerve and tried to dazzle him into consenting, by offering him a safe seat in the Huddersfield division and a small place in the Government if he'd consent to put up as a bracketted Imperialist hyphened Socialist. Then the old man kicked Tagg out of the house, and swore to do the same with his Government within three years. At least that's what I heard about the time, but very likely there isn't a word of truth in it;" a tolerably safe inference on Mr Hammet's part, as, in point of fact, he had concocted Mr Tagg's romance on the spur of the moment.

"No," volunteered Salt. "I don't think that that is the true story, or I should have heard something about it. It's rather curious that you should have mentioned it. I believe——But it's scarcely worth taking up your time with."

"Not at all: I mean that I am quite interested," protested Mr Hammet.

"Well—of course it sounds rather absurd in the broad light of day, but I believe, as a matter of fact, that he was led into founding the League simply as the result of a dream."

"A dream!" exclaimed Mr Hammet, deeply surprised. "What sort of a dream?"

"Well, it naturally must have been a rather extraordinary dream to affect him so strongly. In fact you might perhaps call it a vision."

"A vision!" repeated Mr Hammet, thoroughly absorbed in the mysterious element thus brought in. "Do I understand that this is Sir John's own explanation?" Hampden's sudden return to activity had, indeed, from time to time been a riddle of wide interest.

"Oh no," Salt hastened to correct. "I expect that he would be the last man to admit it, or to offer any explanation at all. Of course the history of the world has been changed in every age through dreams and visions, but that explanation nowadays, in a weighty matter, would run the risk of being thought trivial and open to ridicule."

"But what do you base your deductions upon, then?" demanded Mr Hammet, rather fogged by the serious introduction of this new light. "Is Sir John a believer in clairvoyance?"

"I am afraid that I must not state the real grounds for several reasons, if you won't think me discourteous," replied Salt firmly. "But this I may say: that I had occasion to see Sir John late one night, and then he had not the faintest intention of coming forward. Early the following morning I saw him again, and by that time the whole affair was cut and dried. Of course you are at liberty to confirm or contradict the story just as you like, if you should happen to come across it again."

In a state of conscious bewilderment through which he was powerless to assert himself, Mr Hammet submitted to polite dismissal. The visible result of his interview was half a column of peptonised personalities in The Tocsin, rendered still easier of assimilation to the dyspeptic mind by being well cut up into light paragraphs and garnished with sub-headings throughout. The unseen result, except to the privileged eyes of half a dozen people, was a confidential report which found its way ultimately into the desk of the Home Secretary. The following points summarised Mr Hammet's deductions.

"The Unity League probably has a membership of half a million. It may be safely assumed that it does not exceed that figure by a hundred thousand at the most.

"While largely recruiting by the device of holding out a suggestion of some indefinite and effective political scheme, the policy of the League will be that of laisser faire, and its influence may be safely ignored. Very little of its vast income is spent in propagandism or organisation. On the contrary, there is the certainty that considerable sums are lying at short notice at the banks, and strong evidence that equally large sums have been sent out of the country through the agency of foreign houses.

"Many men of so-called 'good position' enjoy obvious sinecure posts under the League, and all connected with the organisation appear to draw salaries disproportionate to their positions, and in some cases wildly disproportionate.

"The plain inference from the bulk of evidence is that the League is, and was formed to be, the preserve for a number of extravagant and incapable unemployed of the so-called upper and upper-middle classes, who have organised this means of increasing their incomes to balance the diminution which they have of late years experienced through the equalising legislation of Socialism. The money sent abroad is doubtless a reserve for a few of the higher officials to fall back on if future contingencies drive them out of this country.

"This information has been carefully derived from a variety of sources, including John Hampden's secretary, a man called Salt. Salt appears to be a simple, unsuspicious sort of fellow, and with careful handling might be used as a continual means of securing information in the future should there be any necessity."

The simple, unsuspicious secretary had dismissed Mr Hammet with scarcely another thought as soon as that gentleman had departed. In order to fit himself for the requirements of his new sphere of action, Salt had, during the past two years, compelled himself to acquire that art of ready speech which we are told is the most efficient safeguard of our thoughts. But he hated it. Most of all he despised the necessity of engaging in such verbal chicane as Mr Hammet's mission demanded. Of that mission he had the amplest particulars long before the representative of The Tocsin had passed his threshold. He knew when he was coming, why he was coming, and the particular points upon which information was desired. He could have disconcerted Hammet beyond measure by placing before him a list of all those persons who had been so delicately sounded, together with an abstract of the results; and finally, he received as a matter of ordinary routine a copy of the confidential report three hours before it reached Mr James Tubes. Armies engaged in active warfare have their Intelligence Departments, and the Secret Service of the Unity League was remarkably complete and keen.

"My name is Irene Lisle," said the next caller, and there being nothing particular to say in reply Salt expressed himself by his favourite medium—silence; but in such a way that Miss Lisle felt encouraged to continue.

"I have come to you because I am sick of seeing things go on as they have been going for years, and no one doing anything. I believe that you are going to do something."

"Why?" demanded Salt with quiet interest. It mattered—it might matter a great deal—why this unknown Miss Lisle should have been led to form that conclusion.

"I have a great many friends—some in London, others all over the country. I have been making enquiries lately, through them and also by other means. It is generally understood that your membership is about half a million, and you tacitly assent to that." She took up a scrap of waste paper that lay before her, and writing on it, passed it across the desk. "That, however, is my estimate. If I am right, or anything like it, you are concealing your strength."

Salt took the paper, glanced at it, smiled and shook his head without committing himself to any expression. But he carefully burned the fragment with its single row of figures after Miss Lisle had left.

"I have attended your meetings," continued Miss Lisle composedly, "for, of course, I am a member in the ordinary way. I came once as a matter of curiosity, or because one's friends were speaking of it, and I came again because, even then, I was humbled and dispirited at the shameful part that our country was being made to play before the world. I caught something, but I did not grasp all—because I am not a man, I suppose. I saw meeting after meeting of impassive unemotional, black-coated gentlemen lifted into the undemonstrative white-heat of purposeful enthusiasm by the suggestion of that new hope which I failed to understand. At one of the earliest Queen's Hall meetings I particularly noticed a young man who sat next to me. He was just an ordinary keen-faced, gentlemanly, well-dressed, athletic-looking youth, who might have been anything from an upper clerk to a millionaire. He sat through the meeting without a word or a sign of applause, but when at the finish twenty volunteers were asked for, to give their whole time to

50

serving the object of the League, he was the first to reach the platform, with a happier look on his face, in the stolid English style, than I should have ever expected to see there. It was beyond me. Then among the audiences one frequently heard remarks such as 'I believe there's something behind it all'; 'I really think Hampden has more than an idea'; 'It strikes me that we are going to have something livelier than tea and tennis,' and suggestions of that kind. Some time ago, after a meeting at Kensington, I was walking home alone when you overtook me. Immediately in front were two gentlemen who had evidently been to the meeting also, and they were discussing it. At that moment one said emphatically to the other: 'I don't know what it is, but that it is something I'll swear; and if it is I'd give them my last penny sooner than have things as they are.' Sir John Hampden, who was with you, looked at you enquiringly, and you shook your head and said, 'Not one of our men.' 'Then I believe it's beginning to take already,' he replied."

Two things occurred to Salt: that Miss Lisle might be a rather sharp young lady, and that he and Hampden had been unusually careless. "Anything else?" was all he said.

"It's rather a long wild tale, and it has no particular point," explained the lady.

"If you can spare the time," he urged. The long pointless tale might be a pointer to others beside Miss Lisle.

"I was cycling a little way out in the country recently," narrated Miss Lisle, "when I found that I required a spanner, or I could not go on. It was rather a lonely part for so near London, within ten or twelve miles, I suppose, and there was not a house to be seen. I wheeled my bicycle along and soon came to a narrow side lane. It had a notice 'Private Road' up, and I could not see far down it as it wound about very much, but it seemed to be well used, so I turned into it hoping to find a house. There was no house, for after a few turns the lane ended suddenly. It ended, so to speak, in a pair of large double doors—like those of a coach-house—for before me was a stream crossed by an iron bridge; immediately beyond that a high wall and the doors. But do you care for me to go on?"

"If you please," said Salt, and paid the narrative the compliment of a close and tranquil attention.

"It was rather a peculiar place to come on unexpectedly," continued Miss Lisle. "It had originally been a powder works, and the old notices warning intruders had been left standing; as a matter of fact a stranger would probably still take it to be a powder mill, but one learned locally that it was the depot and distributing centre of an artificial manure company with a valuable secret process. Which, of course, made it less interesting than explosives."

"And less dangerous," suggested Salt, smiling.

"I don't know," shot back Miss Lisle with a glance. "Mark the precautions. There was the stream almost enclosing this place—the size, I suppose, of a considerable farm—and in the powder mill days it had been completely turned into an island by digging a canal or moat at the narrowest point of the bend. Immediately on the other side of the water rose the high brick wall topped with iron spikes. The one bridge was the only way across the stream, the one set of double doors, as high as the wall, the only way through beyond. Inside was thickly wooded. I don't suggest wild animals, you know, but savage dogs would not surprise me.

"As I stood there, concluding that I should have to turn back, I heard a heavy motor coming down the lane. It came on very quickly as though the driver knew the twisting road perfectly, shot across the bridge, the big gates fell open apparently of their own accord, and it passed inside. I had only time to note that it was a large trade vehicle with a square van-like body, before the gates had closed again."

Miss Lisle paused for a moment, but she had by no means reached the end of her pointless adventure.

"I had seen no one but the motor driver, but I was mistaken in thinking that there was no one else to see, for as I stood there undecided a small door in the large gate was opened and a man came out. He was obviously the gate-keeper, and in view of the notices I at once concluded that he was coming to warn me off, so I anticipated him by asking him if he could lend me a spanner. He muttered rather surlily that if I waited there he would see, and went back, closing the little door behind him. I thought that I heard the click of a self-acting lock. Presently he came back just as unamiable as before and insisted on screwing up the bolt himself—to get me away the sooner, I suppose. He absolutely started when I naturally enough offered him sixpence—I imagine the poor man doesn't get very good wages—and went quite red as he took it."

"And all ended happily?" remarked Salt tentatively, as though he had expected that a possible relevance might have been forthcoming after all.

"Happily but perplexingly," replied Miss Lisle, looking him full in the face as she unmasked the point of her long pointless story. "For the surly workman who was embarrassed by sixpence was my gentlemanly neighbour of the Queen's Hall meeting, and I was curious to know how he should be serving the object of the League by acting as a gate-keeper to the Lacon Equalised Superphosphate Company."

Salt laughed quietly and looked back with unmoved

composure. "No doubt many possible explanations will occur to you," he said with very plausible candour. "The simplest is the true one. Several undertakings either belong to the League or are closely connected with it, for increasing its revenue or for other purposes. The Lacon is one of these."

"And I don't doubt that even the position of doorkeeper is a responsible one, requiring the intelligence of an educated gentleman to fill it," retorted Miss Lisle. "It must certainly be an exacting one. You know better than I do how many great motor vans pass down that quiet little lane every hour. They bear the names of different companies, they are ingeniously different in appearance, and they pass through London by various roads and by-roads. But they have one unique resemblance: they are all driven by mechanics who are astonishingly disconcerted by the offer of stray sixpences and shillings! It is the same at the little private wharf on the canal a mile away. It was quite a relief to find that the bargemen were common human bargees!"

Salt still smiled kindly. The slow, silent habit gives the best mask after all. "And why have you come to me?" he asked.

"Because I know that you are going to do something, and I want to help. I loathe the way things are being done down there." The nod meant the stately Palace of Westminster, though it happened to be really in the direction of Charing Cross, but it was equally appropriate, for the monuments of the Government, like those of Wren, lay all around. "Who can go on playing tennis as usual when an ambassador who learned his diplomacy in a Slaughter-housemen's Union represents us by acting alternately as a fool and a cad before an astounded Paris? Or have an interest in bridge when the Sultan of Turkey is contemptuously ordering us to keep our fleet out of sight of Mitylene and we apologise and obey? I will be content to address envelopes all day long if it will be of any use. Surely there are other secret processes down other little lanes? I will even be the doorkeeper at another artificial manure works if there is nothing else!"

Salt sat thinking, but from the first he knew that for good or ill some degree of their confidence must be extended to a woman. It is the common experience of every movement when it swells beyond two members: or conspiracies would be much more dangerous to their foes.

"It may be monotonous, perhaps even purposeless as far as you can see," he warned. "I do not know yet, and it will not be for you to say."

Miss Lisle flushed with the pleasurable thrill of blind sacrifice. "I will not question," she replied. "Only if there should be any need

53

you might find that an ordinary uninteresting middle-class girl with a slangy style and a muddy complexion could be as devoted as a Flora Macdonald or a Charlotte Corday."

Salt made a quiet deprecating gesture. "A girl with a fearless truthful face can be capable of any heroism," he remarked as he began to write. "Especially when she combines exceptional intelligence with exceptional discretion. Only," he added as an afterthought, "it may be uncalled-for, and might be inconvenient in a law-abiding constitutional age."

"I quite understand that now; the conscientious addressing of circulars shall bound my horizon. Only, please let me be somewhere in it, when it does come."

"I say, Salt," drawled an immaculately garbed young man, lounging into the room, "do you happen——"

Miss Lisle, who had been cut off from the door by a screen, rose to leave.

"Oh, I say, I beg your pardon," exclaimed the young man. "They told me that you were alone."

"I shall be disengaged in a moment," replied Salt formally. "At ten o'clock to-morrow morning then, Miss Lisle, please." She bowed and withdrew, the Honourable Freddy Tantroy, who had lingered rather helplessly, holding the door as she went out and favouring her with a criticising glance.

"Always making rotten ass of myself," murmured that gentleman plaintively. "General Office fault. Engaging lady clerk? Not bad idea, but you might have gone in for really superior article while you were about it. Cheaper in the end. Oh, I don't know, though."

"Miss Lisle came with the best of recommendations," said Salt almost distantly. One might have judged that he had no desire for Mr Tantroy's society, but that reasons existed why he should not tell him so.

"Yes, I know," nodded Freddy sagely; "they do. Hockey girl, I should imagine. Face of the pomegranate type, carved by amateur whose hand slipped when he was doing the mouth. Prefer the pink and pneumatic style myself. Matter taste."

Salt made no reply. The only possible reply was the one he denied himself. He occupied the time by burning a scrap of paper with a single row of figures.

"I say, Salt. I was really coming about something, but I've forgotten what," announced the honourable youth after a vacuous pause. "Oh, I remember. That elusive old cheesecake of a hunk of mine. Do you happen to know where the volatile Sir John is to be unearthed?"

54

"I imagine that your uncle is in Paris at this moment," replied Salt. "He is expected back to-morrow."

"Paris!" exclaimed Freddy with some interest. "Good luck at the Pink Windmill, old boy! Anything in the air, Salt? Projected French landing at Brighton pier next week? Seriously, don't you think League bit of gilded fizzle? Expected something with coloured lights long ago."

"I think that we have every reason to be satisfied with the progress," replied Salt. "The weight of a great organisation must exercise some influence in the end."

"Oh yes," retorted Mr Tantroy with a cunning look. "That's the other face of double-headed Johnny they have stuffed in museums. Well, all in good time, little Freddy, if you sit quiet." He carried out this condition literally for a couple of minutes, gazing pensively at a slender ring he wore. Then: "I'll tell you what, Salt," he continued. "I wish you'd use benign influence with Sir John. Tired of apeing the golden ass, and I am thinking of settling down. Want an office here and absolutely grinding hard work ten to four, and couple of thousand a year or so until I'm worth more. Fact is, met girl I could absolutely exist for ever with in gilded bird-cage. Been Vivarium lately?"

"No," replied Salt.

"Oh, well, no good trying my rotten powers description. Must go with me some night and see. She hangs by her toes to a slack wire eighty-five feet above the stage and sings:

'Things are strangely upside down, dear boys.
Nowadays.'

No getting away from it, she is positively the most crystallised damson that ever stepped out of lace-edged box. No fear monotony in home with girl like that. The very thought of it——! Well, come out and have drink, Salt?"

"Thanks, no," replied Salt. "I've quite got out of the habit."

"Great Scott!" exclaimed Freddy, aghast. "You better try some of those newspaper things that Johnnies with funny addresses and members of the Greek Royal Family write up to say have done them no end. I say, Salt, I suppose there is spare office in this palatial suite that I could have if I grappled with the gilded effort?"

"I really don't know that there is." He had not the most shadowy faith in the Honourable Freddy's perseverance, even in intention, for a week. To expect any real work from him was out of the question. "We are rather overcrowded here as it is."

"If I were you, Salt, I should insist upon the old man removing

55

better premises somewhere. Place seems absolutely congealed with underlings. Just listen to that in next room: it's like hive of gilded bees. What is it?"

"Simply routine work going on," said Salt half-impatiently. "Sorry I can't spare the time to come out with you."

"Oh, that's all right-angled," said Freddy, taking the hint and rising. "Sorry. Pramp, pramp. You think I shall find Sir John here Friday if I look in?"

"Yes, here; but desperately busy."

"Er, thanks," drawled Freddy, with just a suggestion of vice. "Perhaps my uncle will be able to spare me five minutes when he has done with you."

He drifted languidly through the door and sauntered down the passage. At the door of the room where the monotonous voice rose and fell in the ceaseless repetition of short sentences, he paused to light a cigarette. For perhaps a full minute he remained quite motionless, the cigarette between his lips, the match pressed ready against the corrugations of the jewelled box he held.

"Listretton, Fergus, 572 Upper Holloway Road, N.

"Listwell-Phelps, J. Walter, F.R.S., Department of Ethopian Antiquities, British Museum, W.C.

"Litchit, Miss, Dressmaker, 15 The Grove, Westpoint-on-Sea.

"Little, Rev. H. K., The Vicarage, Lower Skerrington, Dorset.

"Little, Lieutenant-General Sir Alfred Vernon, C.B., V.C., 14a Eaton Square, S.W.

"Littlejohn, John George, Byryxia, Cole Park, Twickenham."

Freddy Tantroy lit his cigarette and passed on. The prosaic list of new members dictated to an entering clerk did not interest him. Five names a minute, three hundred an hour, three thousand a day; an ordinary day, weeks after any special meeting, and in the flat season of the year. But it did not interest Mr Tantroy. Immersed in a scheme for taxing baths, soda-water syphons, and asparagus beds, and further occupied with the unexpectedly delicate details of withdrawing from India, it did not interest the Government.

It was only the ordinary routine work of the Unity League.

CHAPTER VII

"SCHEDULE B"

On the following day Sir John Hampden returned from Paris. A week later and he had again left London. At the office of the League it was impossible to learn where he had gone; perhaps fishing, it was suggested. In any case he was taking a well-earned holiday and did not want to be troubled with business, so that nothing was being forwarded. A little later any one might know for the asking that he was in Berlin—and returning the next day. There was never any secret made of Sir John's movements if the office knew them, only he occasionally liked to cut himself completely off from communication in order to ensure a perfect rest. As soon as the office knew where he was, every one else could know too; only it invariably happened that he was on his way back by that time. The incident was repeated. Callers at Trafalgar Chambers found all the heads communicative and very leisured. It came out that nothing much was being done just then; it was not the time of the year for politics. For all the good they were doing three-quarters of the offices might be closed for the next few months and three-quarters of the staff take a holiday. In fact, that was what they were doing to a large extent. It was Mr Salt's turn as soon as Sir John got back.

That time it was St. Petersburg.

For a man who had been a sailor George Salt displayed a curious taste when he came to take his holiday. The sea had no call for him, nor the coast-line any charm. The inland resorts, the golf centres, moors, lakes, mountains and rivers, all were passed by. It was not even to an "undiscovered" village or some secluded country house that he turned his footsteps in hope of perfect change. On the contrary, where the ceaseless din of industry made rest impossible; where the puny but irresistible hands of generations of mankind had scarred the face of earth like a corroding growth, where the sky was shut out by smoke, vegetation stifled beneath a cloak of grime, day and night turned into one lurid vulcanian twilight, in which by bands and companies, by trains and outposts, dwarfish men toiled in the unlovely rhythm of hopeless, endless labour: the lupus-spots of nature; there Salt spent his holiday. Coal was the loadstone that drew him on, and in a vast contour his journey through that month defined the limits of the coal-fields of the land.

In the subsequent histories of this period no mention of Salt's significant appearance in the provinces finds a place. Yet in presenting a dispassionate review of the succeeding events it is impossible to ignore its influence; although, to adopt a just proportion, it is not necessary to deal with it at length. It was not a vital detail of the scheme on which the League had staked its cause; it was less momentous than any of Hampden's three Continental missions; but by disarming opposition in certain influential quarters when the crisis came, it removed a possible cause of dissension from the first. That is its place.

It was an indication of the extreme care with which the operations had been developed, that even at this point there were still only two men who had any real knowledge of what the plan of campaign would be. There were those who did not hesitate to declare that a hostile demonstration was being arranged by a foreign power with whom Hampden had come to an understanding. At a favourable moment a pretext for a quarrel would be found, relations would be broken off immediately, ambassadors recalled, and within three days England would be threatened with war. If necessary, an actual invasion would take place, and in view of the sweeping reductions in the army and navy no one thought it worth while to express a doubt that an actual invasion could take place. After arranging for a suitable indemnity the invaders would withdraw, leaving a provisional government in power, with Hampden at its head. This was the extremists' view, and the majority, feeling at heart that however England might be internally riven and their liberties assailed, nothing could ever justify so unpatriotic a course, held that Hampden was incapable of the step. Others suggested civil war; passive resistance to the payment of rates and taxes on so organised a scale as to embarrass the Government for supplies; an alliance, on a basis not readily discernible, with the rank and file of the Socialist party; the secret importation of a sufficient number of aliens to turn an election; and a variety of other ingenious devices, easy to suggest but difficult to maintain. Those who, like Miss Lisle, observed the most, talked the least.

Among the working men of the country—the class that the League had come into being to control—it had passed into the category of a second Buttercup League and was ignored. A few, better informed, accepted the conclusions that Mr Hammet and his associates had arrived at, and laughed quietly in their sleeves at the thought of the coming humiliation of the confiding members. Last of all there remained a scattered few here and there, who, through natural suspicion or a shrewder wisdom than their fellows, had of late begun to detect in the existence of the League a real menace to themselves, and to urge the powers, and Mr Tubes in particular, to counteract its aims. It might have been a race, a desperate race, but for one simple thing. Hampden had asked for three years in which to complete his plans, and both friends and foes, deducing from every experience of the past, ranging from the opening of an exhibition to the closing of a war, had conceded that this meant four at least. But Hampden and the man who had been a sailor had no intention of being embarrassed by a race. Not three years meaning four, but three years meaning two, had underlain the boast, and at the end of two years, although there was still much to be gained by time and an unfettered choice of the moment of attack, there was no probability of being forestalled on any important point.

Such was the position when Salt set out on his provincial holiday.

He had nothing to learn; elementary detail of that kind belonged to another journey, when, more than two years ago, he had made the self-same tour. He did not go to offer peace or war; that die had been cast blindly—who shall say how many years before?—in Northampton boot factories, Lancashire mills, Durham coal-pits, in Radical clubs and Labour cabinets. But in war, and in civil war most of all, every blow aimed at the foe must spend its expiring force upon a friend—and therefore Salt went to the coal-fields.

At each centre he was met by a high official of the League who had local knowledge. The man made his report; it concerned a list he brought, a list of names. Sometimes it contained only three or four names, sometimes as many dozens. If to each name there stood the word "Content," Salt passed on to his next centre. If some were reported to be holding out or dissatisfied, Salt remained. When he resumed his methodical way the word "Content" had been added to every name.

Only once did failure threaten to mar his record. A Lancashire colliery proprietor, a man who had risen from the lowest grade of labour, as men more often did in the hard, healthy days of emulous rivalry than in the later piping times of union-imposed collective indolence, did not wish to listen. Positive, narrow, over-bearing, he was permeated with the dogmatic egotism of his successful life. He had never asked another man's advice; he had never made a mistake. As hard as the ground out of which he had carved his fortune, he hated and despised his men; they knew it, and hated and respected him in return. His own brother worked as a miner in his "1500 deep" and received a miner's wage. He hated his master with the rest. Lomas was the "closest" employer in the north central coal-field, and the richest. But there were fewer widows and orphans in Halghcroft than in any other pit village of its size, and Lomas spent nothing in insurance. Under his immediate eye cage cables did not snap, tram shackles part, nor did unexpected falls of shoring occur. His men did not smoke at their work, and no mysterious explosion had ever engaged the attention of a Board of Trade enquiry.

Salt found him sitting in his shirt sleeves in a noble room, furnished in the taste and profusion of a crowded pantechnicon with the most costly specimens of seventeen periods of decorative art. He received him with his usual manner, and that was the manner of a bellicose curmudgeon towards an unwelcome deputation of suppliants. For emphasis, between the frank didactic aphorisms which formed his arguments and his rules of life, he banged with his fist a lapis lazuli table, and lowered his voice in a confidential aside to inform his visitor that three thousand pounds was the figure that the little piece of furniture had cost him, and that in matters of taste he stuck at nothing—an unnecessary piece of information after one had cast an astonished glance around that bizarre room.

In Lomas's future there loomed a knighthood—the consummation in his mind of all earthly ambition and the possible fruit of a lavish charity of the kind that is scarcely the greatest of the three, and his policy was wholly dictated by a fear of endangering his chances. He would have resented the suggestion, in the face of several munificent donations that he had recently made to certain funds, and a gracious acknowledgment which he had received, that the King was not following his career with a personal interest. What, then, was the King's attitude towards the Unity League and its plan of campaign? Had Salt anything to show? It was useless to protest the inviolability of royal neutrality; Lomas only banged the lapis lazuli. That was good enough for outsiders, he retorted: now, between themselves? The strong man who was restrained by diplomatic conventions could make no headway with the strong man who was frankly primitive in his selfishness, and Salt withdrew, baffled, but unperturbed. But the sequel was that before he left his hotel the following day Lomas had waited upon him with full acquiescence to the terms, and the central coal-field was "Content."

The inference might be that at last the intentions of the League must have been disclosed. The reality was nothing of the kind. What had been revealed to these men, then—the largest employers of labour of any class throughout the country—to which they had signified their consent? it may be asked. And the truth was that nothing had been revealed; that even the officers of the League who sounded them were in the dark. In the past, industrial struggles had always been between capital and labour. That vaster encounter, upon which the League was now concentrating its energies, was not to be on such clearly defined lines, and in the strife capital might suffer side by side with labour. Against that contingency the coal influence had now been indemnified in the name of the Unity League and the future Government, and the guarantee had been accepted. It was a far-reaching precaution in the end; it narrowed the issue, and it secured more than neutrality in a quarter where open hostility might have otherwise been proclaimed. It just tended to realise that perfection of detail and completeness of preparation that mark the successful campaign.

But if there was nothing more to learn in the sense that the data upon which the League had based its plans had long since been complete, it was impossible for a thoughtful observer to pass through the land without learning much. Even two years of increasing privilege had left a deeper mark. A lavish policy of "Bread and Circuses" was again depleting the countryside, choking the towns, and destroying the instinct of citizenship, just as it had speeded the decline of another world-power two thousand years before. While wages had remained practically stationary, the leisure of the working man had been appreciably increased, and it was now being discovered that the working man had no way of passing his leisure except in spending money. Betting and drunkenness had increased in direct ratio to the lengthened hours of enforced idleness, and other disquieting indications of how the time was being spent, were brought home to those who moved among the poor. Where the money came from, the books of the great thrift societies at once revealed. There was no longer any necessity for the working man to save; his wages were guaranteed, his risks of sickness and every other adversity were insured against, his old age was pensioned, his children were, if necessary, State-adopted.

Even the Trades Unions had abolished their subscriptions and dissipated their reserves. There was no need of thrift now, for the Government was the working man's savings bank, and had cut out the debit pages of his pass-book. It was almost the Millennium. The only drawback was that, with all this affluence around, the working man found himself very much in the condition of a financial Ancient Mariner. There was a great deal of money being spent on him, and for him, and by him, but he never had any in his pocket. And the working man's wife was even worse off.

Other classes there were which found themselves in the same position, but not by the same process. The rich were taxed up to the eyes, but the rich had obvious means of retrenchment. But the great mass of the middle class had no elastic extravagances upon which they could economise. Even under favourable conditions they were

61

for the most part fulfilling Disraeli's pessimistic dictum: to the generality, manhood had been a struggle. It had passed into a failure. It stood face to face with the certainty of becoming a disaster. Inevitably there were tragedies.... So it happened that the one vivid haunting picture that George Salt carried down into later years from this period was not a lurid impression of some blackened earth-gnarled scene of Dantesque desolation, not even a memory of any of the incidents of his own personal triumph, but the sharp details of an episode that lay quite off the high-road of his work.

He was walking along a pretty country lane one evening (for it is a characteristic of many of these unhappy regions that almost to the edge of man's squalid usurpation Nature spreads her most gracious charms) when a sudden thunderstorm drove him to seek the hospitality of a labourer's cottage.

The man who opened the door was not a labourer, although he was shabbily dressed. He looked sombrely at his visitor. "What is it?" he asked, standing in the doorway with no sign of invitation.

"It is raining very heavily," replied Salt. "I should like to shelter, if you will permit me."

The man seemed to notice the downpour, which had now become a continuous stream, for the first time. "I'm very busy," he said churlishly.

"If I might stand just inside your doorway?" suggested Salt.

"No, come in," said the host with an air of sudden resolution. "After all——" He led the way out of the tiny entrance-hall into a room. Salt could not refrain from noticing that although the furniture was meagre, the walls were covered with paintings.

"I am an artist," said the brusque tenant of the cottage, noticing the involuntary glance around. "Come—in return for shelter you shall tell me what you think of these things."

"I am not a critic," replied Salt, stepping from picture to picture, "and it would be presumptuous, therefore, for me to give an opinion on works that I do not understand, although I can recognise them as striking and unconventional."

"Ah," commented the artist. "And that?"

He indicated a portrait with a nod. It was in an earlier, a smoother, and less characteristic style. To the man who was no artist it was a very beautiful painting of a very beautiful girl.

"My dead wife," said the artist, as Salt stood in silent admiration. "I have buried her this afternoon."

The man who had never known or even seen her felt a stab as he looked up at the lovely, smiling face.

"Well," said the painter roughly, "why don't you say how sorry you are, or some platitude of that sort?"

Salt turned away, to leave the other alone meeting the sweet eyes. "Because I cannot say how sorry I am," he replied with gentle pity.

"Oh, my beloved!" he heard the whisper. "Not long, not long."

"You are packing," Salt continued a minute later. "Let me help you—with some."

A heap of straw and shavings littered the floor; boxes and cases stood ready at hand.

"No," replied the man, looking moodily at his preparations. "I have changed my mind. I have to go on a journey to-night, but I shall leave this place as it is and secure the doors and windows instead."

He brought tools, and together they nailed across the cottage windows the stout old-fashioned shutters that secured them. Neither spoke much.

"Come," said the artist, when the melancholy work was complete; "the storm is over. Our roads lie together for a little way." He locked the outer door, and stood lingering reluctantly with his hand upon the key. "A moment," he said, unlocking the door again, and entering. "Only a moment. Wait for me at the gate."

Salt waited as he was directed beside a dripping linden. The storm had indeed passed over, but the sky was low and grey. Little rivulets meandered in changing currents down the garden path; from beneath the narrow lane came the continuous sobbing rush of some unseen swollen water-course. The hand of despair lay heavy across the scene; it seemed as though Nature had wept herself out, but was uncomforted. Salt pictured the lonely man standing before the soulless, smiling creation of his own hand.

The door opened, the lock again creaked mournfully as its rusty bolt was driven home, and without a backward glance the artist came slowly down the walk, twisting the clumsy key aimlessly upon his finger. He stopped at a tangled patch where the anemone struggled vainly among the choking bindweed, and the hyacinths and lupines had been beaten down to earth.

"Her garden!" he said aloud, and a spasm crossed his face. "But now how overgrown." On a thought he dropped the key gently among the luxuriant growth and turned away.

"I will tell you why my wife died," said the artist suddenly, after they had passed round a bend of the road that hid the cottage from their sight. "It should point a moral, and it will not take long."

"It may plead a cause," replied Salt.

"Ah!" exclaimed his companion, looking at him sharply. "Who are you, then?"

"You do not know me, but you may know my business. I am Salt of the Unity League."

"Strange," murmured the other. "Well, then, Mr Salt, my name is Leslie Garnet, and, as I have told you, I am an artist. Ten years ago, at the age of thirty, I came into a small legacy—three hundred pounds a year, to be precise. Up to that time I had been making a somewhat precarious living by illustration; on the strength of my fortune—which, of course, to a successful man in any walk of life would be the merest pittance—I rearranged my plans.

"Black and white work was drudgery to me, and it would never be anything else, because it was not my medium, but it was the only form of pictorial art that earned a livelihood. Pictures had ceased to sell. At the same time I had encouragement for thinking that I could do something worthy of existence in the higher branch of art.

"I don't want to trouble you with views. I made my choice. I determined to live frugally on my income, give up hack work, to the incidental advantage of some other poor struggler, and devote myself wholly to pictures which might possibly bring me some recognition at the end of a lifetime—more probably not—but pictures which would certainly never enrich me. I do not think that the choice was an ignoble one—but, of course, it was purely a personal matter.

"It was very soon afterwards that I got married. Had I thought of that step earlier I might have acted differently. As it was, Hilda would not hear of it. There seemed no need; we were very comfortable on our small income in a tiny way.

"Nine years ago that. You know the course of events. My income was derived from a prudently invested capital, so disposed as to give the highest safe return. Not many years had passed before the Government then in power fixed seven per cent. as the highest rate of interest compatible with commercial morality, and confiscated all above. My fixed system of living was embarrassed by a deduction of fifty pounds a year. The next year an open-minded Chancellor, in need of a few millions to spend on free amusements for the working class, was converted to the principle that two per cent. of immorality still remained, so five was made the maximum, and my small income was thus permanently reduced to two hundred pounds.

"We received this second blow rather blankly, but Hilda would not hear of surrender. As a matter of fact, I soon found out that there was practically no chance of it, and that in throwing up all connections when I did, I had burned my boats. Artists of every kind were turning to illustration work, but half of the magazines were dead. We gave up the flat that had been made pretty and home-like with inexpensive taste, and moved into three dreary rooms.

"You know what the next development would be, perhaps? Yes, the Unearned Incomes Act. And you will understand how it affected me.

"I was assessed in the same class as the Duke of Belgravia and Mr Dives-Keeps, the millionaire, as a gentleman of private income, capable of earning a living, but electing to live in idleness on invested capital not of my own creating. I was married, could not plead 'encumbrances' in any form, well-educated, strong and healthy, and in the prime of life. So I came under 'Schedule B,' and must pay a tax of ten shillings and sixpence in the pound. It was nothing that I might actually work twelve hours every day. Officially I must be living in voluptuous idleness, because the work of my hands did not bring me in an income bearing any appreciable proportion to my private means. The Government that denounced Riches in every form and had come in on the mandate of the poor and needy, recognised no other standard of attainment but Money. Therefore 'Schedule B.'

"Of course the effect of that was overwhelming. I could not afford a studio, I could not afford a model. I could scarcely afford materials. My wife, who had long been delicate, was now really ill, between anxiety and the unaccustomed daily work to which she bound herself. One of the companies from which I derived a portion of my income failed at this time: ruined by foreign competition and home restrictions. In a panic I endeavoured to get work of any kind. I had not the experience necessary for the lowest rungs of commerce; I was unknown in art. Who would employ a broken-down man beginning life at thirty-eight? I was too old.

"I was warned that appeal was useless, but I did appeal before the Commission. It was useless. I learned that mine was a thoroughly bad case from every official point of view, with no redeeming feature: that I was, in fact, a parasite upon the social system; and I narrowly escaped having the assessment raised.

"It was then that we left London and came to this cottage. My wife's health was permanently undermined, and change of air was necessary even to prolong her life. Her native county was recommended; that is why we chose this spot. When I reviewed affairs I found that I had a clear fifty pounds a year. And there, a few miles to the west, where you see that tracery of wheels and scaffolding against the sun, and there, a few miles to the north, where you see that pall of smoke upon the air, there lie hundreds and hundreds of cottages where gross luxury is rampant, where beneath one roof family incomes of ten times mine are free from any tax at all.

"That is enough for you to fill in the detail," continued Garnet bitterly, as he revived the memory of the closing scenes. "Doctors, things that had to be bought, bare existence. What remained of the investments sold for what a forced sale would bring—you know what that means to-day. The end you have seen. And there, Mr Salt, is the story to your hand. Here is the churchyard.... Killed, to make a Labour holiday!"

He opened the rustic gate of the hillside churchyard and led the way to a newly-turned mound, where the perfume hung stagnantly from the rain-lashed petals of a great sheaf of Bermuda lilies.

"I remain here," he said quietly, after a few minutes' silence by the grave-side. "Your road lies straight on, along the field path. You can even see the smoke of Thornley from here, lying to your right."

Salt did not reply. Looking intently in the opposite direction, he was locating with a seaman's eye another cloud of smoke that rose above the tree-tops in the valley they had left.

"Your house!" he exclaimed, pointing. "Man!" he cried suddenly, with a flash of intuition, "what are you doing? You fired the straw before we left!"

A sharp report was the only answer. Salt turned too late to arrest his arm, only in time to catch him as he fell. He lowered him—there was nothing else to do—lowered him on to the wet sods that flanked the mound, and knelt by his side so that he might support him somewhat. To one who had been on battle-fields there was no need to wonder what to do. It was a matter not of minutes but of seconds. The mute eyes met his dimly; he heard the single whisper, "Hilda," and then, without a tremor, Garnet, self-murdered, pressed a little more heavily against his arm and lay across the yet unfinished grave of his State-murdered wife.

CHAPTER VIII

TANTROY EARNS HIS WAGE

"I think," observed Salt reflectively, soon after his return, "that you had better take a short holiday now, Miss Lisle."

Miss Lisle looked up from her work—she was not addressing circulars, it may be stated—with an expression not quite devoid of suspicion.

"I will, if you wish me to do so, sir," she replied meekly. "But, personally, I do not require one."

"You have been of great use to us while I was away," he explained kindly, but with official precision, "and now that I am back again you have the opportunity."

Miss Lisle coloured rather rapturously at the formal praise, but the astute young woman did not allow her exaltation to beguile her senses.

"A week's holiday?" she asked.

"I would suggest a fortnight," he replied.

"That would be until the end of June?"

Salt agreed.

"Then nothing is likely to happen before the end of June?"

He laughed frankly. There was no trace of the mystery and restraint, of the electric tension in the air, that forerun portentous events, as we are told, to be noticed about the office of the League.

"A great deal may happen before that time, but nothing, I think I can assure you, that comes within your meaning."

"Is there any particular place that you would like me to go to?"

"Oh, not at all. Forget Trafalgar Chambers and business entirely for the time."

Possibly Miss Lisle had looked for some hidden meaning behind the simple suggestion of a holiday: had anticipated "another secret process down another little lane." At any rate, she did not rejoice at the prospect; on the contrary, she declined it.

"Thank you, sir," she replied, "but unless it is for your convenience, I should prefer to go on addressing circulars."

Salt frowned slightly and smiled slightly, and inwardly admitted to himself that he had probably expected worse things when he had first accepted Miss Lisle's services.

"I am a very plain, straightforward person in all my dealings," he remarked, "and you, outside the strict line of work here, have an oblique vein that taxes the imagination. Further, it carries the sting that with all you generally arrive at the same conclusion as I do, only a little earlier."

"I have a loathsome, repulsive nature, I know," admitted Irene cheerfully. "Trivial, ill-mannered, suspicious. I require strict discipline. That is why I am better here."

"So far I have not been inconvenienced by the two first characteristics. It is a mistake, perhaps, to be over-suspicious."

"Yes," agreed the lady with a level glance. "It only ends in you finding people out, when otherwise you might have gone on believing in them to the last."

Salt had only known Miss Lisle for a few months, and for a third of the period he had not seen her. But he knew that when she showed a disposition to take up his time something more than the amenities of conversation lay behind her words. He remembered that level glance. It foreshadowed another "long pointless tale."

"For instance?" he suggested encouragingly.

"If I left this office locked when I went out to lunch, for instance, and found it still locked but the papers slightly disarranged on my return," she replied.

"Anything more?"

"It is very unpleasant to set traps, of course, but if I put a little dab of typewriter ink on the inner handle of the door when I next went out, and subsequently found a slight stain of a similar colour on my white glove after shaking hands with some one, the suspicion would be deepened."

"I think that the matter is of sufficient importance for you to tell me all you know," he said gravely. "If you hesitate to be definite for fear of making a mistake, I will take pains to verify your suspicions and I will accept all responsibility."

"Then I accuse Mr Tantroy of being a paid spy in the service of the Government."

"Tantroy!" exclaimed Salt with a momentary feeling of incredulity. "Tantroy! It seems impossible, but, after all, it is possible enough. You know, of course, that he has a room here now, and might even think in his inexperience that he was at liberty to come into this office at any time."

"But not to take impressions of my keys and have duplicates made; nor to copy extracts in my absence; nor to open and examine the cipher typewriter."

"Has that been left unlocked?" he demanded sharply.

"No," she replied. "You have the only key that I know of. But it has been unlocked, and I infer that the code has been copied."

For quite three minutes there was silence. Salt was thinking, not idly, but estimating exactly the effect of what had happened.

Miss Lisle was waiting, with somewhat rare perception, until he was ready to continue.

"Sooner or later something of the sort was bound to come," he summed up quietly, without a trace of discomfiture. "It is only the personality that is surprising. His interests are identical with ours; he has everything to gain by our success. Why; why on earth?"

"I think that I can explain that in three words," suggested Miss Lisle. "Velma St Saint."

Salt looked enquiringly. He had forgotten the Hon. Freddy's deity for the moment.

"Of the Vivarium," added Irene.

"Oh, the lady who hangs by her toes," he remarked with enlightenment.

"'The World's Greatest Inverted Cantatrice'!" quoted Miss Lisle. "That is her celebrated 'Upside Down' song that the organ is playing in the street below. A few years ago she got a week's engagement at the Elysium at a salary of eighty pounds. She calculated from that that she could afford to spend four thousand a year, and although all theatrical incomes have steadily declined ever since until she only gets ten pounds a week now, she has never been able to make any difference in her style of living.... Of course there is a deficit to be made up."

"It is just as well. If it had not been Tantroy it would have been some one abler. Now what has he done, what has he learned?"

"Duplicate keys of this door and of my desk have been made. The lock of the cipher typewriter case is not of an elaborate pattern, and any one bringing a quantity of keys of the right size would probably find one to answer. I don't think that either your desk or the safe has been opened; certainly not since I began to notice. The papers to which he would have access are consequently not highly important."

"Letters?" suggested Salt. "For instance, my letters lying here until you forwarded them. There is a post in at eight o'clock in the morning; others after you have left up to ten at night. There would be every opportunity for abstracting some, opening them at leisure, and then dropping them into the letter-box again a little later."

"No," said Miss Lisle. "I took precautions against that."

"How?" he demanded, and waited very keenly for her answer.

"Simply by arriving here before eight and remaining until ten."

"Thank you." It was all he said, but it did not leave Miss Lisle with the empty feeling that virtue had merely been its own reward.

"Perhaps I ought to add that Mr Tantroy tried to get information from me," she remarked distantly. "He—he came here

69

frequently and wished me to accept presents; boxes of chocolate at first, I think, and jewellery afterwards. It was a mistake he made."

"Yes," assented Salt thoughtfully, "I think it was. There is one other thing, Miss Lisle. You could scarcely know with whom he was negotiating on the other side?"

"No," she admitted regretfully; "I had not sufficient time. That was why I did not wish to go away just now."

"I do not think that you need hesitate to leave it now. I am not taking it out of your hands, only carrying on another phase that you have made possible. It will simplify matters if I have the office to myself. Could you find an opportunity for telling Tantroy casually that you are taking a fortnight's holiday?"

Her answer hung just a moment. Had he known Tantroy better he might have guessed. "Yes, certainly," she replied hastily, with a little stumble in her speech.

Perhaps he guessed. "No," he corrected himself. "On second thoughts, it does not matter."

"I do not mind," she protested loyally.

"If it were necessary I should not hesitate to ask you," he replied half brusquely. "It is not."

"Very well. I will go to-morrow."

That evening, when he was alone. Salt unlocked the typewriter case to which Miss Lisle had alluded, took out the machine, and seating himself before it proceeded to compose a letter upon which he seemed to spend much consideration. As his fingers struck the keys, upon the sheet of paper in the carrier there appeared the following mystifying composition:

Kbeljsl

wopmjvsjxkivslilscalkwespljkjscwecsspssp
fxfejsloxmjcneoeqjdncs——

It was, in fact, as Miss Lisle had said, a code typewriter. The letters which appeared on the paper did not correspond with the letters on the keys. According to the keyboard the writing should have been:

Mydrstr

nwhvsltscmpltrprtbfrmndthrsmstbndbtthtth
prpslhvfrmltdsfsblndth——

and signified, to resolve it into its ultimate form:

My Dear Estair,—I now have Salt's complete report before me, and there seems to be no doubt that the proposal I have formulated is feasible, and the——

Written without vowels, stops, capitals, or spaces, this gave a very serviceable cryptograph, but there was an added safeguard. After completing the first line the writer moved a shift-key and brought another set of symbols into play—or, rather, the same symbols under a different arrangement. The process was repeated for the third line, and then the fourth line returned to the system of the first. Thus three codes were really in operation, and the danger of the key being found by the frequent recurrence of certain symbols (the most fruitful cause of detection) was almost overcome. Six identical machines were in existence. One has been accounted for; Sir John Hampden had another; and a third was in the possession of Robert Estair, the venerable titular head of the combined Imperial party. A sociable young publican, who had a very snug house in the neighbourhood of Westminster Abbey, could have put his hand upon the fourth; the fifth was in the office of a super-phosphate company carrying on an unostentatious business down a quiet little lane about ten or a dozen miles out of London; and the sixth had fallen to the lot of a busy journalist, who seemed to have the happy knack of getting political articles and paragraphs accepted without demur by all the leading newspapers by the simple expedient of scribbling "Urgent" and some one else's initials across the envelopes he sent them in. Communications of the highest importance never reached the stage of ink and paper, but the six machines were in frequent use. In bonâ fide communications the customary phraseology with which letters begin and end was not used, it is perhaps unnecessary to say. So obvious a clue as the short line "kbeljsl" at the head of a letter addressed to Estair would be as fatal to the secrecy of any code as the cartouched "Cleopatra" and "Ptolemy" were to the mystery of Egyptian hieroglyphics. That Salt wrote it may be taken as an indication that he had another end in view; and it is sometimes a mistake to overrate the intelligence of your opponents. When the letter was finished he put it away in his pocket-book, arranged the fastenings of both safe and desk so that he could tell if they had been disturbed, and then went home.

The next morning his preparations advanced another step. He brought with him a new letter copying-book, a silver cigarette-case with a plain polished surface, and a small jar of some oily preparation. With a little of the substance from the jar he smeared the cigarette-case all over, wiped away the greater part again until nothing but an almost imperceptible trace remained, and then

71

placed it carefully within his desk. The next detail was to write a dozen letters with dates extending over the last few days. All were short; all were quite unimportant; they were chiefly concerned with appointments, references to future League meetings, and the like. Some few were written in cipher, but the majority were plain reading, and Salt signed them all in Sir John's name, appending his own initials. To sign the long letter which he had already written he cut off from a note in the baronet's own handwriting the signature "John Hampden," fastened it lightly at the foot of the typewritten sheet, and then proceeded to copy all the letters into the new book. The effect was patent: one letter and one alone stood out among the rest as of pre-eminent importance. The completion was reached by gumming upon the back of the book a label inscribed "Hampden. Private," treating the leather binding with a coating of the preparation from the jar, and finally substituting it in the safe in place of the genuine volume. Then he burned his originals of all the fictitious letters and turned to other matters.

It was not until two days later that Mr Tantroy paid Salt a passing visit. He dropped in in a friendly way with the plea that the burden of his own society in his own room, where he apparently spent two hours daily in thinking deeply, had grown intolerable.

"You are always such a jolly busy, energetic chap, Salt, that it quite bucks me up to watch you," he explained.

Salt, however, was not busy that afternoon. He only excused himself to ring for a note, which was lying before him already addressed, to be taken out, and then gave his visitor an undivided attention. He was positively entertaining over his recent journeyings. Freddy Tantroy had never thought that the chap had so much in him before.

"Jolly quaint set of beggars you must have had to do with," he remarked. "Thought that you were having gilded flutter Monte Carlo, or Margate, or some of those places where crowds people go."

Salt looked across at him with a smile. "I think that there was an impression of that sort given out," he replied. "But, between ourselves, it was strictly on a matter of business."

"We League Johnnies do get most frightfully rushed," said Freddy sympathetically. "Bring it off?"

"Better than I had expected. I don't think it will be long before we begin to move now. You would be surprised if I could tell you of the unexpected form it will take."

"Don't see why you shouldn't," dropped Tantroy negligently.

Salt allowed the moment to pass on a note of indecision.

"Perhaps I am speaking prematurely," he qualified. "Things are only evolving at the moment, and I don't suppose that there will be anything at all doing during the next few weeks. I have even sent Miss Lisle off on a holiday."

"Noticed the fair Irene's empty chair," said Freddy. "For long?"

"I told her to take a fortnight. She can have longer if she wants."

"Wish Sir John could spare me; but simply won't hear of it. Don't fancy you find girl much good, though."

"Oh, she is painstaking," put in her employer tolerantly.

"No initiative," declared Tantroy solemnly. "No idea of rising to the occasion or of making use of her opportunities."

"You noticed that?" To Freddy's imagination it seemed as though Salt was regarding him with open admiration.

He wagged his head judicially. "I knew you'd like me to keep eye on things while you were away," he said, "so I looked in here occasionally as I passed. Don't believe she had any idea what to do. Invariably found her sitting here in gilded idleness at every hour of the day. If I were you, should sack her while she is away."

Salt thought it as well to change the subject.

"By the way," he remarked, "I came across what seemed to me a rather good thing in cigarettes at Cardiff, and I wanted to ask your opinion about them. It's a new leaf—Bolivian with a Virginian blend, not on the market yet. I wish you'd try one now."

There was nothing Freddy Tantroy liked better than being asked to give his opinion on tobacco from the standpoint of an expert. He took the case held out to him, selected a cigarette with grave deliberation, and leaned back in his chair with a critical air, preparing to deliver judgment. Salt returned the case to its compartment in the desk.

"It has a very distinctive aroma," announced Freddy sagely, after he had drawn a few whiffs, held the cigarette under his nose, waved it slowly in the air before him, and resorted to several other devices of connoisseurship.

"I thought so too," agreed Salt. He had bought a suitable packet of some obscure brand in a side street, as he walked to the office two days before.

"Cardiff," mused Tantroy. "Variety grotesque holes you seem to have explored, Salt."

"Oh, I had to see a lot of men all over the place. I got a few packets of these from a docker who had them from a South American merchant in a roundabout way. Smuggled, of course." All along, his conversation had touched upon labourers, mill-hands, miners, and other sons of toil. Apparently, as Tantroy noted, he had scarcely associated with any other class. He was lying deliberately, and in a manner calculated to alienate the sympathy of many excellent people; for there is a worthy and not inconsiderable class with an ineradicable conviction that although in a just cause the sixth commandment may be suspended, as it were by Act of Parliament, and the killing of your enemy become an active virtue, yet in no case is it permissible to tell him a falsehood. If it is necessary to deceive him the end must be gained by leading him to it by inference. But Salt belonged to a hard-grained school which believed in doing things thoroughly, and when on active service he swept the sophistries away. He had to mislead a man whose very existence he believed to be steeped in treachery and falsehood, and, as the most effectual way, he lied deliberately to him.

"Frantic adventure," drawled Tantroy. "Didn't know League dealt in people that kind."

"Of course, I saw all sorts," corrected Salt hastily, as though he feared that he had indicated too closely the trend of his business; "only it happened that those were the most amusing," and to emphasise the fact he launched into another anecdote. At an out-of-the-way village there was neither hotel nor inn. His business was unfinished, and it was desirable that he should stay the night there. At last he heard of a small farm-house where apartments were occasionally let, and, making his way there, he asked if he could have a room. The woman seemed doubtful. "Of course, as I am a stranger, I should wish to pay you in advance," said Salt. "It isn't that, sir," replied the hostess, "but I like to be sure of making people comfortable." "I don't think that we shall disagree about that," he urged. "Perhaps not," she admitted, "but the last gentleman was very hard to please. Everything I got him he'd had better somewhere else till he was sick of it. But," she added in a burst of confidence, "look what a swell he was! I knew that nothing would satisfy him when I saw him come in a motor-car puffed out with rheumatic tyres, and wearing a pair of them blasé kid boots."

Tantroy contributed an appreciative cackle, and Salt, leaning back in his chair, pressed against a pile of books standing on his desk so that they fell to the ground with a crash.

By the time he had picked them up again a telegram was waiting at his elbow. He took it, opened it with a word of apology, and with a sharp exclamation pulled out his watch. Before Tantroy could realise what was happening, Salt had caught up his hat and gloves, slammed down his self-locking desk, and, after a single hasty glance round the room, was standing at the door.

"Excuse me, won't you?" he called back. "Most important. Can just catch a train. Pull my door to after you, please," and the next minute he was gone.

Left to himself, Tantroy's first action was not an unnatural one in the circumstance. He picked up the telegram which Salt had left in his wild hurry and read it. "Come at once, if you wish to see Vernon alive," was the imperative message, and it appeared to have been handed in at Croydon half an hour before. He stepped to the window, and from behind the curtains he saw Salt run down the steps into the road, call a hansom from the rank near at hand, and disappear in the direction of Victoria at a gallop.

Mr Tantroy sat down again, and his eyes ran over the various objects in the room in quick succession. The code typewriter. He had all he wanted from that. Salt's desk. Locked, of course. The girl's desk. Locked, and, as he knew, not worth the trouble of unlocking with his duplicate key. The safe——His heart gave a bound, his eyes stood wide in incredulous surprise, and he sprang to his feet and stealthily crossed the room to make sure of his astounding luck. The safe was unlocked! The door stood just an inch or so ajar, and Salt, having failed to notice it in his hurried glance, was on his way to Croydon!

Living in a pretentious, breathless age, drawn into a social circle beside whose feverish artificiality the natural artificiality inseparable from any phase of civilisation stood comparable to a sturdy, healthy tree, badly brought up, neglected, petted, the Honourable Frederick Tantroy had grown to the form of the vacuous pose which he had adopted. Beneath it lay his real character. A moderately honest man would not have played his part, but an utterly weak one could not have played it. It demanded certain qualities not contemptible. There were risks to be taken, and he was prepared to take them, and in their presence his face took on a stronger, even better, look. He bolted the door on the inside, picked up a few sheets of paper from the desk-top, and without any sign of nervousness or haste began to do his work.

It was fully three hours later when Salt returned; for with that extreme passion for covering every possible contingency that marked his career, he had been to Croydon. Many a better scheme has failed through the neglect of a smaller detail. The room, when he entered it and secured the door, looked exactly as when he left, three hours before. For all the disarrangement he had caused, Tantroy might have melted out of it.

On the top of his desk, at the side nearest to the safe, lay a packet of octavo scribbling paper. He took out the sheets and twice counted them. Thirty-one, and he had left thirty-four. His face betrayed no emotion. Satisfaction at having outwitted a spy was merged in regret that there must need be one, and pain on Hampden's account that his nephew should be the traitor. He unlocked his desk and carefully lifted out the cigarette-case, pulled open the safe door, and took up the fictitious letter-book. To the naked eye the finger-prints on each were scarcely discernible, but under the magnifying lenses of the superimposing glass all doubt was finally dispelled. They were there, they corresponded, they were identical. Thumb to thumb, finger to finger, and line to line they fitted over one another without a blur or fault. It was, as it often proved to be in those days, hanging evidence.

Salt relocked the safe, tore out the used pages of the letter-book, and reduced them to ashes on the spot. The less important remains of the book he took with him to his chambers, and there burned them from cover to cover before he went to bed.

It had served its purpose, and not a legitimate trace remained. Around the stolen copy the policy of the coming strife might crystallise, and towards any issue it might raise Salt could look with confidence. Finally, if the unforeseen arose, the way was clear for Sir John to denounce a shameless forgery, and who could contradict his indignant word?

CHAPTER IX

SECRET HISTORY

Under succeeding administrations, each pledged to a larger policy to themselves and a smaller one towards every one else, most of the traditional outward forms of government had continued to be observed. Thus there was a Minister for the Colonies, though the Colonies themselves had shamefacedly one by one dropped off into the troubled waters of weak independence, or else clung on with pathetic loyalty in spite of rebuff after rebuff, and the disintegration of all mutual interests, until nothing but the most shadowy bond remained. There was a Secretary of State for War in spite of the fact that the flag which the Government nailed to the mast when it entered into negotiations with an aggrieved and aggressive Power, bore the legend, "Peace at any Price. None but a Coward Strikes the Weak." There had been more than one First Lord of the Admiralty whose maritime experience had begun and ended on the familiar deck of the Koh-I-Noor. There were practically all the usual officers of ministerial rank—and the recipients of ministerial salaries.

Apart from the enjoyment of the title and the salary, however, there were a few members of the Cabinet who exercised no real authority. Lord Henry Stokes had been the last of upper class politicians of standing to accept office under the new régime. Largely in sympathy with the democratic tendency of the age, optimistic as to the growth of moderation and restraint in the ranks of the mushroom party, and actuated by the most sterling patriotism, Lord Henry had essayed the superhuman task of premiership. Superhuman it was, because no mortal could have combined the qualities necessary for success in the face of the fierce distrust and jealousy which his rank and social position excited in the minds of the rawer recruits of his own party; superhuman, because no man possessing his convictions could have long reconciled with them the growing and not diminishing illiberality of those whom he was to lead. There were dissensions, suspicions, and recriminations from the first. The end came in a tragic scene, unparalleled among the many historic spectacles which the House has witnessed. A trivial point in the naval estimates was under discussion, and Lord Henry, totally out of sympathy with the bulk of his nominal following, had risen to patch up the situation on the best terms he could. At the end of a studiously moderate speech, which had provoked cheers from the opposition and murmurs of dissent from his own party throughout, he had wound up his plea for unity, toleration, and patriotism, with the following words: "It is true that here no Government measure is at stake, no crisis is involved, and honourable members on this side of the House are free of party trammels and at liberty to vote as seems best to each. But if the motion should be persisted in, an inevitable conclusion must be faced, an irretrievable step will have been taken, and of the moral outcome of that act who dare trace the end?"

There was just a perceptible pause of sullen silence, then from among the compact mass that sat behind their leader rose a coarse voice, charged with a squiggling laugh.

"We give it up, 'Enry. If it's a riddle about morals, suppose you ask little Flo?"

It was an aside—it was afterwards claimed that it was a drunken whisper—but it was heard, as it was meant to be heard, throughout the crowded Chamber. From the opposition ranks there was torn a cry, almost of horror, at the enormity of the insult, at the direful profanation of the House. Responsible members of the Government turned angrily, imploringly, frantically upon their followers. At least half of these, sitting pained and scandalised, needed no restraint, but from the malcontents and extreme wings came shriek upon shriek of boisterous mirth, as they rocked with laughter about their seats. As for Lord Henry, sitting immobile as he scanned a paper in his hand, he did not appear to have heard at first, nor even to have noticed that anything unusual was taking place. But the next minute he turned deadly pale, began to tremble violently, and with a low and hurried, "Your help, Meadowsweet!" he stumbled from the Hall.

For twenty years he had been a member of the House, years of full-blooded politics when party strife ran strong, but never before had the vaguest innuendo from that deep-seared, unforgotten past dropped from an opponent's lips. It had been reserved for his own party to achieve that distinction and to exact the crowning phase of penance in nature's inexorable cycle.

Apologists afterwards claimed that too much had been made of the incident—that much worse things were often said, and passed, at the meetings of Boards of Guardians and Borough Councils. It was as true as it was biting: worse things were said at Borough Councils, and the Mother of Parliaments had sunk to the rhetorical level of a Borough Council.

Stokes never took his seat again, and with him there passed out of that arena the last of a hopeful patriotic group, whose only failure was that they tried to reconcile two irreconcilable forces of their times.

It did not result, however, that no men of social position were to be found among the Labour benches. There was a demand, and there followed the supply. Rank, mediocrity, and moral obsequiousness were the essentials for their posts. There were no more Stokeses to be had, so obliging creatures were obtained who were willing for a consideration to be paraded as the successors to his patriotic mantle. They were plainly made to understand their position, and if they ventured to show individuality they soon resigned. Nominally occupying high offices, they had neither influence, power, nor respect; like Marlborough in compliance they had "to do it for their bread." They were ruled by their junior lords, assistants, and underlings in various degrees. Many of these men, too strong to be ignored, were frankly recognised to be impossible in the chief offices of State. As a consequence the Cabinet soon became an empty form. Its councils were still held, but the proceedings were cut and dried in advance. The real assembly that dictated the policy of the Government was the Expediency Council, held informally as the necessity arose.

The gathering which was taking place at the Premier's house on this occasion had been convened for the purpose of clearing the air with regard to the policy to be pursued at home. The Government had come into power with very liberal ideas on the question of what ought to be done for the working classes. They had made good their promises, and still that free and enlightened body, having found by experience that they only had to ask often enough and loudly enough to be met in their demands, were already clamouring for more. The most moderate section of the Government was of opinion that the limit had been reached; others thought that the limit lay yet a little further on; the irresponsibles denied that any limit could be fixed at all. That had been the experience of every administration for a long time past, and each one in turn had been succeeded by its malcontents.

Mr Strummery, the Premier, did not occupy the official residence provided for him. Mrs Strummery, an excellent lady who had once been heard to remark that she could never understand why her husband was called Prime Minister when he was not a minister at all, flatly declared that the work of cleaning the windows alone of the house in Downing Street put it out of the question. Even Mr Strummery, who, among his political associates, was reported to have rather exalted ideas of the dignity of his position, came to the conclusion, after fully considering the residence from every standpoint, that he might not feel really at home there. It was therefore let, furnished, to an American lady who engineered wealthy débutantes from her native land into "the best" English society, and the Strummerys found more congenial surroundings in Brandenburg Place. There, within a convenient distance of the Hampstead Road and other choice shopping centres, Mrs Strummery, like the wife of another eminent statesman whose statue stood almost within sight of her bedroom windows, was able to indulge in her amiable foible for cheap marketing. And if the two ladies had this in common, the points of resemblance between their respective lords (the moral side excluded) might be multiplied many-fold, for no phrase put into Mr Strummery's mouth could epigrammatise his point of view more concisely than Fox's inopportune toast, "Our Sovereign: the People." History's dispassionate comment was that the sentiment which lost the abler man his Privy Councillorship in his day, gained for the other a Premiership a century later.

"One thing that gets me is why no one ever seems to take any notice of us when we have a Council on," remarked the President of the Board of Education with an involuntary plaint in his voice. He was standing on the balcony outside the large front room on Mr Strummery's first floor—a room which boasted the noble proportions of a salon, and possibly served as one in Georgian days.

79

Certainly Brandenburg Place did not present a spectacle of fluttering animation at the prospect of seeing the great ones of the land assembling within its bounds. At one end of the thoroughfare a milkman was going from area to area with a prolonged melancholy cry more suggestive of Stoke Poges churchyard than of any other spot on earth; at the opposite end a grocer's errand boy, with basket resourcefully inverted upon his head, had sunk down by the railings to sip the nectar from a few more pages of "Iroquois Ike's Last Hope; or, The Phantom Cow-Puncher's Bride." Midway between the two a cat, in the act of crossing the road, had stopped to twitch a forepaw with that air of imperturbable deliberateness in its movements that no other created thing can ever succeed in attaining. In a house opposite some one was rattling off the exhilarating strains of "Humming Ephraim," but even when a hansom cab and two four-wheelers drove up in quick succession to the Premier's door, no one betrayed curiosity to the extent of looking out of the window. The Minister of Education noted these things as he stood on the balcony, and possibly he felt another phase of the gratitude of men that often left Mr Wordsworth mourning. "I can remember the time when crowds used to wait hours in the rain along Downing Street—our people, too—to catch a sight of Estair or Nettlebury. I won't exactly say that it annoys me, because I've seen too much of the hollowness of things for that, but it certainly is rummy why it should be so."

"A very good thing, too," commented the Premier briskly from the room. "I don't know that we could have a greater compliment. The people know that we are plain, straightforward men like themselves, and they know that we are doing our work without having to come and see us at it. They don't regard us almost as little deities—interesting to see, but quite different and above themselves. That's why."

Every one in the room said "Hear! Hear!" as though that exactly defined his own sentiments; and every one in the room looked rather sad, as though at the back of their collective minds there lurked a doubt whether it might not be more pleasant to be regarded almost as little deities.

"You needn't go as far back as Estair and Nettlebury," put in Vossit of the Treasury. "See how they fairly 'um round Hampden whenever he's about."

"Not us," interposed another man emphatically. "Let them go on their own messin' way; it'll do us no harm. You never saw a working man at any of their high and mighty meetings."

"So much the worse, for they didn't want them. But there ought to have been working men there, from the very first meeting until now." The speaker was one of the most recent additions to the potent circle of the Brandenburg Place councils, and the freedom of criticism which he allowed himself had already been the subject of pained comment on the part of a section of his seniors.

"Well," suggested some one, with politely-pointed meaning, "I don't know what's to prevent one individual from attending a meeting if he so wants. He'd probably find one going on somewhere at this minute if he looked round hard. Doesn't seem to me that any one's holding him back."

"Now, now," reproved Mr Guppling, the Postmaster-General, "let the man speak if he has anything on his mind. Come now, comrade, what do you mean?"

"I don't know what I mean," replied the comrade, at which there was a general shout of laughter. "I don't know what I mean," he continued, having secured general attention by this simple device of oratory, "because I am told in those Government quarters where I ought to be able to find information, that no information has been collected, no systematic enquiries made, nothing is known, in fact. Therefore, I do not know what I mean because I do not know—none of us know—what the Unity League means. But I know this: that a hostile organisation of over a million and a half strong——"

Dissent came forcibly from every quarter of the room. "Not half!" was the milder form it took.

"——of over a million and a half strong," continued the speaker grimly—"perhaps more, in fact, than all our Trades Unions put together—with an income very little less than what all the Trades Unions put together used to have, and funds in hand probably more, is a living menace in our midst, and ought to have been closely watched."

"It keeps 'em quiet," urged the Foreign Under-Secretary.

"Too quiet. I don't like my enemy to be quiet. I prefer him to be talking large and telling us exactly what he's going to do."

"They're going to chuck us out, Tirrel; that's what they're going to do," said a sarcastic comrade playfully. "So was the Buttercup League, so was the Liberal-Conservative alliance. Lo, history repeats itself!"

"I see a long line of strong men fallen in the past—premiers, popes, kings, generals, ambassadors," replied Tirrel. "They all took it for granted that when they had got their positions they could keep them without troubling about their enemies any more. That's generally the repeating point in history."

Mr Strummery felt that the instances were perhaps getting too near home. "Come, come, chaps, and Comrade Tirrel in particular," he said mildly, "don't imagine that nothing is being done in the

81

proper quarter because you mayn't hear much talk about it. Our Executives work and don't talk. I think that you may trust our good comrade Tubes to keep an eye on the Unity League."

"Wish he'd keep an eye on the clock," murmured a captious member. "Not once," he added conclusively, "but three times out of four."

There was a vigorous knock at the front door, and the hurried footsteps of some one ascending the stairs with the consciousness that he was late.

"Talk of Tubes and you'll have a puncture," confided a comrade of humorous bent to his neighbour, and on the words the Home Secretary, certainly with very little breath left in him, entered the room and made his apologies.

The special business for which the Council had been called together was to consider a series of reports from the constituencies, and to decide how to be influenced by their tenor. The Government had no desire to wait for a general election in order to find out the views of the electors of the country; given a close summary of those sentiments, it might be possible to fall in with their wishes, and thereby to be spared the anxiety of an election until their septennial existence had run its course; or, if forced by the action of their own malcontents to take that unwelcome step, at least to cut the ground from beneath their opponents' feet in advance.

If there was not complete unanimity among those present, there was no distinct line of variance. Men of the extremest views had naturally not been included, and although the prevailing opinion was that the conditions of labour had been put upon a fair and equitable basis during their tenure of office—or as far in that direction as it was possible to go without utterly stampeding capitalists and ratepayers from the country—there were many who were prepared to go yet a little further if it seemed desirable.

Judging from the summarised reports, it did seem desirable. From the mills of Lancashire and Yorkshire, the coal-pits of the north and west, the iron fields of the Midlands, the quarries of Derbyshire, the boot factories of Northampton and the lace factories of Nottingham, from every swarming port around the coast, and from that vast cosmopolitan clearing house, the Capital itself, came the same tale. The people did not find themselves so well off as they wished to be; they were, in fact, rather poorer than before. There was nothing local about it. The Thurso flag-stone hewer shared the symptoms with his Celtic brother, digging out tin and copper from beneath the Atlantic waters beyond Pendeen; the Pembroke dock-hand and the Ipswich mechanic were in just the same position. When industries collapsed, as industries had an unhappy character

82

for doing about the period, no one had any reserves. It was possible to live by provision of the Government, but the working man had been educated up to requiring a great deal more than bare living. When wages went down in spite of all artificial inflation, or short time was declared, a great many working-class houses, financed from week to week but up to the hilt in debt, went down too. The agricultural labourer was the least disturbed; he had had the least done for him, and he had never known a "boom." The paradox remained that with more money the majority of the poor were poorer than before, and they were worse than poor, for they were dissatisfied. The remedy, of course, was for some one to give them still more money, not for them to spend less. The shortest way to that remedy, as they had been well taught by their agitators in the past, was to clamour for the Government to do something else for them, and therefore they were clamouring now.

"That is the position," announced Mr Tubes, when he had finished reading the general summary. "The question it raises may not be exactly urgent, but it is at least pressing. On the one hand, there is the undoubted feeling of grievance existing among a large proportion of electors—our own people. On the other hand, there is the serious question of national finances not to be overlooked. As the matter is one that must ultimately concern me more closely than anybody else, I will reserve my own opinion to the last."

The view taken by those present has already been indicated. Their platform was that of Moderate Socialism; they wished it always to be understood that they were practical. They had the interest of their fellow working men (certainly of no other class of the community) at heart, but as Practical Socialists they had a suspicion (taking the condition of the Exchequer into consideration) that for the moment they had reached the limit of Practical Socialism. There was an undoubted dilemma. If a mistake of policy on their part let in the impractical Socialists, the result would be disastrous. Most of them regarded the danger as infinitesimal; like every other political party during the last two centuries, they felt that they could rely on the "sound common-sense of the community." Still, admitting a possibility, even if it was microscopic, might it not be more—say practically socialistic (the word "patriotic" had long been expunged from their vocabulary) in the end to make some slight concessions? If there existed a more material inducement it was not referred to, and any ingenuous comrade, using as an argument in favour of compliance a homely proverb anent the inadvisability of quarrelling with one's bread and butter, would have been promptly discouraged. Yet, although the actors themselves in this great morality play apparently overlooked the consideration, it is impossible for the spectator to ignore the fact. Some few members of the Cabinet might have provided for a rainy day, but even to many of official class, and practically to all of the rank and file, a reversal at the polls must mean that they would have to give up a variety of highly-esteemed privileges and return to private life in less interesting capacities, some in very humble ones indeed.

It ended, as it was bound to end, in compromise. They would not play into the hands of the extreme party and ignore the voice of the constituencies; they would not be false to their convictions and be dictated to by the electors. They would decline to bring in the suggested Minimum Wage Bill, and they would not impose the Personal Property Tax. They would meet matters by extending the National Obligations Act, and save money on the Estimates. They would be sound, if commonplace.

The formal proceedings having been concluded, it was open for any one to introduce any subject he pleased in terms of censure, enquiry or discussion. Comrade Tirrel was on his feet at once, and returned to the subject that lay heavy on his mind.

"Is the Home Secretary in possession of any confidential information regarding the Unity League?" he demanded; "and can he assure us, in view of the admittedly hostile object of the organisation, that adequate means are being taken to neutralise any possible lines of action it may adopt?"

"The answer to the first part of the question is in the affirmative," replied Mr Tubes in his best parliamentary manner. "As regards the second part, I may state that after considering the reports we have received it is not anticipated that the League offers any serious menace to the Government. Should the necessity arise, the Council may rely upon the Home Office taking the requisite precautions."

"The answer is satisfactory as far as it goes. Being in possession of special information, will the Home Secretary go a step further and allay the anxiety that certainly exists in some quarters, by indicating the real intentions and proposed modus operandi of the League?"

Mr Tubes conferred for a moment with his chief. "I may say that on broad lines the League has no definite plan for the future, and its intentions, as represented by the policy of its heads, will simply be to go on existing so long as the deluded followers will continue their subscriptions. I may point out that the League has now been in existence for two years, and during that time it has done nothing at all to justify its founders' expectations; it has not embarrassed us at any point nor turned a single by-election. For two years we heard practically nothing of it, and there has been no fresh development to justify the present uneasiness which it seems to be causing in the minds of a few nervous comrades. Its membership is admittedly imposing, but the bare fact that a million and a half of people are foolish enough——"

There was a significant exchange of astonished glances among the occupants of Mr Strummery's council chamber. Murmurs grew, and Mr Guppling voiced the general feeling by calling the Home Secretary's attention to the figures he had mentioned "doubtless inadvertently."

"No," admitted Mr Tubes carelessly, "that is our latest estimate. From recent information we have reason to think that the previous figure we adopted was too low—or the League may have received large additions lately through some accidental cause. We are now probably erring as widely on the other side, but it is the safe side, and I therefore retain that figure."

Mr Tirrel had not yet finished, but he was listened to with respectful attention now.

"Is the Home Secretary in a position to tell us who this man Salt is?" was his next enquiry.

The Home Secretary looked frankly puzzled. "Who is Salt?" he replied, innocently enough.

"That is the essential point of my enquiry," replied the comrade. "Salt," he continued, his voice stilling the laughter it had raised, "is the Man behind the Unity League. You think it is Hampden, but I tell you that you are mistaken. Hampden is undoubtedly a dangerous power; the classes will follow him blindly, and he is no mere figure-head, but it was Salt who stirred Hampden from his apathy, and it is Salt who pulls the wires."

"And who is Salt?" demanded the Premier, as Mr Tubes offered no comment.

Tirrel shook his head. "I know no more than I have stated," he replied; "but his secret influence must be tremendous, and all doubt as to the identity of the man and his past record should be set at rest."

Mr Tubes looked up from the papers he had before him with a gleam of subdued anger in his eye. "I think that our cock-sure kumred has geete howd of another mare's neest," he remarked, relapsing unconsciously into his native dialect as he frequently did when stirred. "I remember hearin' o' this Saut in one o' th' reports, and here it is. So far from being a principal, he occupies a very different position—that of Hampden's private secretary, which would explain how he might have to come into contact with a great many people without having any real influence hissel. He is

85

described in my confidential report as a simple, unsuspicious man, who might be safely made use of, and, in fact, most of my information is derived from that source."

There was a sharp, smothered exclamation from one or two men, and then a sudden stillness fell upon the room. Mr Tubes was among the last to realise the trend of his admission.

"Are we to understand that the greater part—perhaps the whole—of the information upon which the Home Office has been relying, and of the assurances of inaction which have lulled our suspicions to rest, have been blindly accepted from this man Salt, the head and fount of the League itself?" demanded Tirrel with ominous precision. "If that indicates the methods of the Department, I think that this Council will share my view when I suggest that the terms 'simple' and 'unsuspicious' have been inaccurately allotted—to Salt."

Mr Tubes made no reply. Lying at the bottom of the man's nature smouldered a volcanic passion that he watched as though it were a sleeping beast. Twice in his public career it had escaped him, and each time the result had been a sharp reverse to his ambitions. Repression—firm, instant, and unconditional—was the only safeguard, so that now recognising the danger-signal in his breast, he sat without a word in spite of the Premier's anxious looks, in spite of the concern of those about him.

"I will not press for a verbal reply," continued Tirrel after a telling pause; "the inference of silence makes that superfluous. But I will ask whether the Home Secretary is aware that Salt has been quietly engaged in canvassing the provinces for a month, and whether he has any information about his object and results. Yes," he continued vehemently, turning to those immediately about him, "for a month past this simple, unsuspecting individual from whom we derive our confidential information has been passing quietly and unmarked from town to town; and if you were to hang a map of England on the wall before me, I would undertake to trace his route across the land by the points of most marked discontent in the report to which we have just listened."

A knock at the locked door of the room saved the Home Secretary for the moment from the necessity of replying. It was an unusual incident, and when the nearest man went and asked what was wanted, some one was understood to reply that a stranger, who refused to give his name, wished to see Mr Tubes. Perhaps Mr Tubes personally might have welcomed a respite, but the master of the house anticipated him.

"Tell him, whoever he may be, that Mr Tubes cannot be disturbed just now," he declared.

86

"He says it's important, very important," urged the voice, with a suggestion of largess received and more to come, in its eagerness.

"Then let him write it down or wait," said Mr Strummery decisively, and the matter was supposed to have ended.

The momentary interruption had broken the tension and perhaps saved Tubes from a passionate outburst. He rose to make a reply without any sign of anger or any fear that he would not be able to smooth away the awkward impression.

"As far as canvassing in the provinces is concerned," he remarked plausibly, "it is open for any man, whatever his politics may be, to do that from morning to night all his life if he likes, so long as it isn't for an illegal object. As regards Salt having been engaged this way for the past month, it is quite true that I have had no intimation of the fact so far. I may explain that as my Department has not yet come to regard the Unity League as the one object in the world to which it must devote its whole attention, I am not in the habit of receiving reports on the subject every day, nor even every week. It may be, however——"

There was another knock upon the door. Mr Tubes stopped, and the Premier frowned. In the space between the door and the carpet there appeared for a second a scrap of paper; the next moment it came skimming a few yards into the room. There was no attempt to hold further communication, and the footsteps of the silent messenger were heard descending the stairs again.

Mr Vossit, who sat nearest to the door, picked up the little oblong card. He saw, as he could scarcely fail to see, that it was an ordinary visiting-card, and on the upper side, as it lay, there appeared a roughly-pencilled sign—two lines at right angle drawn through a semicircle, it appeared superficially to be. As he handed it to Mr Tubes he reversed the position so that the name should be uppermost, and again he saw, as he could scarcely fail to see, that the other side was blank. The roughly-pencilled diagram was all the message it contained.

"It may be, however——" the Home Secretary was repeating half-mechanically. He took the card and glanced at the symbol it bore. "It may be, however," he continued, as though there had been no interruption, "that I shall very soon be in possession of the full facts to lay before you." Then with a few whispered words to the Premier and a comprehensive murmur of apology to the rest of the company, he withdrew.

Fully a quarter of an hour passed before there was any sign of the absent Minister, and then it did not take the form of his return. The conversation, in his absence, had worked round to the engaging alternative of whether it was more correct to educate one's son at

Eton or at Margate College, when a message was sent up requesting the Premier's attendance in another room. After another quarter of an hour some one was heard to leave the house, but it was ten minutes later before the two men returned. It was felt in the atmosphere that some new development was at hand, and they had to run the curious scrutiny of every eye. Both had an air of constraint, and both were rather pale. The Premier moved to his seat with brusque indifference, and one who knew Tubes well passed a whispered warning that Jim had got his storm-cone fairly hoisted. The door was locked again, chairs were drawn up to the table, and a hush of marked expectancy settled over the meeting.

The Prime Minister spoke first.

"In the past half-hour a letter has come into our possession that may cause us to alter our arrangements," he announced baldly. "How it came into our possession doesn't matter. All that does matter is, that it's genuine. Tubes will read it to you."

"It is signed 'John Hampden,' addressed to Robert Estair, and dated three days ago," contributed the Home Secretary just as briefly. "The original was in cipher. This is the deciphered form:

"'My Dear Estair,—I now have Salt's complete report before me, and there seems to be no doubt that the proposal I have formulated is feasible, and the moment almost ripe. Salt has covered all the most important industrial centres, and everywhere the reports of our agents are favourable to the plan. Not having found universal happiness and a complete immunity from the cares incident to humanity in the privileges which they so ardently desired and have now obtained, the working classes are tending to believe that the panacea must lie, not in greater moderation, but in extended privilege.

"'For the moment the present Government is indisposed to go much further, not possessing the funds necessary for enlarged concessions and fearing that increased taxation might result in a serious stream of emigration among the monied classes. For the moment the working men hesitate to throw in their lot with the extreme Socialists, distrusting the revolutionary and anarchical wing of that party, and instinctively feeling that any temporary advantage which they might enjoy would soon be swallowed up in the reign of open lawlessness that must inevitably arise.

"'For the moment, therefore, there is a pause, and now occurs the opportunity—perhaps the last in history—

88

for us to retrieve some of the losses of the past. There are scruples to be overcome, but I do not think that an alliance with the moderate section of the Labour interest is inconsistent with the aims and traditions of the great parties which our League represents. It would, of course, be necessary to guarantee to our new allies the privileges which they now possess, and even to promise more; but I am convinced, not only by past experience but also by specific assurances from certain quarters, that they would prefer to remain as they are, and form an alliance with us rather than grasp at larger gains and suffer absorption into another party which they dare not trust.

"'From the definite nature of this statement you will gather that the negotiations are more than in the air. The distribution of Cabinet offices will have to be considered at once. B—— might be first gained over with the offer of the Exchequer. He carries great weight with a considerable section of his party, and is dissatisfied with his recognition so far. Heape is a representative man who would repay early attention, especially as he is, at the moment, envious of R——'s better treatment. But these are matters of detail. The great thing is to get back on any terms. Once in power, by a modification of the franchise we might make good our position. I trust that this, a desperate remedy in a desperate time, will earn at least your tacit acquiescence. Much is irretrievably lost; England remains—yet.

"Yours sincerely,
"John Hampden.'"

Six men were on their feet before the signature was reached. With an impatient gesture Strummery waved them collectively aside.

"We all know your opinion on the writer and the letter, and we can all put it into our own words without wasting time in listening," he said with suppressed fury. "In five minutes' time I shall entirely reopen the consideration of the reports which we met this afternoon to discuss."

"Has any effort been made to learn the nature of Estair's reply?" enquired Tirrel. If he was not the least moved man in the room he was the least perturbed, and he instinctively picked out the only point of importance that remained.

"It probably does not exist in writing," replied Mr Tubes,

avoiding Tirrel's steady gaze. "I find that he arrived in town last night. There would certainly be a meeting."

"Was Bannister summoned to this Council?" demanded another. It was taken for granted that "B" stood for Bannister.

"Yes," replied the Premier, with one eye on his watch. "He was indisposed."

"I protest against the reference to myself," said Heape coldly.

Mr Strummery nodded. "Time's up," he announced.

That is the "secret history" of the Government's sudden and inexplicable conversion to the necessity of the Minimum Wage Bill and to the propriety of imposing the Personal Property Tax. A fortnight later the Prime Minister outlined the programme in the course of a speech at Newcastle. The announcement was received almost with stupefaction. For the first time in history, property—money, merchandise, personal belongings—was to be saddled with an annual tax apart from, and in addition to, the tax it paid on the incomes derived from it. It was an entire wedge of the extreme policy that must end in Partition. It was more than the poorer classes had dared to hope; it was more than the tax-paying classes had dared to fear. It marked a new era of extended privilege for the one; it marked the final extinction of hope even among the hopeful for the other.

"It could not have happened more opportunely for us even if we had arranged it in every detail," declared Hampden, going into Salt's room with the tidings in huge delight, a fortnight later.

"No," agreed Salt, looking up with his slow, pleasant smile. "Not even if we had arranged it."

CHAPTER X

THE ORDER OF ST MARTIN OF TOURS

Sir John Hampden paused for a moment with arrested pen. He had been in the act of crossing off another day on the calendar that hung inside his desk, the last detail before he pulled the roll-top down for the night, when the date had caught his eye with a sudden meaning.

"A week to-day, Salt," he remarked, looking up.

90

"A week to-day," repeated Salt. "That gives us seven more days for details."

Hampden laughed quietly as he bent forward and continued the red line through the "14."

"That is one way of looking at it," he said. "Personally, I was rather wishing that it had been to-day. I confess that I cannot watch the climax of these two years approaching without feeling keyed up to concert pitch. I suppose that you never had any nerves?"

"I suppose not. If I had, the Atlantic water soon washed them out."

"But you are superstitious?" he asked curiously. It suddenly occurred to him how little he really knew of the man with whom he was linked in such a momentous hazard.

"Oh yes. Blue water inoculates us all with that. Fortunately, mine does not go beyond trifles, such as touching posts and stepping over paving stones—a hobby and not a passion, or I should have to curb it."

"Do you really do things like that? Well, I remember Northland, the great nerve specialist, telling me that most people have something of the sort—a persistent feeling of impending calamity unless they conform to some trivial impulse. I am exempt."

"Yes," commented Salt; "or you would hardly be likely to cross off the date before the day is over."

"Good Heavens!" exclaimed Hampden. "What an age we live in! Is it tannin or the dregs of paganism? And you think it would be tempting Providence to do it while there are five more hours to run?"

"I never do it, as a matter of fact," admitted Salt with perfect seriousness. "Of course, I know that nothing would happen in the five hours if I did, but, all the same, I rather think that something would."

"I hope that something will," said Hampden cheerfully. "Dinner, for example. Did I ever strike you as a gourmet, Salt? Well, nevertheless, I am a terrific believer in regular meals, although I don't care a straw how simple they are. You may read of some marvellous Trojan working under heavy pressure for twenty-four hours, and then snatching a hurried glass of Château d'Yquem and a couple of Abernethy biscuits, and going on again for another twenty-four. Don't believe it, Salt. If he is not used to it, his knees go; if he is used to it, they have gone already. If I were a general I solemnly declare that I would risk more to feed my men before an engagement, than I would risk to hold the best position all along the front. Your hungry man may fight well enough for a time, but the moment he is beaten he knows it. And, strangely enough, we

91

English have won a good many important battles after we had been beaten."

He had been locking up the safe and desk as he ran on, and now they walked together down the corridor. At the door of his own office Salt excused himself for a moment and went in. When he rejoined the baronet at the outer door, he held in his hand a little square of thin paper on which was printed in bold type

JULY 14.

"You will regret it," said Hampden, not wholly jestingly. He saw at once that it was the tag for the day, torn from his calendar, that Salt held.

"No," he replied, crumpling up the scrap of paper and throwing it away, "I may remember, but I shall not regret. When you have to think twice about doing a thing like that, it is time to do it.... You have no particular message for Deland?"

"None at all, personally, I think. You will tell him as much as we decided upon. Let him know that his post will certainly be one of the most important outside the central office. What time do you go?"

"The 10 train from Marylebone. Deland will be waiting up for me. There is an early restaurant train in the morning—the 7.20, getting in at 10.40. I shall breakfast en route, and come straight on here."

"That's right. Look out for young Hampshire in the train; he will probably wait on you, but you won't recognise him unless you remember the Manners-Clinton nose in profile. He regards it as a vast joke, but he is very keen. And sleep all the time you aren't feeding. Can't do better. Good night."

Salt laughed as he turned into Pall Mall, speculating for a moment, by the light of his own knowledge, how little time this strenuous, simple-living man devoted to the things he advocated. If he had been able to follow Sir John's electric brougham for the remainder of that night he would have had still more reason to be sceptical.

When Hampden reached his house and strode up to the door with the elastic step of a young man, despite his iron-grey hair and burden of responsibility, instead of the bronze Medusa knocker that had dropped from the hands of Pietro Sarpi and Donato in its time, his eyes encountered the smiling face of his daughter as she swung open the door before him. She had been sitting at an open window of the dull-fronted house until she saw the Hampden livery in the distance.

"There is some one waiting in the library to see you," she said, as he kissed her cheek. "He said that he would wait ten minutes; you had already been seven."

"Who is it?" he asked in quiet expectation. It was not unusual for Muriel to watch for him from the upper room, and to come down into the hall to welcome him, but to-night he saw at once that there was a mild excitement in her manner. "Who is it?" he asked.

She told him in half a dozen whispered words, and then returned to the drawing-room and the society of a depressing companion, who chanced to be a poor and distant cousin, while Sir John turned toward the library.

"Tell Styles to remain with the brougham if he is still in front," he said to a passing footman. The visit might presage anything.

A young man, an inconspicuous young man in a blue serge suit, rose from the chair of Jacobean oak and Spanish leather where he had been sitting with a bowler hat between his hands and a cheap umbrella across his knees, and made a cursory bow as he began to search an inner pocket.

"Sir John Hampden?" he enquired.

"Yes," replied the master of the house, favouring his visitor with a more curious attention than he received in return. "You are from Plantagenet House, I believe?"

The young man detached his left hand from the search and turned down the lapel of his coat in a perfunctory display of his credentials. Pinned beneath so that it should not obtrude was an insignificant little medal, so small and trivial that it would require the closest scrutiny to distinguish its design and lettering.

But Sir John Hampden did not require any assurance upon the point. He knew by the evidence of just such another medallion which lay in his own possession that upon one side, around the engraved name of the holder, ran the inscription, "Every man according as he purposeth in his heart;" upon the other side a representation of St Martin dividing his cloak with the beggar. It was the badge of the Order of St Martin of Tours.

The Order of St Martin embodied the last phase of organised benevolence. In the history of the world there had never been a time when men so passionately desired to help their fellow men; there had never been a time when they found it more difficult to do so to their satisfaction. From the lips of every social reformer, from the reports of the charitable organisations, from the testimony of the poor themselves the broad indictment had gone forth that every casual beggar was a rogue and a vagabond. Promiscuous alms-giving was tabulated among the Seven Curses of London.

Organised charity was the readiest alternative. Again obliging counsellors raised their conscientious voices. Organised charity was wasteful, inelastic, unsympathetic, often superfluous. The preacher added a warning note: Let none think that the easy donation of a cheque here and there was charity. It was frequently vanity, it was often a cowardly compromise with conscience, it was never an absolution from the individual responsibility.

So brotherly love continued, but often did not fructify, and the man who felt that he had the true Samaritan instinct, as he passed by on the one side of the suburban road, looked at his ragged neighbour lying under the hedge on the other side in a fit which might be epilepsy but might equally well be soap-suds in the mouth, and assured himself that if only he could believe the case to be genuine there was nothing on earth he would not do for the man.

It was a very difficult age, every one admitted: "Society was so complex."

There was evidence of the generous feeling—ill-balanced and spasmodic, it is true—on every hand. The poor were bravely, almost blindly, good to their neighbours in misfortune. The better-off were lavish—or had been until a few years previously—when they had certified proof that the cases were deserving. If a magistrate or a police court missionary gave publicity to a Pathetic Case, the Pathetic Case might be sure of being able to retire on a comfortable annuity. If only every Pathetic Case could have been induced to come pathetically into the clutches of a sympathetic police court cadi, instead of dying quite as pathetically in a rat-hole, one of the most pressing problems of benevolence might have been satisfactorily solved.

The Order of St Martin of Tours was one of the attempts to reconcile the generous yearnings of mankind with modern conditions. Its field of action had no definable limit, and whatever a man wished to give it was prepared to utilise. It was not primarily concerned with money, although judged by the guaranteed resources upon which it could call if necessary, it would rank as a rich society. It imposed no subscription and made no outside appeal. Upon its books, against the name of every member, there was entered what he bound himself to do when it was required of him. It was a vast and comprehensive list, so varied that few ever genuinely applied for the services of the Order without their needs being satisfied. The city man willing to give a foolish and repentant youth another chance of honest work; the Sussex farmer anxious to prove what a month of South Down fare and Channel breezes would do for a small city convalescent; the prim little suburban lady, much too timid to attempt any personal contact with the unknown depths of sin and suffering, but eager to send her choicest flowers and most perfect fruit to any slum sick-room; the good-hearted laundry girl who had been through the fires herself, offering to "pal up to any other girl what's having a bit of rough and wants to keep straight without a lot of jaw,"—all found a deeper use in life beneath the sign of St Martin's divided cloak. Children, even little children, were not shut out; they could play with other, lonely, little children, and renounce some toys.

The inconspicuous young man standing in Sir John Hampden's library—he was in a cheap boot shop, but he gave his early closing day to serve the Order as a messenger, and there were millionaires who gave less—found the thing he searched for, and handed to Sir John an unsealed envelope.

"I accept," said the baronet, after glancing at the slip it contained. This was what he accepted:

ORDER OF ST. MARTIN OF TOURS.

Case. . . John Flak, 45 Paradise Buildings, Paradise Street, Drury Lane, W.C.

Cause . . Street Accident.

Requirement . . Service through the night.

Recommender . . L. K. Stone, M.D., 172 Great Queen Street, W.C.

Waltham, Master.

He could have declined; and his membership would have been at an end. But in a mission of personal service he could not accept and appoint a substitute. The Order was modern, business-like, reasonable, unemotional, and quite prepared to take humanity as it was. It did not seek to impose the ideal Christian standard, logically recognising that if a man gave all he possessed, a system of Christian laws (a Cæsar whom he was likewise bidden to obey) would at once incarcerate him in a prison for having no visible means of subsistence, and, if he persisted in his unnatural Christian conduct, in a lunatic asylum, where in its appointed season he would have the story of the Rich Ruler read for his edification.

The Order was practical and "very nice to do with;" but it had a standard, and as a protest against that widespread reliance in the omnipotence of gold that marred the age it allowed no delegation of an office of mercy. On all points it was open; its thin medallion symbolised no mysteries or secret vows; nor, and on this one point it was unbending, as far as lay in the power of the Order should any second-hand virtue find place beneath its saintly ensign.

A few years before, Paradise Street, with that marked

inappropriateness that may be traced in the nomenclature of many London thoroughfares, had been the foulest, poorest, noisomest, most garbage-strewn and fly-infested region even in the purlieus of Drury Lane. It was not markedly criminal, it was merely filthy; and when smell-diseases broke out in central London it was generally found that they radiated from Paradise Street like ripples from a dead dog thrown into a pond. Presently a type foundry in the next street, growing backwards because it was impossible to expand further in any other direction, pushed down the flimsy tenements that stood between and reared a high wall, pierced with windows of prismatic glass, in their place. Soon public authorities, seeing that the heavens did not fall when a quarter of Paradise Street did, suddenly and unexpectedly tore down another quarter as though they had received a maddened impulse and Paradise Street had been a cardboard model. The phœnix that appeared on this site was a seven-storied block of workmen's dwellings. It could not be said to have given universal satisfaction. The municipal authorities who devised it bickered entertainingly over most of the details that lay between the foundations and the chimney-pots; the primitive dwellers in Paradise Street looked askance at it, as they did at most things not in liquid form; social reformers complained that it drove away the very poor and brought in a class of only medium poor; and ordinary people noticed that in place of the nearest approach to artistic dirt to be found in the metropolis, some one had substituted uninteresting squalor.

Hampden dismissed his carriage in Lincoln's Inn Fields and walked the remainder of the way. He had changed into a dark lounge suit before he left, but, in spite of the principle he had so positively laid down, he had not stayed to dine. The inevitable, morbid little group marked the entrance to Paradise Buildings, but the incident was already three hours old, and the larger public interest was being reserved for the anticipated funeral.

A slipshod, smug-faced woman opened the door of No. 45 in response to his discreet knock. He stepped into a small hall where coal was stored in a packing-case, and, on her invitation, through into the front room. Five more untidy women, who had been drinking from three cups, got up as he entered, and passed out, eyeing him with respectful curiosity as they went, and each dropping a word of friendly leavetaking to the slatternly hostess.

"Don't be down'arted, my dear."

"See you later, Emm."

"Let's know how things are going, won't you?"

"You'll remember about that black alpaker body?"

"Well, so long, Mrs Flak. Gord bless yer."

Sir John waited until the hall door closed behind the last frowsy woman.

"I am here to be of any use I can," he said. "Did Dr Stone mention that some one would come?"

"Yes, sir. Thank you, sir," she replied. She stood in the middle of the room, a picture of domestic incapacity, with a foolish look upon her rather comely features. The room was not bare of furniture, was not devoid of working-class comforts, but the dirty dishes, the dirty clothing, the dirty floor, told the plain tale.

"I do not know any particulars of the case yet." He saw at once that he would have to take the lead in every detail. "Did the doctor speak of coming again, or leave any message?"

"Yes, sir," she replied readily. She lifted an ornament on the mantelpiece and gave him a folded sheet of paper, torn from a note-book, that had been placed there for safety. He had the clearest impression that it would never have occurred to the woman to give it to him unasked.

"To rep of O. St M.," ran the pencilled scrawl. "Shall endeavour to look in 8-8.30.—L.K.S."

Even as he took out his watch there came a business-like knock at the door, an active step in the hall, and beneath the conventional greeting, the two men were weighing one another.

Dr Stone had asked the Order to send a man of common-sense who could exercise authority if need be, and one who would not be squeamish in his surroundings. For reasons of his own he had added that if with these qualifications he combined that of being a Justice of the Peace, so much the better. Dr Stone judged that he had the man before him. Hampden saw a brisk, not too well shaven, man in a light suit, with a straw hat and a serviceable stick in his hands, until he threw them on the table. There was kindness and decision behind his alert eyes, and his manner was that of a benevolent despot marshalling his poor patients—and he had few others—as a regiment before him, marching them right and left in companies, bringing them sharply to the front, and bidding them to stand there and do nothing until they were told.

"You haven't been into the other room yet?" he asked. "No, well——"

He stopped with his hand on the door knob, turned back like a pointer on the suspicion of a trail, and looked keenly at the woman, then around the bestrewn room. If her eyes had slid the least betraying glance, Hampden did not observe it, but the doctor, without a word, strode to the littered couch, put his hand behind a threadbare cushion, and drew out a half-filled bottle. There was a gluggling ripple for a few seconds, and the contents had disappeared down the sink, while the terebinthine odour of cheap gin hung across the room.

"Not here, Mrs Flak," he said sharply; and without changing her expression of vacuous good-nature, the woman meekly replied, "No, sir."

Dr Stone led the way into the inner room and closed the door behind them. A man, asleep, insensible, or dead, lay on the bed, his face half hidden in bandages.

"This is the position," explained the doctor, speaking very rapidly, for his time was mapped out with as little waste as there is to be found between the squares on a chess board. "This man went out of here a few hours ago and walked straight into an empty motor 'bus that was going round this way. That's how they all put it: he walked right into the thing. Why? He was a sober enough man, an attendant of some kind at one of the west end clubs. Because, as I have good reason to suppose, he was thinking absorbingly of something else.

"Well, they carried him in here; it ought to have been the hospital, of course, but it was at his own doorstep it took place, you see, and it doesn't really matter, because to-morrow morning——!"

"He will die then?" asked Hampden in a whisper, interpreting the quick gesture.

"Oh, he will die as sure as his head is a cracked egg-shell. Between midnight and dawn, I should say. But before the end I look confidently for an interval of consciousness, or rather sub-consciousness. If I am wrong I shall have kept you up all night for nothing; if I am right you will probably hear something that he wants to say very much."

"Whatever was in his mind when he met with the accident?"

"That is my conviction. There has already been an indication of partial expression. Curiously enough, I have had two exactly similar cases, and this is going just the same way. In one it was a sum of money a man had banked under another name to keep it from his wife and for his children; in the second it was a blow struck in a scuffle, and an innocent man was doing penal servitude for it."

"That is what you wished to have some one here for chiefly, then?" asked Hampden.

"Everything, practically. You see the kind of people around? The wife is a fool; the neighbours are the class of maddening dolts who leave a suicide hanging until a policeman comes to cut him down. They would hold an orgie in the next room. In excitement the women fly to gin as instinctively as a nun flies to prayer. Order them out if they come, but I don't think that they will trouble you after I have spoken to the woman as I go. If there is anything to be caught it will have to be on the hop, so to speak. It may be a confession, a deposition of legal value, or only a request; one cannot guess. Questioning, when the sub-conscious stage is reached, might lead to something. It's largely a matter of luck, but intelligence may have an innings."

"Is there nothing to be done—in the way of making it easier for him?"

Dr Stone made a face expressive of their helplessness and shrugged his shoulders; then mentioned a few simple details.

"He will never know," he explained. "Even when he seems conscious he will feel no pain and remember nothing of the accident. The clock will be mercifully set back." He smiled whimsically. "Forgive me if it never strikes." He turned to go. "The nearest call office is the kiosk in Aldwych," he remarked. "I am 7406 Covent Garden." No paper being visible he wrote the number on the wall. "After 10.30 as a general thing," he added.

So the baronet was left alone with the still figure that counterfeited death so well, the man who would be dead before the dawn. He stepped quietly to the bed and looked down on him. The lower half of the face was free from swathing, and the lean throat and grizzled beard struck Sir John with a momentary surprise. It was the face of an elderly man; he had expected to find one not more than middle-aged as the companion of the young woman in the other room.

There was a single chair against the wall, and he sat down. There was nothing else to do but to sit and wait, to listen to the sounds of voluminous life that rose from the street beneath, the careful creaking movements in the room beyond. From the shallow wainscotting near the bed came at intervals the steady ticking of a death-watch. It was nothing, as every one knew, but the note of an insect calling for its mate, but it thrilled and grew large in the stillness of the chamber ominously.

A low tap on the door came as a relief. He found the woman standing there.

"Is there anything different?" she asked, hanging on to the door. "I kept on thinking I heard noises."

"No, there is no change," he replied. "Will you come in?"

She shrank back at the suggestion. "Gord 'elp us, no!" she cried. "It's bad enough out there."

"What are you afraid of?" he asked kindly.

She had no words for it. Self-analysis did not enter into her daily life. But, sitting there alone among the noises, real and imagined, she had reached a state of terror.

99

"There is nothing at all dreadful, nothing that would shock you," he said, referring to the appearance of the dying man. "You are his wife, are you not?"

The foolish look, half stubborn, half vacuous, flickered about her face. "As good as," she replied. "It's like this——"

"I see." He had no desire to hear the recital of the sordid details.

"His wife's in a mad-house. Won't never be anywhere else, and I've been with him these five years, an honest woman to him all the time," she said, bridling somewhat at the suggestion of reproach. "No one's got no better right to the things, I'm sure." Her eloquence was stirred not so much to defend her reputation as by the fear that some one might step in to claim "the things."

"There will be plenty of time to talk about that when—when it is necessary," he said. "Has he no relations about here who ought to be told?"

"Nah," she said decisively; "no one but me. Why, he didn't even have no friends—no pals of his own class, as you may say. Very close about himself he was. All he thought of was them political corkses, as they call um." She came nearer to the door again, the gossiping passion of her class stronger than her fear, now that the earlier restraint of his presence was wearing off. "It's the only thing we ever had a 'arsh word about. It's all right and well for them that make a living at it, but many and many a time my 'usband's lost 'alf a day two and three times a week to sit in the Distingwidged Strangers' Gallery. You mightn't 'ardly think it, sir, but he was hand and foot with some of the biggest men there are; he was indeed."

Hampden was looking at her curiously. He read into her "'arsh word" the ceaseless clatter of her nagging, shameless tongue when the old man brought home a few shillings less than he was wont; the aftermath of sullen silence, the unprepared meals and neglected home. He pictured him a patient, long-suffering old man, and pitied him. And now she took pride and boasted of the very things that she had upbraided him with.

"Vickers he knew," she continued complacently, "and Drugget. He's shaken hands with Mr Strummery, the Prime Minister, more than onest. Then Tubes—you've heard speak of him?—he found Mr Tubes a very pleasant gentleman. Oh, and a lot more I can't remember."

Hampden disengaged himself from further conversation with a single formal sentence, and returned to his vigil. There he was secure from her callous chatter. He saw the renewed look of terror start into her eyes when a board behind her creaked as the door was closing. He heard the startled shriek, but her squalid avarice cut off his sympathies. He sat down again and looked round at the already familiar objects in the room. The form lying on the bed had not changed a fraction of its rigid outline; but he missed something somewhere in the room, and for a minute he could not identify it. Then he remembered the ticking of the death-watch. It had ceased. He looked at his watch; it was not yet nine o'clock.

He had not been back more than ten minutes when the subdued tapping—it was rather a timid scrape, as though she feared that a louder summons might call another forth—was repeated.

"I don't see that it's no good my staying here," she gasped. "I've been sitting there till the furniture fair began to move towards me, and every bloomin' rag about the place had a face in it. It's giving me the fair horrors."

He could not ignore her half-frenzied state. "What do you want to do?" he asked.

"I want to go out for a bit," she replied, licking her thin feline lips. "You don't know what it's like. I want to hear real people talk and not see things move. I'll come back soon; before Gord, I will."

"Yes, how will you came back?"

"I won't. May it strike me dead if I touch a drop. I'll go straight into Mrs Rugg's across the street, and she's almost what you might call a teetotaler."

"The man you call your husband is dying in there, and he may need your help at any minute," he said sternly. It needed no gift of divination to prophesy that if the woman once left the place she would be hopelessly drunk before an hour had passed. "Don't sit down doing nothing but imagining things," he continued. "Make yourself some tea, and then when one of your friends comes round to see you, you can let her stay. But only one, mind."

He saw the more sullen of her looks settle darkly about her face as he closed the door. He waited to hear the sound of the kettle being moved, the tea-cup clinking, but they never came. An unnatural, uncreaking silence reigned instead. He opened the door quietly and looked out. That room was empty, and, as he stood there, a current of cooler air fell across his cheek. Half a dozen steps brought him to the entrance to the little hall—the only other room there was. It also was empty, and the front door stood widely open. There was only one possible inference: "Mrs Flak" had fled.

Sir John had confessed to possessing nerves, and to few men the situation would have been an inviting one. Still, there was only one possible thing to do, and he closed the door again, noticing, as he did so, that the action locked it. As he stood there a moment before returning to the bedroom and its tranquil occupant lying in his rigid, unbreathing sleep, a slight but continuous sound caught his ear. It was the most closely comparable (to attempt to define it) with the whirring of a clock as the flying pinion is released before it strikes. Or it might be that the doctor's simile prompted the comparison. It was not loud, but the room beyond seemed very, very still.

It was not a time to temporise with the emotions. Hampden stepped into the next room and stood listening. He judged—nay, he was sure—that the sound came from the bedroom, but it was not repeated. Instead, something very different happened, something that was either terrifying or natural, according to the conditions that provoked it. Quite without warning there came a voice from the next room, a full, level, healthy voice, even strong, and speaking in the ordinary manner of conversation.

"Will you please tell Mr Tubes that I am waiting here to see him?"

CHAPTER XI

MAN BETWEEN TWO MASTERS

There was something in the situation that was more than gruesome, something that was peculiarly unnerving.

In his anticipation of this moment as he had sat almost by the bedside, Hampden had conjectured that the dying man would perhaps lift a hand or move his head uneasily with the first instinct of returning consciousness. A sigh, a groan, might escape him, incoherent words follow, then broken but rational expressions of his suffering, and entreaties that something might be done to ease the pain. Or perhaps, after realising his position, he would nerve himself to betray no unmanly weakness, and, in the words of the significant old phrase, "turning his face to the wall," endure in stoical silence to the end. It would be painful, perhaps acutely distressing, but it would not be unnatural.

There had been no groan, no sigh or broken words, no indication of weakness or suffering behind that half-closed door, nothing but the curious clock-like sound that had gone before the voice. And that voice! It was as full and strong, as vibrant and as ordinary as his own could ever be. Standing in the middle of the

102

living-room Sir John could not deceive himself. It came from the other room where a minute before he had left the dying—yes, the almost dead—man lying with stark outline on the bed. There was no alternative: it was from those pallid lips that the words had come, it was by that still, inanimate man that they were spoken.

The suddenness of the whole incident was shocking in itself, but that was not all; the mere contrast to what he had looked for was disconcerting, but there was something more; the curious unexpected nature of the request, if request it was, was not without its element of mystery, but above and beyond all else was the thought—the thought that for a dreadful moment held his heart and soul in icy bonds—what sight when he returned to the inner room, as return at once he must, what gruesome sight would meet his eyes?

What phantoms his misgivings raised, every man may conjecture for himself. Follow, then, another step in imagination, and having given a somewhat free and ghastly fancy rein, push the chamber door cautiously and inch by inch, or fling it boldly open as you will; then pause upon the threshold, as Hampden did, in sharp surprise.

Nothing was altered, no single detail had undergone the slightest change! On the bed, rigid and very sharp beneath the single unclean sheet, lay the body of the mangled man. Not a fold of his shroud-like wrapping differed from its former line, it did not seem possible that a breath had stirred him.

Had the voice been a trick of the imagination? Hampden knew, as far as mortal man can be sure of any mortal sense, that the voice had been as real as his life itself. Then——? It occurred to him in a flash: here was the stage of under-consciousness of which Dr Stone had spoken. Of his pain, the accident, where he at that moment lay, and all his real surroundings, the sufferer knew nothing, and never would know. But out of the shock and shattering, some of the delicate machinery of the brain still kept its balance, and would continue to exercise its functions to the end.

It was an ordeal, but it had to be done. It was the purpose for which he had been summoned. Sir John moved to the bedside, nerved himself to watch the ashen face, and said slowly and distinctly: "Mr Tubes is not here. Do you wish to see him?"

There was just a perceptible pause, and then the bloodless lips replied. But not the faintest tremor of a movement stirred the body otherwise from head to foot, and in the chilling absence of expression the simile occurred to Hampden of bubbles rising from some unseen working to the surface of an inky pool.

"I have come on purpose. Let him be told that it is most important."

Hampden had to feel his way. The woman had mentioned that Flak was at least on terms of acquaintanceship with Mr Tubes. The doctor had surmised that the man had something he must say before he died. But was this the one true line, or a mere vagary of the sub-conscious state—a twist in the tortuous labyrinth that would lead to nothing?

"He is not here at present," he said. "If you will tell me what you wish to say I will write it down, so that it cannot fail to reach him."

"No. I cannot tell any one else. I must see him."

"Mr Tubes is a very busy man. You know that he is the Home Secretary. Is it of sufficient importance to telegraph for him?"

This time the answer followed on his last word with startling rapidity. Until the last phase that was the only variation in the delivery of the sentences—that sometimes there was a pause as though the working of the mind had to make a revolution before it reached the point of the mental clutch, at others it dropped into its gear at once.

"It is important enough to send a coach and four for him," was the reply.

Hampden might not be convinced of this but he was satisfied of one thing: the coherence of idea was being regularly maintained. How long would it last? It occurred to him to put the question.

"I shall have to go out either to send the telegram myself or to find some one who will take it," he explained. "Until Mr Tubes comes or sends his reply will you remain here?"

It was rather eerie to be holding conversation with the fragment of a man's brain with the man himself for all practical purposes eliminated. But he seemed to have arrived at a practical understanding with the centre of sub-consciousness.

"I will remain," was the unhesitating reply, and Hampden felt assured that the line would not be lost.

He had not definitely settled in his mind what to do when he opened the door leading on to the common stairs. A small child who had been loitering outside in a crouching position staggered back in momentary alarm at his sudden appearance. It was a ragged girl, perhaps ten or twelve years old, with cruelly unwieldy boots upon her stockingless feet, matted hair, and a precocious face full of unchildish knowledge. The inference that she had been applying either an eye or an ear to the keyhole was overwhelming.

Her fear—it was only the slum child's instinct of flight—died out when she saw the gentleman. Toffs (so ran her experience) do not hit you for nothing.

"Ee's in there yet, ain't ee?" she whispered, coming back boldly and looking up confidentially to his face. "I 'eard yer talking, but I couldn't tell what yer said. 'Ow long d'yer think 'e'll last?"

Sir John looked down at the child, the child who had never been young, in shuddering pity.

"It was me what picked 'is 'at up, but they wouldn't let me go in," she continued, as though the fact gave her a standing in the case. "Did yer see it in there?" She looked proudly at her right hand with horrid significance.

"Come in here," he said, after considering. "Can you run an errand?"

Her face reflected gloating eagerness as she entered, her attitude had just a tinge of pleasurable awe. He did not permit her to go further than the hall.

"Is it to do with 'im?" she asked keenly. "Yehs!"

"It is to go to the post office in Fleet Street," he explained. "You must go as fast as ever you can."

"I can go anywhere as well as any boy, and as fast if I take my boots off. When that there Italian knifed her man—him what took up with Shiny Sal—in the Lane a year ago, it was me what fetched the police."

He left her standing there—her face to the chink of the door before he had turned away—and went into the next room to write the message. He desired to make it neither too insistent nor too immaterial. "John Flak, of 45 Paradise Buildings, Paradise Street, Drury Lane, has met with fatal accident, and earnestly desires to see you on important business," was the form it took. He had sufficient stamps in his pocket for the payment, and to these he added another for a receipt.

"You can read?" he asked, returning to her.

"Yehs!" she replied with her curious accent of lofty scorn at so ingenuous a question. "I read all the murders and sewercides to Blind Mike every Sunday morning."

"Well, go as fast as you can to the post office in Fleet Street, and give them this paper where you see 'Telegrams' written up. Then wait for another piece of paper which they will give you, and bring it back to me. Here is sixpence for you now, and you shall have another shilling when you come back." He was making it more profitable for her to be honest than to be dishonest, which is perhaps the safest way in an emergency.

It was nearly ten o'clock when he looked at his watch on her departure; it was not ten minutes past when she returned. She was

105

panting but exultant, and watched his face for commendation as she gave him the receipt, as a probationary imp might watch the face of the Prince of Darkness on bringing in his first human soul. One boot she had dropped in her wild career, but so far from stopping to look for it, she had thrown away the other then as useless.

Leaving the ghoul-child seated on the coal to thrill delightfully at every unknown sound, Hampden returned to the bedside. Much of the first, the absolutely cold horror of the situation, was gone. He judged it better not to allow too long an interval of silence in which that dim consciousness might slip back into the outer space of trackless darkness. Now that he knew what to expect it was not very unlike speaking to one who slept and held converse in his sleep.

"I have sent for Mr Tubes, but, making due allowance, he can scarcely get here in less than an hour," he said. "If in the meantime there is anything that you wish to tell me, to make doubly sure, it will be received as a most sacred confidence."

There was a longer pause than any before, so long that the watcher by the bedside was preparing to speak again; then the lips slowly opened, and the same full, substantial voice made reply.

"I will wait. But he must be quick—quick!"

The words seemed to disclose a fear, but there was no outward sign of failing power. Hampden ventured on another point.

"Are you in pain?" he asked.

The reply came more quickly this time, and, perhaps because he was looking for some such indication, the listener fancied that he caught the faintest stumbling, a little blurring of the outline here and there.

"No, I am in no pain. But I have a terrible anxiety that weighs me down."

There was nothing to be gained by further questioning. Sir John returned to the other room. The fire was low and the grate choked with ashes; he had begun to replenish it when a curious sound startled him. He only heard it between the raspings of the poker as he raked the ashes out, but it was not to be mistaken. It was the sharp, dry, clock-like whirring that had been the first indication of life and speech beyond the bedroom door more than an hour before.

A board creaked behind him, and he turned with an exclamation to see the dreadful child standing in the middle of the room. Barefooted, she had slipped noiselessly in from the hall at the first tremor of that unusual sound, and now, with her dilated eyes fixed fearfully on the door, her shrinking form bent forward, she slowly crept nearer step by step. Her face quivered with terror, her

106

whole body shook, but she went on as surely as though a magnet drew her.

"What are you doing?" cried Hampden sharply. "Why did you not stay where I told you?"

She turned her face, but not her eyes, towards him. "Yer heard it, didn't yer?" she whispered. "Ain't that what they call the death-rattle what comes?"

He took her by the shoulder and swung her impatiently round. "Go back, you imp," he commanded. "Back and stay there, or you shall go out."

She crept back, looking fearfully over her shoulder all the way. Something else was happening to engage Hampden's attention. In the next room the man was speaking, speaking spontaneously, as he had done once before, but beyond all doubt the voice was weaker now. The momentary interruption of the child's presence had drowned the first part of the sentence, but Hampden caught a word that strung up every faculty he possessed—"League."

"——League will then suddenly issue a notice to all its members, putting an embargo—a boycott, if you will—on——"

The voice trailed off, and, although he sprang to the door, Sir John could not distinguish another word. But that fragment alone was sufficiently startling. To the President of the Unity League it could only have one meaning; for it was true! Some—how much?—of their plan lay open. And to how many was it known? The terrible anxiety of this poor, battered wreck, unconsciously loyal to his class in death, to give the warning before he passed away, seemed to indicate that nothing but the frayed thread of one existence stood in the League's path yet.

Was there anything to be done? That was Hampden's first thought. There was plainly one thing: to learn, if possible, before Mr Tubes's arrival, how much was known.

Nothing was changed; only the death-watch ticked again. He leaned over the bed in his eagerness, and, stilling the throbbing excitement of his blood, tried to speak in a tone of commonplace indifference.

"Yes, continue."

There was no response.

"Repeat the sentence," he commanded, concentrating his voice in his desperation, and endeavouring by mere force of will to impose its authority on the indefinite consciousness.

Just as well might he have commanded the man to get up and walk.

Had that last elusive thread that held him to mortality been broken? Hampden bent still lower. The pallid face was no more pallid than before, but before it could scarcely have been more death-like. The acutest test could not have found a trace of breath. He put together the gradual failing of the voice that little more than an hour ago had been as full and vigorous as his own, the unfinished sentence, the silence——

Suddenly he straightened himself by the bedside with a sense of guilt that struck him like a blow. What was he thinking—hoping? Who was he—Sir John Hampden, President of the Unity League? Not in that room! The man who watched by the bedside stood there even as the humblest servant of the Order of St. Martin, pledged while in that service to succour in "trouble, sorrow, need, sickness, or any other adversity."

It did not occur to him to debate the point. His way seemed very straight and clear. His plain duty to the dying man was to try by every means in his power to carry out his one overwhelming desire. Its successful accomplishment might aim a more formidable blow at his own ambition than almost anything else that could happen. It could not ward off the attack upon which the League was now concentrating—nothing could do that—but an intimate knowledge of the details of that scheme of retaliation might act in a hundred adverse ways. Hampden did not stop to consider what might happen on the one side and on the other. A thousand years of argument and sophistries could not alter the one great fact of his present duty. He had a very simple conscience, and he followed it.

If he could have speeded Mr Tubes's arrival he would have done so now. He went into the hall to listen. The street child was still there, sitting on the coal, as sharp-eyed and wakefully alert as ever. He had forgotten her.

"Come, little imp," he said kindly, "I ought to have packed you off long ago." It was, in point of fact, nearly eleven o'clock.

"Ain't doin' no aharm to the coal," she muttered.

"That's not the question. You ought to have been at home and in bed by this time of night."

She looked up at him sharply with a suspicion that such innocence in a grown-up man could not be unassumed.

"Ain't got no bed," she said contemptuously. "Ain't got no 'ome."

A sentence rang through his mind: "The birds of the air have nests."

"Where do you sleep?" he asked.

"Anywhere," she replied.

"And how do you live?"

"Anyhow."

108

The lowest depths of human poverty had not been abolished by Act of Parliament after all.

A knock at the door interrupted the reflection. The child had already heard the step and sought to efface herself in the darkest corner.

Hampden had not noticed the significance of the knock. He opened the door, prepared to admit the Home Secretary. So thoroughly had he dissociated his own personality from the issue, that he felt the keenest interest that the man should arrive before it was too late. He opened the door to admit him, and experienced an actual pang of disappointment when he saw who stood outside.

He had sent a telegram instead. Whatever the telegram said did not matter very much. Hampden instinctively guessed that he was not coming then—was not on his way. Anything less than that would be too late.

He took the orange envelope and opened it beneath the flaring gas that piped and whistled at the stairhead.

"There is no reply," he said quietly, folding the paper slowly and putting it away in his pocket-book. Were it not that the gain to Hampden of the League was so immense one might have thought, to see him at that moment, that he felt ashamed of something in life.

Members of Parliament had every department of the postal system freely at their service. The statement may not be out of place, for this was what the telegram contained:

"Deeply regret to hear of Comrade Flak's accident, and will have it fully enquired into. Was it while he was engaged at work? Cannot, however, recall any business upon which he could wish to see me. Probably a mental hallucination caused by shock. Have been terribly busy all day, and am engaged at this moment with important State papers which must be finished before I go to bed. If it is thought desirable I will, on receiving another wire, come first thing in the morning, but before deciding to take this course I beg you to consider incessant calls made on my time. Let everything possible be done for the poor fellow.

"James Tubes."

The burden of failure pressed on Hampden as he walked slowly to the bedroom. In that environment of death his own gain did not touch him at all, so completely had he succeeded in eliminating for the time every consideration except an almost fanatical sense of duty to the articles of the Order. It would be better, he felt, if the shadowy consciousness that hovered around the bed could have sunk finally into its eternal sleep, without suffering the pang of being recalled only to hear this, but something in the atmosphere of the room, a brooding tension of expectancy that seemed to quicken in the silence, warned him that this was not to be.

"A reply has been received from Mr Tubes in answer to our telegram."

"He is here?" There was no delay this time; there was an intense eagerness that for a brief minute overcame the growing weakness.

"No. He cannot come. He regrets, but he is engaged on matters of national importance."

Silence. Painful silence. In it Hampden seemed to share the cruel frustration of so great a hope deferred.

"There is this," he continued, more for the sake of making any suggestion than from a belief in its practicability; "I might go and compel him to come. If he understood the urgency——"

"It is too late.... A little time ago there was a thin white mist; now it is a solid wall of dense rolling fog. It is nearer—relentless, unevadable...."

"I can still write down what you have to say. Consider, it is the only hope."

"I cannot judge.... I had a settled conviction that no other ear.... Stay, quick; there are the notes! Incomplete, but they will put him on the track.... Swear, swear that you will place them in his hand unread."

"I swear to do as you ask me. Go on quickly."

"To-night, now. Do not ... do not let ... do not wait...."

"Yes, yes. But the notes? Where are they? How am I to know them?" The voice was growing very thin and faltering, weaker with every word. The disappointment had sapped all its failing strength at a single blow.

"The notes ... yes. You will explain.... The black wall ... how it towers!..." He was whispering inaudibly.

Hampden leaned over the dying man in a final effort.

"Flak!" he cried, "the notes on the Unity League! Where are they? Speak!"

"The envelope"—he caught a breath of sound—"... coat lining.... I must go!"

Twenty minutes later Sir John picked up his motor brougham in New Oxford Street. He had telephoned immediately on leaving Paradise Buildings for it to start out at once and wait for him near Mudie's corner. In Paradise Street he had seen a bacchanalian group surrounding "Mrs Flak," high priestess, who chanted a song in praise of home and the domestic virtues. It was at this point that he missed the ghoul-child from his side.

A south-east wind was carrying the midnight boom of the great clock at Westminster as far as Kilburn when he turned out of the High Road, and the little clocks around had taken up the chorus, like small dogs envious of the baying of a hound, as he stopped before the Home Secretary's house.

There was a light still burning in a room on the ground floor, and it was Mr Tubes himself who came to the door.

"I have to place in your hands an envelope of papers entrusted to me by a man called Flak who died in Paradise Street an hour ago," said Hampden, and with the act he brought his night of duty as a faithful servant of his Order to an end.

"Oh, that's you," said Mr Tubes, peering out into the darkness. "I had a wire about it. So the poor man is dead?"

"Yes," replied Hampden a shade drily. "The poor man is dead."

Mr Tubes fancied that he saw the lamps of a cab beyond his garden gate, and he wondered whether he was being expected to offer to pay the fare.

"Well, it's very good of you to take the trouble, though, between ourselves, I hardly imagine that the papers are likely to be of any importance," he remarked. "Now may I ask who I am indebted to?"

Hampden had already turned to go. He recognised that in the strife which he was about to precipitate, the man who stood there would be his natural antagonist, and he regretted that he could not find it in his nature to like him any better than he did.

"What I have done, I have done as a servant of the Order of St Martin," he replied. "What I am about to do," he added, "I shall do as Sir John Hampden."

And leaving Mr Tubes standing on the doorstep in vast surprise, the electric carriage turned its head-lights to the south again.

111

CHAPTER XII

BY TELESCRIBE

What Sir John Hampden was "about to do" he had decided in the course of the outward journey.

There was nothing in his actions, past or prospective, that struck him as illogical. He would have said, indeed, that they were the only possible outcome of the circumstance.

For the last four hours, as the nameless emissary of the Order to whose discipline he bound himself, he had merged every other feeling in his duty to the dying man and in the fulfilment of a death-bed charge.

That was over; now, as the President of the Unity League, he was on his way to try by every means in his power to minimise the effect of what he had done; to anticipate and counteract the value of the warning he had so scrupulously conveyed.

It was a fantastic predicament. He had sat for perhaps half an hour with the unsealed envelope in his pocket, and no eye had been upon him. He had declared passionately, year after year, that class and class were now at war, that the time for courteous retaliation was long since past, that social martial law had been proclaimed. Yet as he drove back to Trafalgar Chambers he would have given a considerable sum of money—the League being not ill provided, say fifty thousand pounds—to know the extent of those notes.

When he reached the offices it was almost half-past twelve. Salt would be flying northward as fast as steam could take him, and for the next two hours at least, cut off from the possibility of any communication. The burden of decision lay on Hampden alone.

He had already made it. Within an hour he would have pledged the League to a line of policy from which there was no retreat. Before another day had passed the Government could recall the little band of secret service agents and consign their reports to the wastepaper basket. Every one would know everything. Everything? He smiled until the remembrance of that cheap frayed envelope in Mr Tubes's possession drove the smile away.

Next to his own office stood the instrument room. Here, behind double doors that deadened every sound, were ranged the telephones, the tape machines, the Fessenden-d'Arco installation, and that most modern development of wireless telegraphy which had come just in time to save the over-burdened postal system from chronic congestion, the telescribe.

Hampden had not appeared to move hurriedly, but it was just seventeen seconds after he had sent his brougham roving eastward that he stood before the telephone.

"1432 St Paul's, please."

There was a sound as of rushing water and crackling underwood. Then the wire seemed to clear itself like a swimmer rising from the sea, and a quiet, far-away voice was whispering in his ear: "Yes, I'm Lidiat."

"I am at Trafalgar Chambers," said Hampden, after giving his name. "I want you to drop anything you are on and come here. If my motor is not waiting for you at the corner of Chancery Lane, you will meet it along the Strand."

At the other end of the wire, Lidiat—the man who possessed the sixth code typewriter—looked rather blankly at his pipe, at the little silver carriage clock ticking on the mantelpiece, at the fluted white-ware coffee set, and at his crowded desk. Then, concluding that if the President of the Unity League sent a message of that kind after midnight and immediately rang off again he must have a good reason for it, he locked up his room as it stood, took up a few articles promiscuously from the rack in the hall, and walked out under the antique archway into Fleet Street.

In the meantime the Exchange was being urged to make another attempt to get on with "2743 Vincent," this time with success.

"Mr Salt is not 'ere, I repeat, sir," an indignant voice was protesting. "He is out of town."

"Yes, yes, Dobson, I know," replied "St James's." "I am Sir John Hampden. What train did your master go by?"

"Beg pardon, sir," apologised "Vincent." "Didn't recognise your voice at first, Sir John. The wires here is 'issing 'orrible to-night. He went by the 10 o'clock from the Great Central, and told me to meet the 10.40 Midland to-morrow morning."

"He did actually go by the 10 train?"

"I 'anded him the despatch case through the carriage window not five minutes before the whistle went. He was sitting with his—"

"Thank you, Dobson. That's all I wanted to know. Sorry if you had to get up. Good night," and Sir John cut off a volume of amiable verbosity as he heard the bell of his Launceston ring in the street below.

"Fellow watching your place," said Lidiat, jerking his head in the direction of a doorway nearly opposite, as Hampden admitted him. Had he himself been the object of the watcher's attention it

113

would have been less remarkable, for had not the time and the place been London after midnight, Lidiat's appearance must have been pronounced bizarre. Reasonable enough on all other points he had a fixed conviction that it was impossible for him to work after twelve o'clock at night unless he wore a red silk skull cap, flannels, and yellow Moorish slippers. Into this æsthetic costume he had changed half an hour before Hampden rang him up, and in it, with the addition of a very short overcoat and a silk hat that displayed an inch of red beneath the brim, he now stepped from the brougham, a large, bovine-looking man, perfectly bald, and still clinging to his pipe.

Hampden laughed contemptuously as he glanced across the street.

"They have put on half a dozen private enquiry men lately," he explained. "They are used to divorce, and their sole idea of the case seems to be summed up in the one stock phrase, 'watching the house.' Possibly they expect to see us through the windows, making bombs. Why don't they watch Paris instead? Egyptian Three Per Cents. have gone up 75 francs in the last fortnight, all from there, and for no obvious reason."

Lidiat nodded weightily. "We stopped too much comment," he said. "Lift off?"

"There are only two short flights," apologised Hampden. "Yes; I saw that even the financial papers dismissed it as a 'Pied Piper rise.' Here we are."

They had not lingered as they talked, although the journalist ranked physical haste and bodily exertion—as typified by flights of stairs—among the forbidden things of life.

Hampden had brought him to the instrument room. In view of what he was asking of Lidiat, some explanation was necessary, but he put it into the narrowest possible form. It was framed not on persuasiveness but necessity.

"Salt is away, something has happened, and we have to move a week before we had calculated."

Lidiat nodded. He accepted the necessity as proved; explanation would have taken time. His training and occupation made him chary of encouraging two words when one would do, between midnight and the hour when the newspapers are "closed up" and the rotaries begin to move.

"I should like," continued Hampden, "in to-day's issue of every morning paper a leader, two six-inch items of news, one home one foreign, and a single column six-inch advertisement set in the middle of a full white page."

Lidiat had taken off his hat and overcoat and placed them

114

neatly on a chair. It occurred to him as a fair omen that Providence had dealt kindly with him in not giving him any opportunity of changing his clothes. He now took out his watch and hung it on a projecting stud of the telephone box.

"Yes, and the minimum?" He did not think, as a lesser man with equal knowledge of Fleet Street might have done, that Hampden had gone mad. He knew that conventionally such a programme was impossible, but he had known of impossible things being done, and in any case he understood by the emphasis that this was what Hampden would have done under freer circumstances.

"That is what I leave to you. The paragraphs and comment at some length I shall look for. The provinces are out of the question, I suppose? The eight leading London dailies must be dealt with."

"You give me carte blanche, of course—financially?"

"Absolutely, absolutely. Guarantee everything to them. Let them arrange for special trains at all the termini. Let them take over all the garages, motor companies, and cab yards in London as going concerns for twelve hours. They will all be in it except The Tocsin and The Masses. We can deal with the distributing houses later. You see the three points? It is the patriotic thing to do at any cost; they can have anything they like to make up time; and it is absolutely essential."

"Yes," said Lidiat; "and the matter?"

Hampden had already taken a pencilled sheet of paper from his pocket. He had written it on his way up to Kilburn. He now handed it to the journalist.

"Between four and five o'clock that will be telescribed over the entire system," he explained. "Those who are not on the call will see it in the papers or hear from others. Every one will know before to-night."

He watched Lidiat sharply as he read the statement. Apart from the two principals, he was the first man in England to receive the confidence, and Sir John had a curiosity, not wholly idle, to see how it would strike him. But Lidiat was not, to use an obsolete phrase, "the man in the street." He absorbed the essence of the manifesto with a trained, practical grasp, and then held out his hand for the other paper, while his large, glabrous face remained merely vacant in its expression.

The next paper was a foreign telegram in cipher, and as Lidiat read the decoded version that was pinned to it, the baronet saw, or fancied that he saw, the flicker of a keener light come into his eyes and such a transient wave across his face, as might, in a man of impulse, indicate enthusiasm or appreciation.

"Are there to be any more of these—presently?" was all he said.

"I think that I might authorise you to say that there will be others to publish, as the moment seems most propitious."

"Very good. I will use the instruments now."

"There is one more point," said Hampden, writing a few short lines on a slip of paper, "that it might be desirable to make public now."

Lidiat took the paper. This was what he read:

"You are at liberty to state definitely that the membership of the Unity League now exceeds five million persons."

There was a plentiful crop of grey hairs sown between Charing Cross and Ludgate Hill in the early hours of that summer morning. With his mouth to the telephone, Lidiat stirred up the purlieus of Fleet Street and the Strand until office after office, composing room after composing room, and foundry after foundry, all along the line, began to drone and hum resentfully, like an outraged apiary in the dead of night. When he once took up the wire he never put it down again until he had swept the "London Dailies: Morning" section of Sell and Mitchell from beginning to end. Those who wished to retort and temporise after he had done with them, had to fall back upon the telescribe—which involved the disadvantage to Fleet Street of having to write and coldly transmit the indignant messages that it would fain pour hot and blistering into its tormentor's ear. For two hours and a half by the watch beneath his eye he harrowed up all the most cherished journalistic traditions of the land, and from a small, box-like room a mile away, he controlled the reins of the Fourth Estate of an Empire—a large, fat, perspiring man of persuasive authority, and conscious of unlimited capital at his back.

By the end of that time chaos had given place to order. The Scythe had shown an amenable disposition with a readiness suggesting that it possibly knew more than it had told in the past. The Ensign was won over by persuasion and the condition of the Navy, and The Mailed Fist was clubbed and bullied and cajoled with big names until it was dazed. For seven minutes Lidiat poured patriotism into the ear of The Beacon's editor, and gold into the coffers of The Beacon's manager, and then turned aside to win over The Daily News-Letter by telling it what The Daily Chronicler was doing, and the Chronicler by reporting the News-Letter's acquiescence. The Morning Post Card remained obdurate for half an hour, and only capitulated after driving down and having an interview with Hampden. The Great Daily—well, for more than a year The Great Daily had been the property and organ of the League, only no one had suspected it. The little Illustrated Hour, beset by the difficulty of half-tone blocks, and frantic at the thought of having to recast its plates and engage in the mysteries of "making ready" again after half its edition had been run off, was the last to submit. So long was it in making up its mind, that at last Lidiat sarcastically proposed an inset, and, taking the suggestion in all good faith, the Illustrated Hour startled its sober patrons by bearing on its outside page a gummed leaflet containing a leaderette and two news paragraphs.

So the list spun out. Lidiat did not touch the provinces, but sixteen London dailies, including some sporting and financial organs, marked the thoroughness of his work. At half-past three he finally hung up the receiver; and taking the brougham, rode like another Wellington over the field of his still palpitating Waterloo. His appearance, bovine and imperturbable despite the shameful incongruity of his garb when revealed in the tremulous and romantic dawn of a day and of an epoch, and further set off by the unimpeachable correctness of the equipage from which he alighted, was a thing that rankled in the minds of lingering compositors and commissionaires until their dying days.

A few minutes after his departure Hampden returned to the telephone and desired to make the curious connection "1 Telescribe."

"Who is there?" he asked, when "1 Telescribe" responded.

The man at the other end explained that he was a clerk on the main platform of "1 Telescribe"—name of Firkin, if the fact was of Metropolitan interest.

"Is Mr Woodbarrow there yet?"

It appeared, with increased respect, that Mr Woodbarrow was in his own office and could be informed of the gentleman's name.

"Please tell him that Sir John Hampden wishes to speak with him."

In two minutes another voice filtered through the wire, a voice which Hampden recognised.

"What are you running with now, Mr Woodbarrow?" he asked, when brief courtesies had been exchanged.

Mr Woodbarrow made an enquiry, and was able to report that a 5 H.P. Tangye was supplying all the power they needed at that hour. Nothing was coming through, he explained, except a few press messages from America, a little business from Australia, and some early morning news from China.

"I should be obliged if you would put on the two

117

Westinghouses as soon as you can, and then let me know when you can clear the trunk lines for a minute. Within the next hour I want to send an 'open board' message."

There was no response to this matter-of-fact request for an appreciable five seconds, but if ever silence through a telephone receiver conveyed an impression of blank amazement at the other end, it was achieved at that moment.

"Do I rightly understand, Sir John," enquired Mr Woodbarrow at the end of those five seconds, "that you wish to repeat a message over the entire system?"

"That is quite correct."

"It will constitute a record."

"An interesting occasion, then."

"Have you calculated the fees, Sir John?"

"No, I have not had the time. You will let me know when the power is up?"

Mr Woodbarrow, only just beginning to realise fully the magnitude of the occasion and tingling with anticipation, promised to act with all possible speed, and going to his own room Sir John took up an agate pen and proceeded to write with special ink on prepared paper this encyclical despatch.

A library of books had been written on the subject of the telescribe within two years of its advent, but a general description may be outlined untechnically in a page or two. It was, for the moment, the last word of wireless telegraphy. It was efficient, it was speedy, it was cheap, and it transmitted in facsimile. It had passed the stage of being wondered at and had reached that of being used. It was universal. It was universal, that is, not in the sense that tongues are universally in heads, for instance, but, to search for a parallel, as universal as letter-boxes are now on doors, book-cases in houses, or cuffs around men's wrists. There were, in point of number, about three millions on the index book.

It was speedy because there was no call required, no intervention of a connecting office to wait for. That was purely automatic. Above the telescribe box in one's hall, study, or sitting-room, was a wooden panel studded with eight rows of small brass knobs, sixteen knobs in each row. These could be depressed or raised after the manner of an electric light stud, and a similar effect was produced: a connection was thereby made.

All the country—England and Wales—was mapped out into sixteen primary divisions, oblong districts of equal size. The top row of brass knobs corresponded with these divisions, and by pulling down any knob the operator was automatically put into communication with that part of the system, through the medium of the huge central station that reared its trellised form, like an Eiffel Tower, above the hill at Harrow, and the subsidiary stations which stood each in the middle of its division.

The second stage was reached by subdividing each primary division into sixteen oblong districts, and with these the second row of knobs corresponded. Six more times the subdividing process was repeated, and each subdivision had its corresponding row. The final division represented plots of ground so small that no house or cottage could escape location.

Pulling down the corresponding studs on the eight rows instantly and automatically established the connection. The written communication could then be transmitted, and in the twinkling of an eye it was traced on a sheet of paper in the receiving box. There was no probability of the spaces all being occupied with telescribes for some years to come. A calculation will show that there was provision for a good many thousand million boxes, but only three million were fixed and attuned at this period.

That, briefly, was the essential of the telescribe system. It was invaluable for most purposes, but not for all. Though speedier than the letter, it lacked its privacy when it reached its destination, and it also, in the eyes of many, lacked the sentimental touch, as from hand to hand, which a letter may convey. It carried no enclosures, of course, and, owing to the difficulties of ink and paper, printed matter could not be telescribed at all. It cost twice as much as a letter, but as this was spread in the proportion of three-quarters to the sender and one quarter to the receiver the additional cost was scarcely felt by either. Thus it came about that although the telescribe had diminished the volume of telegrams by ninety per cent., and had made it possible still to cope with a volume of ordinary postal correspondences which up to that time had threatened to swamp the department, it had actually superseded nothing.

At four o'clock Mr Woodbarrow called up Sir John and reported that the two great engines were running smoothly, and that for three minutes the entire system would be closed against any message except his. In other words, while the "in" circuit was open to three million boxes, the "out" circuit was closed against all except one. It was not an absolutely necessary precaution, for overlapping telescripts "stored latent" until the way was clear, but it was not an occasion on which to hesitate about taking every safeguard.

The momentous order was already written. Hampden opened the lid of a small flat box supported on the telescribe shelf by four vulcanite feet, put the paper carefully in, and closed the lid again. He had pulled down the eight rows of metal studs in anticipation of

Woodbarrow's message, and there was only one more thing to do. A practical, unemotional man, and not unused, in an earlier decade, to controlling matters of national importance with energy and decision, he now stood with his hand above the fatal switch, not in any real doubt about his action, but with a kind of fascinated time-languor. A minute had already passed. To pull down the tiny lever and release it would not occupy a second. At what period of those three minutes should he do it? How long dare he leave it? He caught himself wondering whether on the last second—and with an angry exclamation at the folly he pressed the lever home.

There was no convulsion of nature; a little bell a foot away gave a single stroke, and that was all the indication that the President of the Unity League had passed the Rubicon and unmasked his battery.

This was what he had written and scattered broadcast over the land:

"THE UNITY LEAGUE

"The time has now arrived when it is necessary for the League to take united action in order to safeguard the interests of its members.

"In directing a course which may entail some inconvenience, but can hardly, with ordinary foresight, result in real hardship, your President reminds you of the oft-repeated warning that such a demand would inevitably be made upon your sincerity. The opportunity is now at hand for proving that as a class our resource and endurance are not less than those of our opponents.

"On or before the 22nd July, members of the League will cease until further notice to purchase or to use coal in the form of (a) Burning Coal (except such as may be already on their premises), (b) Coke (with the exception as before), (c) Gas, (d) Coal-produced electricity.

"The rule applies to all private houses, offices, clubs, schools, and similar establishments; to all hotels, restaurants, boarding-houses and lodging-houses, with the exception (for the time) of necessary kitchen fires, which will be made the subject of a special communication, to all greenhouses and conservatories not used for the purposes of trade; and to all shops, workshops, and similar buildings where oil or other fuel or illuminant not produced or derived from coal can be safely substituted.

"Members of the League who have no coal in stock,

and who do not possess facilities for introducing a substitute immediately, are at liberty to procure sufficient to last for a week. With this exception members are required to cancel all orders at present placed for coal. The League will take all responsibility and will defend all actions for breach of contract.

"Members of the League are earnestly requested to co-operate in this line of action both as regards the letter and the spirit of the rule.

"Members are emphatically assured that every possible development of the campaign has been fully considered during the past two years, and it is advanced with absolute confidence that nothing unforeseen can happen to mar its successful conclusion.

"Nothing but the loyal co-operation of members is required to ensure the triumph of those Principles of Government which the League has always advocated, and a complete attainment of the object for which the League came into existence.

"John Hampden, President.
"Trafalgar Chambers,
"London, 15th July 1918."

In the past the world had seen very many strikes on the part of workers, not selfishly conceived in their essence, but bringing a great deal of poverty and misery in their train, and declared solely for the purpose of benefiting the strikers through the necessity of others. In the more recent past the world had seen employers combine and declare a few strikes (the word will serve a triple purpose) for just the same end and accompanied by precisely similar results. It was now the turn of the consumers to learn the strike lesson, the most powerful class of all, but the most heterogeneous to weld together. The object was the same but pursued under greater stress; the weapons would be similar but more destructive; the track of desolation would be there but wider, and the end——On that morning of the 15th of July the end lay beyond a very dim and distant shock of dust and turmoil that the eye of none could pierce.

CHAPTER XIII

THE EFFECT OF THE BOMB

Mr Strummery having finished his breakfast with the exception of a second glass of hot water, which constituted the amiable man's only beverage, took up his copy of The Scythe. He had already glanced through The Tocsin, in which he had a small proprietary interest, but he also subscribed to The Scythe, partly because it brought to his door a library which he found useful when he had to assume an intimate knowledge of a subject at a day's notice, partly because the crudely blatant note of The Tocsin occasionally failed to strike a sympathetic cord.

He had found that morning in his telescribe receiver the Trafalgar Chambers manifesto which had been flashed to friend and foe alike. He had read it with a frown; it savoured of impertinence that it should be sent to him. He finished it with a laugh, half-contemptuous, half-annoyed. He saw that it was a stupid move unless the League had abandoned all hope of forming the League-Labour alliance; in any case, it was a blow that stung but could not wound. All the chances were that nothing would come of it; but, if a million people did give up burning coal for say a month, if a million people did that—well, it would be very inconvenient to themselves, but there would certainly be a good many tens of thousand pounds less wages paid out in districts that seemed to be far from satisfactory even as it was.

The Tocsin did not refer to the matter at all. Mr Strummery opened The Scythe, and was rather surprised to see, beneath five lines of heavy heading on the leader page, a full account of Sir John Hampden's sudden move. Instinctively his eye turned to the leader columns. As he had half expected there was a leader on the subject, not very long but wholly benedictory. In rather less measured phrases than the premier organ usually adopted and with other signs of haste, readers were urged to enter whole-heartedly into this development of bloodless civil war of which the impending Personal Property Act had been the first unmasked blow. He glanced on, not troubling about the views advanced until a casual statement drew a smothered exclamation from his lips. "An argument which will be used in a practical form by the five million adult members now on the books of the League—" ran the carelessly-dropped information. "It is a lie—a deliberately misleading lie," muttered the Premier angrily; but it was the truth. He read on. The article concluded: "In

122

this connection the strong action taken by M. Gavard, as indicated in the telegrams from Paris which we print elsewhere, may be purely a coincidence, but it is curiously akin to those 'mathematical coincidences' that fall into their places in a well-planned campaign."

Mr Strummery had no difficulty in finding the telegrams alluded to. Rushed through in frantic haste, the type had stood a hair's breadth higher than it should, and in the resulting blackness the words of the headlines leapt to meet his eye.

THE INDUSTRIAL WAR IN FRANCE

Prohibitive Tax on Coal

From Our Special Correspondent
Paris Wednesday Night.
"It is authoritatively stated that the industrial crisis which has been existing in the north, and to some extent in the Lyonnais districts, for the past six months is on the eve of a settlement. Yesterday M. Gavard returned from S. Etienne, and after seeing several of his colleagues and some leading members of the Chamber of Commerce, left at once for Lens. Early this morning he was met at the Maison du Peuple by deputations from the Syndicate of Miners, the 'Broutchouteux,' the Association of Mine Owners, the Valenciennes iron masters, and representatives of some other industries.

"The proceedings were conducted in private, but it is understood in well-informed circles here that in accordance with the plenary powers conferred on him by the Chambers in view of the critical situation, M. Gavard proposed to raise the small existing tax on imported coal to an ad valorem tax of 55 p.c. The mine owners on their side will guarantee a minimum wage of 8f. 15c., and commence working at once, reinstating all men within a week of the imposing of the tax. The amalgamated industries acquiesce to a general immediate advance of 1f. 75c. per ton (metric) in the price of coal, and will start running as soon as the first portion of their orders can be filled.

"Troops are still being massed in the affected districts, but after last Thursday's pitched battle a tone of sullen apathy is generally preserved. There was, however, severe rioting at Anzin this morning, and about 200 casualties are reported."
Paris. Later.

123

"The terms of settlement contained in my earlier message are confirmed. They will remain in operation for a year. The tax will come into force almost immediately, three days' grace being allowed for vessels actually in French ports to unload. In view of your Government's subsidy to English coal exportation and its disastrous effects on French mining, and, subsequently, on other industries, the imposition of the tax will be received with approval in most quarters."

As the Prime Minister reached the end of the paragraph he heard a vehicle stop at his door, followed by an attack on bell and knocker that caused Mrs Strummery no little indignation. It was Mr Tubes arriving, after indulging in the unusual luxury of a cab, and the next minute he was shown into his chief's presence. Both men unconsciously frowned somewhat as they met, but the ex-collier was infinitely the more disturbed of the two.

"You got my 'script?" he asked, as they shook hands.

"No; did you write?" replied Mr Strummery. "To tell the truth, this meddling piece of imbecility on Hampden's part, and his gross impertinence in sending it to me, put everything else out of my head for the moment. You have seen it?"

"You wouldn't need to ask that if you'd passed a newspaper shop," said Mr Tubes grimly. "The newsbills are full of nothing else. 'COAL WAR PROCLAIMED,' 'HAMPDEN'S REPLY TO THE P.P. TAX,' 'UNITY LEAGUE MANIFESTO,' and a dozen more. I had private word of it last night, but too late to do anything. That's why I asked half a dozen of them—Vossit, Guppling, Chadwing, and one or two more—to meet me here at half-past nine. Happen a few others will drop in now."

"Well, don't let them see that you think the world is coming to an end," said the Premier caustically. "Nothing may come of it yet."

"That's all very well, Strummery," said Mr Tubes, with rising anger. "All very well for you; you don't come from a Durham division. I shall have it from both sides. Twenty thousand howling constituents and six hundred raving members."

"Let them rave. They know better than press it too far. As for the miners, if they have to lose by it we can easily make grants to put them right." A sudden thought struck him; he burst out laughing. "Well, Tubes," he exclaimed boisterously, "I can excuse myself, but I should have thought that a man who came from a Durham constituency would have seen that before. Hampden must either be mad, or else he knows that his precious League won't stand very much. Don't you see? We are in the middle of summer

124

now, and for the next three months people will be burning hardly any coal at all!"

The Home Secretary jumped up and began to pace the room in seething impatience, before he could trust himself to speak.

"Don't talk like that before the House with fifty practical men in it, for God's sake, Strummery," he exclaimed passionately. "Hampden couldn't well have contrived a more diabolical moment. Do you know what the conditions are? Well, listen. No one is burning any coal, and so it will be no hardship for them to do without. But every one is on the point of filling his cellar at summer prices to last all through the winter. And Hampden's five million—"

"I don't believe that," interposed the Premier hastily.

"Well, I do—now," retorted his colleague bitterly. "His five million are the five million biggest users of domestic coal in the country. They use more than all the rest put together. And they all fill their cellars in the summer or autumn."

"Then?" suggested Mr Strummery.

"Then they won't now," replied Mr Tubes. "That's all. The next ten weeks are the busiest in the year, from the deepest working to the suburban coal-shoot. Go and take a look round if you want to see. Every waggon, every coal-yard, every railway siding, every pit-bank is chock-full, ready. Only the cellars are empty. If the cellars are going to remain empty, what happens?" He threw out his left hand passionately, with a vigorous gesture. It suggested laden coal carts, crowded yards, over-burdened railways, all flung a stage back on to the already congested pit-heads, and banking up coal like the waters of the divided Red Sea into a scene of indescribable confusion.

The Prime Minister sat thinking moodily, while his visitor paced the room and bit his lips with unpleasant vehemence. In the blades of morning sun, as he crossed and recrossed the room, one saw that Mr Tubes, neither tall nor stout but large, loosely boned, loosely dressed and loosely groomed, had light blue eyes, strong yellow teeth which came prominently into view as he talked, and a spotted sallow complexion, which conveyed the unfortunate, and unjust, impression of being dirty.

"We shall have to do something to carry them on till the winter, that's all," declared Mr Strummery at length. "There's no doubt that the Leaguers will have to use coal then."

"It's no good thinking that we can settle it off-hand with a few thousand pounds of strike pay, Strummery," said the Home Secretary impatiently, "because we can't. You have to know the conditions to see how that is. If there's a strike, the article has to be supplied from somewhere else at more money, and every one except those who want to strike keep on very much as before. But here, by God, they have us all along the line! Anything from fifty to a hundred thousand miners less required at one end, and anything from five to ten thousand coal carters at the other. And between? And dependent on each lot all through?" His ever-ready arm emphasised the situation by a comprehensive sweep. "You've heard say that coal is the life-blood of the country, happen?" he added. "Well, we're the heart."

"What do you suggest, then?"

"It's all a matter of money. If it can be done we must make up the difference; buy it, pay for it, and store it. There are the dockyards, the barracks, and we could open depôts here and in all the big towns. In that way we could spread it over as long a period as we liked. Then there's export. I think that has touched its limit for the time, but we might find it cheaper in the end to stimulate it more."

"Yes; but what about this French business? Are you allowing for that in your estimate?"

"What French business?"

"The French tax," said the Premier impatiently, pointing to the open Scythe. "You've seen about it, haven't you?"

He had not. He snatched up the paper, muttering as he read the first few lines that he had glanced through The Tocsin before he came out, and that had been all. His voice became inaudible as he read on. When he had finished he was very pale. He flung the paper down and walked to the window, and stood there looking out without a word. The declaration of the coal war had filled him with smouldering rage; the Paris telegram had effectually chilled it. Before, he had felt anger; now he felt something that, expressed in words, was undistinguishable from fear.

The men whom he had asked to meet him there were beginning to arrive. They had already heard Vossit and Chadwing pass upstairs talking. There was a step in the hall outside that could only belong to Tirrel. He had not been summoned, but, as Mr Tubes had anticipated, a few others were beginning to drop in. Guppling and two men whom he had met on the doorstep came in as Mr Tubes was finishing the Paris news.

"It's not much good talking about it now," he said, turning from the window, "but if I had known of this, or even that the other would be out, I should have come here myself without bringing all these chaps down too. Not but what they'd have come, though. But when I wrote to them I'd just got the information, you understand, and it was thought that Hampden wouldn't be doing anything for a week at least."

126

"He was too clever for you again?" said Strummery vindictively, as he rose to go upstairs.

"So it seems," admitted Mr Tubes indifferently.

CHAPTER XIV

THE LAST CHANCE AND THE COUNSEL OF EXPEDIENCE

In the salon, where a month before they had drafted the outline of the Personal Property Bill, under the impression that government was a parlour game and Society a heap of spelicans, eight or nine men were already assembled. One or two sat apart, with ugly looks upon their faces. Mr Vossit was dividing his time between gazing up to the ceiling and making notes in a memorandum book as the points occurred to him. Sir Causter Kerr, Baronet of the United Kingdom, and Chevalier of the Order of the Golden Eagle, who in return for a thousand pounds a year permitted himself to be called First Lord of the Admiralty in a Socialist Government, was standing before a steel engraving with the title in German, "Defeat of the British at Majuba Hill, 27th February 1881," but, judging from the slight sardonic grin on his thin features, he was thinking of something else. Sir Causter Kerr had assuredly not been invited to the meeting. The rest of the company stood together in one group, where they talked and laughed and looked towards the door from time to time, in expectation of their host's arrival.

The talk and laughter dropped to a whisper and a smile as Mr Strummery entered and Mr Tubes followed, and with short greetings passed to their places at the table. The Prime Minister was popular, or he would not have held that position, but Mr Tubes was not. He was Home Secretary by virtue of the voice of the coal interest, so much the largest labour organisation in the country that if its wishes were ignored it could, like another body of miners in the past, very effectively demand to "know the reason why."

"Well, Jim, owd lad," said Cecil Brown hilariously, taking advantage of the fact that formal proceedings had not yet commenced, "hast geete howd o' onny more cipher pappers, schuzheou?" Cecil Brown, it may be explained, held that he had the

127

privilege of saying offensive things to his friends without being considered offensive, and as no one ever thought of calling him anything else but "Cecil Brown," he was probably right. Of the Colonial Office, he was in some elation at the moment that his usually despised Department was quite out of this imbroglio.

"Ah, that was a very red, red herring, I'm more than thinking now," said Mr Guppling reflectively.

"Certainly a salt fish, eh, Tirrel?" said Cecil Brown.

Mr Strummery rapped sharply on the table with his knuckles, to indicate that the proceedings had better begin. A hard-working, conscientious man, he entirely missed the lighter side of life. He sometimes laughed, but in conversation his face never lit up with the ready, spontaneous smile; not because he was sad, but because he failed to see, not only the utility of a jest, but its point also. That conversational sauce which among friends who understand one another frequently takes the outer form of personal abuse, was to him merely flagrant insult.

Mr Tubes leaned across and spoke to his chief; and looking down the table the Premier allowed his gaze to rest enquiringly on Sir Causter Kerr.

A man who had been invited jumped up. "I called on Comrade Kerr on my way here and took the liberty of asking him to come, because I thought that we might like to know something of the condition of the navy," he explained.

"For what purpose?" enquired Mr Strummery smoothly.

"Because," he replied, flaring up suddenly with anger, "because I regard this damned French tax, without a word of notice to us or our representative, as nothing more or less than a casus belli."

The proceedings had begun.

"Case of tinned rabbits!" contemptuously retorted a Mr Bilch, sitting opposite. "What d'yer think you're going to do if it is? Why, my infant, the French fleet would knock you and your belli into a packing casus in about ten minutes if you tried it on. You'll have to stomach that casus belli, and as many more as they care to send you."

Mr Bilch was a new man, and was spoken of as a great acquisition to his party, though confessedly uncertain in his views and frequently illogical in his ground. His strength lay in the "happy turns" with which his speech was redolent, and his splendid invulnerability to argument, reason, or fact. He had formerly been a rag-sorter, and would doubtless have remained inarticulate and unknown had he not one day smoothed out a sheet of The Tocsin from the bin before him as he ate his dinner. A fully reported speech was therein described as perhaps the greatest oratorical masterpiece ever delivered outside Hyde Park. Mr Bilch read the speech, and modestly fancied that he could do as well himself. From that moment he never looked back, and although he was still a plain member he had forced his way by sheer merit into the circle of the Council Chamber.

"It is against our principles to consider that contingency," interposed the Premier; "and in any case it is premature to talk of war when the courts of arbitration——"

"That's right enough," interrupted the man who had first spoken of war, "and when it was a matter of fighting to grab someone else's land to fatten up a gang of Stock Exchange Hebrews, I was with you through thick and thin, but this is different. The very livelihood of our people is aimed at. I've nothing to say against the Hague in theory, but when you remember that we've never had a single decision given in our favour it's too important to risk to that. But why France should have done this, in this way and just at this moment, is beyond me."

Yet it was not difficult to imagine. When many English manufactories were closed down altogether, or removed abroad because the conditions at home were too exacting for them, less coal was required in England. Less coal meant fewer colliers employed, and this touched the Government most keenly. The same amount of coal must be dug, especially as the operation of the Eight Hours Act had largely increased the number of those dependent on the mines; therefore more must be exported. The coal tax had long since gone; a substantial bounty was now offered on every ton shipped out of the country. It made a brave show. Never were such piping times known from Kirkcaldy to Cardiff. English coal could be shot down in Rouen, Nantes, or Bordeaux, even in Lille and Limoges, at a price that defied home competition. Prices fell; French colliery proprietors reduced wages; French miners came out on strike—a general strike—and for the time being French collieries ceased to have any practical existence. But France was requiring a million tons of coal a week, and having done the mischief, England could only, at the moment, let her have a quarter of a million a week, while German and Belgian coal had been knocked out of the competition and diverted elsewhere. The great industries had to cease working; chaos, civil war and anarchy began to reign....

"Why France should have done this is beyond me."

There was another reason, deeper. It was a commonplace that England had been cordially hated in turn by every nation in and out of Europe, but with all that there was no responsible nation in or out of Europe that dare contemplate a weak, a dying, England.

129

France looked at the map of Europe, and the thought of the German Eagle flying over Dover Castle and German navies patrolling the seas from Land's End to The Skawe haunted her dreams. Russia wanted nothing in the world so much as another Thirty Years' Peace. Spain had more to lose than to gain; Italy had much to lose and nothing at all to gain. All the little independent states and nations remembered the Treaties of Vienna and Berlin, and trembled at the thought of what might happen now. Germany alone might have had visions, but Germany had a nightmare too, and when the man who ruled her councils with a strong if tortuous policy saw wave after wave of the infectious triumph of Socialism reach his own shores, he recognised that England's weakness was more hostile to his ambitions than England's strength.

No one wanted two Turkeys in Europe.

"I don't see why we shouldn't make a naval demonstration, at all events," some one suggested hopefully. "That used to be enough, and the French Government must have plenty to look after at home."

"Naval demonstration be boiled!" exclaimed Mr Bilch forcibly. "Send your little Willie to Hamley's for a tin steamer, and let him push it off Ramsgate sands if you want a naval demonstration, comrade. But don't show the Union Jack inside the three-mile limit on the other side of the Channel, or you'll have something so hot drop on your hands that you won't be able to lick it off fast enough."

"I fail to see that," said Mr Vossit. "Heaven forbid that I should raise my voice in favour of bloodshed, but if it were necessary for self-preservation our navy is at least equal to that of any other power."

"Is it?" retorted Mr Bilch, with so heavily-laden an expression of contemptuous derision on his face that it seemed as though he might be able to take it off, like a mask, and hang it on some one else. "Is it? Oh, it is, is it? Well, ask that man there. Ask him, is all I say. Simply ask him." His contorted face was thrust half-way across the table towards Mr Vossit, while his rigid arm with extended forefinger was understood to indicate Sir Causter Kerr.

"As the subject has been raised, perhaps the First Lord of the Admiralty will reassure us on that point," said the Premier.

"Dear, dear, no," replied Causter Kerr blandly. "We couldn't carry it through, Premier. You must not think of going to extremes."

There was a moody silence in which men looked angrily at Kerr and at one another.

"Are we to understand that the navy is not equal to that of any other power?" demanded Mr Vossit.

"On paper, yes, comrade," replied Kerr, with a pitying little

130

smile, "but on deep water, where battles are usually fought, no. It is a curious paradox that in order to be equal to any other single power England must be really very much stronger. I should also explain that from motives of economy no battleships have been launched or laid down during the last three years, and only four cruisers of questionable armament. Then as regards gunnery. From motives of economy actual practice is never carried out now, but the championship, dating from last year, lies at present with the armoured cruiser Radium:—stationary regulation target, 1-1/2 miles distant, speed 4 knots, quarter charges, 3 hits out of 27 shots. As regards effective range——"

"Tell them this," struck in Mr Bilch, "they'll understand it better. Tell them that the Intrepidy could sail round and round the Channel Fleet and bloody well throw her shells over the moon and down on to their decks without ever once coming into range. Tell them that."

"The picture so graphically drawn by Comrade Bilch is substantially correct," corroborated Sir Causter Kerr. "The Intrépide, together with three other battleships of her class, has an effective range of between four and five thousand yards more than that of any English ship.... But you have been told all this so often, comrades, that I fear it cannot interest you." Sir Causter was having his revenge for two years of subservience at a thousand pounds a year.

"Then perhaps you will tell us, as First Lord of the Admiralty—the job you are paid for doing—what you imagine the navy is kept up for?" demanded a comrade with fierce resentment.

"As far as I have been encouraged to believe, in that capacity," replied Kerr with easy insolence, "I imagine that its duties consist nowadays in patrolling the lobster-pots, and in amusing the visitors on the various seaside promenades by turning the searchlights on."

"We won't ask you to remain any longer," said the Premier.

Sir Causter Kerr rose leisurely. "Good morning, comrades," he remarked punctiliously, and going home wrote out his resignation, "from motives of patriotism," and sent a copy of the letter to all the papers.

A man who had been standing by the door listening to the conversation now came forward with a copy of an early special edition of the Pall Mall Gazette in his hand.

"You needn't sweat yourselves about being equal to a single power or not," he remarked with an unpleasant laugh. "Look at the 'fudge' there." And he threw the paper on the table, as though he washed his hands of it and many other things.

Mr Bilch secured it, and turning to the space which is left

131

blank for the inclusion of news received up to the very moment of going to press, he read aloud the single item it contained.

COAL WAR

Berlin, Thursday Morning.

"The action which France is reported to have taken had for some time been anticipated here. On all sides there is the opinion, amounting to conviction, that Germany must at once call into operation the power lying dormant in the Penalising Tariff and impose a tax on imported coal. It is agreed that otherwise, in her frantic endeavours to restore the balance of her export trade, England would flood this country with cheap coal and precipitate a state of things similar to that from which France is just emerging.

"Emphasis is laid on the fact that such a measure will be self-protective and in no way aggressive. It is not anticipated that the tax will exceed 2 mks. 50 pf., or at the most 3 mks. per ton."

"Export value, eight and elevenpence," murmured a late arrival, one of the fifty practical men in the House. "Yes, I imagine that two marks fifty will just about knock the bottom out."

"Is there nothing we can offer them in exchange?" demanded some one. "Nothing we can hit them back with?"

Cecil Brown, who was suspected of heterodoxy on this one point, crystallised the tariff question into three words.

"Nothing but tears," he replied.

"If there's one thing that fairly makes me hot it's the way we always have to wait for some one else to tell us what's going on," said the comrade who had brought in the Pall Mall Gazette, looking across at the Foreign Office Under-Secretary resentfully. "A fellow in Holborn here pokes the paper under my nose and asks me what we're going to do about it, and there I don't even know what is being done at us. What I want to know is, what our ambassadors and Foreign Office think they're there for. It's always the same, and then there'll be the questions in Parliament, and we know nothing. Makes us look like a set of kiddin' amateurs."

The fact had been noticed. Former governments had not infrequently earned the title in one or two departments. Later governments had qualified for it in every department. The reason lay on the surface; the members of those parliaments and the men who sent them were themselves bunglers and amateurs in their daily work and life. Except in the stereotyped product of machinery,

132

accuracy was scarcely known. The man who had built a house in England at that period, the man who had had a rabbit-hutch built to order, the man who had stipulated for one article to be made exactly like a copy, the man who had been so unfortunate as to require "the plumbers in," the man who had to do with labour in any shape or form, the man who had been "faithfully" promised delivery or completion by a certain stated time, the woman who shopped, the person who merely existed with open eyes, could all testify out of experiences, some heartrending, some annoying, some simply amusing, that precision and reliability scarcely existed among the lower grades of industry and commerce. It was a period of transition. The worker had cast off the love, the delicacy, the intelligence of the craftsman, and he had not yet attained to the unvarying skill of the automaton. In another century one man would only be able to fix throttle valve connections on to hot-water pipes, but his fixing of throttle valves would be a thing to dream about, while the initial letter A's of his brother, whose whole life would be devoted to engraving initial letter A's on brass dog-collar plates, would be as near unswerving perfection as mundane initials ever could be.

"Makes us look like a set of tinkerin' amateurs."

"One inference is plain enough," said Mr Guppling, smoothing over the suggestion. "These three things weren't going to happen all together of their own accord. There's a deep game somewhere, and seeing what's at stake our powers ought to be wide enough for us to put our hands on them and stop it."

There was a murmur of approval. Having been taken by surprise, the idea of peremptorily "stopping it" was a peculiarly attractive one.

But there were malcontents who were not to be appeased so easily, and a Comrade Pennefarthing, who had arrived in the meantime, raised an old cry in a new form.

"I won't exactly say that we've been betrayed," he declared, glancing at the group of orthodox Ministers who sat together, "but game or no game I will say that we've been damned badly served with information."

Comrade Tirrel stood up. He had not yet spoken at all, and he was accorded instant silence, for men were beginning to look to him. "It is now nearly eleven o'clock," he said in his quick, incisive tone, "and some of us have been here for upwards of an hour. We met to consider a situation. That situation still remains. May I ask that the Home Secretary, who is doubly qualified for the task, should tell us the extent of the danger and its probable effect?"

If Mr Tubes possessed a double qualification he also laboured under a corresponding disability. As the representative of a mining constituency, a practical expert, and a leading member of a Government which existed by the goodwill of the workers—largely of the miners—it would be scarcely to his interest to minimise the gathering cloud. As the Minister for the Home Department, the blacker he made the picture the greater the volume of obloquy he drew upon his head for not having foreseen the danger; the more relief he asked for, the fiercer the opposition he would encounter from hostile sections and from the perturbed heads of a depleted Treasury.

"We are still very much in the dark as to what has really happened, is happening, and will happen," he remarked tamely. "An appreciable drop in the demand for coal, whether for home or export, will certainly have a disturbing effect on the conditions of labour in many departments. But the difficulties of estimating the effects are so great——"

There were murmurs. Whatever might be the failings of Socialistic oratory, flatness and excess of moderation did not lie among them.

"Figures," suggested Tirrel pointedly.

"Perhaps Comrade Tirrel will take the job in hand instead of me," said Tubes bitterly, but without any show of anger. "Doubtless he'd get a better hearing."

"No," replied Tirrel gravely, "the moment is too critical for recrimination. If the Home Secretary lays the position frankly before us, he will have no cause to complain of an unsympathetic hearing, nor, as far as I can speak, of a whole-hearted support in taking means to safeguard it."

It occurred to Mr Tubes then, for the first time in his life—and it was almost like a shock to feel it—that the man who had always seemed to throw himself into sharp antagonism to himself might be actuated by higher motives than personal jealousy after all. He continued his speech.

"If we accept the figure of five millions as a correct return of the Unity League membership, and if we assume that they will all obey the boycott, then we are face to face with the fact that on the basis of a four ton per person average, twenty million tons of coal must be written off the home consumption."

"But the four tons per head average includes the entire industrial consumption of the country," objected Mr Vossit.

"That is so," admitted Mr Tubes, "but it also includes a great many people whose use of coal is practically nil. An alternative basis is to assume that two millions of the members are house-holders. Then taking ten tons a year as their average household

134

consumption—and admitting that all the wealthiest men in the country are included the average is not too high—we arrive at just the same result.

"The exports, on the other hand, do not depend on estimate: we have the actual returns. France takes fifteen million tons in round numbers. For the purpose of facing the worst, we may therefore assume that the work of digging and handling thirty-five million tons will be suddenly cut off."

"Germany," some one reminded him.

"Germany is wholly conjectural at present. I have no objection to taking it into account as well, if it is thought desirable, but I would point out that we are being influenced by the merest rumour."

"No," objected Tirrel, but without any enmity, "I think that we must regard Germany as lost. We are just beginning to touch the outskirts of a vast organisation which has been quietly perfecting its plan of operation for years. I do not regard a German tax as settled because of this one rumour, but I do regard it as settled because at this precise moment the rumour has been allowed to appear."

"Germany ten millions," accepted Mr Tubes. "Total decrease, forty-five million tons."

"Don't you be too sure of that, comrade," warned Mr Bilch. "Why, it's not twelve o'clock yet by a long way. There'll be half a dozen editions out before the 'Three o'clock winners.'" Mr Bilch evidently regarded his shaft that each fresh edition might contain a new country imposing a tax humorously, but several comrades looked towards the Home Secretary enquiringly.

"The other large importers are Italy, Russia, Sweden, Egypt, Spain and Denmark," said Mr Tubes, who could have talked coal statistics for hours if necessary. "All these, with the possible exception of Russia, must import. It is unlikely that the estimate I have given will be exceeded from that cause."

"And the result?"

"Above and below, about a million men are now employed in raising 236,000,000 tons. It is simple arithmetic.... In less than a month about two hundred thousand more men will be out of work."

Mr Chadwing, Chancellor of the Exchequer, moved uneasily in his chair.

"That is the full extent?" enquired Cecil Brown.

"No," admitted the Home Secretary. "That is the inevitable direct result. Forty-five million tons less will be carried by rail, or cart, or ship, or all three. A fair sprinkling of railway-men, carters, dockers, stokers, sailors, and other fellows will be dropped off too. There will be fewer railway trucks built this next year, less doing in the fire-grate trade, several thousand horses not wanted, a slight falling off in road-mending work. There is not a trade in England, from steeple-building to hop-picking, that will not be a little worse off because of those 45,000,000 tons. Then the two hundred thousand out-of-work miners will burn less coal at home, the ships and the engines will burn less, and the workshops and the smithies will burn less, and the whole process will be repeated again and again, for coal is like a snowball in its cumulative effects, and it cannot stand still."

If Mr Tubes had come to compromise, he had remained to publish broadcast.

Perhaps no one quite understood the danger yet, for the mind, used to everyday effects, does not readily grasp the extent of a calamity, and six hours before there had not been a cloud even the size of a man's hand on their horizon. The Premier thought it was impolitic on his colleague's part; the Treasury officials looked on it as a move to force their hands; the Foreign Under-Secretary was suspicious that Mr Tubes was leading away by some mysterious by-path from the unpreparedness of his own Department to Foreign Office remissness. They all continued to look silently at the Home Secretary as he continued to stand.

"The indirect effects will involve about two million people to some extent," he summed up.

"That, at least, is the worst?" said Cecil Brown with an encouraging smile, for Mr Tubes remained standing.

The Prime Minister made an impatient movement; the Treasury heads looked at one another and said with their eyes, "He is really overdoing it"; the Foreign Office man scowled unconsciously, and Cecil Brown continued to smile consciously.

"The worst is this: that a great many pits are working to-day at a bare profit, partly in the hope of better things, partly because we stimulate the trade. The crisis we are approaching will hang over the coal fields like a blight, and one crippled industry will bring down another. All the poorer mines will close down. You need only look back to '93 to see that. Neither I nor any one else can give you a forecast of what that will involve, but you may be sure of this: that although '93 with its 17,000,000 tons of a decrease half-ruined the English coal fields for a decade, '93 was a shrimp to what this is going to be."

"Then let us stimulate the trade more, until the crisis is over," suggested Cecil Brown.

Mr Tubes gave a short, dry laugh. "I commend that course to Comrade Chadwing," he said, as he sat down.

The Chancellor of the Exchequer was busy with his papers.

136

"Let me dispel any idea of that kind at once," he remarked, without looking up. "The moment is not only an unfortunate one—it is an utterly impossible one for making any extra disbursement however desirable."

"Well," said Mr Bilch, looking round on the moody assembly paternally, "it seems that the situation is like this here, mates: The navy is no messin' good at all, same as I told you; the army's a bit worse; Treasury empty, yes; the Home Office don't know what's going on at home, and the Foreign Office possesses just the same amount of valuable information as to what is happening abroad. Lively, ain't it? Well, it's lucky that Bilch is still Bilch."

No one rose to his mordant humour. Even Cecil Brown had forgotten how to smile.

"If our comrade has any suggestion to make——" said the Premier discouragingly.

"Yes, sir," replied Mr Bilch. "I have the wisdom of the serpent to rub into your necks if you'll only listen. We haven't any navy, so we can't fight if we wanted to; we haven't any money, so we can't pay out. Tubes here doesn't know what's going to happen at home, and Jevons doesn't rightly know what has happened abroad. What is to be done? I'll tell you. Wait. Wait and see. Wait, and let them all simmer down again. Why," he cried boisterously, looking round on them in good-humoured, friendly contempt, "to see your happy, smiling faces one would think that the canary had died or the lodger gone off without paying his rent. For why? Because a bloke in a frock-coat and a top hat gets on to a wooden horse and blows a tin trumpet, and the export trade in a single article of commerce is temporarily disarranged—perhaps!"

Mr Strummery nodded half absent-mindedly; the Treasury men smiled together; Mr Chadwing murmured "Very true"; and nearly every one looked relieved. Comrade Bilch was certainly a rough member, but the man had a shrewd common-sense, and they began to feel that they had been hasty in their dismal forebodings.

"Haven't we been threatened with this and that before?" demanded Mr Bilch dogmatically. "Of course we have, and what came of it? Nothing. Haven't there been strikes and lock-outs, some big some little, every year? According to Comrade Tubes, this is going to be the champion. That remains to be seen. What I say is, don't play into their hands in a panic. Wait and see what's required. That don't commit us to anything."

"It may be too late then," said Mr Tubes, but he said "may" now and not "will."

"There may be no need to do anything then," replied Mr Bilch. "And remember this: that the minute you begin to shout 'Crisis!' you

137

make one. All round us; all at us. My rag-bags! what a run on the old bank there would be! But if you go on just as usual, taking no notice of no one? Why, before long there will come a wet day or a cold night, and Johnny Hampden's aunt will say to Johnny Hampden's grandmamma: 'My dear, I feel positively starved. Don't you think that we might have a little fire without Johnny knowing?' And the old lady will say: 'Well, do you know, my pet, I was just going to say the same thing myself. Suppose you run out and buy a sack of coal?' And before you can say 'coughdrop' every blessed aunt and mother and first cousin of the Unicorn League will be getting in her little stock of coal."

It was what every one wished to believe, and therefore they were easily persuadable. It was a national characteristic. The country had never entered into a war during the past fifty years without being assured by every authority, from the Commander-in-Chief down to the suburban barber, that as soon as the enemy got a little tap on the head they would be making for home, howling for peace as they went. All these men had known strikes; many had been involved in them: some had controlled their organisation. They had seen the men of their own class loyally and patiently facing poverty and hardship for the sake of a principle, and enduring day after day and week after week, and, if necessary, month after month; they had seen the women of their own class preaching courage and practising heroism by the side of their men while their bodies were racked by cold and hunger and their hearts were crushed by the misery around; they had seen even the children of their class learning an unnatural fortitude. They accepted it as a commonplace of life, an asset on which they could rely. But they did not believe that any other class could do it. It did not occur to them to consider whether the officers of an army are usually behind the rank and file in valour, sacrifice, or endurance.

Doubtless there were among them some who were not deceived, but they wilfully subordinated their clearer judgment to the policy of the moment.

Tirrel was the one exception.

"There can be no more fatal mistake of the dangerous position into which we have been manœuvred than to assume that we shall be easily delivered from it by the weakness of our opponents before we have the least indication that weakness exists," he declared, as soon as Mr Bilch had finished, speaking vigorously, but without any of the assertiveness and personal feeling that had gained him many enemies in the past. "I agree with every word that Comrade Tubes has spoken. We all do; we all must admit it or be blind. What on earth, then, have we to hope for in a policy of drift, of sitting tight and doing nothing in the hope of things coming round of their own accord? It is madness, my comrades, sheer madness, I tell you, and a month hence it will be suicide."

He dropped his voice and swept the circle of faces with a significant glance.

"It is through such madness on the part of others that we are here to-day."

Mr Chadwing smiled the thin smile of expediency.

"It is one thing for a comrade with no official responsibility to say that a certain course does not satisfy him," he said; "it may be quite another thing for those who have to consider ways and means to do anything different. Perhaps Comrade Tirrel will kindly enlighten us as to what in our position he would do?"

"I see two broad courses open," replied Tirrel, without any hesitation in accepting the challenge. "Both, as you will readily say, have their disadvantages, but neither is so fatal as inaction. The first is aggressive. The Unity League has declared war on us. Very well, let it have war. I would propose to suspend the habeas corpus, arrest Hampden and Salt, declare the object and existence of the Unity League illegal, close its offices and confiscate its funds. There are between five and ten million pounds somewhere. Do you reflect what that would do? It would at least keep two hundred thousand out-of-work miners from actual starvation for a year. Prompt action would inevitably kill the boycott movement at home. The foreign taxes, my comrades, you would probably find to have a very marked, though perhaps undiscoverable, connection with the home movement, and when the latter was seen to be effectually dealt with, I venture to predict that the former could be compromised. If the confiscated funds were not sufficient to meet the distress, I should not hesitate to requisition for State purposes in a time of national emergency all incomes above a certain figure in a clean sweep."

A medley of cries met this despotic programme throughout. Even Tirrel's friends felt that he was throwing away his reputation; and he had more enemies than friends.

"You'd simply make the situation twice as involved," exclaimed Mr Vossit as the mouthpiece of the babel. "The liberty of the subject! It would mean civil war. They'd rise."

"Who would rise?" demanded Tirrel.

"The privileged classes."

"But they have risen," he declared vehemently. "This is civil war. What more do you want?"

It was a question on which they all had views, and for the next five minutes the room was full of suggestions, not of what they themselves wanted, but of what would be the probable action of the classes if driven to extremities.

"Very well," assented Tirrel at last; "that is what they will do next as it is, for they consider that they are in extremities."

"Well, comrade," said Mr Bilch broadly, "you don't seem to have put your money on a winner this event. What's your other tip?"

"Failing that, the other reasonable course is conciliation. I would suggest approaching Hampden and Salt to find out whether they are open to consider a compromise. The details would naturally require careful handling, but if both sides were willing to come to an understanding, a basis could be found. As things are, I should consider it a gain to drop the Personal Property Tax, the Minimum Wage Bill, to guarantee the inviolability of capital against further taxation while we are in office, and to make generous concessions for the fuller representation of the monied classes in Parliament, in return for the abandonment of a coal war, the dispersal in some agreed way of the League reserves, the reduction of the subscription to a nominal sum, and a frank undertaking that the League would not adopt a hostile policy while the agreement remained in force."

This proposal was even less to the temper of the meeting than the former one had been, and the latter half of it was scarcely heard among the fusillade of hostile cries. No one laughed when a hot-headed comrade stood upon a chair and howled "Traitor!"

Tirrel looked round on the assembly. Practically every man who had a tacit right to join in the deliberative Council had arrived, and the room was full; but there was not a single member among them willing to face the necessity for strong and immediate action, and they were hostile to the man who just touched the secret depths of their unconfessed and innermost misgivings. Mr Tubes felt that he had done his duty, and need not invite reference to his delicate position by further emphasising unpalatable truths; he had presented the spectacle of a weak man startled into boldness, now he was sufficiently himself again to go with the majority. The more responsible members of the Government distrusted Tirrel in every phase; the smaller fry relied on the wisdom of orthodoxy, and agreed that the man who could blow the hotness of extirpation and the coldness of conciliation with the same breath must prove an unworthy guide; and on every hand there was the tendency of settled authority to deprecate novel and unmatured proceedings.

Tirrel had become the Hampden of an earlier decade among his party.

"You call me 'Traitor,'" he said, turning to the man who had done so. "Write down the word, comrade, and then, if you will bring it to me without a blush six months hence, I will wear it round my neck in penance."

He bowed to the Premier and withdrew, not in anger or with a mean sense of injustice, but because he felt that it would be sheer mockery to share the deliberations of a Council when their respective views, on a matter which he believed to be the very crux of their existence, were antagonistic in their essences.

After his departure the progress was amazing. His ill-considered proposals had cleared the air. Every one knew exactly what he did not want, and that was a material step towards arriving at the opposite goal.

At the end of a few hours a very effective and comprehensive scheme for quietly and systematically doing nothing had been almost unanimously arrived at. Several quires of paper had been covered with suggestions, some of them being accepted as they stood, some recommended for elaboration, some passed for future consideration, some thrown out. The ambassador in Paris was to retire (on the ground of ill-health) if he could not satisfactorily explain the position. A special mission was to be sent to Berlin to get really at the bottom of things, and, if possible, have the tax either not put on or taken off, according to the situation when they arrived there. A legal commission was to rout out every precedent to see if the Unity League was not doing something outside the powers of a trade union (a very forlorn hope); and all over the country enquiries were to be made and assurances given, all very discreetly and without the least suggestion of panic.

The only doubtful point was whether every one else would play the game with the same delicate regard for Ministerial susceptibilities, or whether some might not have the deplorable taste to create scenes, send deputations, demand work with menace, claim the literal fulfilment of specific pledges, incite to riot and violence, stampede the whole community, and otherwise act inconsiderately towards the Government, when they discovered the very awkward circumstances in which their leaders had involved them.

The first indication of a jarring note fell to the lot of the President of the Board of Trade in the shape of a telegram which reached him early on the following morning. This was its form:

"From the Council of the Amalgamated Union of Chimney Sweepers and Federated Carpet Beaters. (Membership, 11,372).—Seventeen million estimated chimneys stop smoking. No soot, precious little dust. Where the Hell do we come in?

"Blankintosh, Secretary."

141

A few years before, it had been officially discovered that there were four or five curiously adaptable words, without which the working man was quite unable to express himself in the shortest sentence. When on very ceremonious occasions he was debarred their use, he at once fell into a pitiable condition of aphasia. Keenly alive to the class-imposed disadvantages under which these men existed, the Government of that day declared that it was a glaring anomaly that the poor fellows should not be allowed to use a few words that were so essential to their expression of every emotion, while the rich, with more time on their hands, could learn a thousand synonyms. The law imposing a shilling fine for each offence (five shillings in the case of "a gentleman," for even then there was one law for the rich and another for the poor) was therefore repealed, and the working man was free to swear as much as he liked anywhere, which, to do him justice, he had done all along.

It was for this reason that Mr Blankintosh's pointed little message was accepted for transmission; but there was evidently a limit, for, when the President of the Board of Trade, an irascible gentleman who had, in the colloquial phrase, "got out of bed on the wrong side" that morning, dashed off a short reply, it was brought back to him by a dispirited messenger two hours later with the initials of seventeen postmasters and the seventeen times repeated phrase, "Refused. Language inadmissible."

CHAPTER XV

THE GREAT FIASCO

The Government allowed the 22nd day of July to pass without a sign. They were, as their supporters convincingly explained to anxious enquirers, treating the Unity League and all its works with silent contempt. They were "doing nothing" strategically, they wished it to be understood; a very different thing from "doing nothing" through apathy, indecision, or bewilderment, but very often undistinguishable the one from the other in the result.

On the 22nd day of July seventeen million "estimated chimneys" ceased to pollute the air. The League was not concerned with the exact number, and they accepted the chimney sweepers' figures. It was more to the purpose that the order was being loyally and cheerfully obeyed. The idea of fighting the Government with the Government's own chosen people, appealed to the lighter side of a not unhumorous nation.

Ever since the institution of a Socialistic press, and from even remoter times than the saplinghood of the "Reformer's Tree," Fleet Street party hacks and Hyde Park demagogues had been sharpening their wit upon the "black-coated" brigade, the contemptible bourgeoisie of "Linton Villas," "Claremonts," and "Holly Lodges," taunting them with self-complacency, political apathy, and social parasitism. The proportion of moral degradation conferred by a coat intentionally black, in comparison with one that is merely approaching that condition through the personal predilections of its owner, has never yet been defined, and the relative æsthetic values of the architectural pretensions of villadom, compared with the unswerving realism of the "Gas Works Views," "Railway Approach Cottages," and "Cement Terraces," of the back streets, may be left to the matured judgment of an unprejudiced posterity. The great middle class in all its branches had never hitherto made any reply at all. Now that it had begun to retort in its own effective way, the Government agreed that the best counterblast would be—to wait until it all blew over.

There were naturally defections from the first. A friendly spy in Mr Tubes's secret service managed to secure the information without much trouble that within seven days of the publication of the order no less than 4372 notices of resignation had been received at headquarters. He was hastening away with this evidence of the early dissolution of the League when his grinning informant called him back to whisper in his ear that during the same period there had been 17,430 new members enrolled, and that while the resignations seemed to have practically ceased the enrolments were growing in volume. In addition to these there were battalions who joined in the policy of the League through sympathy with its object without formally binding themselves as members.

In some of its aspects the success of the movement erred in excess. There were men, manufacturers, who in their faith and enthusiasm wished to close their works at once, and, regardless of their own loss, throw their workmen and their unburnt coal into the balance. It was not required; it was not even desirable then. The League's object was to disorganise commerce as little as possible beyond the immediate boundaries of the coal trade. They were not engaged in an internecine war, and every one of their own people deprived of employment was a loss. Cases of hardship there would

143

be; they are common to both sides in every phase of stubborn and prolonged civil strife, but from the "class" point of view coal had the pre-eminent advantage that its weight and bulk gave employment to a hundred of the "masses" to every one of themselves. There were also two circumstances that discounted any sense of injustice on this head. Firstly, there was a spirit of sacrifice and heroism in the air, born of the time and the situation; and secondly, it soon became plain that the League was engaged in vast commercial undertakings and was absorbing all the men of its own party who were robbed of their occupation by the development of the war.

A firm starting business with an unencumbered capital of ten million sterling, enjoying a "private income" of five millions a year, and not troubled with the necessity of earning any dividend at all, could afford to be a generous employer.

From the first moment it was obvious that oil must take the place of coal. That was the essence of the strife. The Tocsin set to work in frantic haste to prove that it was impossible; to show that all the authorities of the past and present had agreed that no real substitute for coal existed. It was quite true, and it was quite false. It was not a world struggle. Abroad, foreign coal was being substituted for English coal. At home only half a million tons a week were in issue at the first. Afterwards, as coal stagnation fed coal stagnation, the tonnage rose steadily, but the calorific ratio of coal and oil, the basis of all comparison, simply did not exist, except on paper, for the two fuels in domestic use.

The Tocsin's second article convinced its readers that all the lamp companies in the world could not keep up with the abnormal demand for lamps, stoves, and oil-cookers, that the ridiculous proposal of the League would involve, if it were not providentially ordained that it was foredoomed to grotesque failure by the dead weight of its own fatuous ineptitude.

In practice the two single firms of Ripplestone of Birmingham, and Schuyler of Cleveland, U.S.A., at once put on the market a varied stock that filled every requirement. There was no waiting. As The Tocsin bitterly remarked, it soon became apparent that the demand had been foreseen and "treacherously provided against during the past two years."

The third Tocsin article on the situation dealt statistically with the oil trade of the world. It necessarily fell rather flat, because The Tocsin Special Commissioner entered upon the task with the joyous conviction that the world's output would not be sufficient for the demand, the world's oil ships not numerous enough to transport it. As he dipped into the figures, however, he made the humiliating discovery that the increased demand would do little more than ruffle the surface of the oil market. The Baku oil fields could supply it without inconvenience; the United States could do it by contract at a ten per cent. advance; the newly-discovered wells of Nova Scotia alone would be equal to the demand if they diverted all their produce across the Atlantic.

He threw down his pen in despair, and then picked it up again to substitute invective for statistics. Before his eyes the motor-tanks of the Anglo-Pennsylvanian Oil Company, of London and Philadelphia, and the Anglo-Caucasian Oil Company, of London and Baku, were going on their daily rounds. It was still a matter for wonder how well equipped the sudden call had found those two great controlling oil companies. It was yet to be learned that for their elaborate designations there might be substituted the simple name "Unity League."

It was submitting The Tocsin young man to rather a cruel handicap to send him to the British Museum Reading Room for a few hours with instructions to prove impossible what Salt and Hampden had been straining every nerve for two years to make inevitable.

Three articles exhausted his proof that a successful coal boycott under modern conditions was utterly impossible.

He went out into the city and the suburbs, interviewing coal merchants and coal agents with the object of drawing a harrowing picture of the gloom and depression that had fallen upon these unfortunate creatures at the hands of their own class League.

He found them all bearing up well under the prospect, but much too busy to give him more than a few minutes of their time. Every one of them had been appointed an oil agent to the League firms, and League members were ordering their oil through them, just as heretofore they had ordered coal. It was very easy, profitable work for them; they had nothing to do but to transmit the orders to the League firms and the fast business-like motor-tanks distributed the oil. But half of the coal carters were now under notice to leave, and there were indications that work was very scarce. Each motor-tank displaced twenty men and twenty horses. Already, it was said, thousands of horses had been sent out to grass from London alone.

Externally, as far as the Capital was concerned at all events, things were going on very much the same as before, when the struggle was a fortnight old. Elsewhere signs were not lacking. The Government had received disquieting reports from its agents here and there, but so far it was meeting the situation by refusing to acknowledge that it existed. A march of the Staffordshire miners had been averted by the men's leaders being privately assured that it would embarrass the Government's plans. The march had been

145

deferred under protest; so far the organisation answered to the wheel. But the Midlands were clamorously demanding exceptional relief for the exceptional conditions. Monmouth had seen a little rioting, and in Glamorgan the bands of incendiaries called "Beaconmen," who set fire to the accumulations of coal stacked at the collieries, had already begun their work. Cardiff was feeling the effect of having a third of its export trade in coal suddenly lopped off, and Newport, Swansea, Kirkcaldy, Blyth, Hull, Sunderland, Glasgow, and the Tyne ports were all in the same position. Most of the railways had found it necessary to dispense with their entire supernumerary staff, and most of the railway workshops had been put on short time. In London alone, between four and five thousand out-of-work gas employés were drawing Government pay.

About the third week in August the Premier, Mr Tubes, and the Chancellor of the Exchequer had a long private conference. As a result Mr Strummery called an Emergency Council. It was a thin, acrimonious gathering. Some one brought the tidings that seven more companies in South London were substituting Diesel oil engines for steam. He had all the dreary developments statistically worked out on paper. Nobody wanted to hear them, but he poured them out into the unwilling ears, down to the climax that it represented two hundred and forty-seven fewer men required at the pits.

It served as a text, however, for Mr Chadwing to hang his proposal on. After a month of inaction, the Government was at length prepared to go to the length of admitting that abnormal conditions prevailed. Oil had thrown a quarter of a million of their people out of employment. Let oil keep them. He proposed to retaliate with a 50 per cent. tax on imported oil, to come into operation under Emergency Procedure on the 1st of September.

There were men present to whom the suggestion of taxing a raw article, necessary to a great proportion of the poor, was frankly odious. They were prepared to attack the proposal as a breach of faith. A few words from Mr Strummery, scarcely more than whispered, explained the necessity for the tax and the menace of the situation.

Those who had not been following events closely, paled to learn the truth.

The Treasury was living from hand to mouth, for the City had ceased to take up its Bills. Unless "something happened" before the New Year dawned, it would have to admit its inability to continue the Unemployed Grant. Already a quarter of a million men and their dependents, in addition to the normal average upon which the estimates were based, had been suddenly thrown upon the

146

resources of the Department. If Mr Tubes's forecast proved correct, double that number would be on their hands within another month. The development of half a million starving men who had been taught to look to the Government for everything, looking and finding nothing, could be left to each individual imagination.

The Oil Tax came into operation on the 1st of September. Under the plea of becoming more "business-like," a great many of the Parliamentary safeguards had been swept away, and such procedure was easy. All grades of petroleum had already advanced a few pence the gallon under the increased demand, and the poorer users had expressed their indignation. When they found, one day, that the price had suddenly leapt to half as much again, their wrath was unbounded. It was in vain for Ministers to explain that the measure was directed against their enemies. They knew that it fell on them, and demanded in varying degrees of politeness to be told why some luxury of the pampered, leisured classes had not been chosen instead. The reason was plain to those who studied Blue Books. So highly taxed was every luxury now that the least fraction added to its burden resulted in an actually decreased revenue from that source.

But if the mere tax and increase had impressed the poor unfavourably, a circumstance soon came to light that enraged them.

In spite of the tax the members of the Unity League were still being supplied with oil at the old prices, and they were assured that they would continue to be supplied without advance, even if the tax were doubled!

The poor, ever suspicious of the doings of those of their own class when set high in authority, at once leapt to the conclusion that they were being made the victims of a double game. It was nothing to them that the Anglo-Pennsylvanian and the Anglo-Caucasian companies were now trading at a loss; it was common knowledge that their richer League neighbours had not had the price of their oil increased, and they knew all too well that they themselves had. With the lack of balanced reasoning that had formerly been one of the Government's best weapons, they at once concluded that they alone were paying the tax, and the unparalleled injustice of it sowed a crop of bitterness in their hearts.

If that was the net result at home, the foreign effect of the policy was not a whit more satisfactory. Studland, the Consul-General at Odessa, one of the most capable men in the Service, cabled a despatch full of temperate and solemn warning the moment he heard of the step. It was too late then, if, indeed, his words would have been regarded. Russia replied by promptly trebling her existing tax on imported coal, and at the same time

147

gave Germany rebate terms that practically made it a tax on English coal. It was said that Russia had only been waiting for a favourable opportunity, and was more anxious to develop her own new coal fields in the Donetz basin than to import at all. As far as the Treasury was concerned, the oil tax yielded little more than was absorbed by the thirty thousand extra men thrown out of work by Russia's action. The Government had given a rook for a bishop.

A little time ago the Cabinet had been prepared to greet winter as a friend. Without quite possessing the ingenuousness of their amiable Comrade Bilch, they had thought cynically of the pampered aristocrats shivering in Mayfair drawing-rooms, of the comfort-loving middle classes sitting before their desolate suburban hearths, of blue-faced men setting out breakfastless for freezing offices, and of pallid women weeping as they tried to warm the hands of little children, as they put them in their icy beds.

And now? All their cynical sympathy had apparently been in vain. There were not going to be any cold breakfasts, freezing offices, or shivering women and children. Warming stoves and radiators raised the temperature of a room much quicker than a fire did, and kept it equable without any attention. Oil cookers took the place of the too often erratic kitchen range. Mrs Strummery innocently threw the Premier into a frenzy one morning by dilating on the advantages of a "Britonette" stove which she had been shown by a Tottenham Court Road ironmonger. The despised, helpless "classes" were going on very comfortably. They were going on even gaily; "Oil Scrambles" constituted a new and popular form of entertainment for long evenings; from Wimbledon came the information that "Candle Cinderellas" would have a tremendous rage during the approaching season; and in Cheapside and the Strand the penny hawkers were minting money with the novel and diverting "Coal Sack Puzzle."

But the winter was approaching, though no longer as a friend. If England should say to-morrow what Lancashire was saying that day, there were portents of stirring times in the air. Already Northumberland, Durham, and Yorkshire were muttering in their various uncouth dialects, and Lanark was subscribing to disquieting sentiments in its own barbarous tongue. Derbyshire was becoming uneasy, Staffordshire was scarcely answering to the wheel, and Nottingham was in revolt against what it considered to be the too compliant attitude of the Representation Committee. The rioting in Monmouth was only restrained from becoming serious in its proportions by the repeated assurances from Westminster that the end was in sight; and the "Beaconmen" of Glamorgan were openly boasting that before long they would "light such a candle" that the ashes would fall upon London like a Vesuvian cloud.

Still nearer home was the disturbing spectacle of the railway-men thrown out of work, the coal carters, the stablemen, the gasworkers, the canal boatmen, the general labourers, the tool-makers, the wheel-wrights, the chimney sweepers, the brushmakers. The sequence of dependence could be traced, detail by detail, through every page of the trade directory.

They had all been taught to clamour to the Government in every emergency, and this administration they regarded as peculiarly their own. It was not a case of Frankenstein's Monster getting out of hand; this Monster had created its Frankenstein, and could dissolve him if he proved obstinate. All that Frankenstein had ventured to do so far had been to reduce the Unemployed Grant to three quarters of its normal rate "in view of the unprecedented conditions of labour," and where two or more unemployed were members of one family, to make a further small deduction. The action had not been well received. "In view of the unprecedented conditions of labour" the unemployed had looked for more rather than for less. When the rate was fixed they had been given to understand that it represented the minimum on which an out-of-work man could be decently asked to live. Why, then, had their own party reduced it? Funds? Tax some luxury!

Even the Government assurance, an ingenious adaptation of truth by the light of Mr Chadwing's figures, that they "did not anticipate having to impose the reduced grant for many more weeks, but at the same time counselled economy in every working-class home," did not restore mutual good feeling. The general rejoinder was that the Government had "better not," and the reference to economy was stigmatised as gratuitously inept.

In the meantime the situation was reacting unfavourably upon Mr Strummery and the chief officers of State, not only in Parliament but even in the Cabinet itself. Consultations between the Premier and half a dozen of his most trusted Ministers were of daily occurrence. One day, towards the end of September, Mr Strummery privately intimated to all the "safe" members of the Council that it was necessary to meet to consider what further steps to take.

The meeting was a "packed" one in that the Tirrels, the Browns, and the Bilches of the party were not invited and knew nothing of it. There was no reason why Mr Strummery should not call together a section of his followers if he wished, and discuss policy with them, but at the moment it was dangerous, because the conclave was just strong enough to be able to impose its will upon Parliament, and yet individually it was composed of weak men. It

149

was dangerous because half a dozen weak men, rendered desperate by the situation into which they were being inevitably driven, had resolved to act upon heroic lines. As Balzac had remarked, "There is nothing more horrible than the rebellion of a sheep," but the horrible consequences generally fall upon its own head in the end.

Mr Chadwing's statement informed the despondent gathering that on the existing lines it would be necessary to suspend the wholesale operation of the relief fund about the middle of December. By reducing the grant in varying degrees it would be possible to carry on for perhaps three months beyond that date, but to reach the furthest limit the individual relief would have become so insignificant that it would only result in an actual crisis being precipitated earlier than would be the case if they went on as they were doing.

That was all that the Chancellor of the Exchequer had to say. The uninitiated men looked at one another in mute enquiry. There was something in the air. What was coming?

The Premier rose to explain. He admitted that they had underrated the danger of the situation at first. Measures that might have sufficed then were useless now. Oil was the pivot of the whole question. The oil tax had not realised expectations. To raise the tax would only alienate the affections of their own people without reaching the heart of the matter. They had already taken one bite at a cherry.

He paused and looked round, an indifferent swimmer forced by giant circumstance to face his Niagara.

He proposed as a measure of national emergency to prohibit the importation of oil altogether.

There was a gasp of surprise; a moment of stupefaction. Strange things were again being done in the name of Liberty.

Mr Tubes's voice, enumerating the results and advantages of the step, recalled their wandering thoughts. There was little need for the recital; the effect of so unexpected a coup leapt to the mind at once.

The Leaguers must either burn coal or starve. The home oil deposits had long ceased to be worked. Wood under modern conditions was impracticable; peat was equally debarred, and neither could meet a sudden emergency in sufficient quantity; electricity meant coal, and was far from universal. The League movement must collapse within a week.

There were other points, all in favour of the course. Although it might slightly inconvenience many working-class homes it would not take their money as a heavier tax would, and it must convince all that the end was well in sight. It would induce the poor to use more coal, more gas, in itself a step towards that desired end. It would teach Russia a sharp lesson, and Russia's sins were the freshest in their minds.

All were convinced, and all against their will. There was something sinister in the proposal; the thought of it fell like a shadow across the room.

"It is not a course I would recommend or even assent to as a general thing," said Mr Strummery. "But we are fighting for the existence of our party, for the lives of thousands of our people. It is no exaggeration. Think of the awful misery that must sweep the country in the coming winter if the League holds out. If we do not break the wicked power of those two men, there is no picture of national calamity to be found in the past that can realise the worst."

"It is their game," said Mr Tubes bitterly. "The cowards are striking at the women and children through the men."

He ignored the fact that his party had struck the first blow, and had had the word "War!" figuratively nailed to the staff of their red banner for years. In war one usually strikes some one, and on the whole it is perhaps less reprehensible to strike women and children through men than vice versa. But it was an acceptable sentiment on the face of it, and it sounded all right at the moment.

"Moreover," added the Premier, "there will be this danger in the situation: that blinded by passions and desperate through misery, the people may fail to realise who are the real causes of their plight."

Yes, there was that possibility to be faced by thoughtful Socialistic Ministers. The people are not very subtle in their reasoning. The most pressing fact of their existence would be that the Government, which had promised to keep them from starvation in return for their votes, had had their votes and was allowing them to starve.

"I think that we must all agree to the necessity of the step," said one of the minor men, "though our feelings are all against it."

"Quite so," admitted Mr Strummery. "Let us hope that being a sharp remedy it will only need to be a short one."

Surprise was the essence of the coup, and the "business-like" procedure of Parliament permitted this when the Government was backed by a large automatic majority. The expeditious passing of the measure was a foregone conclusion, yet a few shrewd warning voices were raised against it even among the stalwarts. The regular opposition voted against it as a matter of course. The most moderate section of the Labour Party and the extreme Socialists, who both elected to sit on the opposition side of the House, refrained from voting, and a few Ministers, who were distracted

151

between their private opinions and their party duty, were diplomatically engaged elsewhere.

The Bill first received the attention of the House on the 25th of September, the day after the Premier had called his informal meeting. It became law on the 28th, and three days later, the 1st of October, Great Britain was absolutely "closed" against the introduction of mineral burning oils on any terms.

The country received the measure with mixed feelings, but on the whole with the admission that it would be effective and with an expression of dislike. The coal mining districts hailed it with enthusiasm, and the same reception was accorded it among the affected industries, but outside these it was nowhere popular, and in certain working-class quarters it evoked the bitterest hostility. It was felt even by those who stood to gain much by the overthrow of the League that their instincts rebelled against the means; possibly the underlying feeling was distrust of the exercise of power so despotic. It was admitted that the League's action with respect to coal stood on a different plane. Any member could at once resign; it was questionable if one could not use coal and still remain a member. Certainly no coercion was used. But in the matter of oil a necessary commodity was absolutely ruled out, and, whether he wished or nor, every one must obey. By the 8th of October the retail price of petroleum of an average quality was 2s. 9d. the gallon, and the price was rising as the end of the stock came in sight.

One curious circumstance excited remark. The Unity League members were still being supplied at the original price. The League was keeping its word gallantly to the end. The Government had calculated that the two interested companies might have a reserve that would last a week. The average stock which the consumer might be supposed to have in hand would carry them on for a further five days, and the economy which they would doubtless practise might hold off the climax for five more. The 17th of October came to be confidently mentioned in Government circles as the date of the Unity League's surrender.

It might have been merely coincidence, but on the 17th of October Mr Strummery chose to entertain a few of his colleagues to dinner in the House.

In spite of the host's inevitable jug of boiling water, an air of genial humour, almost of gaiety, pervaded the board. Mr Tubes was entertainingly reminiscent; Chadwing succeeded in throwing off the weight of the Treasury; Comrade Stubb, fresh from the soil, proved to have a dry humour of his own; and Cecil Brown, who was always socially welcome, made a joke which almost surprised the Premier into a smile.

Mr Tubes was in the middle of a sentence when Cecil Brown, with his face turned towards the door, laid his hand upon the speaker's arm.

"A minute, Tubes," he said. "There is something unusual going on out there."

"Perhaps it is——" began Chadwing, and stopped. The same thought had occurred to at least three of them. Perhaps they were coming to tell them that Hampden had accepted his defeat. Whatever it might be, a dozen members who had entered the room in a confused medley were making their way towards the Premier's table. A man who seemed to concentrate their attention was in their midst; some were apparently trying to hold him back, while others urged him on. While yet some distance off he broke away from them all, and running forward, reached the table first.

It was Comrade Bilch, so dishevelled, red, and heated, that it did not occur to any one to doubt that he was drunk. For a second he stood looking at them stupidly, and then he suddenly opened his mouth and poured out so appalling a string of vile and nauseating abuse that men who were near drew aside.

"Why, in Heaven's name, don't you take him away?" exclaimed Cecil Brown, appealing to those who formed the group beyond the table.

They would have done so, but Comrade Bilch raised his hand as though to enjoin attention for a moment. A change seemed to have come over him even in that brief passage of time. He walked up to the table and leaned heavily upon it with both fists, while his breath came in throbs, and the colour played about his face like the reflection of a raging fire. When he spoke it was without a single oath; all his uncleanness had dropped away from him as though he recognised its threadbare poverty in the face of the colossal news he brought.

"Gentlemen," he said, leaning forward and breathing very hard, "you would have it, and you have got your way. You've made oil contraband, and not a drop can be landed in Great Britain now. It can't be brought, but it can be used when it is here, and the Unity League that you have done it all to starve has got two hundred million gallons safely stowed away at Hanwood! Yes, while our people will have to grope and freeze through the winter, they are quite comfortably provided for, and you, whether you leave the bar on or whether you take it off, you have made us the laughing-stock of Europe!"

An awed silence fell on the group. Not the most shadowy suspicion of such a miscarriage had ever stirred the most cautious. All their qualms had been in the direction of swallowing the

153

unpalatable measure, not of doubting its efficacy. They seemed to be the puny antagonists of some almost superhuman power that not only brushed their most elaborate plans aside, but actually led them on to pave the way to their own undoing.

Mr Tubes was the first to speak. "It can't be true," he whispered. "It is impossible."

"Oh, everything's impossible with you, especially when it's happened," retorted Mr Bilch contemptuously. "Pity you didn't live when there were real miracles about."

"But the time?" protested some one. "How could they do it in the time?"

"Time!" said Mr Bilch, "what more do you want? They've had two years, and they've used two years. If those——" He stopped suddenly, jerked his head twice with a curious motion, and fell to the ground in a fit.

There were plenty of good friends to look after him without troubling the Ministerial group. The dinner-party broke up in the face of so inauspicious a series of events, and before another hour had passed the story of the gigantic fiasco had reached every club in London, and was being cabled to every capital in Christendom.

CHAPTER XVI

THE DARK WINTER

The autumn of 1918 had proved unusually mild. It was said that many of the migratory birds delayed their exodus for weeks beyond their normal times, and in sheltered gardens and hedgerows in the south of England flowers and fruit were making an untimely show; but about midday on the 24th of November it began to grow dark, and, without any indication of fog, it grew darker, until the greater part of England and Wales was plunged into a nocturnal gloom. As there was a marked fall in the temperature, men looked up to the clouds and predicted snow, but they were wrong. Had it snowed it might have been the White Winter of 1918, for that night the frost began, and the 24th of November had already become an ill-omened date to usher in a frost. It did not belie its character. The next day broke clear but bitter, and those who read newspapers learned with curious interest that during the night the seven-tailed comet of 1744 had been observed by several astronomers, to the great confusion of their science, for its appearance was premature by a round hundred thousand years. The phenomenon afterwards grew into a portent to the vulgar mind, for that was the beginning of the great frost that lasted seven weeks without an intermission.

Outside certain limits, life was proceeding very much as before. The condition of the upper classes was not materially different from what it had been before the policy of retaliation had been declared. The Personal Property Tax had not been proceeded with, and the Minimum Wage Bill had been dropped for the time. There were diplomatic explanations; the real reason was that the Cabinet was too sharply divided over the expediency of anything in those days to make the passing of important measures practicable. While none had the courage to go to an extreme either in aggression or in conciliation, there was a multitude of counsel vehemently wrangling over the wisdom of little concessions and little aggressions.

In London the great increase in the number of unemployed began to be observable in the early autumn. The obsolete "marches of unemployed" were revived, but, as might have been foreseen, except among the poor themselves, they met with no financial encouragement. Even the poor were becoming careful of their pence. They saw what the winter must mean, for every one knew of a score of deserving cases around his own door, and it was commonly reported that the Government contemplated reducing the Unemployed Grant to two-thirds its normal basis before the year was out. That was the Cabinet's idea for "breaking it gently." So, meeting with no response in the suburbs, the City, or the West End, the processions groaned occasionally, broke a few windows, enhanced the bitter feeling existing against their class by frightening more than a few ladies, and were finally kept in check by the special constabulary raised in the suburbs, the City, and the West End. Finding so little profit for their exertions, they abandoned their indiscriminate peregrinations, and took to demonstrating before St Stephen's and to hooting outside the houses of Cabinet Ministers until the processions and meetings were disallowed.

There was no public charity that winter, either organised or spontaneous, for the benefit of the working-class poor. The conditions of labour would have warranted a Mansion House Fund being opened in September, but no one suggested it, and no one would have contributed to it. Abroad it was generally recognised that England was involved in civil war to which it behoved them to act as neutrals. The Socialists in Belgium collected and despatched the sum of £327, 14s. 6d. for the relief of their "persecuted confraternity in England," but as the pomp and circumstances attending the inauguration of the Fund had led their persecuted confraternity in England to expect at least a quarter of a million sterling, some intemperate remarks greeted the consummation of the effort, and it was not repeated.

To those who did not look very deeply into the situation it appeared that a long, hard winter must operate against the interests of the League. Their opponents would burn more coal. The Government, indeed, issued an appeal asking them to do so, and thus to relieve the tension in the provinces. The response was not promising. The Government was, in effect, told to mind its own business, and particularly that detail of its business which consisted in the guarantee of a full and undocked living wage to every worker in or out of work. The contention so far had been that with the surfeit, coal would be so cheap that even the poorest could burn it unstintingly. But soon a new and rather terrible development grew out of the complex situation. Coal became dear, not only dear in the ordinary sense of the word—winter prices—but very, very dear. The simple truth was that a disorganised industry always moves on abnormal lines, and coal was a routed, a shattered, industry.

There was no oil to be had by any but members of the League; in some places there was no gas to be had, for many of the small gas companies, and some of the large ones, had found it impossible to continue amidst the dislocation of their trade, and the cheapest coal was being retailed in the streets of London at two shillings the hundred-weight. The Government had left oil contraband after the discovery of the League's secret store down the quiet country lane, for they recognised that to remove the embargo immediately would kill them with ridicule. They promised themselves that the freedom of commerce should be restored at the first convenient opportunity. In the meanwhile they decided to do as they had done in other matters: they bravely ignored the fact that the League members were any better off than any one else, and declined to believe the evidence that any store existed.

That was the state of affairs before the winter set in, and in London alone. The Capital was feeling some of the remoter effects of the blow, but from the provinces, from the actual battle-fields, there came grim stories. Northumberland, which had been loth to accept the Eight Hours Bill, now traced the whole of the trouble to that head, and declared that the only hope was for the Government to make a complete surrender to the Unity League, on the one condition that it restored a normal demand for coal both at home and abroad. Durham, on the contrary, held that it was necessary for the Government to crush or wear out the League. In both counties there had been fierce conflict between the rival factions, and blood had been freely shed. After a single day's rioting at Newcastle and Gateshead seventeen dead bodies had been collected by the ambulances.

The "Beaconmen" in Glamorgan were setting fire to the pits themselves in a spirit of fanaticism. In one instance a fire had spread beyond the intended limits, and an explosion, in which three score of their unfortunate fellow-workmen perished, had been the net result. The Midlands were the least disturbed, and even there Walsall had seen a mass meeting at which thirty thousand colliers and other affected workmen had called insistently with threats upon the Government, in pathetic ignorance of the Treasury's plight, to purchase the nation's coal pits at once, and resume full time at all of them, as the only means of averting a national calamity.

And all this had been taking place in the mild autumn, while the Government was still paying out sufficient relief funds to ensure that actual starvation should not touch any one, long before it had been driven to take the country into its confidence. The spectre of cold and hunger had not yet been raised to goad the men to madness; so far they regarded existence at least as assured, and the question that was stirring them to rebellion was not the fundamental one of the "right to live," but the almost academic issue of the right to live apart from the natural vicissitudes of life.

The Government had other troubles on hand. The two principal causes for anxiety among these, if not actually of their own hatching, had certainly sprung from a common stock.

The Parliament sitting at College Green deemed the moment opportune for issuing a Declaration of Independence and proclaiming a republic. Three years before, all Irishmen had been withdrawn from the British army and navy on the receipt of Dublin's firmly-worded note to the effect that since the granting of extended Home Rule, Irishmen came within the sphere of the Foreign Enlistment Act. These men formed the nucleus of a very useful army with which Ireland thought it would be practicable to hold out in the interior until foreign intervention came to its aid. Possibly England thought so too, for Mr Strummery's Ministry contented itself with issuing what its members described as a firm and dignified protest. Closely examined, it was discoverable that the dignified portion was a lengthy recapitulation of ancient history; the firm portion a record of Dublin's demands since Home Rule had been conceded, while the essential part of the communication informed the new republic that its actions were not what his Majesty's Ministers had expected of it, and that they would certainly

157

reserve the right of taking the matter in hand at some future time more suitable to themselves.

The other harassment was that Leicester lay at the mercy of an epidemic of small-pox which threatened to become historic in the annals of the scourge. In the second month the average daily number of deaths had risen to 120, and there was no sign of a decrease. In the autumn it was hoped that the winter would kill the disease; in the winter it was anticipated that it would die out naturally under the influence of the spring sunshine. The situation affected Mr Chadwing more closely than any of his colleagues, for Leicester had the honour of returning the Chancellor of the Exchequer as one of its members. Under normal conditions Mr Chadwing made a practice of visiting his constituency and addressing a meeting every few weeks, but during the six months that the epidemic raged he found himself unable to leave London. His attitude was perfectly consistent, in spite of the hard things that some of his supporters said of him in his absence: like the majority of his constituents, he had a Conscientious Objection to vaccination, but he also had an even stronger conscientious objection to encountering small-pox infection.

The 24th of November ushered in a new phase of the strife. It marked the beginning of the Dark Winter. Early in December the newspapers began to draw comparisons between the weather then prevailing and the hard winters on record. At that date it was noticeable how many rustic-looking vagrants were to be seen walking aimlessly about the streets of London. The unemployed from the country were beginning to flock in for the mere sense of warmth. The British Museum, St. Paul's Cathedral, the free libraries, and other places where it was possible to escape from the dreadful rigour of the streets, were crowded by day. At night long queues of miserable creatures haunted the grids of restaurants, the sheltered sides of theatres, the windows of printing houses, and any spot where a little warmth exhaled. On the nights of the 4th, the 5th, and the 6th of December the thermometer on Primrose Hill registered 3° below zero. On the 7th pheasants were observed feeding among the pigeons in the main street of Highgate, and from that time onwards wild birds of the rarer kinds were no unusual sight in the London parks and about the public buildings. In the country it was remarked that the small birds had begun to disappear, and the curious might read any morning of frozen goldfinches being picked up in Camberwell, larks about Victoria Park, and starlings, robins, blackbirds, and such like fry everywhere. By this time dairymen had discovered that it was impossible to deliver milk unless they carried a brazier of live charcoal on their cart or hand-truck. Local correspondents in the provinces had ceased to report ordinary cases of death from cold and exposure; there were cases in the streets of London every night.

Early in December Sir John Hampden was approached unofficially by a few members of Parliament, including one or two of minor official rank, to learn his "terms." The suggestions were tentative on both sides, and nothing was stated definitely. But out of the circumlocution it might be inferred that he expressed his willingness to rescind the boycott, and to devote five million pounds to public relief at once, in return for certain modifications of the franchise and an immediate dissolution. Nothing came of the movement, and during the first week of December the Government sent round to the post-offices and to all the Crown tax collectors notices that the licences ordinarily falling due on the 1st of January must be taken out on or before the 15th of the current month, and the King's Taxes similarly collected in advance. The League did not make any open comment on this departure, but every member merely ignored it, and when the 16th of December was reached, it devolved upon the officers of the Crown to enforce the payment by legal process. In the language of another age, the Government was faced by five million "Passive Resisters." It soon became apparent that instead of getting in the taxes a fortnight before their time, the greater part of the revenue from that source would be delayed at least a month later than usual.

On the 20th of December one million and three-quarters State-supported unemployed of various grades presented themselves at the appointed trades unions committee rooms, workhouse offices, employment bureaux, Treasury depôts, from which the Fund was administered, to receive their weekly "wage." As they passed in they were confronted by a formal notice to the effect that the disbursement was then reduced to half its usual amount. As they passed out they came upon another formal notice to the effect that after the following week the Grant would be "temporarily suspended." Possibly that also embodied an idea of "breaking it gently."

The cry of surprise, rage, and terrified foreboding that rose from every town and village of the land when the direful news was at length understood, can never be described. Its echoes were destined to roll through the pages of English history for many a generation. The immediate result was that rioting broke out in practically all parts of the country except the purely agricultural. The people who had been promised a perpetual life of milk and honey had "murmured" when they were offered bread and water. Now there seemed every prospect of the water reaching them as ice,

159

and the bread-board being empty, and their "murmuring" took a sharper edge. In some places there were absolute stampedes of reason. In justice it has to be remembered that by this time the most pitiless winter of modern times had been heaping misery on misery for a month, that the chance of finding work or relief was recognised to be the forlornest hope, and that very, very few had a reserve of any kind.

The indiscriminate disturbances of the 20th of December were easily suppressed. A people that has been free for generations loses the gift for successful rioting in the face of armed discipline, even of the most inadequate strength. But for constitutional purposes the body of one dragooned rioter in England was worth more than a whole "Vladimir's battue" east of the Baltic.

On the 27th of December the certified unemployed drew their diminished pittance for the last time. They left the buildings in many places with the significant threat that they would return that day week, and if there was nothing for them would "warm their hands" there at the least. There was renewed rioting that day also. The forces of law and order had been strengthened; the rioters appeared to have been better organised. In one or two towns the rioting began to approach the Continental level. Bolton was said to have proved itself far from amateurish, and Nuneaton was spoken of as being distinctly promising. At the end of that day public buildings had to be requisitioned in several places to lay out the spoils of victory and defeat.

Two days later every newspaper contained an "open letter" from Sir John Hampden to the Government, in which he unconditionally offered them, on behalf of the Unity League and in the name of humanity, sufficient funds to pay the half grant for four weeks longer. It was a humane offer, but its proper name was strategy. It embarrassed the Government to decide whether to accept or decline. It embarrassed them if they accepted, and if they declined it embarrassed them most of all. They declined; or, to be precise, they ignored the offer.

By this time England might be said to be under famine. London, in its ice-bound straits, began curiously to assume the appearance of a mediæval city. By night one might meet grotesquely clad bands of revellers returning from some ice carnival (for the Thames had long been frozen from the Tower to Gravesend) by the light of lanterns and torches which they carried. None but those who had nothing to lose ventured out into the streets at night except by companies. Thieves and bludgeoners lurked in every archway, and arrests were seldom made; beggars importuned with every wile and in every tone, and new fantastic creeds and extravagant new

160

parties sent out their perfervid disciples to proclaim Utopias at every corner.

To add to the terror of the night there suddenly sprang into prominence the bands of "Running Madmen" who swept through the streets like fallen leaves in an autumn gale. Barefooted, gaunt, and wildly dressed in rags, they broke upon the astonished wayfarer's sight, and passed out again into the gloom before he could ask himself what strange manner of men they were. Never alone, seldom exceeding a score in any band, they ran keenly as though with some purposeful end in view, for the most part silently, but now and then startling the quiet night with an inarticulate wail or a cry of woe or lamentation, but they turned from street to street in aimless intricacy, and sought no definite goal. They were never seen by day, and whence they came or where they had their homes none could say, but the steady increase in the number of their bands showed that they were undoubtedly the victims of a contagious mania such as those that have appeared in the past from time to time.

Almost as ragged and unkempt was the army that by day marched under the standard of Brother Ambrose towards the sinless New Jerusalem. Reading the abundant signs all round with an inspired and fatalistic eye, Ambrose uncompromisingly announced that all the portents of the Millennium were now fulfilled, and that the reign of temporal power on earth was at an end. Each day his eloquence mounted to a wilder flight, each day he dreamed new dreams and saw fresh visions, and promised to his followers more definitely the spoil of victory, and parcelled out the smiling, fruitful land. Drawn by every human passion, recruits poured into his ranks, and when he marched in tattered state to mark the boundaries of the impending Golden City, the Legions of the Chosen rolled not in their thousands, but in their tens of thousands, singing hymns and interspersing ribaldry.

A very different spectacle was afforded by the bands of the Gilded Youth which by day patrolled the approaches to houses of the better class, wherever smoke had been seen issuing from the chimneys, and by night with equal order and thoroughness turned out the public gas lamps in the streets, until many of the authorities at last gave up the lighting of the lamps as a useless formality.

It was impossible for the occupants of a house that had incurred their enmity to have them removed by force, or to maintain an attitude of unconcern in the face of their demonstration, yet everything they did came under the term of "Peaceful Picketing" within the provisions of the Act, and an attempt to fix responsibility upon the Unity League for the high-handed action of its agents in a few cases where the Gilded Youth had gone beyond their powers, failed ignominiously through the precedent afforded by the final settlement of the celebrated Tawe Valley Case.

In the provinces the rioters were burning coal, burning coal-pits, smashing machinery and destroying property indiscriminately, blind to the fact that some of the immediate effects were falling on their fellow-workmen, and that most of the ultimate effects would fall upon themselves. In London and elsewhere the bands of the Gilded Youth were going quietly and systematically about their daily work, "peacefully" terrorising house-holders into submission, and carefully turning out the public lamps at night as soon as they were lit. To the reflective mind it was rather a dreadful power that the time had called into being: an educated mob that "rioted peacefully" and did nothing at all that was detrimental to its own interest.

Each morning people assured one another that so unparalleled a frost could last no longer, but each night the air seemed to be whetted to a keener edge, and each day there came fresh evidences of its power. Early in January it was computed that all the small birds that had not taken refuge in towns were dead, partly through the cold itself, but equally by starvation, for the ground yielded them nothing, and the trees and shrubs upon which they had been able to rely for food in former winters had long since perished. There were none but insignificant hollies to be seen in English gardens for the next generation, and in exposed situations forest trees and even oaks were split down to the ground.

All this time there was very little destructive rioting going on in London on any organised scale, but every night breadths of wood pavement were torn up by the homeless vagrants, who were now allowed to herd where they could, and great fires set burning at which the police warmed themselves and mingled supinely with the crowd. By day the police went in pairs, by night they patrolled in companies of five. For the emergency of serious rioting the military were always kept in readiness; against the more ordinary depredations on private property the owners were practically left to defend themselves. In those dark weeks watch duty became one of the regular occupations among the staff of every London business, and short shrift was given to intruders. Inquests went like marriages in busy churches at Easter-tide—in batches, and the morning cart that picked up the frozen dead had only one compartment.

The time was past when the effects of the vast disorganisation could be localised. Every trade and profession, every trivial and obscure calling, and every insignificant little offshoot of that great trunk called Commerce was involved in depression; it was not too much to say that every individual in the land was feeling some ill effect. Frantic legislation had begun it ten years before; the coal war had brought it to a climax, and the grip of the long, hard winter had pressed like a hostile hand upon the land.

It had resolved itself into a war of endurance. Coal was no longer the pivot; it was money, immediate money with which to buy bread at the bakers' shops, where they carried on their trade with the shutters up and loaded weapons laid out in the upper rooms.

Not the least curious feature of the struggle was the marked disinclination of the starving populace to pillage or bloodshed. Doubtless they saw that whatever they might individually profit by a reign of terror, their cause and party had nothing to gain from it. Such an outburst must inevitably react unfavourably upon the Government of the day, and it was their party then in power. But they had not the mob instinct in them; they were not composed of the ordinary mob element. In the bulk they were neither criminals nor hooligans, but matter-of-fact, disillusionised working men, and the instincts of their class have ever been steady and law-abiding. In Cheapside a gang of professional thieves blew out the iron shutter of a jeweller's shop with dynamite, and securing a valuable haul of jewellery in the momentary confusion, sought to hide themselves among the mob. Far from entering into their aspirations, the mob promptly conveyed them to the nearest police station, and returned to the owner the valuable articles that had been scattered about the street. The climax of the incident was reached by half a dozen of the most stalwart unemployed gladly accepting a few shillings each to guard the broken window until the shutter was repaired.

At the collieries, the mills, the workshops, and the seats of labour there were outrages against property, but away from the immediate centres there was neither cupidity nor resentment. Whenever disturbances of the kind took place they were invariably in pursuit of food or warmth. The men were dispirited, and by this time they regarded their cause as lost. Their leaders, in and out of Parliament, were classed either as incompetent generals in a war, or as traitors who had misled the people. The people only asked them now to make the terms of surrender so that they might live; and they did not hesitate to declare roundly that the old times when they had had to look after themselves more, and had not been body and soul at the disposal of semi-political Unions, were preferable on the whole.

The position of the Cabinet was daily growing more critical. Its chiefs were execrated and insulted whenever they were seen. All the approaches to the House were held by military guards, and the members reached its gates singly, and almost by stealth. Every day placards, written and printed, were found displayed in public places, calling on the Government that had no money to let in one that had. "You thought more of your position than of our needs when Hampden offered us help," ran one that Mr Strummery found nailed to his front door. "You have always thought more of your positions than of our needs. You have used our needs to raise yourselves to those positions. Now, since you no longer represent the wishes of the People, give way to others."

The delay of the Government in throwing up an utterly untenable position was inexplicable to most people. Many said that the reason was that Hampden refused to take office under the existing franchise, and no one but Hampden could form an administration in that crisis that could hope to live for a day. Whatever the reason might be, it was obvious that the Government was drifting towards a national tragedy that would be stupendous, for in less than a month's time, it was agreed on all hands, the daily tale of starved and famished dead would have reached its thousands.

Still the Government hung on, backed in sullen submission by its automatic majority. Changes in the Cabinet were of almost daily record, but the half dozen men of prominence remained. Cecil Brown was the last of the old minor men to be dropped. A dog trainer, who had taken up politics, succeeded him. "It is too late now," Cecil Brown was reported to have said when he learned who was to be his successor. "They want bread, not circuses!"

CHAPTER XVII

THE INCIDENT OF THE 13TH OF JANUARY

"I do not altogether like it," said A.

"Do you prefer to leave things as they are, then?" demanded B.

A. went over and stood by the window, looking moodily out.

"It is merely a necessity," said C.

"The necessity of a necessity," suggested D. happily.

"Perhaps you are not aware," said B., addressing himself to the man standing at the window, "that the suggestion of arresting Salt did not come from us in the first case."

"Is that so?" replied A., coming back into the room. "I certainly assumed that it did."

"On the contrary," explained B., "it was Inspector Moeletter who reported to his superiors that he had succeeded in identifying the mysterious man who was seen with Leslie Garnet, the artist, about the time of his death. He would have got his warrant in the ordinary way, only in view of the remarkable position that Salt occupies just now, Stafford very naturally communicated with us."

"The only point that troubles us," remarked C. reflectively, "is that none of us can persuade himself in the remotest degree that Salt killed Garnet."

"I certainty require to have the evidence before I can subscribe to that," said B. "The man who is daily killing hundreds—"

"Ah, that is the difference," commented D.

"Where are the Monmouth colliers now?" asked C., after a pause.

"Newbury, this morning," replied D. "Reading, to-night."

"And the Midland lot?"

"Towcester, I think."

"If Hampden formally asks for protection for the oil store at Hanwood, after the miners' threat to burn it, what are you going to do?" asked A.

"I should suggest telling him to go and boil himself in it, since he has got it there," replied C.

"There will be no need to tell him anything but the bare fact, and that is that with twenty-five thousand turbulent colliers pouring into London and adding to the disaffected element already here, we cannot spare a single man," replied B.

"I quite agree with that," remarked D., drawing attention to his freshly-scarred cheek. "I had a tribute of the mob's affection as I came in this morning."

"That's your popularity," said C. "Your photograph is so much about that no one has any difficulty in recognising you. How do you get on in that way, B.?"

"I?" exclaimed B. with a startled look. "Oh, I always drive with the blinds down now."

"Are any extra military coming in before Friday?" asked A.

"Yes, the Lancers from Hounslow. They come into the empty Albany Street Barracks to-night. Then I think that there are to be some extra infantry in Whitehall, from Aldershot. Cadman is seeing to all that."

"But you know that the Lancers are being drawn from Hounslow?" asked C. with a meaning laugh.

"Yes, I know that," admitted B. "Why do you laugh, C.?"

C.'s only reply was to laugh again.

"I will tell you why he laughs," volunteered D. "He laughs, B., because the Lancers withdrawn from Hounslow to Regent's Park, Salt under arrest at Stafford, and the Monmouth colliers coming along the Bath road and passing within a mile or two of Hanwood, represent the three angles of a very acute triangle."

"There is still Hampden," muttered B.

"Yes; what is going to happen to Hampden?" asked C., with a trace of his mordant amusement.

A., who was walking about the room aimlessly, stopped and faced the others.

"I'll tell you what," he exclaimed emphatically. "I said just now that I didn't like the idea of smuggling Salt away like this, and, although it may be advisable, I don't. But I wish to God that we had openly arrested the pair of them as traitors, and burned their diabolical store before every one's eyes three months ago."

"Ah," said D. thoughtfully, "it was too early then. Now it's too late."

"It may be too late to have its full effect," flashed out B., "but it won't be too late to make them suffer a bit along with our own people."

"Provided that the oil is burned," said D.

"Provided that no protection can be sent," remarked C.

"Provided that Salt is arrested," added A.

There was a knock at the door. It explained the attitude of the four men in the room and their scattered conversation. They had been awaiting some one.

He came into the room and saluted, a powerfully-built man with "uniform" branded on every limb, although he wore plain clothes then.

"Detective-Inspector Moeletter?" said B.

"Yes, sir," said the inspector, and stood at attention.

"You have the warrant?" continued B.

Moeletter produced it, and passed it in for inspection. It was made out on the preceding day, signed by the Stipendiary Magistrate of Stafford, and it connected George Salt with Leslie Garnet by the link of Murder.

"When you applied for this warrant," said B., looking hard at the inspector, "you considered that you had sufficient evidence to support it?"

Moeletter looked puzzled for a moment, as though the question was one that he did not quite follow in that form. For a moment he seemed to be on the verge of making an explanation; then he thought better of it, and simply replied: "Yes, sir."

166

"At all events," continued B. hastily, "you have enough evidence to justify a remand? What are the points?"

"We have abundant evidence that Salt was in the neighbourhood about the time of the tragedy; that fact can scarcely be contested. Coming nearer, an old man, who had been hedging until the storm drove him under a high bank, saw a gentleman enter Garnet's cottage about half-past five. Without any leading he described this man accurately as Salt, and picked out his photograph from among a dozen others. About an hour later, two boys, who were bird-nesting near Stourton Hill church, heard a shot. They looked through the hedge into the graveyard and saw one man lying apparently dead on the ground, and another bending over him as though he might be going through his pockets. Being frightened, they ran away and told no one of it for some time, as boys would. Of course, sir, that's more than six months ago now, but the description they give tallies, and I think that we may claim a strong presumption of identity taking into consideration the established time of Salt's arrival at Thornley."

"That is all?" said B.

"As regards identity," replied the inspector. "On general grounds we shall show that for some time before his death Garnet had been selling shares and securities which he held, and that although he lived frugally no money was found in the remains of his house or on his person, and no trace of a banking account or other investment can be discovered. Then we allege that 'George Salt' is not the man's right name, although we have not been able to follow that up yet. He is generally understood to have been a sailor recently, and the revolver found beside the body was of a naval pattern. I should add that the medical evidence at the inquest was to the effect that the wound might have been self-inflicted, but that the angle was unusual."

B. returned the warrant to the inspector.

"That will at least ensure a remand for a week for you to continue your investigations?"

"I think so, sir."

"Without bail?"

"If it is opposed."

"We oppose it, then. Did you bring any one down with you?"

Inspector Moeletter had not done so. He had not been able to anticipate what amended instructions he might receive in London, so he had thought it as well to come alone.

"For political reasons it is desirable that nothing should be known publicly of the arrest until you have your prisoner safely at Stafford," said B. "At present he is motoring in the southern counties. I have information that he will leave Farnham this afternoon between three and half-past and proceed direct to Guildford. Is there any reason why you should not arrest him between the two places?"

Inspector Moeletter knew of none.

"It will be preferable to doing so in either town from our point of view," continued B., "and it is not known whether he intends leaving Guildford to-night."

The inspector took out an innocent-looking pocket-book, whose elastic band was a veritable hangman's noose, and noted the facts.

"Is a description of the motor-car available?" he enquired.

B. picked up a sheet of paper. "It is a large car, a 30 H.P. Daimler, with a covered body, and painted in two shades of green," he read from the paper. "The number is L.N. 7246."

"I would suggest bringing him straight on in the car," said Moeletter. "It would obviate the publicity of railway travelling."

B. nodded. "There is another thing," he said. "It is absolutely necessary to avoid the London termini. They are all watched systematically by agents of the League—spies who call themselves patriots. You will take the 7.30 train with your prisoner, but you will join it at Willesden. I will have it stopped for you."

"I shall need a man who can drive the motor to go down with me," the detective reminded him.

B. struck a bell. "Send Sergeant Tolkeith in," he said to the attendant.

Sergeant Tolkeith was apparently being kept ready in the next room, to be slipped at the fall of the flag, so to speak. He came in very smartly.

"You will remain with Inspector Moeletter while he is in London, and make all the necessary arrangements for him," instructed B. "I suppose that there are men at Scotland Yard available now who can drive every kind of motor?"

Sergeant Tolkeith hazarded the opinion that there were men at Scotland Yard at that moment who could drive—he looked round the room in search of some strange or Titanic vehicle to which the prowess of Scotland Yard would be equal—"Well, Anything."

"A man who knows the roads," continued B. "Though, for that matter, it's a simple enough route—the Portsmouth road all the way to Kingston, and then across to Willesden. You had better avoid Guildford, by the way, coming back. Now, what other assistance will you require?"

"How many are there likely to be in the car, sir?"

"No one but Salt, I am informed. He has been touring alone for a week past, at all events."

"In that case, sir, we had better take a couple of men from Guildford and drive towards Farnham. We can wait at a suitable place in the road and make the arrest. Then when the irons are on I shall need no one beyond the driver I take with me. The two local men—you'll want Mr Salt's chauffeur detained for a few hours, I suppose, sir?"

"Yes, certainly; until you are well on your way. And any one else who may happen to be in the car. I will give you authority covering that."

"The two local men can take him, or them, back to Guildford—it will be dark by the time they get there—for detention while enquiries are being made. Then if a plain-clothes man meets me at Willesden we can go on, and our driver can take the car on to Scotland Yard."

"You see no difficulty throughout?" said B. anxiously. The inspector assured him that all seemed plain sailing. It was not his place to foresee difficulties in B.'s plans.

"Then I shall expect you to report to me from Stafford about 10.30 to-night that everything is satisfactory. Let me impress on you as a last word the need of care and unconcern in this case. It must be successfully carried out, and to do that there must be no fuss or publicity."

"Sergeant," said Detective-Inspector Moeletter, when they were outside, "between ourselves, can you tell me this: why they think it necessary to have three mute gentlemen looking on while we arrange a matter of this sort?"

"Between ourselves, sir," replied Sergeant Tolkeith, looking cautiously around, "it's my belief that it's come to this: that they are all half-afraid of themselves and can't trust one another."

"D.," remarked C., as they left together a few minutes later, "does anything strike you about B.?"

"It strikes me that he looks rather like an undertaker's man when he is dressed up," replied D.

"Does it not strike you that he is afraid?"

"Oh," admitted D., stroking his wounded cheek, "that's quite possible. So am I, for that matter."

"So may we all be in a way," said C.; "but it is different with him. I believe that he is in a blue funk. He's fey, and he's got Salt on the brain. Just remember that I venture on this prophecy: if Salt through any cause does not happen to get arrested, B. will throw up the sponge."

The office of the Unity League in Trafalgar Chambers was

169

little more than an empty hive now. The headquarters of the operations had been transferred to the colony at Hanwood, and most of the staff had followed. With the declaration of the coal war, an entirely different set of conditions had come into force. The old offices had practically become a clearing house for everything connected with the League, and the high tide of active interest swept on elsewhere.

Miss Lisle remained, a person of some consequence, but in her heart she sighed from time to time for a sphere of action "down another little lane."

On the afternoon of the 13th of January she returned to the office about half-past three, and going to the instrument room unlocked the telescribe receiver-box and proceeded to sort the dozen communications which it contained—the accumulation of an hour—before passing them on to be dealt with. Most fell into clearly-defined departments at a glance. It was not until she reached the last, the earliest sent, that she read it through, but as she read that her whole half-listless, mechanical manner changed. With the first line apathy fell from her like a cloak; before she had finished, every limb and feature conveyed a sense of tingling excitement. In frantic haste she dragged the special writing materials across the table towards her, dashed off a sprawling, "Stop Mr Salt at any cost.—Lisle," and flashed it off to the League agency at Farnham.

A couple of minutes must pass before she could get any reply. She picked up the cause of her excitement, and for the second time read the message it contained:

"If you want to keep your Mr Salt from being arrested on a charge of murder, warn him that Inspector Moeletter from Stafford will be waiting for him on the road between Farnham and Guildford at three o'clock this afternoon with a warrant. No one believes in it, but he will be taken on in his motor to Willesden, and on to Stafford by the 7.30, and kept out of the way for a week while things have time to happen at Hanwood. There will be just enough evidence to get a remand, as there was to get a warrant. This is from a friend, who may remind you of it later and prove who he is by this sign."

The letter finished with a rough drawing of a gallows and a broken rope. It was written in a cramped, feigned hand and addressed to Sir John Hampden. It might have been lying in the box for an hour.

The telescribe bell gave its single note. Irene opened the box in feverish dread. An exclamation of despair broke from her lips as some words on the paper stood out in the intensity of their significance even before she took the letter from the box.

This was what Farnham replied:

"Hope nothing is the matter. Mr Salt left here quite half an hour ago, in his motor, for Guildford. He will stay there the night, or proceed to Hanwood according to the time he is occupied. Please let me know if there is any trouble."

Half an hour! There was not the remotest chance of intercepting him. Already, under ordinary circumstances, he would be in the outskirts of Guildford. It only remained to verify the worst. She wrote a brief message asking Mr Salt if he would kindly communicate with her immediately on his arrival, and despatched it to the agency at Guildford. If there was no reply to that request during the next half-hour she would accept the arrest as an established fact. And there being nothing apparently to do for the next half-hour, Miss Lisle, very much to the surprise of ninety-nine out of her hundred friends could they have seen her, went down on her knees in the midst of a roomful of the latest achievements of science and began to pray that a miracle might happen.

"I suppose that I may smoke?" said Salt. He was sitting handcuffed in his own motor-car, charged with murder, and formally cautioned that anything he should say might be used as evidence against him. It was scarcely a necessary warning in his case; with the exception of an equally formal protest against the arrest, he had not opened his lips until now. He and Moeletter had sat silently facing one another in the comfortably-appointed, roomy car, Salt with his face to the driver and leaning back in his easy seat with outward unconcern, the detective braced to a more alert attitude and with his knees almost touching those of his prisoner. For a mile or more—for perhaps seven or eight minutes by time, for the new driver was cautious with the yet unknown car—they had proceeded thus.

Yet Salt was very far from being unconcerned as he leaned back negligently among the cushions. He was thinking keenly, and with the settled, tranquil gaze that betrayed nothing, watching alertly the miles of dreary high-road that stretched along the Hog's Back before them. He had long foreseen the possibility of arrest, and he had taken certain precautions; but to safeguard himself effectually he would have had to abandon the more important part of his work, and the risk he ran was the smaller evil of the two. But he had not anticipated this charge. Some legal jugglery with "conspiracy" had been in his mind.

"I suppose that I may smoke?" Half a mile ahead a solitary wayfarer was approaching. Salt might have noted him, but there was nothing remarkable in his appearance except that pedestrians— or vehicles either, for that matter—were rare along the Hog's Back on that bitter winter afternoon.

171

"Why, certainly, sir; in your own car, surely," replied the inspector agreeably. He was there to do his duty, and he had done it, even down to the detail of satisfying himself by search that his prisoner carried no weapon. Beyond that there was no reason to be churlish, especially as every one had to admit that there was no telling what might have happened in a week's or a month's time. "Can I help you in any way?"

"Thank you, I will manage," replied Salt, and in spite of his manacles he succeeded without much difficulty in taking out his cigarette-case and a match-box. He lit a cigarette, blew out the match, and then looked hesitatingly round the rather elegant car, at the rich velvety carpet on the floor, at the half-burned vesta in his hand. Then with easy unconcern he lowered the window by his side and leaned forward towards it.

It was a perfectly natural action, but Inspector Moeletter owed at least one step in his promotion to a habit of always being on his guard against natural-seeming actions of that kind. His left foot quickly and imperceptibly slid across the carpet, so that if Salt made any ill-judged attempt to leave the car he must inevitably come to grief across that rigid barrier; with a ready eye Moeletter noted afresh the handle of the door, the size of the window frame, and every kindred detail. His hands lay in unostentatious readiness by his side, and he felt no apprehension.

But Salt had not the faintest intention of attempting any sensational act. He dropped the match leisurely from between his fingers, cast a glance up to the sky, where the lowering clouds had long been threatening snow, and then drew in his head. But in some way, either from his position, a jolt of the car, or a touch against the sash, as he did so his cap was jerked off, and, despite a quick but clumsy attempt to catch it in his fettered hands, it was whirled away behind in their eddying wake.

"Please stop," he said, turning to Moeletter. "I am afraid that I shall find it too cold without."

The detective was not pleased, but there was nothing in the mishap that he could take objection to. Further, he had no wish to make his prisoner in any way noticeable during the latter part of their journey. "Pull up, Murphy," he called through the tube by his shoulder, and with a grinding that set its owner's teeth on edge, the car came to a standstill in two lengths.

Moeletter had intended that the driver should recover the cap, but he was saved the trouble. The solitary pedestrian had happened to be on the spot at the moment of the incident, and he was standing by the open window almost as soon as the car stopped. Forgetful of his indignity, Salt stretched out a manacled hand and received his property. "Thank you," he said with a pleasant smile. "I am much obliged."

"Go on," said Moeletter, through the tube.

"I think that I had better get used to these—'darbies' is the professional name, is it not, Inspector?—to these 'darbies' before I look out again," remarked Salt good-humouredly.

The telescribe bell announced another message. It found Irene sitting at the table in the instrument room with ordnance maps around her and the index book of the League's most trusted agents lying open on the shelf. She just glanced at the clock as she jumped up. It was 4.15, exactly the last minute of the half-hour that she had fixed as the limit of uncertainty. The message might even yet be from Salt. But it was not; it was this instead:

"Fear Mr Salt has been arrested. He is in his motor-car, handcuffed, proceeding towards Guildford, in charge of man who has appearance of belonging to police force. Driver is not Mr Salt's man. Mr S. made opp. for me to see sit., but said nothing. Passed just W. of Puttenham 3.55. Roads good, but snow beginning. Car trav only 10-12 m. hour. Shall remain here on chance being use. Don't hesitate."

A hall-formed plan was already floating in the space between Miss Lisle's adventurous brain and the maps. The Puttenham message crystallised it. There was now something to go on. The route she knew already; the times and mileages also lay beneath her hand. The scheme had a hundred faults, and only one thing to recommend it—that it might succeed. For ten minutes she flung herself into the details of the maps, jotting down a time, a distance, here and there a detail of the road. "Puttenham" might remain at his box till dawn, but all the work, all the chance, was forward—before the car. At the end of ten minutes Irene picked up the accumulation of her labours and rang up the telephone exchange.

"What is it, Murphy?" demanded the inspector through the tube, as the car came to a dead stop. "Something else in the way?"

"I can't quite make it out, sir," was the reply. "We're just outside the long railway arch, and there seems to be something on fire towards the other end. Terrible lot of smoke coming through."

"Can't we run up to it?"

"This is an unusually long bridge—fifty or sixty yards, I should say. I hardly like to take you on into that smoke, sir."

"Oh, very well. Jump down and see what it is. Only be as sharp as you can."

It was now pitch dark, and a driving, biting storm of snow and hail was blowing across their path from the east. When the constable-chauffeur had learned sufficient of the car to give him

173

confidence, the storm had swept down, and their progress had been scarcely any faster. There had been delays, too. By Ripley a heavy farm waggon had broken down almost before their eyes, and it had been ten minutes before a spare chain horse could be obtained to drag it to the roadside. Further on some men felling a tree in a coppice had clumsily allowed it to fall across the road, and another ten minutes elapsed before it was cut in two and rolled aside. Fortunately they were not pressed for time. Fortunately, also, the driver knew the way, for few people were afoot to face that dreadful stream of snow and ice with the lashing wind and the numbing cold. Two, two or three, or perhaps four men had chanced to be at hand when the car stopped, making their way towards the bridge, but the wreathing snow soon cut them off. Occasionally, when the wind and drift hung for a moment, a figure or two showed dimly and gigantic in the murk of the tunnel. Nothing of the fire could be seen, but the smoke continued to pour out, and the mingled odour of burned and unburned oil filled the car.

In a few minutes the driver returned. When he had left his seat Moeletter had leaned forward, and with a gruff word of half apology had laid a hand upon the rug across Salt's knees, so that he held, or at least controlled, the connecting links of the handcuffs, while at the same time his other hand had dropped quietly down to his hip-pocket. He now lowered the window on the further side, still keeping his left hand on the rug.

"Oil cart ablaze, sir," gasped the driver, between paroxysms of coughing. "Road simply running fire, and the fumes awful." His face was almost completely protected beneath cap, goggles, and a storm shade that fell from the cap over the shoulders and buttoned across the mouth, but no covering had seemed effectual against the suffocating reek of the burning oil. The fire had melted the snow off his clothes, and he stood by the door with a bar of darkness just falling across his face, and the electric light through the lowered window blazing upon his gleaming leathers, his gauntlets and puttee leggings, and the cumbrous numbered badge that the regulations then imposed.

"It will be some time before the road is passable?" asked Moeletter with a frown.

"Oh, hours perhaps," was the sputtering reply. "Would suggest going by Molesey Bridge, sir. Best way now."

"Is it much out?"

"The turning is half a mile back. From there it is no further than this way."

"And you know the way perfectly?"

The driver nodded. "Perfectly, sir."

174

"Very well; go on. We have plenty of time yet, but you might get a few more miles out of her, if you think you can."

The driver jumped up to his seat, the horn gave its bull-like note of warning, and gliding round the car began to head back towards Esher with the open common on either side and the pelting wind behind. It slackened for a moment at the fork in the high-road, turned to the right, and then began to draw away northward with an increased speed that showed the driver to be capable of rising to his instructions.

"It is fortunate that the inspector is not a motoring man," thought Salt to himself with an inward smile. "This is very much too good." But the inspector only noticed that with the increased speed the car seemed to run more smoothly, and even then he had no means of judging what the increase had become. The man whose car it was knew that a very different explanation than mere speed lay behind the sudden change that made the motion now sheer luxury. He knew with absolute conviction what had happened, and he would have known without any further evidence that the driver who now had his hand upon the wheel was a thousand miles ahead of constable-chauffeur Murphy in motor-craft.

It was not the first suggestion of some friendly influence at work that had stirred his mind. The incident of the stranded waggon across the road by Ripley was little in itself. Even when they were a second time delayed by the fallen tree a few miles further on nothing but an unreasoning hope could have called it more than coincidence. But with the third episode a matured plan began to loom through the meaningless delays. Oil was here, and where there was oil in England at that day the hand of the Unity League might be traced not far away. In his mind's eye Salt ran over half a dozen miles of the Portsmouth road. As far as he could remember, if it was intended to block the road there was scarcely a more suitable spot than the long railway bridge to be found between Esher and Kingston, and, followed the thought, if it was intended to force Moeletter to accept the bridge at Molesey, no point in all the high-road south of the fork would have served.

The three accidents had taken place each at the exact point where it would best serve its purpose.

Salt did not even glance at the driver when he returned from the fire. He leaned back in his seat in simple enjoyment, and Inspector Moeletter thought from his appearance that he was going to sleep.

There was little to be gained by looking out, apart from the policy of unconcern. The huge white motor-car that was waiting in the cross-road by Esher station had its head-lights masked, and in the snow-storm and the night it could not have been seen ten yards away. The driver of the green car sounded his horn for the road as he swept by, and ten seconds later the white car glided out from its place of concealment like a ghostly mastodon, and, baring its dazzling lamps, began to thrash along the road in the other's wake.

What would be their route when they had crossed the bridge? That was Salt's constant thought now, not because he was troubled by the chances, but because it was the next point in the unknown plan that would serve to guide him. He had not long to wait under the dexterous pilotage of the unknown hand outside. The flat, straight road became a tortuous village street, the lights of the Molesey shops and inns splashed in splintering blurs across the streaming windows, an iron bridge shook and rumbled beneath their wheels, and they were in Middlesex.

The horn brayed out a continuous warning note, the car swung off to the left, and Salt, with his eyes closed, knew exactly what had been arranged.

But there was yet Inspector Moeletter to be reckoned with. He was ignorant of the roads, but he had a well-developed gift of location, and the abrupt turn to the left when he had seen what appeared to be a broad high-road leading straight on from Molesey Bridge, gave him a moment's thought. He turned to the speaking-tube.

"Are you sure that this is right, Murphy?" he asked sharply. "Kingston must lie away on the right."

"We go through Hampton this way, sir, and into the Kingston road at Twickenham," came the chattering reply in a half-frozen voice. "It is just as near, and we don't meet the wind."

It was quite true, although the inspector might not know it, but the ready explanation seemed to satisfy him. Another circumstance would have set his mind at rest. At Hampton the route took them equally to the right. Salt did not know the road intimately, but he knew that if his surmise was correct, they must very soon draw away to the left again. What would happen then? For three or four miles they would run between hedges and encounter nothing more urban than a scattered hamlet. Twickenham they would never see that night. Inspector Moeletter was far from being unsophisticated, and his suspicion had already once, apparently, been touched. How would the race end?

The car slowed down for a moment, but so smoothly that it was almost imperceptible, and with a clanging bell an electric tram swung into their vision and out again. Salt was taking note of every trifle in this enthralling game. Why, he asked himself, had so expert a driver slackened speed with plenty of room to pass? He saw a possible explanation. They had been meeting and overtaking trams at intervals all the way from Molesey Bridge. In another minute they would have left the high-road and the tram route, and the driver wished to hide the fact from Moeletter as long as possible. He had therefore waited to meet this tram so that the inspector might unconsciously carry in his mind the evidence of their presence to the last possible point.

They were no longer on the high-road; they had glided off somewhere without a warning note or any indication of speed or motion to betray the turn they had taken. The houses were becoming sparser, fields intervened, with here and there a strung-out colony of cottages. Soon even the scattered buildings ceased, or appeared so rarely that they only dotted long stretches of country lanes, and at every yard they trembled on the verge of detection. Nothing but the glare of light inside the vehicle and the storm and darkness beyond could have hid for a moment from even the least suspicious of men the fact that they were no longer travelling even the most secluded of suburban high-roads. And now, as if aware that the deception could not be maintained much longer, the driver began to increase the speed at every open stretch. Again nothing but his inspired skill and the perfectly-balanced excellence of the car could disguise the fact that they flew along the level road; while among the narrow winding lanes they rushed at a headlong pace, shooting down declines and breasting little hills without a pause. The horn boomed its warning every second, and from behind came the answering note of the long white motor. It had crept nearer and nearer since they left the high-road, and its brilliant head-lights now lit up the way as far as the pilot car. Little chance for Moeletter to convoy his prisoner out of those deserted lanes whatever happened now!

What means, what desperate means, he might have taken in a gallant attempt to retrieve the position if he had suspected treachery just a minute before he did, one may speculate but never know.

As it was, the uneasy instinct that everything was not right awoke too late for him to make the stand. It was less than ten minutes after meeting the last tram that he peered out into the night doubtfully, but in those ten minutes the green car had all but won its journey's end.

"Murphy," he cried imperiously, with his mouth to the tube and a startled eye on Salt, "tell me immediately where we are."

"A minute, sir," came the hasty answer, as the driver bent forward to verify some landmark. "This brake——

"Stop this instant!" roared the inspector, rising to his feet in rage and with a terrible foreboding.

177

There was a muffled rattle as they shot over a snow-laden bridge, a curious sense of passing into a new atmosphere, and then with easy precision the car drew round and stopped dead before the open double doors of its own house. No one spoke for a moment. There was another muffled roar outside, the sound of heavy iron doors clashing together, and the great white car reproduced their curve and drew up by their side.

From the driver's seat of the green car the Hon. Bruce Wycombe, son and heir of old Viscount Chiltern and the most skilful motorist in Europe, climbed painfully down, and, pulling off his head-gear, opened the door of the car with a bow that would have been more graceful if he had been less frozen.

"Welcome to Hanwood after your long journey, Inspector Moeletter!" he exclaimed most affably.

CHAPTER XVIII

THE MUSIC AND THE DANCE

Along the great west road, ten thousand Monmouth colliers were streaming towards London, in every stage of famine and discomfort. What they intended to do when they reached the Capital they had no clearer idea than had the fifteen thousand Midlanders at Barnet. All they knew was that they were starving at home, and they could be no worse off in London. Also in London there was to be found the Government, the Government that had betrayed them.

The conception of the march had been wild, the execution was lamentable. The leaders might have taken Napoleon's descent on Moscow as their model. Ten hand-carts exhausted their commissariat. They were to live on the land they passed through; but the land was agricultural and poor, the populace regarded the Monmouth colliers as foreigners, and the response was scanty. Only one circumstance saved the march from becoming a tragedy of hundreds instead of merely, as it was, a tragedy of scores.

The men were being fed from London. By whom, and why, not even their leaders knew, but each night a railway truck full of provisions was awaiting their arrival at a station on their route, and each day the men's leader-in-chief was informed where the next supply would be. It influenced them to continue their journey pacifically when they must otherwise, sooner or later, have abandoned all restraint and marched through anarchy. It enabled them to reach London. It added another element to the Government's distraction in their day of reckoning. It was a Detail.

But at Windsor there were no provisions waiting. No one knew why. The station authorities had nothing to suggest. After a week's regular supply the leaders had come to expect their daily truck-load, had come to rely implicitly upon it, and had made no other arrangements. They conferred together anxiously; it was all there was for them to do. Windsor was not sympathetic towards them. They had not expected it to be, but they had expected to be independent of Windsor's friendship. Two thousand special constables escorted them in and shepherded them assiduously. Otherwise there might have been disturbances, for a Castle guard comprised the extent of Windsor's military resources then. As it was, the miners reached the Royal Borough hungry, and left it famished. A rumour spread along the ranks as they set out that an unfortunate mistake had been made, but that supplies would be awaiting them in Hyde Park.

If that was a detail, as it might well have been, it was not wholly successful. The men were hungry and dispirited, but London was not their immediate goal. For weeks they had been telling the vacillating Cabinet what ought to be done with the oil at Hanwood, and as they set out they had boasted to their brothers across the Rhymney that before they returned they would show them how to fire a beacon that would singe the hair of five million Leaguers. Midway between Windsor and London they proceeded to turn off from the highway under the direction of their leaders, and debouching from the narrow lanes on to the fields beyond, they began to advance across the country in a straggling, far-flung wave.

On the previous day both the Home Office and the War Office had received applications for protection from the Company at Hanwood, backed by evidence which left no possible doubt that the Monmouth unemployed contemplated an organised attack on the oil store. The two departments replied distantly, that in view of the existing conditions within the Metropolis and the forces at their disposal, it was impossible to despatch either troops or constabulary to protect private property in isolated districts. Hanwood acknowledged these replies, and gave notice with equal punctilio that they would take the best means within their power for safeguarding their interests, and at the same time formally notified the Government that they held them responsible, through their failure to carry out the obligations of their office, for all the

179

developments that the situation might lead to—an exchange of civilities which in private life is sometimes attained much more simply by two disputants consigning each other to the society of the Prince of Darkness in four words.

Whatever there might be behind the intimation, there was little to indicate it at dusk that afternoon. The stranger or the native passing along Miss Lisle's secluded lane would have noticed only two circumstances to suggest anything unusual in the air.

A few hundred feet above the trees within the wall, a box-kite was straining at its rope in the rising gale. From the basket car a man watched every movement of the countryside through his field-glasses, and conversed from time to time through a telephone with the kite section down below. A second wire ran from the field telephone to a room of the offices where Salt was engaged with half a dozen of the chiefs of the Council of the League. Sir John Hampden was not present. He was remaining in London to afford the Government every facility for negotiating a settlement whenever they might desire it.

In the lane, a group of men with tickets in their hats were loitering about the bridge. They comprised a Peaceful Picket within the meaning of the Act. They had been there since daybreak, and so far no one had shown any wish to dispute their position.

The war-kite and the picket in the lane were the "eyes" of the opposing belligerents.

The League had nothing to gain by submitting the issue to the arbitrament of lead and fire. No one had anything to gain by it, but after a bout at fisticuffs a defeated child will sometimes pick up a dangerous stone and fling it. The League had accepted the challenge of those who marched beneath the red banner for war on constitutional lines. Some of those who marched beneath the red banner were now disposed to try the effect of beating their ploughshares into swords, and however much the League might have preferred them to keep to their bargain, the most effective retort was to turn their own pacific sickles into bayonets.

In the staff room Salt was addressing his associates—half military, half political—who now represented the innermost Council of the League. Some of them had been members of former Ministries, others soldiers who had worn the insignia of generals, but they rendered to this unknown man among them an unquestioning allegiance, because of what he had already done, because he inspired them with absolute reliance in what he would yet succeed in doing, and, not least, because he had the air that fitted the position.

"More than two years ago," he was saying, "the first draft of

180

the formation and operations of the League contained a section much to the following effect:

"'It is an essential feature of the plan that the League should work on constitutional lines from beginning to end and in contemplation of bringing about the desired reforms without firing a solitary shot or violating a single law.

"'Nevertheless, it is inevitable that when the position becomes acute civil disorders will arise out of the involved situation, and demonstrations of the affected people will threaten the Government of the day on the one hand and the proposed League on the other.

"'In these circumstances it will be prudent to contemplate, as a last phase of the struggle, an organised military attack on the property of the League, masked under the form of a popular riot, but instigated or connived at by responsible authorities. I propose, therefore, to establish the League stores in a position naturally suited for defence, and to adopt such further precautions as will render them secure against ordinary attack.'

"We have now reached that closing phase of the struggle," continued Salt. "On the evidence of this report from Sir John Hampden we may assume that within twenty-four hours our aggressive work will be over. Will our opponents, in the language of the street, 'go quietly'?"

"It has fallen to my lot to read the Riot Act on three occasions," said one of the company, "and I have seen disturbances in Ireland; but I have never before known an unorganised mob to surround a position completely and then to sit down to wait for night."

"Lieutenant Vivash wishes to speak to Mr Salt personally," said a subordinate, appearing at the door.

Salt stepped into the ante-room, and spoke through the telephone.

"Yes, Vivash," he said to the man in the kite a quarter of a mile away. "What is it?"

"Two general service wagons with bridge-making tackle have just been brought up, and are waiting in Welland Wood," reported Vivash. "There is a movement among the colliers over Barfold Rise. With them are about two hundred men carrying rifles. They are not in uniform, but they march."

Salt turned to another instrument and jerked the switch rapidly from plate to plate as he distributed his orders.

"Captain Norris, strengthen the Territorials at the outer wire North."

"Send up two star rockets to recall the motor-cycle scouts."

"Tell Disturnal to have the searchlights in immediate readiness."

"Fire brigade, full strength, turn out with chemical engine, and stand under earthwork cover at central tank."

He turned again to the kite telephone to ask Vivash a detail. There was no response.

"Get on with Lieutenant Vivash as soon as you can, and let me know at once," he said to the one who was in charge, as he returned to the staff room.

In less than a minute the operator was at the door again.

"I am afraid there is something the matter, sir," he explained. "I can get no reply either from Lieutenant Vivash or from the kite section."

"Ring up the despatch room. Let some one go at once to Mr Moore and return here with report."

"Yes, sir." He turned to go. "Here is Mr Moore," he exclaimed, standing aside from the door.

They all read some disaster in his face as he entered.

"I am deeply sorry to say that Lieutenant Vivash has been shot."

"Is he seriously hurt?" asked some one.

"He is dead. He was shot through the head by a marksman in Welland Wood."

Salt broke the shocked silence.

"We have lost a brave comrade," he said simply. "Come, General Trench, let us visit the walls."

It was dark when they returned. Salt passed through the room, calling to his side the man with whom he had been most closely associated at Hanwood, and traversing some passages led the way up a winding staircase into the lantern of the tower. Here, under the direction of an ex-officer of Royal Engineers, two powerful searchlights were playing on every inch of doubtful ground that lay within their radius beyond the entanglement that marked the outer line of the defences.

Nothing had been seen; not a solitary invader had yet shown himself within the zone of light. The officer in charge was explaining a technical detail of the land when, without the faintest warning, a fulgent blaze of light suddenly ran along the edge of a coppice half a mile away, and a noise like the crackling of a hundred new-lit fires drifted on the wind. With the echo, a thick hedge to the east and a wood lying on the west joined in the vicious challenge. A few bullets splashed harmlessly against the steel shield that ingeniously protected the lantern.

The searchlights oscillated uncertainly from sky to earth

under the shock of the surprise, and then settled down to stream unwinkingly into the eyes of the enemy, while in the double darkness the defenders hugged the earth behind the wire and began to reply with cool deliberation to the opening volleys.

There was a knock upon the door of the little lantern room, and a telescribe message was placed before Salt. It bore a sign showing that it had come over the private system which the League maintained between Hanwood and the head office. He read it through twice, and for almost the first time since he had left his youth behind, he stood in absolute indecision.

"It is necessary for me to go at once to London," he said, turning to his companion, when he had made an irrevocable choice. "You will take command in my absence, Evelyn, under the guidance of the Council."

"May I venture to remind you, sir, that we are completely surrounded?" said Orr-Evelyn through his blank surprise.

"I have not overlooked it. You will——"

There was a sullen roar away in the north, a mile behind the coppice that had first spoken. Something whistled overhead, not unmelodiously, and away to the south a shell burst harmlessly among the ridges of a ploughed field. The nearer searchlight elevated its angle a fraction and centred upon a cloud of smoke that hung for a moment until the gale whirled it to disintegration. The army, like the navy, had reverted to black powder. It was Economy; and as it was not intended ever to go to war again, it scarcely mattered.

"Marsham will engage that gun from both platforms D and E. Make every effort to silence it with the least delay; it is the only real menace there is. Hold the entanglement, but not at too heavy a cost. If it should be carried——Come to my room."

"You have considered the possible effect of your withdrawal at this moment, Salt?" said Orr-Evelyn in a low voice, as they hastened together along the passages.

"I can leave the outcome in your hands with absolute reliance," replied Salt. "If Hanwood is successfully held until to-morrow, it will devolve upon Sir John Hampden to dictate terms to the Government. The end is safely in sight independent of my personality.... My reputation——!" He dismissed that phase with a shrug.

He threw open the door of his private office. A shallow mahogany case, about a foot square, locked and sealed, was sunk into the opposite wall. Salt knocked off the wax and opened the case with a key which he took off the ring and gave to Orr-Evelyn as he spoke. Inside the case were a dozen rows of little ivory studs, each

183

engraved with a red number. Fastened to the inside of the lid was a scale map of the land lying between the outer wall and the wire fence. Every stud had its corresponding number, surrounded by a crimson circle, indicated on the plan.

"If the entanglement should be carried you will take no further risk," continued Salt. "Captain Ford will give you the general indication of the attack from the lantern. There are two men detailed to each block of mines who will signal you the exact moment for firing each mine. Those are the numbered indicators above the box. Good-bye."

He paused at the door; time was more than life to him, but he had an ordered thought for everything.

"If you hear no more of me, and what might be imagined really troubles you, Evelyn, you can make use of this," he remarked, and laid the telescript he had received upon a table.

It was not the time for words, written or spoken, beyond those of the sheerest necessity. Half an hour passed before Orr-Evelyn had an opportunity of glancing through the letter that had called Salt from his post. When he had finished it he took it down, and read it aloud to the headquarter staff amidst the profoundest silence, in passionate vindication of his friend and leader. This was what they heard:

"Unity League, Trafalgar Chambers.

"The building is surrounded by mob. Seaton Street, Pantile Passage, and Pall Mall and the Haymarket, as far as I can see, densely packed with frantic men. All others in building had left earlier. I shall remain. Wires cut, and fear that you may not receive this, as other telescribe messages for help unanswered. Mob howling continuously for Sir John Hampden and Mr Salt; dare not look out again, stoned. Shall delay advance, doors and stairs, as long as possible, and burn all important League books and papers last resource.

"Good-bye all, my dear friends.
"Irene Lisle."

CHAPTER XIX

THE "FINIS" MESSAGE

The storm had not decreased its violence when, three minutes later, Salt stood unperceived on the broad coping outside an upper storey of the tower, and, sinking forward into the teeth of the gale, was borne upwards with rigid wings as a kite ascends.

In accordance with his instructions the two searchlights had turned their beams steadily earthward for the time, and in the absolute blackness of the upper air he could pass over the firing lines of friends and foes in comparative safety. As he rose higher and higher before turning to scud before the wind, he saw, as on a plan, the whole field of operations, just distinguishable in its masses of grey and black, with the points of interest revealing themselves by an occasional flash. Immediately beneath him, beneath him at first, but every second drawing away to the south-west as he drifted in the gale he breasted, lay Hanwood, with its three outer lines of defence. From above it seemed as though a very bright needle was every now and then thrust out from the walls into the dark night and drawn back again. On each of the platforms D and E two 4.7-inch quick-firing guns appeared to be rocking slightly in the wind. By all the indication there was of smoke or noise, or even flame, the gunners might have been standing idly behind their shields; but over the steep scarp of the little hill, a mile and a half away, shells were being planted every ten yards or so, with the methodical regularity of a farmer dropping potatoes along a furrow.

Salt might not have quite expected that there would be the necessity to fire those guns when, a year before, he had obtained for Hanwood its complement of the finest artillery that the world produced, but when the necessity did arise, there was no need for the League gunners to use black powder.

When he had reached the height he required, simply leaning against the wind, Salt moved a pinion slightly and bore heavily towards the right. It was the supreme moment for the trial of skill, as the long flight that followed it was the trial of endurance. If his nerve had failed, if a limb had lost its tension for the fraction of a second, his brain reeled amidst that tearing fury of the element, or a single ring or swivel not answered to its work, he would have been crumpled up hopelessly, beyond the chance of recovery, and flung headlong to the earth. As it was, the wind swept him round in a great half circle, but it was the wind his servant, not his master, and he turned its lusty violence to serve his ends. He caught a passing glimpse of the coppice whence the attack had first been opened; he saw beneath him the line of guns ensconced behind the hill, one already overturned and centred in confusion; and then the sweeping arc reached its limit, and he came, as it seemed, to anchor in mid-air, with the earth slipping away beneath him as the banks glide past a smoothly-moving train, and a thousand weights and forces dragging at his aching arms.

He had nothing to do but to maintain a perfect balance among the conflicting cross winds that shot in from above and below, and from north and south, and to point his course towards the glow in the sky that marked the Capital. A dozen words could express it, but it required the skill of the practised wingman, the highest development of every virile quality, and the spur of a necessity not less than life and death, to dignify the attempt above the foolhardy. Whether beyond all that the accomplishment lay within the bounds of human endurance was a further step. It would at that time have been impossible to pronounce either way with any authority, for not only had the attempt never been made, but nothing approaching the attempt had been made. A breeze that ran five miles an hour was considered enough for any purpose; to take to the air when the anemometer indicated fifteen miles an hour was not allowed at the practice grounds, and the record in this direction lay with an expert who had accomplished a straight flight in a wind that travelled a little less than thirty miles an hour. The storm on the night of the 15th of January tore across the face of the land with a general velocity of fifty or sixty miles an hour, rising at times even higher.

Under the racking agony of every straining tendon and the heady pressure of the wind, a sense of mundane unreality began to settle upon the flier. He saw the earth and its landmarks being drawn smoothly and swiftly from beneath him with the detachment of a half-conscious dream. He saw—for he remembered afterwards—the Thames lying before him like a whip flicked carelessly across the plain. A town loomed up, black and inchoate, on his right, developed into streets and terraces, and slid away into the past. It was Richmond. The river, never far away, now slipped beneath him at right angles, reappeared to hold a parallel course upon his left, and flung a horse-shoe coil two miles ahead. A colony of strange shining roofs and domes next challenged recognition. They were the conservatories at Kew, looking little more than garden frames, and they were scarcely lost to view before he was over the winding line of Brentford's quaint old High Street, now, as it appeared, packed with a dense, moving crowd. The irresistible pounding of the gale was edging the glow of London further and further to his right. Instinctively he threw more weight into the lighter scale, and slowly and certainly the point of his destination swung round before his face again.

Thenceforward it was all town. Gunnersbury became Chiswick, Chiswick merged into Hammersmith, Kensington succeeded, in ceaseless waves of houses that ran north and south, and long vistas of roofs that stretched east and west. It was a kaleidoscope of contrasts. Scenes of saturnalian gaiety, where ant-like beings danced in mad abandonment round fires that blocked the road, or seemed to gyrate by companies in meaningless confusion, bounded districts plunged into an unnatural gloom and solitude, where for street after street neither the footstep of a wayfarer nor the light of a public lamp broke the uncanny spell. Immediately beyond, by the glare of the flambeaux which they carried, an orderly concourse might be marching eastward, and fringing on their route a garish gutter mart, where busy costermongers drove their roaring trade and frugal housewives did their marketing with less outward concern than if the crisis in the State had been a crisis in the price of butter.

The multitudinous sounds beat on his ears through the plunging gale like a babel of revelry heard between the intermittent swinging of an unlatched door. The sights in their grotesque perspective began to melt together lazily. The upper air grew very cold. The weights hung heavier every mile, the contending forces pulled more resistlessly. Strange fancies began to assail him as the brain shrank beneath the strain; doubts and despairs to gather round like dark birds of the night with hopeless foreboding in the dull measure of their funereal wings. In that moment mind and body almost failed to contend against the crushing odds; nothing but his unconquerable heart flogged on his dying limbs.

It was scarcely more than half an hour after she had written her despairing message that from her post at the head of the broad stone staircase Irene Lisle heard a noise in the garret storey above that sent her flying back to her stronghold. It was the last point from which she had expected an attack. Through the keyhole of the door behind which she had taken refuge, she saw a strangely outlined figure groping his way cumbrously down the stairs, and then, without a word or cry, but with a face whiter than the paper that had summoned him, she threw open the door to admit Salt.

He walked heavily along the corridor and turned into his own room, while she relocked the door and followed him. There was mute enquiry in her eyes, but she did not speak.

A powerful oil-stove stood upon the hearth-stone, throwing its beams across the room. He stood over it while the beaded ice melted from his hair and fell hissing on the iron. He opened his mouth, and the sound of his voice was like the thin piping of a reed. She caught a word, and began to unbuckle the frozen straps of his gear. When he was free he tried to raise his hand to a pocket of his coat, but the effort was beyond the power of the cramped limb. Irene interpreted the action, and, finding there a flask, filled the cup and held it to his lips.

She got a blue, half-frozen smile of thanks over the edge of the cup. "Ah," he said, beginning to find his voice again, and stamping about the room, "we owe Wynchley Slocombe a monument, you and I, Miss Lisle. Now you must write a telescript for me, please; for I cannot."

"If you will remain here, where it is warmer, I will bring the materials," she suggested.

He thanked her and allowed her to go, watching her with thoughtful eyes that were coming back to life. She paused a moment at the top of the stairs to listen down the shaft, and then sped quickly through the smoke to the instrument room on the floor beneath.

Salt glanced round the office. On and about his desk all the books and papers that might be turned to a hostile purpose had been stacked in readiness, and by them stood the can of oil that was to ensure their complete destruction. He stepped up to the window and looked out cautiously. Every pane of glass was broken—every pane of glass in Trafalgar Chambers was broken, for that matter—but it was not easy for an unprepared mob to force an entrance. When the Unity League had taken over the whole block of building in its expansion many alterations had been carried out, and among these had been to fix railings that sprang from the street and formed an arch, not only over the basement, but over the ground floor windows also. If the shutters on the windows had been closed in time, the assailants would have been baffled at another point, but the shutters had been overlooked, and the mob, after lighting great fires in the street, was now flinging the blazing billets through the lower windows.

In a very brief minute Irene was back again with the telescribe accessories. She seated herself at a table, dipped her pen into the ink, and looked up without a word.

"Trafalgar Chambers.

"6.25 P.M.," dictated Salt. "Most of the miners drawn off and passing through Brentford. Over Barfold Rise half battery of 18-pounders, one out of action. In Spring Coppice and Welland Wood about four companies

188

regulars each. Reconnoitre third position assuming same proportion. Act."

He stood considering whether there was anything more to add usefully. The sound of Irene's agate pen tapping persistently against the table caught his ear.

"You are not very much afraid?" he asked with kindly reassurance in his voice as he looked at her hand.

"No, not now," she replied; but as she wrote she had to still the violent trembling of her right hand with the left.

"All going well here. Send messenger Hampden with report immediately after engagement," he concluded.

"I will try to sign it myself." He succeeded in sprawling a recognisable "George Salt" across the paper, and after it wrote "Finis," which happened to be the pass-word for the day.

"Your message came through; this may possibly do the same," he remarked. He turned off the radiator as orderly as though he had reached the close of a working day, and they went out together, locking the doors behind them.

"They were attacking Hanwood when you left?" she asked with the tensest interest. They had sent off the telescript, and it seemed to Irene that they had reached the end of things.

"Yes," he replied. "But all the same," he added, as a fresh outburst of cries rose from the street, and the light through the shattered window attracted a renewed fusillade of missiles, "I think that we have kept our promise to let you be in the thick of it."

She shook her head with the very faintest smile. "That seems a very long time ago. But you, how could you come? When I sent I never thought ... I never dreamed——"

"It was possible to leave," he said. "My work is done. Yes," in reply to her startled glance, "it has all happened!"

"You mean——?" she asked eagerly.

He took a paper from his pocket-book. It was, as she saw immediately, a telescript from Sir John Hampden. It had reached him at Hanwood an hour before he left.

"I have this afternoon received a deputation of Ministerialists who have the adherence of a majority in the House without taking the Opposition into account," she read. "The Parliamentary Representation Committees throughout the country are frantically insisting upon members accepting any terms, if we will give an undertaking that the normal balance of trade and labour shall be restored at once. The Cabinet is going to pieces

189

every hour, and the situation can no longer either be faced or ignored by the Government. There will be a great scene in the House to-night. The deputation will see me again to-morrow morning with a formal decision. I have confidential assurances that a complete acceptance is a foregone conclusion. The arrival of the Midland colliers to-night, if not of those from Monmouth, will precipitate matters."

Tears she could not hold back stood in her eyes as she returned to him the paper. "Then it has not been in vain," she said softly.

"No," he replied. "Nothing has been in vain."

They stood silently for a minute, looking back over life. So might two shipwrecked passengers have stood on a frail raft waiting for the end, resigned but not unhopeful of a larger destiny beyond, while the elements boiled and roared around them.

"It was very weak of me to send that message," said Irene presently; "the message that brought you. I suppose," she added, "that it was the message that brought you?"

"Yes, thank God!" he replied.

"And if it had been impossible for you to come? If it had been an utterly critical moment in every way, what would you have done?"

He laughed a little, quietly, as he looked at her. "The question did not arise, fortunately," he replied.

"No," she admitted; "only I felt a little curious to know, now that everything is over. It is, isn't it? There is nothing to be done?"

"Oh yes," he replied with indomitable cheerfulness. "There is always something to be done."

"A chance?" she whispered incredulously. "A chance of escape, you mean?"

"It is possible," he said. "At least, I will go and hear what they have to say."

"No! no!" she cried out, as a dreadful scene rose to her imagination. "You cannot understand. Don't you hear that?... They would kill you."

"I do not suppose that I shall find myself popular," he said with a smile, "but I will take care. You—I think you must stay here."

"Cannot I come with you?" she pleaded. "See, I am armed."

He took the tiny weapon that she drew from her dress and looked at it with gentle amusement. It was a pretty thing of ivory and nickeled steel, an elaborate toy. He pressed the action and

190

shook out the half-dozen tiny loaded caps—they were little more than that—upon his palm.

"I would rather that you did not use this upon a mob," he said, reloading it. "It would only exasperate, without disabling. As for stopping a rush—why, I doubt if one of these would stop a determined rabbit. You have better weapons than this."

"I suppose you are right. Only it gave me a little confidence. Then you shall keep it for a memento, if you will."

"No; it might hold off a single assailant, I suppose. I should value this much more, if I might have it." He touched a silk tie that she had about her neck, as he spoke; it was one that she had often worn. She held up her head for him to disengage it.

"Some day," he said, lingering a little over the simple operation, "you will understand many things, Irene."

"I think that I understand everything now," she replied with a brave glance. "Everything that is worth understanding."

He placed the folded tie in an inner pocket, and went down the stone steps without another word. The well was thick with smoke, but the fire had not yet spread beyond the lower rooms. Half-way down he encountered a barricade of light office furniture which the girl had flung across the stairs and drenched with oil. It was no obstacle in itself, but at the touch of a match it would have sprung into a conflagration that would have held the wildest mob at bay for a few precious moments. He picked his way through it, descended the remaining stairs, and unlocked the outer door. Beyond this was an iron curtain that had been lowered. A little door in it opened directly on to the half-dozen steps that led down to Seaton Street.

Salt looked through a crevice of the iron curtain, and listened long enough to learn that there was no one on the upper steps; for the upper steps, indeed, commanded no view of the windows, and the windows were the centres of all interest. Satisfied on this point, he quietly unlocked the door and stepped out.

CHAPTER XX

STOBALT OF SALAVEIRA

To the majority of those who thronged Seaton Street the effect of Salt's sudden—instantaneous, as it seemed—and unexpected appearance was to endow it with a dramatic, almost an uncanny, value. The front rows, especially those standing about the steps, fell back, and the further rows pressed forward. And because an undisciplined mob stricken by acute surprise must express its emotion outwardly—by silence if it has hitherto been noisy, and by exclamation if it has been silent—the shouts and turmoil in the street instantly dwindled away to nothing, like a breath of vapour passing from a window pane.

Salt raised his hand, and he had the tribute of unstirring silence, the silence for the moment of blank astonishment.

"My friends and enemies," he said, in a voice that had learned self-possession from the same school that Demosthenes had practised in, "you have been calling me for some time. In a few minutes I must listen to whatever you have to say, but first there is another matter that we must arrange. I take it for granted that when you began your spirited demonstration here you had no idea that there was a lady in the building. Not being accustomed to the sterner side of politics, so formidable a display rather disconcerted her, and not knowing the invariable chivalry of English working men, she hesitated to come out before. Now, as it is dark, and the streets of London are not what they once were, I want half a dozen good stout fellows to see the lady safely to her home."

"Be damned!" growled a voice among the mass. "What do you take us for?"

"Men," retorted Salt incisively; "or there would be no use in asking you."

"Yes, men, but famished, desperate, werewolf men," cried a poor, gaunt creature clad in grotesque rags, who stood near. "Men who have seen our women starve and sink before our eyes; men who have watched our children dying by a slower, crooler death than fire. An eye for an eye, tyrant! Your League has struck at our women folk through us."

"Then strike at ours through us!" cried Salt, stilling with the measured passion of his voice the rising murmurs of assent. "I am here to offer you a substitute. Do you think that no woman will mourn for me?" He sent his voice ringing over their heads like a

192

prophetic knell. "The cause that must stoop to take the life of a defenceless woman is lost for ever."

As long as he could offer them surprises he could hold the mere mob in check, but there was among the crowd an element that was not of the crowd, a chosen sprinkling who were superior to the swaying passions of the moment.

"Not good enough," said a decently-dressed, comfortable-looking man, who had little that was famished, desperate, or wolfish in his appearance. "You're both there, and there you shall both stay, by God! Eh, comrades?" He spoke decisively, and made a movement as though he would head a rush towards the steps.

Salt dropped one hand upon the iron door with a laugh that sounded more menacing than most men's threats.

"Not so fast, Rorke," he said contemptuously; "you grasp too much. Even in your unpleasant business you can practise moderation. I am here, but there is no reason on earth why I should stay. Scarcely more than half an hour ago I was at Hanwood—where, by the way, your friends are being rather badly crumpled up—and you are all quite helpless to prevent me going again."

They guessed the means; they saw the unanswerable strength of his position, and recognised their own impotence. "Who are you, any way?" came a dozen voices.

"I am called George Salt: possibly you have heard the name before. Come, men," he cried impatiently, "what have you to think twice about? Surely it is worth while to let a harmless girl escape to make certain of that terrible person Salt."

There was a strangled scream in the vestibule behind. Unable to bear the suspense any longer, Irene had crept down the stairs in time to hear the last few sentences. For a minute she had stood transfixed at the horror of the position she realised; then, half-frenzied, she flung herself against Salt's arm and tried to beat her way past to face the mob.

"You shall not!" she cried distractedly. "I will not be saved at that price. I shall throw myself out of the window, into the fire, anywhere. Yes, I'm desperate, but I know what I am saying. Come back, and let us wait together; die together, if it is to be, but I don't go alone."

The crowd began to surge restlessly about in waves of excited motion. The interruption, in effect, had been the worst thing that could have happened. There were in the throng many who beneath their seething passion could appreciate the nobility of Salt's self-sacrifice; many who in the midst of their sullen enmity were wrung with admiration for Irene's heroic spirit, but the contagion to press forward dominated all. Salt had irretrievably lost his hold upon their reason, and with that hold he saw the last straw of his most forlorn hope floating away. In another minute he must either retreat into the burning building where he might at any time find the stairs impassable with smoke, or remain to be overwhelmed by a savage rush and beaten to the ground.

"Men," cried Irene desperately, "listen before you do something that will for ever make to-day shameful in the history of our country. Do you know whom you wish to kill? He is the greatest Englishman——"

There were angry cries from firebrands scattered here and there among the crowd, and a movement from behind, where the new contingents hurrying down the side streets pressed most heavily, flung the nearest rows upon the lower steps. Salt's revolver, which he had not shown before, drove them back again and gave him a moment's grace.

"Quick!" he cried. "My offer still holds good."

One man shouldered his way through to the front, and, seeing him, Salt allowed him to come on. He walked up the steps deliberately, with a face sad rather than revengeful, and they spoke together hurriedly under the shadow of the large-bore revolver.

"If it can be done yet, I'll be one of the posse to see to the young lady," said the volunteer. "I have no mind to wait for the other job that's coming."

"Take care of her; get her back into the hall," replied Salt. "Gently, very gently, friend."

Two more volunteers had their feet upon the steps, one, a butcher, reeking of the stalls, the other sleek and smug-faced, with the appearance of a prosperous artisan.

"I'll pick my men," cried Salt sharply, and his steady weapon emphasised his choice, one man passing on through the iron doorway, the other turning sharp from the insistent barrel to push his way back into the crowd with a bitter imprecation.

It was too much to hope that the position could be maintained. The impatient mob had only been held off momentarily from its purpose as a pack of wolves can be stayed by the fleeing traveller who throws from his sleigh article after article to entice their curiosity. Salt had nothing more to offer them. His life was already a hostage to the honour of those whom he had allowed to pass. Others were pressing on to him with vengeance-laden cries. The terrible irresistible forward surge of a soulless mob, when individuality is merged into the dull brutishness of a trampling herd, was launched.

"Capt'n Stobalt!" cried a lusty voice at his shoulder.

Salt turned instinctively. A man in sailor's dress, with the guns

194

and star of his grade upon his sleeve, had climbed along the arch of the railings with a sailor's resourcefulness, and had reached his ear. Salt remembered him quite well, but he did not speak a word.

"Ah, sir, I thought that warn't no other voice in the world, although the smoke befogged my eyes a bit. Keep back, you gutter rats!" he roared above every other sound, rising up in his commanding position and balancing himself by a stanchion of the gate; "d'ye think you know who you're standing up before, you toggle-chested galley-sharks! Salt? Aye, he's salt enough! 'Tis Capt'n Stobalt of the old Ulysses. Stobalt of Salaveira!"

Three years before, the moment would have found Salt cold, as cold as ice, and as unresponsive, but he had learned many things since then, and sacrificed his pride and reticence on many altars.

He saw before him a phalanx of humanity startled into one common expression of awe and incredulity; he saw the hostile wave that was to overwhelm him spend itself in a sharp recoil. By a miracle the fierce lust of triumphant savagery had died out of the starved, pathetic faces now turned eagerly to him; by a miracle the gathering roar for vengeance had sunk into an expectant hush, broken by nothing but the whispered repetition of his name on ten thousand lips. He saw in a flash a hundred details of the magic of that name; he knew that if ever in his life he must throw restraint and moderation to the winds and paint his rôle in broad and lurid colours, that moment had arrived, and at the call he took his destiny between his hands.

They saw him toss his weapon through the railings into the space beneath, marked him come to the edge of the step and stand with folded arms defenceless there before them, and the very whispers died away in breathless anticipation.

"Yes," he cried with a passionate vehemence that held their breath and stirred their hearts, "I am Stobalt of Salaveira, the man who brought you victory when you were trembling in despair. I saved England for you then, but that was when men loved their country, and did not think it a disgraceful thing to draw a sword and die for her. What is that to you to-day, you who have been taught to forget what glory means; and what is England to you to-day, you whose leaders have sold her splendour for a higher wage?"

"No! No!" cried a thousand voices, frantic to appease the man for whose blood they had been howling scarcely a minute before. "You shall be our leader! We will follow you to death! Stobalt of Salaveira! Stobalt for ever! Stobalt of Salaveira! Stobalt and England!"

The frenzied roar of welcome, the waving hands, the hats flung high, the mingled cries caught from lip to lip went rolling up the street, kindling by a name and an imperishable memory other streets and other crowds into a tumult of mad enthusiasm. Along Pall Mall, through Trafalgar Square, into the Strand and Whitehall, north by Regent Street and the Haymarket to Piccadilly, running east and west, splitting north and south, twisting and leaping from group to group and mouth to mouth, ran the strange but stirring cry, carrying wonder and concern on its wing, but always passing with a cheer.

Seven years had passed since the day of Salaveira, and the memory of it was still enough to stir a crowd to madness. For there had been no Salaveiras since to dim its splendour. Seven years ago the name of Salaveira had brought pallor to the cheek, and the thought of what was happening there stole like an icy cramp round the heart of every Englishman. The nation had grown accustomed to accept defeat on land with the comfortable assurance that nothing could avert a final victory. Its pride was in its navy: invincible!...

The war that came had been of no one's seeking, but it came, and the nation called upon its navy to sweep the presumptuous enemy from off the seas. Then came a pause: a rumour, doubted, disbelieved, but growing stronger every hour. The English fleets, not so well placed as they might have been, "owing to political reasons that made mobilisation inadvisable while there was still a chance of peace being maintained," were unable to effect a junction immediately, and were falling back before the united power of the New Alliance. Hour after hour, day after day, night after night, crowds stood hopefully, doubtfully, incredulously, in front of the newspaper office windows, waiting for the news that never came. The fleets had not yet combined. The truth first leaked, then blazed: they were unable to combine! Desperately placed on the outer line they were falling back, ever falling back into a more appalling isolation. A coaling station had been abandoned just where its presence proved to have been vital; a few battleships had been dropped from the programme, and the loss of their weight in the chain just proved fatal.

Men did not linger much at Fleet Street windows then; they slunk to and fro singly a hundred times a day, read behind the empty bulletins with poignant intuition, and turned silently away. In the mourning Capital they led nightmare lives from which they could only awake to a more definite despair, and the first word of the hurrying newsboy's raucous shout sent a sickening wave of dread to every heart. There was everything to fear, and nothing at all to hope. Could peace be made—not a glorious, but a decent, living peace? Was—was even London safe? Kind friends abroad threw back the answers in the fewest, crudest words. England would

196

have to sue for peace on bended knees and bringing heavy tribute in her hands. London lay helpless at the mercy of the foe to seize at any moment when it suited him.

All this time Commander Stobalt, in command of the Ulysses by the vicissitudes of unexpected war and separated from his squadron on detached service, was supposed to be in Cura Bay, a thousand miles away from Salaveira, flung there with the destroyers Limpet and Dabfish by the mere backwash of the triumphant allied fleet. According to the rules of naval warfare he ought to have been a thousand miles away; according to the report of the allies' scouts he was a thousand miles away. But miraculously one foggy night the Ulysses loomed spectrally through the shifting mist that drifted uncertainly from off the land and rammed the first leviathan that crossed her path, while the two destroyers torpedoed her next neighbour. Then, before leviathans 3 and 4 had begun to learn from each other what the matter was, the Ulysses was between them, sprinkling their decks and tops with small shell, and perforating their water-line and vital parts with large shell from a range closer than that at which any engagement had been fought out since the day when the Treasury had begun to implore the Admiralty to impress upon her admirals what a battleship really cost before they sent her into action. For the Ulysses had everything to gain and nothing but herself to lose, and when morning broke over Salaveira's untidy bay, she had gained everything, and lost so little that even the New Alliance took no pride in mentioning it in the cross account.

It was, of course, as every naval expert could have demonstrated on the war-game board, an impossible thing to do. Steam, searchlights, wireless telegraphy, quick-firing guns, and a hundred other innovations had effaced the man; and the spirit of the Elizabethan age was at a discount. What Drake would have done, or Hawkins, what would have been a sweet and pleasing adventure to Sir Richard Grenville, or another Santa Cruz to Blake, would have been in their heirs unmitigated suicide by the verdict of any orthodox court martial. Largely imbued with the Elizabethan spirit—the genius of ensuring everything that was possible, and then throwing into the scale a splendid belief in much that seemed impossible—Stobalt succeeded in doing what perhaps no one else would have succeeded in doing, merely because perhaps no one else would have tried.

"Stobalt of Salaveira! Come down and lead us!" The wild enthusiasm, the strange unusual cries, went echoing to the sky and reverberating down every street and byway. Behind barred doors men listened to the shout, and wondered; crouching in alleys, tramping the road with no further hope in life, beggars and outcasts heard the name and dimly associated it with something pleasant in the past. It met the force of special constables hastening from the west; it fell on the ears of Mr Strummery, driving by unfrequented ways towards the House. "Stobalt and England! Stobalt for us! Stobalt and the Navy!" It was like another Salaveira night with Stobalt there among them—the man who was too modest to be fêted, the man whose very features were unknown at home, Stobalt of Salaveira!

Imagine it. Measure by the fading but not yet quite forgotten memory of another time of direful humiliation and despair what Salaveira must have been. They had passed a week of fervent exaltation, a week of calm assurance, a week of rather tremulous hope, and for the last quarter a long dumb misery that conveyed no other sense of time in later years than that of formless night. They were waiting for the stroke of doom. Then at midnight came the sudden tumult from afar, sounding to those who listened in painful silence strangely unlike the note of defeat, the frantic, mingled shouts, the tearing feet in the road beneath, the wild bells pealing out, the guns and rockets to add to the delirium of the night, and the incredible burden of the intoxicating news: "Great Victory! Salaveira Relieved!! Utter Annihilation of the Blockading Fleet!!!"

The Philosopher might withdraw to solitude and moralise; the Friend of Humanity stand aside, pained that his countrymen should possess so much human nature, but to the great primitive emotional heart of the community the choice lay between going out and shouting and staying in and going mad. Never before in history had there been a victory that so irresistibly carried the nation off its feet. To the populace it had seemed from beginning to end to contain just those qualities of daredevilry and fortuitous ease that appeal to the imagination. They were quite mistaken; the conception had been desperate, but beyond that the details of the relief of Salaveira had been as methodical, as painstaking, and as far-seeing as those which had marked the civil campaign now drawing to a close.

That was why a famished, starving mob remembered Salaveira. They would have stoned a duke or burned a bishop with very little compunction, but Stobalt ranked among their immortals. They did not even seem to question the mystery of Salt's identity. As the flames began to lap out of the lower windows of Trafalgar Chambers, and it became evident that their work there was done, a stalwart bodyguard ranged themselves about his person and headed the procession. Hurriedly committing Irene to the loyal sailor's charge, Stobalt resigned himself good-humouredly to his position until he could seize an opportunity discreetly to withdraw.

Not without some form of orderliness the great concourse marched into the broader streets. Stobalt had no idea of their destination; possibly there was no preconcerted plan, but—as such things happen—a single voice raised in a pause gave the note. It did not fall on barren ground, and the next minute the countless trampling feet moved to a brisker step, and the new cry went rolling ominously ahead to add another terror to the shadowy phantasmagoria of the ill-lit streets.

"To Westminster! Down with the Government! To Westminster!"

CHAPTER XXI

THE BARGAIN OF FAMINE

Sir John Hampden had not to wait until the morning to meet the deputation of Ministerialists again. Late the same evening a few men, arriving together, presented themselves at one of the barricades that closed the Mayfair street, and were at once admitted. Many of the residential west-end districts which were not thoroughfares for general traffic were stockaded in those days and maintained their street guard. The local officials protested, the inhabitants replied by instancing a few of the cases where an emergency had found the authorities powerless to extend protection, and there the matter ended. It was scarcely worth while stamping out a spark when they stood upon a volcano.

Sir John received the members in the library—a disspirited handful of men who had written their chapter of history and were now compelled to pass on the book to other scribes, as every party must. Only this party had thought that it was to be the exception.

"Events are moving faster than the clock," apologised Cecil Brown, with a rather dreary smile. He was present as the representative of that body in the House which was not indisposed to be courteous and even conciliatory in attitude towards an opponent, while it yielded nothing of its principles: a standpoint unintelligible to most of the rank and file of the party. "Doubtless we are not unexpected, Sir John Hampden?"

"Comrade," corrected a member who was made of sterner

metal. They were there to deliver up their rifles, but this stalwart soldier of Equality clung tenaciously to an empty cartridge case.

"I am no less desirous than yourselves of coming to a settlement," replied Sir John. "If there is still any matter of detail-?"

The plenipotentiaries exchanged glances of some embarrassment.

"Have you not heard?" asked Mr Soans, whose voice was the voice of the dockyard labourers.

"I can scarcely say until I know what you refer to," was the plausible reply. "I have found that all communication has been cut during the last few hours." He lightly indicated the instruments against the wall.

They all looked towards Cecil Brown, the matter being rather an unpleasant one.

"The fact is, the House has been invaded by a tumultuous rabble. They overcame all resistance by the mere force of numbers, and"—he could not think of a less ominous phrase at the moment—"well, simply turned us out.... Quite Cromwellian proceedings. We left them passing very large and comprehensive resolutions," he concluded.

"Your people!" said the uncompromising man accusingly.

"Scarcely," protested Hampden with a smile. "The ends may be the ends of Esau, but the means——"

"Not our people; they couldn't possibly be ours to come and turn on us like that."

"Suppose we say, without defining them further," said Sir John, "that they were simply"—he paused for a second to burn the thrust gently home with a little caustic silence—"simply The People."

Mr Vossit made a gesture of impatience towards his colleague.

"Whether Queen Anne, died of gout or apoplexy isn't very material now," he said with a touch of bitterness. "We are here to conduct the funeral."

"I wish to meet you in every possible way I can," interposed Hampden, "but I must point out to you that at so short a notice I am deprived of the counsel of any of my associates. I had hoped that by the time of the meeting to-morrow morning——"

"Is that necessary if the Memorandum is accepted by the Government?"

"Without discussion?"

Mr Vossit shrugged his shoulders. "As far as I am concerned, Sir John. The concession of a word or two, or a phrase here and there, can make no difference. It is our Sedan, and the heavier you make the terms, the more there will be for us to remember it by."

"I am content," subscribed Mr Guppling. "We have been surprised and routed, not by the legitimate tactics of party strife, but by methods undistinguishable from those of civil war."

Hampden's glance was raised mechanically to an inscribed panel that hung upon the wall in easy view, where it formed a curious decoration. The ground colour was dull black, and on it in white lettering was set forth a trenchant sentiment selected from the public utterances of every prominent member of the Government and labelled with his name. It was a vindication and a spur that he had kept before his eyes through the years of ceaseless preparation, for in each extract one word was picked out in the startling contrast of an almost blinding crimson, and that one word was WAR. Even Sir John's enemies, those who called Salt a machine of blood and iron, admitted him to be a kindly gentleman, and his glance had been involuntary, for he had no desire to emphasise defeat upon the vanquished. The thing was done, however, and following the look every man who sat there met his own flamboyant challenge from the past; for all, without exception, had thrown down the gauntlet once in no uncertain form. War—but that had meant them waging war against another when it was quite convenient for them to do so, not another waging war against themselves out of season. War—but certainly not war that turned them out of office, only war that turned their opponents out of office.

The rather strained silence was broken by the sound of footsteps approaching from the hall.

"We are still short of the Home Secretary and Comrade Tirrel," explained Mr Chadwing to the master of the house. "We divided forces. They were driving I understand. Perhaps——"

It was. They came in slowly, for the Home Secretary faltered in his gait and had a hunted look, while Tirrel led him by the arm. Both carried traces of disorder, even of conflict.

"Oh yes; they held us up," said Tirrel with a savage laugh, as his colleagues gathered round. "He was recognised in Piccadilly by a crowd of those ungrateful dogs from the pits. I shouted to the cabman to drive through them at a gallop, but the cur jumped off his seat howling that he was their friend. I was just able to get the reins; we bumped a bit, but didn't upset, fortunately. I left the cab at the corner of the street, here." He turned his back on the Home Secretary, who sat huddled in a chair, and, facing the others, made a quick gesture indicating that Mr Tubes was unwell and had better be left alone.

"I brought him here, Sir John," he said, crossing over to the baronet and speaking in a half-whisper, "because I really did not know where else to take him. For some reason he appears to be almost execrated just now. His house in Kilburn will be marked and watched, I am afraid. And in that respect I daresay we are all in the same boat."

"He appears to be ill," said Hampden, rising. "I will——"

"Please don't," interrupted Tirrel decisively. "Any kind of attention distresses him, I find. It is a collapse. He has been shaken for some time past, and the attack to-night was the climax. His nerve is completely gone."

"As far as his safety is concerned," suggested the host with an expression of compassion, "I think that we can ensure that here against any irregular force. And certainly it would be the last place in which they would think of looking for him. For the night, at least, you had better leave him in our charge."

"Thank you," said Tirrel; "it is very good of you. I will. Of course," he added, as he turned away, "we shall have to assume his acquiescence to any arrangement we may reach. Unofficially I can guarantee it."

They seated themselves round the large table, Sir John and his private secretary occupying one end, the plenipotentiaries ranging around the other three sides. As they took their places Mr Drugget and another member were announced. They did not appear to have been expected, but they found seats among their colleagues. The Home Secretary sat apart, cowering in an easy-chair, and stretching out his hands timorously from time to time to meet the radiant heat of the great oil stove.

The composition of the meeting was not quite the same as that of the deputation which had paved the way to it earlier in the day. It was more official, for the action of the deputation had forced the hand of the Cabinet—to the relief of the majority of that body, it was whispered. But there was one notable Minister absent.

"I represent the Premier," announced Mr Drugget, rising. "If his attendance in person can be dispensed with, he begged to be excused."

"I offer no objection," replied Hampden. "If in the exceptional circumstances the Prime Minister should desire to see me privately, I will meet him elsewhere."

"The Premier is indisposed, I regret to say."

"In that case I would wait upon him at his own house, should he desire it," proffered Sir John.

"I will convey to him your offer," replied Mr Drugget. "In the meantime I am authorised to subscribe Mr Strummery's acquiescence to the terms, subject to one modification."

"One word first, please," interposed Sir John. "I must repeat what I had already said before you arrived. I am unable just now to consult my colleagues, in concert with whom the Memorandum was drafted. If it is necessary to refer back on any important detail——"

Mr Tubes half rose from his chair with a pitiable look of terror in his eyes and gave a low cry as a turbulent murmur from some distant street reached his ears.

"It's all right, comrade," said Cecil Brown reassuringly. "You're safe enough here, Jim."

"Aye, aye," whispered Tubes fearfully; "but did you hear that shout?—'To the lamp-post!' They fling it at me from every crowd. It haunts me. That is what I—I—yes, that is what I fear."

"No good arguing," muttered Tirrel across the table. "Leave him to himself; there's nothing else to be done just now."

"I can at least express the Premier's views" resumed Mr Drugget. "He would prefer the Bill for Amending the Franchise to be brought forward as a private Bill by a member of the Opposition rather than make it a Government measure. The Government would grant special facilities, and not oppose it. The Premier would advise a dissolution immediately the Bill passed."

There was a knock at the library door. The secretary attended to it with easy discretion, and for a minute was engaged in conversation with some one beyond.

Sir John looked at Mr Drugget in some amazement, and most of the members of his own party regarded their leader's proxy with blank surprise.

"I was hardly prepared for so fundamental an objection being raised at this hour," said the baronet. "It amounts, of course, to bringing an alternative proposal forward."

"The result would be the same; I submit that it is scarcely more than a matter of detail."

"Then why press it?"

Mr Drugget's expression seemed to convey the suggestion that he had no personal wishes at all in the matter, but felt obliged to make the best case he could for his chief.

"The Premier not unnaturally desires that the real authors of so retrogressive and tyrannical an Act should be saddled with the nominal as well as the actual responsibility," he replied. "Possibly he fears that in some remote future the circumstances will be forgotten, and his name be handed down as that of a traitor."

The private secretary took the opportunity of the sympathetic murmur which this attitude evoked to exchange a sentence with Sir John. Then he turned to the door and beckoned to the man who stood outside.

"I must ask your indulgence towards a short interruption, gentlemen," said Hampden, as a cyclist, in grey uniform, entered and handed him a despatch. "It is possible that some of my friends may even now be on their way to join me."

They all regarded the messenger with a momentary curious interest; all except two among them. Over Mr Drugget and the comrade who had arrived with him the incident seemed to exercise an absorbing fascination. After a single, it almost seemed a startled, glance at the soldier-cyclist, their eyes met in a mutual impulse, and then instantly turned again to fix on Hampden's face half-stealthily, but as tensely as though they would tear the secret from behind his unemotional expression.

"It's all very well, Drugget—in justice," anxiously murmured Mr Vossit across the table, "but, as things are, we've got to be quick, and accept considerably less than justice. For Heaven's sake, don't prolong the agony, after to-day's experience."

"If you hang on to that," warned Mr Guppling, "you will only end in putting off till to-morrow not a whit better terms than you can make to-night."

"Wait, wait, wait, wait, wait," muttered Mr Drugget impatiently, not withdrawing his fascinated gaze.

In the silence of the room they again heard the crescive ululation of the street, distant still, but sounding louder than before to their strained imagination, and terrible in its suggestion of overwhelming, unappeasable menace. Mr Tubes started uneasily in his chair.

"Will that wait?" demanded Mr Guppling with some passion.

"A very little time longer; your coming here to-night has thrown us out," pleaded Mr Drugget's companion, in a more conciliatory whisper. "To-morrow morning, a few hours, an hour—perhaps even——"

The messenger had been dismissed without an answer. Looking up with sudden directness, Hampden caught one man's eyes fixed on him with a furtive intensity that betrayed his hopes and fears.

"The attack on Hanwood has completely failed," quietly announced Sir John, holding the startled gaze relentlessly. "The guns have been captured and brought in. The troops have been surrounded, disarmed, and dispersed, with the exception of those of the higher rank who are detained. There have, unfortunately, been casualties on both sides."

"I—I—I—Why do you address yourself to me, Sir John?" stammered the disconcerted man, turning very white, and exhibiting every painful sign of guilt and apprehension.

"Are we to understand that your property at Hanwood has

been attacked by an armed force of regulars?" asked one with sincere incredulity, as Hampden remained silent.

"It is unhappily true."

"And defended by an evidently superior force of armed men, unlawfully assembled there," retorted a militant comrade defiantly.

"In view of the strained position to which the circumstances must give rise, I will take the responsibility of withdrawing the Premier's one objection to the Memorandum as it stands," announced Mr Drugget with dry lips.

"In that case I will ask Mr Lloyd to read the terms of the agreement formally before we append our signatures," said Hampden, without offering any further comment.

A printed copy of the Articles was passed to each delegate; on the table before Sir John lay the engrossed form in duplicate. From one of these the secretary proceeded to read the terms of the agreement, which was frankly recognised on both sides as the death-warrant of socialistic ascendency in England.

From the Government the League required only one thing: the immediate passing of "A Bill to amend the Qualifications of Voters in Parliamentary Elections," to be followed by a dissolution and its inevitable consequence, a general election. But of the result of that election no one need cherish any illusions, for it would be decided according to the new qualification; and shorn of its parliamentary phraseology, the new Act was to sweep away the existing adult suffrage, and, broadly, substitute for it a £10 occupation qualification, with, still worse, a plurality of voting power in multiples of £10, according to the rateable value of the premises occupied. It was wholly immoral according to the democratic tendency of the preceding age, but it was wholly necessary according to the situation which had resulted from it.

A genial Autocrat, Professor, and Poet has set forth in one of his works, for the sake of the warning it conveys, the story of a little boy who, on coming into the possession of a nice silver watch, and examining it closely, discovered among the works "a confounded little hair entangled round the balance-wheel." Of course his first care was to remove this palpable obstruction, with the result that the watch accomplished the work of twenty-four hours in an insignificant fraction of a second, and then refused to have anything more to do with practical chronometry. On coming into possession of their new toy the Socialists had discovered many "confounded little hairs" wrapped away among the works of that elaborate piece of machinery, the English Constitution, all obviously impeding its free working. Recklessly, even gaily, they had pulled them out one after another, cut them across the middle and left pieces hanging if

205

they could not find the ends, dragged out lengths anyhow. For a time the effect had been dazzlingly pyro-technical when seen from below. The Constitution had gone very, very, very fast; it had covered centuries in a few years; and as it went it got faster. But unfortunately it had stopped suddenly. And every one saw that while it remained in the hands of its nominal masters it would never go again.

Had the times been less critical some other means of effecting the same end might have been found. But although it was scarcely more than whispered yet, for four hours England had been involved in actual, deadly, civil war; and water once spilled is hard to gather up. Under ordinary circumstances the expedient of disenfranchising a party would have proved unpopular even with the bitterest among that party's enemies. As it was, it was simply accepted as the necessary counterstroke to their own policy of aggression.

"If the 'most business-like Government of modern times' can instance a single business where eleven shareholders to the amount of a sovereign apiece can come in and outvote ten shareholders who have each a stake of a thousand pounds in the concern, and then proceed to wreck it," was a remark typical of the view people took, "then—why, then the record of the Government will lose its distinction as an absolutely unique blend of fatuous imbecility and ramping injustice, that's all."

So there was to be a general election very soon in which the issue would lie between the League party and the shattered, shipwrecked Administration that had no leaders, no coherence, and scarcely a name to rally to. It was estimated that Labour of one complexion or another might hold between thirty and forty seats, if the working classes cared to support representatives after the Payment of Members Act had been repealed. It was computed that in more than four hundred constituencies League candidates would be returned unopposed. There could be no denying that our countrymen of 1918 (circa) lived through an interesting period of their country's history. The League party would go to the poll with no pledges, and their policy for the present was summed up in the single phrase, "As in 1905." It was to be the cleanest of slates.

"How soon can the Bill become law under the most expeditious handling?" Hampden had asked of those who formed the earlier deputation, and the answer had been, "Three days!" Solely from the "business" point of view it was magnificent, and it was certainly convenient as matters stood. In three more days a general election could be in full swing, waged, in the emergency, on the existing register supplemented by the books of the local authorities and the voters' receipts for rates or taxes. In a single day it could be over. Within a week England would have experienced a change in her affairs as far-reaching as the Conquest or the Restoration.

Mr Lloyd, to return to Sir John Hampden's library, read the first article to the breathless assembly. It had been tacitly agreed that the time had come when the conditions must be accepted without discussion; but when the fateful clause was finished a deep groan, not in empty hostile demonstration, but irresistibly torn from the unfeigned depths of their emotion, escaped many of the Ministers. Boabdil el Chico's sigh, when he reached the point where the towers and minarets of Granada were lost to him for ever, was not more sincere or heart-racked. Even Sir John could not have claimed that he felt unmoved.

The secretary read on. The League entered into certain undertakings. It guaranteed that the normal conditions of the home coal trade should be restored, and the men called back to the pits by an immediate order for ten million tons. Temporary relief work of various kinds would be instituted at once to meet the distress. The Unemployed Grant would be reopened for nine weeks to carry over the winter; for three weeks fully, for three weeks at the rate of two-thirds, and for the last period reduced to one-third. The colliers in London would be carried back to their own districts as fast as the railways could get out the trains.

There were many other points of detail, and they all had a common aim—the obliteration of the immediate past and the restoration of that public confidence which in a country possessing natural resources is the foundation stone of national prosperity. Already there were facts for the present and portents for the future. Men of influence and position, who had been driven out of England by the terrible atmosphere of political squalor cast over an Empire by a Government that had learned to think municipally, were even now beginning to return; and that most responsive seismograph which faithfully reflected every change in the world's condition for good or ill predicted better times. In other words, consols had risen in three months from 54-1/2 to 68 and the bulk of the buying was said to be for investment.

"If it is not trenching on the forbidden ground, I should like to ask for an assurance on one point," said a member with a dash of acrimony. The secretary had finished his task, and then for perhaps ten seconds they had sat in silence, speculating half unconsciously upon the future, as each dimly saw it, that lay beyond the momentous step they were about to take. "I refer to the question of coal export. It is, of course, a more important outlet than the domestic home consumption. Is the League in a position to guarantee that the taxation will be rescinded without delay?"

"I think it would be a very unwarrantable presumption for us to assume that any one outside the governments of the countries interested possesses that influence, and that it would be a very undesirable, a very undiplomatic, proceeding to hint at the possibility of any such concession in the document I have before me," replied Sir John suavely. "Beyond that, I would add that it will be manifestly to the interest of the next government to restore the bulk of foreign trade to a normal level; and that should the League party find itself in office, it will certainly make representations through the usual channels."

"Quite like old times," said Mr Soans dryly. "I suppose that we shall have to be content with that. Let us hope that it will prove a true saying that those who hide can find."

He picked up a pen as he finished speaking, signed the paper that had been passed to him first by reason of his position at the table, and thrust it vehemently from him to his neighbour. Mr Chadwing held up his pen to the light to make sure that it contained no obstruction on so important an occasion, signed his name with clerkly precision, and then carefully wiped his pen on the lining of his coat. Cecil Brown looked down with the faint smile that covered his saddest moments as he added the slender strokes of his signature, and Tirrel dashed off the ink-laden characters of his with tightened lips and a sombre frown. Consciously or unconsciously every man betrayed some touch of character in that act. Mr Vossit made a wry grimace as he passed the paper on; and Mr Guppling, with an eye on a possible line in Fame's calendar, snapped his traitorous pen in two and cast the pieces dramatically to the ground.

When the last signature had been written, some of the members stood up to take their leave at once, but Hampden and Tirrel made a simultaneous motion to detain them. The master of the house gave way to his guest.

"I am not up to cry over spilled milk," said Tirrel with his customary bluntness. "What is done, is done. We shall carry out the terms, Sir John Hampden, and you and your party will be in office in a week. But you are not merely taking over the administration of a constitution: you are taking over a defeated country. I ask you, as the head of your party and the future Premier, to do one thing, and I ask it entirely on my own initiative, and without the suggestion or even the knowledge of my friends or colleagues. Let your first act be to publish a general amnesty. It does not touch me.... But there have been things on both sides. You may perhaps know my views; I would have crushed your League by strong means when it was

208

possible if I had had my way. None the less, there is not the most shadowy charge that could hang over me to-day, and for that reason it is permissible for me to put in this petition. The nation is shattered, torn, helpless. Do not look too closely into the past ... pacify."

"The question has not arisen between my associates and myself, but I do not imagine that we should hold conflicting views, and I may say that for my part I enter cordially into the spirit of the suggestion," replied Hampden frankly. "Anything irregular that could come within the meaning of political action in its widest sense I should be favourable towards making the object of a general pardon.... While we are together, I will go a step further, and on this point I have the expressed agreement of my friends. You, sir, have assumed without any reserve that our party will be returned to office. I accept that assumption. You have also compared our work to the pacification of a conquered nation. That also may be largely admitted. We shall be less a political party returned to power by the even chances of a keenly-fought election, and checked by an alert opposition, than a social autocracy imposing our wishes—as we believe for the public good—on the country. For twenty years, as I forecast the future, there will be no effective opposition. Yet a great deal of our work will have reference to the class whom the opposition would represent, the class upon whose wise and statesmanlike pacification the tranquillity, and largely the prosperity, of the country, will depend."

Some few began to catch the drift of Hampden's meaning, and those who did all glanced instinctively towards Cecil Brown.

"You have used, and I have accepted, the comparison of a conquered nation," continued Sir John. "When a country has been forcibly occupied the work of pacification is one of the first taken in hand by a prudent conqueror. There is usually a Board or Committee of Conciliation, and in that body are to be found some of the foremost of those who resisted invasion while resistance seemed availing.... It would be analogous to that, in my opinion, if a supporter of the present Government was offered and accepted a position in the next. There would be no suggestion—there would be no possibility—of his being in accord with the Cabinet in its general policy. He would be there as an expert to render service to both parties in the work of healing the scars of conflict. If the proposal appears to be exceptional and the position untenable at first sight, it is only because the prosaic parliamentary machinery of normal times has by a miracle been preserved into times that are abnormal."

There was an infection of low laughter, amused, sardonic,

some good-natured and a little ill-natured, and a few cries of "Cecil Brown!" in a subdued key.

"The moment seemed a favourable one for laying the proposal before the members of the Government," went on Hampden, unmoved, "though, of course, I do not expect an answer now. On the assumption that we are returned to power, it is our intention to create a new department to exist as long as the conditions require it, and certainly as long as the next Parliament. Its work will be largely conciliation, and it will deal with the disorganisation of labour. In the same confidential spirit with which you have spoken of the future without reserve, I may say that should I be called upon to form a Ministry, I shall—and I have the definite acquiescence of my colleagues—offer the Presidentship of the Board to Mr Cecil Brown ... the office of Parliamentary Secretary to Mr Tirrel."

If Hampden had wished to surprise, he certainly succeeded. The open laugh that greeted the first name was cut off as suddenly and completely as the light is cut off when the gas-tap is turned, by the gasp that the second name evoked. To many among them the offer had been the merest party move; Cecil Brown's name a foregone conclusion. The addition of Tirrel, whose rather brilliant qualities and quite fantastic sense of honour they were prone to lose sight of behind his vehement battle-front, was stupefying.

It was Tirrel who was the first to break the silence of astonishment on this occasion, not even waiting, with characteristic impetuousness, for his chief-designate to offer an opinion.

"You say that you do not want an answer now, Sir John, but you may have it, as far as I am concerned," he cried, with the defiant air that marked his controversial passages. "From any other man of your party the proposal would have been an insult; from you it is an amiable mistake. You do not think that you can buy us with the bribe of office, but you think that there is no further party work for us to do: that Socialism in England to-day is dead. I tell you, Sir John Hampden, with the absolute conviction of an inspired truth, that it will triumph yet. You will not see it; I may not see it, but it is more likely that the hand of Time itself should fail than that the ideals to which we cling should cease to draw men on. We, who are the earliest pioneers of that untrodden path, have made many mistakes; we are paying for them now; but we have learned. Some of our mistakes have brought want and suffering to thousands of your class, but for hundreds of years your mistakes have been bringing starvation and misery to millions of our class. From your presence we go down again into the weary years of bondage, to work silently and unmarked among those depths of human misery from which our charter springs. I warn you, Sir John Hampden—for I

210

know that the warning will be dead and forgotten before the year is out—that our reign will come again; and when the star of a new and purified Socialism arises once more on a prepared and receptive world the very forces of nature would not be strong enough to arrest its triumphant course."

"Hear! hear!" said Mr Vossit perfunctorily, as he looked round solicitously for his hat. "Well, I suppose we may as well be going."

Cecil Brown recalled his wistful smile from the contemplation of a future chequered with many scenes of light and shade.

"I thank you, Sir John," he replied with a look of friendly understanding, "but I also must go down with my own party."

"I hope that the decision in neither case will be irrevocable," said Hampden with regret, but as he spoke he knew that the hope was vain.

They had already begun to file out of the room, with a touch here and there of that air of constraint that the party had never been quite able to shake off on ceremonial occasions. They left Mr Tubes cowering before the stove, and raising his head nervously from time to time to listen to the noises of the street.

Mr Guppling, determined that his claims should not escape the eye of Fame, paused at the door.

"When we leave this room, John Hampden," he proclaimed in a loud and impressive voice, and throwing out his hand with an appropriate gesture, "we leave Liberty behind us, bound, gagged, and helpless, on the floor!"

"Very true, Mr Guppling," replied Sir John good-humouredly. "We will devote our first efforts to releasing her."

Mr Guppling smiled a bitter, cutting smile, and left the shaft to rankle. It was not until he was out in the street that a sense of the possible ambiguity of his unfortunate remark overwhelmed him with disgust.

CHAPTER XXII

"POOR ENGLAND"

With the account of the signing of the dissolution terms, and a brief reference to the sweeping victory of the League party—already foreshadowed, indeed, to the point of the inevitable—the unknown chronicler, whose version of the Social War this narrative has followed, brings his annals to a close. That war being finished, and by the repudiation of their Socialistic mentors on the part of a large section of the working classes, finished by more than a mere paper treaty, the worthy scribe announces with praiseworthy restraint that there is no more to be said.

"These men," he declares, in the quaint and archaic language of the past,—and he might surely have added "these women" also— "came not reluctantly, but in no wise ambitiously, out of the business of their own private lives to serve their country as they deemed; and that being accomplished to a successful end, would have returned, nothing loth, to more obscure affairs, having sought no personal gain beyond that which grew from public security, an equitable burden of citizenship, and a recovered pride among the nations. Albeit some must needs remain to carry on the work."

Even the not unimportant detail of who remained to carry on the work, and in what capacities, is not recorded, but the distribution of rewards and penalties, on the lines of strict poetic justice, may be safely left to the individual reader's sympathies, with the definite assurance that everything happened exactly as he would have it. At the length of three times as much space as would have sufficed to dispose of these points once and for all, this superexact historian goes on to set out his reasons for not doing so. He claims, in short, that his object was to portray the course of the social war, not to recount the adventures of mere individuals; and with the suggestion of a wink between his pen and paper that may raise a doubt whether he, on his side, might not be endowed with the power of casting a critical eye upon other periods than his own, he indulges in a little pleasantry at the expense of writers who, under the pretext of developing their hero's character, begin with his parent's childhood, and continue to the time of his grandchildren's youth. For himself, he asserts that nothing apart from the course of the social war, its rise and progress, has been allowed to intrude, and that ended, and their work accomplished, its champions are rather heroically treated, very much as the Arabian magician's army was disposed of until it was required again, and to all intents and purposes turned into stone just where they stood.

But from other sources it is possible to glean a little here and there of the course of subsequent events. To this patchwork record the Minneapolis Journal contributes a cartoon laden with the American satirist's invariable wealth of detail.

A very emaciated John Bull, stretched on his bed, is just struggling back to consciousness and life. On a table by his side stands a bottle labelled "Hampden's U. L. Mixture," to which he owes recovery. On the walls one sees various maps which depict a remarkably Little England indeed. Some sagacious economist, in search of a strip of canvas with which to hold together a broken model of a black man, has torn off the greater part of South Africa for the purpose. Over India a spider has been left to spin a web so that scarcely any of the Empire is now to be seen. Upper Egypt is lost behind a squab of ink which an irresponsible urchin has mischievously taken the opportunity to fling. Every colony and possession shows signs of some ill-usage.

"Say, John," "Uncle Sam," who has looked in, is represented as saying, "you've had a bad touch of the 'sleeping sickness.' You'd better take things easy for a spell to recuperate. I'll keep an eye on your house while you go to the seashore."

That was to be England's proud destiny for the next few years—to take things easy and recuperate! There is nothing else for the pale and shaken convalescent to do; but the man who has delighted in his strength feels his heart and soul rebel against the necessity. Fortunate for England that she had good friends in that direful hour. The United States, sinking those small rivalries over which cousins may strive even noisily at times in amiable contention, stretched a hand across the waters and astonished Europe by the message, "Who strikes England wantonly, strikes me": a sentiment driven home by the diplomatic hint that for the time being the Monroe Doctrine was suspended west of Suez.

France—France who had been so chivalrously true to her own ally in that stricken giant's day of incredible humiliation—looked across The Sleeve with troubled, anxious eyes, and whispered words of sympathy and hope. Gently, very tactfully, she offered friendship with both hands, without a tinge of the patronage or protection that she could extend; and by the living example of her own tempestuous past and gallant recovery from every blow, pointed the way to power and self-respect.

Japan, whose treaty had been thrown unceremoniously back to her many years before, now drew near again with the cheerful smile that is so mild in peace, so terrible in war. Prefacing that her own enviable position was entirely due to the enlightened virtues of her emperor, she now proposed another compact on broad and generous lines, by which England—a "high contracting Power," as she was still magnanimously described—was spared the most fruitful cause for anxiety in the East.

"You didn't mind allying with us when you were at the head of the nations," said Japan. "We come to you—now. Besides, all very good business for us in the end. You build up again all right, no time."

Japan's authority to speak on the subject of "building up" was not to be disputed. The nations had forgotten the time, scarcely a quarter of a century before, when they had been amused by "Little Japan's" progressive ambitions. And when Japan had taken over the "awakening" arrangements of a sister-nation on terms that gave her fifty million potential warriors to draw upon and train (warriors whom one of England's most revered generals had characterised as "Easily led; easily fed; fearless of death"), non-amusement in some quarters gave way to positive trepidation.

The sympathetic nations spoke together, and agreed that something must be done to give "Poor England" another chance; as, in the world of commerce, friendly rivals will often gather round the man who has fallen on evil days to set him on his feet again.

So England was to have a fair field and liberty to work out her own salvation. But she was not to wake up and find that it had all been a hideous dream. Egypt had been put back to the time of the Khalifa. India had lost sixty years of pacification and progress. Ireland was a republic, at least in name, and depending largely on Commemoration Issues of postage stamps for a revenue. South Africa was for the South Africans. There were many other interesting items, but these were, as it might be expressed to a nation of shopkeepers, the leading lines.

If the worst abroad was bad enough, there was one encouraging feature at home. With the election of the new government industries began to revive, trade to improve, the money market to throw off its depression, and the natural demand for labour to increase: not gradually, but instantly, phenomenally. It was as though a dam across some great river had been removed, and with the impetus every sluggish little tributary was quickened and drawn on in new and sparkling animation. It was not necessary to argue upon it from a party point of view; it was a concrete fact that every one admitted. There was only one explanation, and it met the eye at every turn. Capital reappeared, and money began to circulate freely again. Why? There was security.

It was not the Millennium; it was the year 19—, and a "capitalistic" government was in office; but the "masses" discovered that they were certainly not worse off than before. Working men

214

now wore, it is true, a little less of the air of being so many presidents of South American republics when they walked about the streets; but that style had never really suited them, and they soon got out of it. The men who had come into power were not of the class who oppress. The strife of the past was being forgotten; its lessons were remembered. What was good and practical of Socialistic legislation was retained. So it came about that the vanquished gained more by defeat than they would have done by victory.

It was undeniable that, in common with mankind at large, they still from time to time experienced pain, sickness, disappointment, hardship, and general adversity. Those who were employed by gentlemen were treated as gentlemen treat their work-people; those who were so unfortunate as to be in the service of employers who had no claim to that title continued to be treated as cads and despots treat their employés. Those among them who were gentlemen themselves extended a courteous spirit towards their masters, and those among them who were the reverse continued to act towards employers and the world around as churls and blusterers act, and so the compensating balance of nature was more or less harmoniously preserved.

And what of the future? Will the nation that was so sharply taught dread the fire like the burned child, or return to the flame as the scorched moth does? Alas, the memory of a people is short, even as the wisdom of a proverb is conflictingly two-edged.

Or, if the warning fades and the necessity grows large again, will there be found another Stobalt to respond to the call? "For those whom Heaven afflicts there is a chance," contributes the Sage of another land; "but they who persistently work out their own undoing are indeed hopeless."

Or may it be that the faith of Tirrel will be justified, and that in the process of time there will emerge from man's ceaseless groping after perfection a new wisdom, under whose yet undreamt-of scheme and dispensation all men will be content and reconciled?

The philosopher shakes his head weightily and remains silent—thereby adding to his reputation. The prophets prophesy; the old men dream dreams and the young men see visions, and the dispassionate speculate. On all sides there is a multitude of the counsel in which, as we must believe, lies wisdom.

It is an interesting situation, and as it can only be definitely settled beyond the dim vista of future centuries, the pity is that we shall never know.

THE END